ALFHEIM:
THE CURSE OF NIDAVELLIR

JOHN STOETER

FOREWORD

It was 2017, and by all accords, a slow night at the bar. It was storming, and for a poolside bar, that meant no business. As an introverted bartender who liked to bang out drinks and not talk to anyone, I was more than okay with that. Then you arrived, disrupting my afternoon of solace, and holy shit, was I annoyed. Nothing pains introverts more than meaningless conversation, and yet there you stood, ready to pebble out nothing but small talk.

You ordered a drink and complained about the price, not in an obnoxious way. Still, anytime a customer complained about a price that I had no control over, it was annoying. *It's a pool bar at a vacation destination; what do you expect,* were the words I wanted to say, but I bit my tongue. Small talk ensued, and you left. Thank god, I thought.

A couple hours later, you came back for a second drink, and I'm not sure anyone had come in between then. That's how slow it had been. You ordered your second drink. You were about to leave, but you hesitated and stuck around. You appeared as if you were hiding from someone or you were nervous. I wasn't really sure, but I was used to seeing spouses hide from their significant other, so I didn't question it either.

Regardless, you sat down and enjoyed your drink, which annoyed the shit out of me, but hey, I could bullshit with the best of them, so there we were bullshitting about absolutely nothing. I'm not sure what compelled you to say this, but you told me you saw something special in me, and you knew I was chasing after something.

You didn't know that I had just started making music again. You didn't know I was in the middle of completing a screenplay, and based on our brief conversation about nothing, there was no way you could have known those things. You kept going on and on about my dreams and how I would achieve them. Somehow you knew I wasn't from Orlando or Kissimmee, and you told me, "Don't stop until you get what you left home for."

I don't know if it's God or Odin or heaven or hell. Nobody does. And nobody knows what the afterlife holds, but I do believe that whoever is above let my dad have a field trip that day. Your wisdom and demeanor were that of my father. That much I will go to the grave believing. So if it was my dad, thank you. Words can't describe how proud of you I am. And if it was just a random man at a bar in Kissimmee, thank you as well. Your comments inspired me that day and still do.

To those reading and chasing their dreams, "Don't stop until you get what you left home for."

CHAPTER ONE

THE WORLD TREE

Michael sat in his car for what felt like an eternity. While the world around him was quiet, his mind grew increasingly loud. The asphyxiating silence that drummed inside his ears intensified with each passing second, ringing like sirens in the precipice of war. Irritating as it was, the sound was welcoming because it created the smallest of distractions, quelling him of the guilt and anxiety that coiled inside him.

He sat there waiting, waiting for himself to find the courage to exit his car and ring the doorbell before him, but his mind raced with thoughts of procrastination instead. He could always come back tomorrow, he thought. Perhaps that would be better. Maybe by then, they would finally have a lead worthy of investigation, but who was he kidding?

His cousin, Peter, had already been missing for two days. After forty-eight hours and no leads, Michael's hopes of finding him were dwindling. His entire body shuddered at the idea of this case turning from a missing person investigation into that of a dead body case. His heart plunged to the pit of his stomach, leaving him with that sinking feeling that could only be attributed to overwhelming grief and heartbreak. That feeling where somehow your gut knew the inevitable, harrowing truths that your mind couldn't bear to formulate.

It couldn't happen again, not like this, he pleaded. Whom he was begging to, he didn't know anymore. He just knew that his family didn't deserve to go through this a second time. Twenty years prior, his sister, Skye, had been involved in a missing person's case. They never found her, and that still haunted him every day of his life.

His innocence had been stripped from him at six years old, leaving him a broken mess. The adoring belief that he shared in Santa, the exuberant joy of Christmas, and the exhilaration he would experience from a tooth fairy visit all marred and destroyed. The world had shown its sharp teeth and scathing claws early on, never letting go of its clutches, shackling him to a lifetime of debilitating fear and self-doubt.

The latest kidnapping only filled him with more trauma. He couldn't bear the toll of another missing child on his conscience. He vowed to his cousin, Emma, that he would bring her son back home. He couldn't fail her. Not like he did his sister. Granted, he was only six then, but that didn't stop the never-ending remorse that harbored inside him, nor did it stop the eternal blame his mother had bestowed upon him all these years.

This case meant a lot to him for a multitude of reasons. The obvious being that Peter was family, but deep down, in the depths of Michael's heart, this case represented an opportunity for redemption. No matter how hard he tried to suppress those dark emotions, they returned with a vengeance every time. He couldn't help but think that finding Peter would heal the aches of his past, exercising any remaining demons that still inhabited him. A means to a new beginning, he hoped.

Provoked by his thoughts, he failed to realize the death grip he had secured on the steering wheel or the incessant tapping of his left foot. This case had consumed him, enrapturing him entirely. Since Peter's disappearance, he'd maybe gotten four or five hours of sleep. His mind and body were on the brink of exhaustion, operating on fumes and desperation.

Regardless, he'd sat in his car long enough. He found his conviction and filed his way towards Emma's doorstep. From the outside, he could hear her newborn wailing tirelessly. He took a deep cleansing breath and knocked on the glass-paneled door, skipping the doorbell for fear of disturbing his little cousin more.

His sloppy, unappealing reflection glared off the glass, staring back at him, doing him absolutely no justice. His hair poked and flared in every which direction, looking as if it hadn't been combed in days, which was sadly accurate. Its frazzled form resembled that of Doc Brown's from *Back to the Future*, only his was jet-black rather than an aging white.

His facial hair was untrimmed and stubbly, growing too quick to keep manicured to perfection but too patchy to ever develop a full beard. His eyes were puffy, filled with blotchy purplish bags underneath.

To make matters worse, he was feverishly pale at the moment as well. It wasn't the type of pale that occurred naturally from genetics; instead, it was locked in your bedroom and avoid sunlight kind of pale. His complexion resembled that of a harsh winter, yet he was currently entrenched in the dog days of summer. It was the hottest summer in recorded history, and he still managed to look like the heir to Dracula's throne.

Typically, he was a strapping looking gentleman, handsome, but in a cute, *he's just a friend* kind of way. A non-threatening, puppy dog kind of cute was the phrase used to describe him many years ago when that kind of thing mattered to him. With proper confidence, he was attractive enough to stand out in a crowd, but that over-the-top kind of charisma was something that he lacked, and it showed.

His sulked stature and demeanor mostly went unnoticed, and for the most part, that was to his liking. Attention scared him just as much as failure, and he feared failure more than life itself. It wasn't so much failure that he feared but more so the resounding and disabling fear that he would let down the people closest to him.

You couldn't fail if no one was around to see it, he always told himself. So, he did his best to hide his passions, therefore, hiding the shortcomings that seemingly came with them. That's why he avoided the spotlight; if there weren't any expectations set upon him, then he couldn't possibly let anyone down, but all eyes were on him now. He would either be the hero that delivered Peter home to safety or the one who failed to find him.

After a lengthy wait, Emma arrived at the door to greet Michael, interrupting his one-on-one therapy session with himself. With her disgruntled newborn in one hand, Emma gave Michael a brief side armed hug with her free hand and invited him inside.

Remarkably, Emma trounced him in his stand-alone beauty pageant. To put it nicely, she looked awful. She lacked sleep desperately, far worse than Michael. The bags under her eyes were double the size of his. Both her eyes and nose were red and puffy from all the crying she'd been doing. Her clothes reeked of baby spit-up and body odor, leaving Michael to wonder when the last time she had showered.

Michael felt terrible for her. He wanted more than anything to help. He wished he had come here with a sliver of hope to provide her with. Instead, he regretted showing up at all. Regretted knocking on the door and bothering her already tiresome day. He felt shame and anguish but mostly just disappointment that he would only be letting her down once more.

"Have you slept at all recently?" Michael asked timidly, tiptoeing around the inevitable nervous breakdown combusting inside her.

"An hour," said Emma. "Maybe two." She paused. Her mouth opened, and Michael's heart fluttered at the question that would inevitably come next, but Emma closed it at the startling screams from the twins.

From the other room, Michael heard the persistent banging and yelling from Will and Cam. The two were always fighting and wrestling, performing whatever new acrobatic moves they could think of from the top of their bunk bed. Flips and jumps that gave their poor mother mini heart attacks every time, and no matter how many times she begged them to stop, they always went back to leaping off the bed the next day.

Emma placed her youngest in the bassinet with her pacifier to coax her to sleep. She rubbed her face softly, singing lightly until she soothed her into a deep sleep. Emma made her way over to the dining room table and gripped her coffee mug tightly. It rattled and shook in her hands subtly, either from stress or jitters, probably both thought Michael.

"Are there any leads?" she asked. "I mean anything. Anything that can lead me back to my baby?" Her body chock-full of anxiety as she rocked anxiously in her chair, staring through him for answers.

It was excruciating to watch, even more so that he couldn't do anything to help her find the solace that she desired. "None that lead anywhere," said Michael, the guilt oozing out of his mouth and into his voice. "Not yet, at least, but we're working tirelessly. We're going to find him, Emma. It's only a matter of time until something pops up."

Emma didn't respond. Her dejected gaze said it all. Her eyes shifted from Michael to her coffee mug, straining tightly to hold in her tears.

"You're positive you had your eyes on them at all times?" asked Michael. "I only ask because something's not adding up. Your timeline and the kid's timeline don't match . . . I understand if time slipped away from you. Your hands are clearly full," he said, motioning to the haphazard mess dispersed across the living room. "I want you to know that no one is blaming you, Emma. None of this is your fault." Michael chose his words carefully, ensuring that they were delivered gently, but Emma thought otherwise.

Her body shifted defensively, as did her tone. "I know it's not my fault," barked Emma, her stare firm and unrelenting. "And I only left them out of eyesight for a minute, maybe two. The amount of time it takes to do a diaper change and by the time I came back," she said, struggling to find the words.

Her gaze set deep into her coffee mug as if it were a crystal ball that held the whereabouts of Peter's location. "By the time I came back, he was gone, Michael. It's just like Skye's disappearance . . . which leads me to this," she said, shifting through the unorganized stack of papers that scattered across her tabletop. "I've been doing some research . . . on fairies."

"On fairies?" Michael stammered, unsure of whether or not he had heard her correctly, knowing damn well that he had. He just needed the confirmation of hearing her say it once more. That would allow him the ample time needed to wrap his head around the outlandish statement.

"It didn't start with fairies, but you know how the internet is. One thing led to another, and ultimately, I landed on fairies. I know how crazy it sounds, and I don't expect you to believe me but hear me out," said Emma filing through her research in a frenzied manner.

Michael stared at her blankly, incredulously even. It made sense for her to resort to fairy tales when reality was unable to provide the answers that she coveted. It was why people resorted to the bible or God in times of desperation. However, God was understandable and relatable, but fairies, that was a first, even for him, and he had been assigned to some looney cases over the years.

"I take it you came across the reptilian race that secretly rules the world as well?" Michael joked to no avail. "I'm all ears," he said, quickly changing his tone to match the seriousness of Emma's. "Do continue."

"The kids say they visited an abandoned kingdom," said Emma. "Now we both know that that's impossible."

"Clearly," said Michael, waiting patiently for whatever point it was that she was trying to sell.

"It's impossible because I was only gone for the length of a diaper change. They couldn't have possibly seen a kingdom and come back in the span of a minute or two. Which leads me to fairies. One thing that's commonplace in fairy abductions is lost time. The castles. The kingdoms. The lost time.

"I think we're looking at something supernatural here. That would explain why we haven't been able to find any leads, and it's precisely why they were never able to find Skye either, Michael. It's the only explanation that links Peter's and Skye's disappearances together. Think about it. It's all right here," she said, handing him some pages that had been printed from a website created during the dial-up stage of internet access.

"The fairies," she exclaimed, almost excitedly. "They take these kids, their abductees, to a place called Faerieland. Will and Cam, they visited Faerieland. WE visited Faerieland! That day, twenty years ago, the day that Skye disappeared, that's what happened. That's where Peter is now. I'm sure of it."

Michael paused hesitantly, his brain churning like old machinery, trying to find the most efficient and formulaic response least likely to upset her. What the hell does someone say back to something like that, he thought. She had clearly lost it. There obviously wasn't an ounce of validity to any of her claims, but he couldn't come right out and say that.

He bit the inside of his cheeks, restraining himself from blurting out the first thing that came to mind. His brain faltered as it attempted to string together the words that would eloquently let her down. "If it makes you feel better, I'll take your research and look it over tonight . . . But I'm going to need more than your certainty and belief in fairies if I'm supposed to present this evidence—and I say that loosely—to the others at the precinct."

"You don't present it to the others," Emma countered. "Not yet, at least. We can investigate it together. I'll go out with you to the woods. Just like old times . . . like when we were kids looking for Skye."

"Absolutely not. You're in no condition to journey out there. There's not a chance in hell that I'm escorting you into the woods, Emma. Are you crazy?"

"Please . . . I need you to do this for me," she said, grasping his hand and cupping it tenderly. "Please, Michael."

For a moment, he entertained it. If it made her feel better, he didn't see the harm in a quick surveillance of the area, but he'd rather not breathe life into the all too real fairy tale festooning inside of her. "Emma, listen. I understand things are tough, but—"

"No, no, you don't! You don't have kids, Michael. You have absolutely no idea what I'm going through right now. You couldn't possibly know. So please don't sugarcoat me with this I know things are tough bullshit."

"You're right. I don't know. I don't have kids, and I can't possibly know how you're feeling right now. It was selfish of me to insinuate such a thing but what I do know is that we didn't get taken to fairyland twenty years ago, and neither did Peter. There's a reasonable explanation to all of this, one that probably includes a sick monster of a man that lurks out there in those woods, and I assure you I'm going to find him."

It was as if Emma had blanked out and ignored everything Michael had said, that or she was unwilling to believe him. "You really don't remember the castle? We saw it. Me, you, Reed, and Skye. We saw it, Michael."

"I remember . . . I remember being kids, and I remember a shady man leading us into the woods. We came back . . . and Skye didn't. That's what I remember."

"That's such bullshit, and you know it. For once in your life, can't you just suspend your disbelief? Why is it so hard for you to admit we saw a castle? We all remembered it up until you turned sixteen, and then I guess it wasn't cool to believe in castles anymore."

"Because there was never a castle to begin with," Michael fired back, raising his voice to match hers. "Some people actually have to grow up and stop believing in fairy tales. You know why? Because they're fake, that's why. Skye was taken by some sex offending lunatic. I'm sorry if you've never come to terms with that. Now it's my job to make sure the same thing doesn't happen to Peter. It's my job to bring him back, and that's exactly what I'm going to do . . . We were kids," Michael replied softly. "We made it up. We're lucky we didn't get taken as well."

Emma tightened her gaze apprehensively, the fire she once had dimmed to a mere flicker. The spark and will to continue arguing now gone and withered away. "We saw a castle, Michael," she murmured as soft as a whisper. She sighed deeply and stared off into the distance as tears began to flood her eyes once more.

"I'm sorry," said Michael, regathering his composure and grabbing her hand gently. "I'm going to find Peter. I promise."

The baby cried softly, startled awake by their previous disagreement. Emma calmly rubbed her daughter's belly, soothing her back to sleep. The loud thumping and banging that came from the twin's room had ceased because of the commotion. The twins poked their heads out of their bedroom door to check on the turmoil.

"Michael," they chanted in unison as they ran over to greet him with hugs.

"Shh," said Emma, glaring at the twins. "I just put her back down," she said quietly.

The pair looked identical; Michael couldn't tell the twins apart unless he talked to them for a few minutes. Will had a higher squealed voice than Cam; that's the only way he could distinguish any difference between the two. He had no idea how Emma did it.

Michael was too shocked by their growth spurt to try to differentiate them. Although he made a reasonable effort to see them every few weeks, they seemed to grow between his visits. Shit, he thought. They had to be edging up on eight or nine now by now. Michael silently counted the years in his head, proving that much to be true.

"Are you gonna help us find our brother?" asked the high and shrilly voice of Will.

"I am," whispered Michael. "But I'm going to need your guys' help. Go on back to your room, and I'll grab you in a little bit. Okay?"

"Yeah," the two of them squealed excitedly, jumping up and down. They stopped immediately after making eye contact with the hardened eyes of their mother. The boys took the hint and evacuated to their room quietly.

Emma stood over the bassinet, massaging the baby's head gently. "I'm gonna get some rest. She won't be down for long."

"Sounds good," said Michael. "I'm going to take them outside and horseplay with them for a little while. If that's okay? I feel like that will help with some of their restless energy."

"That would be nice. They need the sunlight. I haven't let them outside since . . . since it happened. As soon as you leave, bring them back inside and lock the doors," Emma said sternly. "Please," she said, softening her tone.

"You got it. I'll do my best to try to stop by again tomorrow too."

Emma nodded her head and slumped off to her room to get some much-needed rest. Michael made his way to his cousins' room to retrieve them. He opened the door to find Cam on the receiving end of a headlock, courtesy of his twin brother, Will. The two appeared to be really going at it before Michael intervened between them.

"Settle down, cowboys," chimed Michael. "How about we take a little stroll out back and retrace some of your steps?"

Cam squirmed out of the headlock and pushed Will off of him. His face flushed red with frustration. He glared at Will and kicked at his shins before responding to Michael. "Yeah, let's go," he huffed and puffed between breaths.

"After you guys," said Michael.

Michael followed them outside, hustling behind to keep up with their brisk pace. Cam brushed past Will, nudging him hard in the shoulder, proceeding to take the lead of the group. Cam leapfrogged over the small white picket fence that surrounded their backyard. Will quickly followed, emulating his brother. Everything had to be a competition with them. Somebody had to be the fastest, the strongest, the quickest, the smartest. It was never ending between them, and quite frankly, it was exhausting even in brief doses.

Instead of climbing and straddling the fence, Michael simply opened the gate. About twenty or so yards of unkempt grass stood between them and the woods, but it was nothing but forest after that. Cam and Will streaked through the grass, dead set on the forest ahead.

"Aye," Michael shouted at them. "Aye, get your little asses back here. Where do you think you're going?"

The boys turned around, enamored with sass and eye-rolls.

"I thought we were searching for clues in the woods with you?" asked Cam.

"Yeah, that's what you said," replied Will.

"No, I said let's go out back," said Michael. "Not once did I mention the woods. I might go in there but not with you two little heathens."

"Boo."

"Yeah, no fair," said Cam. "That's lame."

"You're lame," said Michael sneeringly, knowing good and well how to play their devious games after years of practice. "Now, where did you guys wander off to from here?"

"Through those trees," Will answered mockingly, pointing towards the vast abundance of trees that littered the area.

"And what tree might that be?" asked Michael, trying to keep the annoyance they caused from simmering across his face.

"That one," said Cam, darting towards the wilderness with Will fleeing behind his footsteps.

Michael let out a long, over-exaggerated sigh but decided to save his breath rather than yell after them. They may have been disobedient little shits, but neither were actually stupid enough to defy him. As Michael predicted, the twins stopped in place, moving twigs and branches around, peering through the branchy veil, eyeing the forest intently.

Michael positioned himself in front of them, boxing them out with his much larger adult frame. "Through here?" he asked.

"Yep," said Will.

"And you're sure it was this exact spot?"

"Yep."

"How far did you go?"

"Not telling unless you take us with you," Will grinned.

"Cam, how far until I reach this so-called kingdom?"

"What do I get if I tell you?" questioned Cam.

"I'll let you punch that smug grin off your brother's face, and I won't tell your mom. How about that?"

Cam thought it over decisively before shaking his head no. "I do that all the time. Gonna have to be better than that."

"Alright, I've had enough," said Michael. He let go of the branches and turned around. He walked back slowly through the scraggly grass, towards the white picket fence and the backyard of Emma's, hoping that the twins were too naive to pick up on his bluff.

"Okay, fine," sighed Will. "The kingdom's like five minutes away."

"Try seven," said Cam. "Can we go with you?" he asked, turning to Michael for approval, inching his face close enough against him to annoy him.

"No," said Michael. "I'll see that you two make it inside safely. Off you go," he said, shooing them away with his hand. "Your work is done. Fantastic job, both of you. I'll be sure to get you some of those sticker badges that we have in the office. The ones for little kids."

"Please, Uncle Mike. We wanna help find our brother."

Michael studied the twins, unsure if their puppy eyes and grieved tones were sincere or an elaborate act contrived to fool him. The one thing that stood out most to him was their overzealous demeanor and willingness to revisit the place their brother had been abducted. They seemed to honestly believe in this kingdom. How much bullshit had Emma been feeding them? he thought. Fairyland, abandoned realms? None of it was real, of course, but Michael supposed that fairy tales were better than the grim reality of what had really happened to Peter.

Had the kids actually seen anything disturbing, their behavior would surely be the telltale sign, but here they stood, eager to explore once more. Michael used their cheerfulness as a symbol of hope. Maybe, just maybe, Peter had gotten lost. That was believable enough, but the faint glimmer of hope washed over him as Michael was reminded of the unsuccessful search and rescue teams that had detailed the perimeter the past forty-eight hours.

"I know," said Michael, clearing his mind. "I know you do, but you each have been more than enough help. When I find Peter, I'll be sure to tell him it was because of your guys' help. I promise."

The twins nodded their heads, neither saying a word, both sharing the same crestfallen expression.

"Let me walk you guys back," said Michael.

"Oh yeah, we forgot to tell you about the fork," said Will, throwing his hand to his head theatrically. He winked at Cam as if Michael would somehow miss the rather obvious gesture.

"Uh-huh. A fork, I'm sure," said Michael, playing along in their game, no longer feeling the remorse he had shown moments before.

"Yeah, yeah. A fork. A big one."

"Which way did you go? Left or right?" asked Michael, his patience wearing thinner.

"Ahh, I can't remember. Dang."

Michael turned to Cam for an answer.

Cam shrugged. "I dunno. I guess you'll have to take us and find out."

"Looks like I'll take both ways and find out myself," responded Michael. "Now off you go. Bye."

"Oooh, did you tell him about the bees?" Cam asked Will.

"Oh yeah," said Will. "The bees. How could I forget? There's a underground hive out there, so watch out for the bees. They're everywhere."

"Maybe cause they're not real," said Michael. "That's how you forgot. I appreciate the help, Lewis and Clark. Now adios. I mean it."

"Oh, and there's a password to enter the kingdom."

"Oh, my fu—" uttered Michael behind clenched teeth. He closed his eyes and felt his lungs expand. His nostrils flared as he exhaled the deep breath held within him. He was at his wits' end with the twins. Any patience that he had left dissipated two annoying comments ago. "Five minutes, you said? That's how long it takes to get there?"

"Yep," said Will. "Five minutes, that's it."

"But it takes seven," Cam said quietly, nudging his brother.

"Shh, no, it doesn't," said Will, winking three times. Each successive wink looked more like a twitch rather than an act done voluntarily.

"If I take you into the woods, will both of you shut up for ten minutes?" asked Michael. "Are either one of you capable of that?"

"We are, I promise. See, zip," said Will, squeezing his hand to his lips and acting out the motion of zipping them together.

"Off we go," hollered Cam.

Michael gave him a darting glare. "What part of zip it don't you understand?"

"Sorry," whispered Cam, motioning his lips shut the same way that Will had.

"After you," said Michael, gesturing them ahead of him. "And not a word of this to your mother."

Michael placed his hand on his holster, toggling his gun. A mindless check to see if it was there, the same way he did with his keys or wallet. He severely doubted that he would need it, but he checked anyway.

It was against his better judgment to have them accompany him, and Michael knew that, but he was desperate for answers. Besides, they would only be gone for ten minutes, any longer, and he would risk Emma finding out, and the last place he wanted to be was on the receiving end of one of her thrashings.

Ten minutes is all it would take to debunk any future talks of fairies and magical kingdoms. Not to mention, Michael knew these woods like the back of his hand. In fact, he knew them so well he was confident the kids were full of shit regarding a fork, but nevertheless, that didn't matter at the moment. All that mattered was that he could absolve the myth of fairies and maybe stumble upon some real clues along the way.

Emma resided at a different house than Michael's childhood home, but the same set of woods connected the two. Michael would venture into these woods damn near every day during his adolescent years, hoping to find a clue of Skye's whereabouts. Even if he knew the odds were slim, it never discouraged him from trying. He used to hold on to that sliver of hope that she still might be alive. He would clutch it tightly, grasping at it like straws because back then, hope was all that he had.

He had more than moved on from that waning hope that used to energize him. He was now closer to a high school reunion than he was high school itself. He couldn't remember the exact moment it happened, but sometime long ago, he had come to terms that Skye was dead. Now he could only hope that a clue of Peter's whereabouts would come at the hands of his two pesky, unrelenting cousins before he had to acknowledge that fate a second time.

"So, what the hell were you guys doing back here anyways?" questioned Michael, needing to hear a voice other than his own. Even if that voice came from one of his annoying cousins, it sure as hell beat the plaguing thoughts that absorbed him. "I know your mother told you never to come back here," continued Michael. "Am I right?"

Michael had read the reports thoroughly. He studied them like he was preparing for the ACT. He'd even did some investigating of his own back here, but the one thing he hadn't been able to do yet is pick the twins' brains without the presence of other surrounding officers. He hoped that in doing so, he would discover a token of truth that they may have concealed from his colleagues.

"Yeah, you're right," said Cam sheepishly with his head sulked into his chest. "We knew better than to be back here."

"We did," said Will. "But c'mon, Michael. We were soooo bored. Ever since the baby, we hadn't done anything fun, so when Cam hit the ball into the woods, it seemed like fun to explore some. Ya know? It'd only be for a few minutes, we thought. So, I convinced Cam, and off we went. We didn't even want Peter to come 'cause he's such a baby, but he would've tattletaled on us, so we hadta bring him."

"Uh-huh, I see," said Michael. "And what happened next? When and where do you remember seeing Peter last?"

"We took this trail here—" said Will.

"Let me tell the story," said Cam, nudging his brother. "We just followed this trail here. We didn't think we'd be back here long but then like . . . like the whole forest changed or something. I dunno. I can't explain it."

"Wow, some story," said Will, rolling his eyes. "I'm telling the stories from now on. That sucked."

"Don't say that word," lectured Michael.

"What? Suck? What's wrong with suck?"

"Just don't say it. You know your mom doesn't like you using that word. She has enough going on as it is, so stopping saying it, please."

"Whatever, fine. Like Cam said, we were just in the woods about to go back, but then we saw this little beat-up brick trail, so we followed it. Took it all the way to that kingdom we told you about."

Their story made no logical sense, but Michael needed to pry what little answers he could from them even if they involved myths and fairy tales. They were the only eyewitnesses he had; for better or worse, Peter's fate relied on their narration of the event, no matter how unbelievable.

"Did you see anyone else in the forest?" Michael asked. "And what about the kingdom? Did you see anyone there?"

"Just us three," said Will. "We didn't see anyone else."

"So, what do you think happened to Peter?"

"Probably got lost, I think."

"No, that's not what happened," said Cam. "He got trapped. Trapped in that kingdom."

"What do you mean trapped?" Michael probed.

"Like he got trapped. When we went back—" Cam was cut off by a hard nudge and a glaring set of eyes from Will. Will shook his head violently, his eyes wide with panic, cautioning his brother from continuing.

"You guys went back? When? Why the hell didn't you tell anyone?"

Cam's head dropped to his chest once more. "We were scared. We didn't think anyone would believe us."

"Believe what?"

"It was gone," said Cam. "Once we saw Peter was missing, we ran back as fast as we could, but the kingdom was gone."

Michael trudged along the beaten trail silently, deep in thought. Trauma can create false memories, repress memories, even recover memories, and in this case, Michael believed the kids had seen something, only they were unwilling to acknowledge it. They created a false memory, an abandoned kingdom just like he and Emma had imagined a castle twenty years prior.

But if they had seen something horrid, why would they be so eager to return? Michael tried his hardest to piece the answers together, but all logic seemed to dissipate from his grasp. The events of that day were a mystery, a mystery that he wasn't any closer to solving.

The once wide trail dwindled beneath their footsteps until it merged into the nothingness of the forest, becoming obsolete. Before them, immersed into the heart of the forest, stood an enormous yew tree with trunk-sized branches that elongated majestically.

Michael marveled at its beauty. The serenity of nature relaxed him and awoke his soul. It had always been a comfort zone for him growing up. A place that he could nestle into safely and seek refuge, forgetting about the repugnant world around him.

He snapped out of his trance, looking to the twins for answers. Where to now, he thought. There was no way they wandered past this tree into the denser, brushier part of the forest.

Cam and Will exchanged bewildered expressions. They poked and prodded at the tree like it was an elaborate prop to a set as if it hadn't been rooted there for hundreds of years. They peered around the tree as if somehow that would make a kingdom sprout out of thin air.

"This wasn't here last time," Will clamored feverishly.

"Yeah," agreed Cam. "Last time, we just kept going along this path, and it turned into the brick trail we were telling you about."

"You mean to tell me this big ass tree wasn't here before?" asked Michael, perplexed, to say the least. Surely the kids were mistaken. The forest was vast; they must have embarked upon a different trail the day Peter had gotten lost.

"Nope."

"Ooh, can we climb it?" asked Will.

Before Michael could respond, the twins attempted to outmuscle the other, scurrying and maneuvering their way up the tree like possums. "Stop," Michael hissed. "Both of you get down! Neither of you are climbing the damn tree. Your mom would kill me if one of you got hurt. We're not even supposed to be back here in the first place."

"I so would've beaten you," said Cam, jumping down from the tree.

"Whatever," said Will, following suit. "Win a fight first."

Just like that, the twins began to brawl at once, dropping to the floor, exchanging grapples and chokeholds.

Michael ignored them. Boys will be boys. He didn't have time for their shenanigans. He examined the area around them, evaluating the surroundings beyond the yew tree. The soft, skinny trail they had been walking on eviscerated beneath him.

This was it, as far they could go. As far as he was willing to go with them, at least. This had to have been a different area. They couldn't have possibly come this way before. Behind the tree was a thick, impenetrable wall of briar and tree brush.

Michael snapped off a small branch from a nearby tree and began to poke around the forest wall that enclosed it. From what he could see, the brush extended quite a ways, a never-ending abyss of tree branches—another dead end.

Sure, he could bring the boys back home and venture into the thicket alone, but even he wasn't thrilled about the sound of that idea. While nature supplied him with bliss, these particular woods filled him with irrevocable fear.

Wilderness had no bounds or limits. It was an ornate and glorious kingdom forged by God himself with no regard to humankind and rightfully so, considering how humans chose to treat her. One day nature's prickle thorns would wear down on them all, initiating their extinction, but not today. Not for him. Not on the fallacy of an abandoned kingdom and the whim of two boys with overbearing imaginations.

"What about the kingdom?" asked Michael. His last resort to get any sort of answers out of today's trip. "Anything you can recall about it in specific?" he asked while gently brushing his shoulder against the tree.

His extremities went numb upon his body coming in contact with the tree. The paralysis percolated throughout his body, traveling slowly, navigating through his veins as if they were an interconnecting highway. The sensation was reminiscent of his foot falling asleep, except he felt that tingling sensation everywhere.

He collapsed to the forest floor under his own weight, unable to support himself. He tried to move but was unable. His limbs constrained to his side, suppressed and frozen in place. His head swelled with symptoms of vertigo and nausea, opening the floodgates to his mind, unveiling visions of his past.

Panic crept over him slowly, suffocating him. One thought emerged before another could finish. He tried to call for his cousins, but his lips remained reluctant to listen. Long lost and forgotten memories swarmed from his subconscious mind to the forefront. Memories shuffled through like a deck of cards, stopping on the day that Skye disappeared. He spent his entire life trying to remember details from that day but was left with nothing more than dissociative amnesia, and now, somehow lying on the floor, immobilized, the memories came flooding back to him.

CHAPTER TWO

FAERIELAND

Michael laid there, enveloped by fear as his conscious and subconscious mind vied for control, reminding him of the exact moment one became consciously aware that they were dreaming. His mind and body existing in two places at once.

He understood that he was currently unconscious and sprawled out along the forest floor. He equally understood that his subconscious state had taken over the steering wheel, replaying the day of the abduction, transporting him back to that hot, steamy afternoon in July, twenty years ago. But instead of re-experiencing that day from his perspective, this time it was from Skye's.

Skye frolicked her way back to the dwarfish tree stump that they had designated as home base during their games of hide-and-seek. It was there that Michael, Reed, and Emma waited for her impatiently. Each of them far more skilled than the younger, absentminded Skye.

They were all within a year of age. Reed was the eldest of the bunch by eight or nine months, while Emma edged Michael in age by a month and a half. They were each six years old at the time, with Reed on the cusp of turning seven. Skye was the youngest of the group, having just celebrated her fifth birthday a month prior.

Reed kicked dirt into the air continuously, creating mini dust storms at his feet. The distraught child voiced his displeasure for everyone to hear. "This is too easy. Why does Skye have to play with us? She always gets caught. It's no fun with her playing."

At that moment, Michael could only see from Skye's perspective. He had no access to her thoughts, nor could he feel her emotions, but judging by her oblivious and distracted point of view, he doubted she cared in the slightest about Reed's comments.

Revisiting this memory as an adult from the vantage point of a child with the attention span of a goldfish was torturing. Here he was re-experiencing the memory he had spent his entire life searching for. Yet, it felt like he was playing an RPG with two broken analog sticks, resulting in the camera swiveling out of control in every direction.

"You know why," replied the younger version of himself. "She's my sister, and whatever we do, my mom is gonna make us include her."

"Can we at least make the field bigger then?" asked Reed, letting out an exaggerated moan. "At least to the woods or something."

Both Michael and Emma exchanged a look of uncertainty.

"I don't think that's a good idea," said Michael.

"C'mon," Reed begged. "Why not?"

"Cause we'll get in trouble for that," said Emma, echoing her opinion alongside Michael.

"Not if we barely go into the woods. Just to the outer edge. We won't go no further. I promise. C'mon guys. Please," Reed beckoned as if his life depended on it.

Emma grimaced and then shrugged her shoulders. "Sure, but you're it first."

Reed's eyes sparkled with joy. His triumphant hands couldn't contain themselves as he looked to Michael for his opinion.

"I guess," said Michael skeptically. "Only to the opening of the woods. Any further, and I'm done, Reed. I mean it," he said sharply.

"Deal," said Reed, unable to hide his grin.

Michael walked over to Skye. He placed his arm around her shoulders and explained the latest set of rules. It was weird seeing himself from someone else's perspective, even stranger seeing himself as a kid from the point of view of someone a foot shorter than him.

His heart tugged inside his chest, his mind urgently pulling to take over like a wrestler in the corner awaiting the hot tag from their partner. Every part of him ached that he wouldn't be able to change the outcome of the events that day. He desperately wished to go back and wrap his arms around his sister tightly and never let her go. The guilt and torment that had shrouded him for so long reemerged, knowing that in a few brief moments, she would be gone forever, leaving him without the chance to say farewell.

With his head down at the base of the stump, Reed began his countdown. "One . . . Two . . ."

At the sound of Reed's voice, each of the kids broke off in a scurry, scrambling for a good place to hide.

Reed's voice bellowed throughout the backyard, echoing off of the tree trunks. "Six . . . Seven . . ."

Skye waltzed into the woods without a care in the world, aimlessly following behind Emma, her idol. They were only cousins, but Skye looked up to her like a sister, following her every move, even replicating the way she walked. She was a near-spitting image of Emma regarding her personality and temperament.

Skye flanked behind Emma like a shadow, cozying up next to her behind a large tree. Emma swatted her away like a fly, a constant, never-ending game between the two, leaving Skye to herself to find a new hiding place. Ultimately, Skye chose a spot one tree over where she could see and mimic Emma.

From behind Skye's scatterbrained, inattentive vision, Michael could see himself as a child, cowered behind the shed, hiding in place. He could still recall the mesmerizing feeling that consumed him that day, but as always, the fear of getting caught by his parents was stronger than his desire to explore the wilderness.

Reed finished his count and scampered directly into the woods, just as Michael expected he would do. The younger Michael raced to the deserted base and hollered in Reed's direction. "Safe," he snickered, proceeding to place one finger on the base delicately.

Reed turned around and shook his head, scowling at Michael's victory. He immediately turned his attention back to Skye and Emma, continuing his trek into the forest.

Upon Reed turning the corner of a tree, Emma bolted, beelining towards the base where Michael sat jovially. The fleet-footed Reed followed closely behind her in a footrace.

Skye turned around at the sound of rustling leaves, her attention already shifting to the next entertaining thing, whatever that might be. From behind a tree emerged a younger-looking gentleman, somewhere in his teens, perhaps slightly older. He appeared from nothing, as if he teleported at will to their exact location.

The gentleman was tall and slender, handsome, and extraordinarily cunning. His amber locks of hair hung to his shoulder, gleaming in the sunlight, dancing and weaving in the wind. Minus the faded scar etched between his brows, the man was otherwise perfect. Teeth, dimples, hair, muscles, skin, each characteristic detailed to the perfection of a near god. Michael didn't think it was possible to create a more charismatic individual. No wonder they followed him to Skye's impending death, he thought.

"Hi," the man said to Skye, approaching her slowly.

"Hi, I'm Skye," she said, painfully unaware of the danger that followed.

"Hi, Skye. You certainly are gorgeous. How would you like to see a castle today?"

"A castle?"

"A castle, indeed. A radiant castle in need of a princess."

"Ooh, I wanna be a princess."

The younger version of Michael arrived at their location just in time. He placed his arm around Skye protectively and pulled her closer to him, weary of the teen beside her. Reed and Emma arrived at them seconds after.

Skye looked up at Michael with youthful exuberance, a look that seared into his heart. "He wants to show us a castle, Mike-Mike."

Before Michael could kindly turn the gentleman away, Reed impeded his way to the forefront, thrilled at the idea of adventure. "A castle?" he questioned delightedly.

An uncomfortable smirk spread across the man's face. "That's right, a castle," he said. "I take your enthusiasm as a yes, shall I?"

"Hell yeah. Let's go," said Reed without a doubt or thought of hesitation.

Michael looked to Emma reluctantly, hoping to seek her support on the matter. "We have to go back inside, or we'll get in trouble," said Michael. "Sorry. Not today."

With his graceful demeanor and suave, the slender teen objected, possessing the kind of charm that could sell a Prius to a redneck or a gas-guzzler to an environmentalist. "It will only be five minutes of your time. After all, how often do you get to see a castle?"

"Is it like Cinderella's castle?" Emma asked eagerly.

"An exact replica, only bigger and more beautiful . . . like you."

Emma blushed sheepishly, tilting her head to the side bashfully. Her eyes glimmered with excitement, replicating those of Reed's. She turned her attention to Michael, practically begging for his approval. "We have to go, Michael. We have to. He said it'll only be five minutes. Pretty please . . . with cherries on top."

Michael responded to the teen tentatively, his voice faltering with uncertainty. "Only five minutes?"

The charming man extended his hand, his untrustworthy gaze sending shivers down Michael's paralyzed, adult spine. This was the moment he made a deal with the devil, and now he was forced to relive it once more.

"Only five minutes," the man said. "I promise." His smile beaming from ear to ear.

Michael reached his hand out carefully, with caution, and shook the gentleman's hand. Emma and Reed both squealed, unable to contain their enthusiasm any longer. They ran to the forefront, nipping at the teens' heels as he walked. Michael and Skye followed behind loosely as the group began their trek to the castle.

While Reed and Emma were on cloud nine, Michael could see the concern vexed across his forehead as Skye scanned her surroundings. Lingering inside his six-year-old mind was the impenetrable fear of getting caught, and the longer they stayed out, the better chance they would all arrive back home to a belt's worth of ass whoopings.

Michael had always been the group's goody-two-shoes, the angel on Emma's shoulder, which made Reed her metaphorical devil. Michael and Reed were polar opposites, Michael being overly cautious and far too sheltered, while Reed always searched for trouble, which left Emma as the perfect balance between the two.

She was their Florida, the coveted swing state who held all the power in their disagreements, so even though Michael feared getting caught, Emma voted yes, which left them wandering behind the heels of the mysterious man who would go on to abduct Skye.

"How much longer?" Reed groaned loudly. "It's already been five minutes."

"We're almost there," the sly teen answered. "I assure you. It's just beyond the hill."

Seemingly, on the gentleman's command, spikes of the castle ascended over the hill as their journey loomed closer. The kids looked at each other in awe, their brisk walk turning to that of a full-on sprint as the compressed trail expanded, transitioning into a solid brick.

The closer they got to the castle, the more surreal it became. Everything radiated in the purest form of high definition, as if Skye had been surveilling the landscape with polarized sunglasses.

The trees and bushes surrounding them emitted every color of the rainbow, manifesting all four seasons together in unison. Different flowers sprouted like wildfire. Yellow daisies, purple lavenders, blue bellflowers, pink tulips, and red poinsettias all bloomed vibrantly along the trail.

A river ran alongside them, leading directly to the castle. Along the riverbank, a herd of deer ate tranquilly, unphased by the travelers nearby. Geese swam throughout the river in harmony. Schools of fish leaped elegantly, somersaulting through the air. It felt and looked like a scene out of an animation movie, and even the adult logic of Michael had a hard time disputing the memory from being otherworldly.

The castle stood luxuriantly, resembling that of a historic cathedral. The kids were on cloud nine. Excitement exuded out of their pores as each of them expressed their delight differently.

Michael stared at the castle in amazement, shaking his hands rapidly in exhilaration as if they were little, uncontrollable propellers. A habit that he gladly grew out of as he got older.

Reed being the troublemaker that he was, ran and chased down squirrels and birds and any other small creatures that he could find. Emma, entranced by the unique array of flowers, picked herself out a bouquet, leaving Skye to mimic behind her.

The once shifty teen even seemed incredibly less creepy and more so like a man who had stumbled across something so tantalizing that he simply couldn't keep it to himself any longer. He had to show someone his breathtaking discovery and that someone happened to be Michael and his family members.

They each took in the moment and enjoyed the dazzling scenery around them. Michael turned to Reed and the rest of the group, his face giddy with delight. "We have to go back and show our parents. They gotta see this," he exclaimed.

Without another thought in the world, the kids sprinted back down the trail and headed home, excited to show their parents the castle they had embarked upon, and as they ran, the flowers faded, the trees withered, and the sky blurred and littered with clouds. The kids, too preoccupied with enthusiasm, failed to notice any of the changes that had taken place. They had a one-track mind with a mission of getting home to their parents. This world was too good to be true. You had to see it to believe it, and they couldn't wait to get back home and show them.

Skye hustled as fast as her little feet would take her, screaming for the rest of them to slow down, but nobody stopped on her behalf. Her feet shuffled, accelerating with every motion of her legs until her left foot hooked into a tree root, twisting her ankle and causing her to stumble. She cried out in pain, hoping for her family to return, but they had already sprinted home without her.

She turned around frantically, searching for help. The castle still danced vaguely in the distance, melting into the mirage of heatwaves. Her voice grew shaky as the panic began to build deep into her throat like phlegm. Her calls for help were soon answered by the gentleman who had guided them there. He ushered his way to her and picked her up gently, escorting Skye back to the castle, to the last place that anybody had seen her alive.

CHAPTER THREE

DARRIUS STOKES

"Michael!" the twins clamored, their voices cracking under stress. "Michael, wake up! Wake up!"

Michael slowly stirred awake, his eyes sifting through the blur of haze and unconsciousness. Smeared together were two distorted figures that he recognized as the twins by the sounds of their voices. His eyes gradually settled, as did his senses. Cam and Will squatted at his side, both sharing pale and ghastly expressions.

"Wha— what happened?" Michael stammered.

"I dunno, you touched that tree and passed out or something," said Will. "But I touched it, and nothing happened, so it must be something wrong with you, I guess."

"Are you okay?" asked Cam.

Michael sat up shakily, still groggy. "Yeah . . . I'm fine. How long was I out for?"

"Maybe five minutes. Not long."

The kids rambled off words a mile a minute, berating Michael with all sorts of questions, but their voices were drowned out by the deafening sound of his own thoughts. Confusion bubbled inside of him. His head was spinning, jumbled with too many questions to answer at once.

After all these years of being unable to remember that day, how the hell was he suddenly able to remember it now? He'd tried for so long to recall it, and now he touches some tree, and voila, he remembers? No, it doesn't work that way. That's impossible.

He had to have been dreaming, but even then, he'd never experienced a dream from another person's perspective before, nor had he encountered a dream comprising that level of accuracy and detail. It had to have been a memory, but as far as he knew, Skye was dead, and even if she was alive, accessing her memories would prove impossible. None of it made any sense.

Maybe it was guilt. The guilt of Skye and now the guilt of Peter had finally driven him mad and taken its toll on him. He tried to convince himself that the occurrence was an episode of sleep deprivation mixed with guilt and trauma, but even he didn't believe that. The memory was all too painstakingly clear to be a figment of his own ingenuity.

That castle was the castle they had seen as children, and that was the man who had kidnapped Skye. He didn't know how it was possible, but somehow, he had seen the gospel truth. He felt it deep within him, deeper than he had ever felt anything before.

All this time, Emma had been right, but that still didn't justify her belief in fairies or add any credibility to her claim. The more Michael tried to suppress any thoughts of supernatural activity, the more those thoughts stirred within him, jarring all logic out the window.

Now, there was no doubt in Michael's mind that the twins had arrived at the same castle that he had seen twenty years prior, but that still didn't explain how a castle could appear and disappear at will. Nor did it explain how a castle could exist in the throes of their backyard, yet remain hidden entirely to the likes of GPS.

Michael walked the kids home and had the twins lock the top bolt behind him. He wiggled the door handle twice on his way out for good measure. His feet escorted him to his car, mindlessly on autopilot. His mind still riddled with confusion.

He'd never had a case like this before, not since Skye, and he was only six then. How does one begin to tackle a case involving disappearing castles? He needed help. He needed someone with a sound mind, someone distanced enough to think straight. Luckily, he wasn't alone. It was time for him to head back to the precinct and meet up with his partner, Darrius.

Michael arrived at the station with his mind still muddled by the transpiring vision the tree had left him with. He reviewed Emma's papers in the all too familiar silence he had come to hate. He rehearsed lines out loud, knitting together a half-assed elevator pitch. If he was going to sell Darrius on the notion of fairies and castles, he needed to at least believe the fabrication himself, something that he was finding harder to do with every strangling line he produced.

Enough was enough, he thought. He would drive himself to another level of deranged if he sat alone with his thoughts any longer. He entered the precinct, pretending to be on the phone until he found his partner and best friend, Darrius Stokes. Darrius was active on the case, chatting with two other veterans, Ortiz and Allen.

Typically, Michael found himself on the receiving end of Ortiz and Allen's wisecracking jokes and hazing remarks, but even they must have taken notice of the urgency and stress that he exhibited. The big fuck you stamped across his forehead did him justice for once. Both of them greeted him with nothing more than a slight head nod before departing, leaving Darrius alone with Michael.

From the moment that Michael had been assigned as Darrius's partner, they became best friends. It had only been a little over a year, but it was one of those friendships that sparked instantly, leaving both feeling as if they had known each other their entire life. From day one, Darrius took Michael in under his guidance and showed him the ropes.

That was one of the many things Michael admired about Darrius was that he treated him as an equal rather than the youthful detective that he was. The hazing and superiority complex demonstrated by his peers wasn't in his nature.

Darrius treated everyone with respect. Everyone earned his respect until they didn't, and then it was damn near impossible to get it back. He was the most genuine, down-to-earth dude Michael had ever met. He saw the best in everyone and made it his mission to bring it out of them. Michael aspired to be just like him one day, and if he achieved nothing more in life than becoming a little more like Darrius and less like himself, then that would be one hell of a life.

Darrius was smooth, much smoother than Michael or anyone else at the department, for that matter. He had an unparalleled charisma, and it showed in the way everyone gravitated towards him. Michael couldn't think of anyone who didn't like the guy, except the criminals he incarcerated, that is.

Darrius was older than Michael, somewhere in his mid-thirties. Father time hadn't been as nice as it could've been to him. A few months back, Darrius started getting streaks of gray hairs, but he pulled them off elegantly, referring to them as his wisdom locks. It was just another element to his charm, another facet of his game to add to his repertoire.

Darrius looked Michael over the same way Ortiz and Allen had, leaving Michael to feel like he had something stuck in his teeth. "You look rough," said Darrius, emphasizing the word rough.

"Oh," replied Michael, patting his hair down to no avail. With each pat, his hair flared upwards again at the release of his hand. Amid his shambolic day, he had forgotten all about his sloppy appearance. "Sorry, it's been quite the day."

"I can tell," said Darrius, following Michael to their office. "What's gotten into you? You got that whole signature Michael Leitner look going on."

"What? I don't have no signature look," retorted Michael, scrunching his eyebrows together.

"You do, though. It's that I'm about to crack this case wide-open look. So, what's up? Spill it."

"That's the thing," said Michael, shutting the office door behind them and motioning for Darrius to take a seat. "I think I do have our first lead. I just don't think you will like it all that much."

"Okay," said Darrius, his stare cold and tense. "Lay it on me. What're we looking at?"

Michael sighed a deep, laboring breath. The air-filled the pit of his stomach and expelled as if Michael needed every breath of air to usher the words he was about to say. "I think . . . I think we're looking at something supernatural here."

"Say what now?" riddled Darrius, taken aback.

"Something supernatural. As in otherworldly," said Michael squeamishly, swallowing his words.

"I'm getting pranked, right? This is one of those funny little videos that will wind up on the internet and go viral, huh? Real funny. Which one of the guys put you up to this?" said Darrius, looking around the office jokingly for hidden cameras.

"Look, I know how crazy it sounds. It's bat shit crazy. I know. When Emma first mentioned supernatural elements, I felt the same way."

"Emma turned you on to this nonsense?"

"Yeah. Well, no, not exactly. Kind of, I don't know. Just listen," said Michael, forgetting any remnant of the bullshit speech he had rehearsed in his vehicle. He was freestyling now, shooting from the hip and failing miserably. "I dismissed it originally, but then I touched this tree that I can only assume to be magic and—"

"A magic tree?" Darrius questioned, cutting Michael off. "It sounds like you did some magic mushrooms. That's what it sounds like."

"I didn't do mushrooms," said Michael. "I mean not now, maybe once or twice years ago, but whatever, that's not the point."

"So, what the hell do you and Emma think are behind the disappearances then? Ghouls? Goblins? The Boogeyman? He seems to have an affinity for kids, so I could see how that would make sense. Is that the type of shit you're talking about here?"

"No, man. Come on. Cut it out, please. I'm being serious. I don't know what's going on out there, but I'm starting to believe that Emma might be right. She thinks it's . . . she thinks it's fairies," said Michael as the nervousness seeped through the tightness of his face.

"Fairies?"

"Yeah," grimaced Michael. "And seeing as how we don't have any leads . . . I don't see the harm in investigating it. Take a look," he said, swiveling his computer monitor towards

Darrius. He showed him a webpage involving fairy abductions and proceeded to tell him about Will and Cam's adventure to the castle while mixing in the aspect of lost time as well. "Then the three of us went back—"

"You brought the kids back there with you? Are you serious, Michael? Do you realize how much trouble you could've gotten in for that? Bringing the kids back to the scene of the crime? That's not just young, rookie detective dumb. That's straight-up IQ level dumb."

"I know," said Michael, unable to make eye contact with him. "I shouldn't have brought them with me. Emma would've killed me had she known, but I had my pistol on me at all times, holstered and ready to go. We were more than safe. I assure you. I had to go back there and squander whatever leads I could get out of them. We had nothing, Dee. I was desperate."

Darrius shook his with disappointment and stared off into the distance. "I understand. I really do. I probably would've done the same thing when I was younger, but that doesn't change the fact that it was incredibly reckless of you. What if something would've happened to them? Or happened to you? You should've called me first."

"And what would you have said? You wouldn't have let me go there alone with them. Even if you did believe me enough to come out there, you wouldn't have taken them with us. I'm not saying it was the right thing to do . . . but I can remember everything from the day Skye disappeared now.

"You know how long I've been trying to remember that day? I'm not even sure how it happened or what happened, to be exact. But I touched this tree—a tree that didn't exist two days ago according to the kids—and after that, the memories of that day flooded back to me," said Michael, making it a point not to mention that those memories belonged to Skye and not himself.

"This tree is humongous, like impossible to miss big, and the twins claim it wasn't there before, and now all of a sudden, I touch it and have some sort of memory type of superpower. It doesn't make any sense."

"You're damn right it doesn't," remarked Darrius. "Do you hear yourself? You need to get some rest, bro. Go back to your place and get some sleep. Me and the boys can handle it today. We got your back, Mike. In the meantime, you and I can finish this conversation tomorrow."

"You're probably right. I could use the rest, but I'm not putting off tomorrow what can be done today. We need answers. That's why I'm going back tonight. Something weird is going on out there, and I need to find out what it is. I want you to come with me."

"He-e-e-ell no! I'm black. Black people don't go into the woods, Mike. Not at night. Not even during the daytime. That's some white people shit. I've seen enough horror movies to know how this trip ends for me."

"I'm serious, Darrius. I need you."

"I'm serious too, and ain't no way I'm going into those creepy-ass woods late at night."

"I know you're skeptical, but every year child disappearances spike around this time. But every twenty years, that number spikes astronomically. That can't be a mere coincidence."

"It's summertime, man. There's no school. The sun's out longer. Kids are outside more. I think you're reaching hard on this one."

"How else do you explain the lost time? And what about the strange disappearances?" Michael stroked his keyboard, browsing pages on the internet before turning the monitor back to Darrius. "This isn't a normal case. At least you can attest to that. Before my sister disappeared, there was another kidnapping. It took place twenty years prior. Adam Barnhart, age six. It checks all the boxes for supernatural elements, including lost time as well as his sister claiming to have seen heaven. Twenty years later, Skye goes missing. Fast forward another twenty, and now Peter is missing. There's no such thing as coincidences on this job, you know that. I just can't believe I didn't find this connection sooner."

Darrius sighed. "I know more than anyone how much this case means to you, but you're clearly stressed. You're overloaded and over your head. You need to take a break and regroup. I think this case is too close to home for you. You should take this one off and let me and the others handle it."

Michael, visibly flustered, closed his eyes and exhaled deeply. "You don't understand, Darrius. I have to find Peter. I never found Skye, and not a day goes by that I don't think about that. I failed her . . . I failed my family. I failed myself . . . I can't afford to fail Peter too."

"It wasn't your responsibility to find her, Michael. You were six years old, for crying out loud. You didn't fail at anything. What happened to her wasn't your fault."

"Tell that to my family," Michael muttered underneath his breath. "I'm the one who lost her. It was my fault, and nobody can convince me otherwise." The guilt seething exceedingly more as of late after seeing Skye on the ground abandoned by him. "If I don't find Peter, I'll just be proving everyone right."

"Proving everyone right about what?"

"Being a failure . . . not being good enough."

"I don't think you're a failure. Far from it, you're one of the youngest detectives in our precinct's history, and you're a damn good one too."

"None of that matters. I'm a good-for-nothing failure and always have been. Everyone thinks it, even Emma. I could see it in her eyes earlier."

Darrius paused long and hard, biding his time. Michael knew him well enough to know that he was articulating some form of wisdom to inject upon him.

"We're a lot alike, me and you, you know that?" Darrius asked rhetorically. "I used to blame myself for my dad's murder. I know, it sounds stupid, right? But some part of me believed I should've done something or tried to save him. At the end of the day, though, I was only a kid. What the hell was I supposed to do? Because of that guilt, I became an officer, just like my pops. I don't remember if it was to make him proud or provide him the justice he deserved. Probably a bit of both looking back on it.

"In due time, I worked my way to detective, buried myself in case after case, just like you. I thought if I apprehended murderers, I'd get some kind of conviction from it all. Funny thing is that didn't bring my dad back. The whole burying myself into my work was merely a bandage. It wasn't the stitches or the healing that I needed. Point being in all of this—you can't save the world if you don't fix yourself first. You're one of the baddest dudes I know, and the moment you realize that the universe better take notice. You have the whole world ahead of you, but what you choose to do with it is up to you, and you won't get very far doubting yourself. If you don't believe in yourself, who will?"

Michael sulked in his chair, merging into it and wearing it like the shell of a turtle. He nodded his head but didn't quite have the words to respond to Darrius.

"Well, you sold me," said Darrius. "I'll meet you tonight."

"Seriously?" exclaimed Michael. "To the woods?"

"Yeah, to the stupid ass woods, knucklehead. You're going with or without me, so I might as well tag along and keep your dumbass out of trouble. With that being said, I'm only going on one condition. We do this my way, and my way only, or I'm out, you hear?" He stared at Michael sternly, resembling the glare of a parent.

Michael nodded his head in agreement. "What's your terms?"

"We go tonight. If we strike out, you're off the case, and me and Ortiz take it from there on out. Do we have a deal?"

"I suppose so." Michael shook Darrius's hand, shaking his head with displeasure at the agreement. He hated the deal, but having the experience and level-headedness of Darrius beside him was instrumental. "Meet me at Emma's at ten . . . and hey, this stays between us, you know that, right?"

"Oh, believe me, I know. I'm not trying to get sent to the psych ward because I went fairy hunting with you," chuckled Darrius. "I'll see you tonight. Get some rest until then." He shut the door behind him and exited the office.

Michael stayed put, researching incessantly, searching for any and everything fairy related. After about thirty minutes, his lack of sleep had finally caught up to him, so he took Darrius's words of advice and crashed on the tiny, uncomfortable futon that was perched in the corner of their office.

When Michael awoke, it was almost time to meet up with Darrius. He packed everything he would need for their trip, including two handguns that he attached to his firearm belt, a Glock 19 in his left holster, and a Ruger SR9 in his right. He stored half a dozen magazines in his pockets, all of them filled with ammo. He threw on his bulletproof vest and exited his office.

He had no idea what he was in store for. Likewise, he didn't know if bullets would work on fairies or whatever supernatural entity it was that they were hunting, but he packed them, just in case. Even he had to take a moment to laugh at the absurdity of it all. He really convinced his partner to go fairy hunting with him. What kind of lunatic does that? He really was thankful to have Darrius at his side. He didn't know of many other people willing to risk their jobs to search for Neverland.

Michael stored his shotgun in the trunk of his car, preparing for any wild encounter such as a coyote or a bear. He was over prepared; that's just the way he was wired. He left the precinct and sped off to Emma's to meet Darrius. When he arrived, Darrius was already there waiting on him.

Darrius loaded the shells into a shotgun of his own and cocked it. "Tinker Bell, here we come, baby."

Michael gave him a look of agitation. "I'm glad you find this so amusing."

"Don't you? I mean, look at us. We're going fairy hunting. Out of all my years of seeing white people shit, this is by far the craziest white person shit I have ever seen. I mean ever. I hope you know that."

"I'm well aware. Trust me," said Michael, striding off towards the woods, gesturing for Darrius to follow him.

The light from his flashlight illuminated the vast and eerie forest before them. Michael guided the way with his flashlight in his left hand while his Glock rested easy in his right hand, atop his left wrist for support.

It was a wet-drizzly night; their footsteps sloshed in the mud as rain sopped the trail. The path felt longer than it did earlier in the day when Michael had traveled it with his cousins. Maybe it was because of the rain, but Michael could feel the anxiety mounting inside him with each trudging step.

No matter what, Michael tried his hardest to prepare for the disappointment that most likely lied ahead. If this lead struck out, then they were back to square one, this time without his help. He needed something concrete to convince Darrius that this case was unlike others and involved some sort of magic or something of occult nature.

The trail beneath them began to narrow and wither away at their feet, which meant the tree was getting closer. In the daytime, the yew tree was calm and tranquil, entrancing and filled with bliss.

In the night, it was the opposite, a reciprocal of the magnificent beauty displayed in the sunlight. The tree was bone-chilling; its herculean branches were as wide as tree trunks, extending throughout as if ten different trees merged together to form one. The branches casted sinister shadows in the distance, playing tricks on their eyes, but neither of them could break free from its haunting and captivating grasp.

"This is the tree," said Michael. "The one I touched earlier and could somehow remember my sister's disappearance afterwards."

Michael tiptoed around the tree cautiously, shining his light upon it as he did. The tree was massive, so much so that it was impossible for him to illuminate the whole thing. Darrius followed behind him, ready to shoot and ask questions later.

Michael knew Darrius lacked belief in fairies, rightfully so, but he also knew his partner feared what surprises nature might have in store for them. That much was apparent by Darrius's furrowed eyebrows and the death grip he held over his shotgun. As if on cue, Michael stopped dead in his tracks, unable to suppress the haunted expression that swept over him.

Darrius clenched his shotgun tighter, his hair raising at the sight of his partner's fear. "Wha— what is it?"

"The tree," said Michael in disbelief. "It's different. When I came here earlier, there was nothing but tree brush behind it." Michael struggled to find his words. "It's . . . it's all gone. This was as far as we could go last time."

Michael gulped, trying his best to clear his face from the fear that tugged at him. He tried equally as hard not to let Darrius see it; after all, this was his idea. He motioned Darrius with his flashlight, gesturing for him to stay close behind.

This had to have been where his cousins ventured off too, Michael thought. A mixture of excitement and trepidation formed inside him, only to be dispelled by the startling caws of a bird. Michael shakily gleamed the flashlight into the direction of the cries. The light gave way to a raven nestled atop one of the mysterious branches of the yew tree.

"Oh, hell nah," exclaimed Darrius. "Get me the hell out of here, stat."

The raven's caws echoed eerily throughout the forest. Michael squinted, examining the bird to the best of his ability. The night shadows and the raven's feathers camouflaged together, revealing nothing but a pair of black and beady eyes. The raven stared them down intently, sending chills down Michael's spine. It felt as if the two had just received an omen of death—a warning from the raven, cautioning them against adventuring any further.

Michael almost heeded the raven's foreboding warnings and Darrius's multiple attempts to leave, but he couldn't turn away. Not now, they had come too far. As much as Michael wanted to curl up in bed and forget about those ominous set of eyes, he couldn't. They had to keep going. Who knew when the tree would open up its trail again and welcome more visitors? It was a risk Michael simply couldn't take. If they turned around, they might never get this opportunity again.

"It's fine," said Michael, attempting to reassure both Darrius and himself. "If the worst thing we encounter tonight is a raven, then that's a win in my book."

Darrius begrudgingly followed Michael farther along the trail. "Easy for you to say, white man. You're not the one who's gonna die out here."

"Huh? What are you talking about?"

"I'm talking about a black man in the woods. They don't make horror movies where we survive."

"Then explain LL Cool J."

"That doesn't count. Everyone knows rappers can't die in a horror movie. It's a part of their contract."

"I highly doubt that, but we're not in a horror movie, so you will be fine. Now can we keep it moving?"

"Nah, instead, we're in a fairytale with ankle-biting fairies and leprechauns."

"Precisely, and after our survival, you can write a horror movie of your own based on the outcome."

"I just might have to," said Darrius, following even closer behind Michael after confronting the raven.

With each step into the dark abyss, the trail slowly illuminated. Initially, Michael thought his eyes were playing tricks on him again, but there was no mistaking it. The further they trekked, the brighter the trail became, to where Michael no longer needed his flashlight, so he turned it off to conserve the battery.

"Hey, turn that back on," hollered Darrius.

"For what?" asked Michael. "We don't need it anymore."

"What do you mean we don't need it anymore? It's dark as shit. Quit playing and turn that thing back on."

Michael, too mesmerized by the glimmering trail surrounding him, ignored Darrius's cries. He watched in awe as every color of the rainbow illuminated the forest floor. The mushrooms, the shrubbery, the tree roots, the blades of grass beneath them all gleamed shades of red and lavender and orange, representing every spectrum imaginable.

Michael's body rattled with excitement; he couldn't believe his eyes. After twenty years of searching, he was finally back on the trail that could lead him to the unsolved mystery of his past.

"Mike, stop playing, man," bellowed Darrius. "Turn that shit back on."

Michael snapped out of his daydream and back to his current reality. "You're kidding, right? It's lit up like crazy out here. No way you can't see."

"No, it's not. What the hell are you talking about?" said Darrius, his voice fading as Michael's pace distanced the two.

"I don't know how you're not seeing it, but I can see everything out here," said Michael, turning around and catching the fear that tremored in Darrius's eyes. Michael turned the flashlight back on, illuminating the dark and eerie forest for Darrius. "It's just like before, when I was a kid, the trail got all fluorescent, just like this."

"Give me that damn thing," said Darrius, snatching the flashlight from him and trading Michael his shotgun so he could use his off hand to guide the light.

The forest became blinding, to where Michael had to remove a hand from the shotgun to shield his eyes. Tiny, bright orbs pranced around the trail like fireflies. About a hundred yards ahead, barely decipherable through the light, was what could only be described as a portal.

The portal was oval, about five feet tall and a few feet wide. The perimeter had crisp, rigid blue edges that danced around it like flames. Inside the fiery outside, another world existed. Glimpses at a time flashed through the filmy, hazy surface. A harsh black and blue purgatory, reminiscent of space, fluttered inside the portal, but every so often, an exquisite landscape peered through the veil, staring back at Michael and inviting him inside.

Within the veil was a rigorously sparkling sunlight, the contrasting dark around him mixed with the light of the foreign landscape blinded him even more. In the patches of black that he saw from blinking his eyes, he could make out what looked to be a meadow of some sort. It was the world that eluded him for so long. Michael was sure of it. After all this time, he had finally found it.

"The portal," said Michael enthusiastically. "It's here. That's where Peter is."

"I don't see anything," whimpered Darrius. The flashlight rattled in his convulsing hands, flickering like a strobe light. "L-L-Let's go back," he said, fighting against the rabid clattering of his teeth. He pounded the head of the flashlight against his quivering palm and tightened it, but the light still pulsed on and off until finally, it shut off for good, shrouding him in a veil of darkness.

"We can't go back," said Michael. "I've been waiting twenty years for this. I have to see what's in there. Wherever this place leads to, I'm going."

Michael's body magnetized to the portal like he was positive, and the portal was negative, the two destined for a crash course. His feet moved without command, as if they had a mind of their own, shuffling towards the portal. This was his sole reason for becoming a detective. It was finally emanating before him; there was no way he could turn around now.

"We're closing in on it," said Michael, reaching back and offering his hand out towards Darrius. "Grab my hand."

"I can't see you, Mike. Where are you?" asked Darrius, flailing his hands around frantically to find Michael.

Michael turned around to help him. He shielded his eyes, protecting against the harsh brightness that emitted from the forest floor. After a few seconds, he was able to eye out a blurry, silhouette-shaped Darrius. He swung his hand outwards towards Darrius and grasped his arm. "Hold on. Things could get bumpy."

"Bumpy?" questioned Darrius. "What do you mean by bumpy?"

"I don't know, but we're about to find out."

Michael turned around, disoriented from the constant probing of his eyesight. There it was, an arm's length away, the portal that had evaded him for so long. Michael sifted through its filmy surface and felt the heart of the portal breathe in and out, as if it were a living, breathing creature. Its texture was like that of lukewarm water or dense fog, something you could feel and not feel at the same time. "The portal. It's—" Before Michael could finish his statement, he vanished. The portal vacuumed him in, absorbing him, the two becoming one and collapsing in on each other.

CHAPTER FOUR

STEINA & REYNIR

Fluorescent blue and purple lights swarmed past Michael, whirling and whooshing together violently yet majestically. The colors raced past him, leaving violet contrails in place. The lights encapsulated him, stretching across the unseen horizon, spreading throughout the vast and desolate void as far it could reach. Michael felt weightless, as if he were flying. The fluttering sensation that accompanied him, combined with the transcendent speeds that orbited around him, left him with bouts of vertigo.

"Darrius?" Michael hollered, desperately hoping to find his best friend. "Darrius? Do you hear me?" He screamed once more but heard no response.

The panic tugged at Michael's mind, attacking it like a virus, targeting Michael's fears and insecurities. Any attempt at an escape seemed improbable. The sheer and insurmountable region that contained him was endless, a never-ending loophole, destined to conceal him for eternity.

Seconds felt like hours as claustrophobia and hopelessness clutched at him until finally, the blue and purple lights evaporated. The portal dissipated, vanishing before him and releasing him into a beautiful and foreign land.

The rich and indulgent wildlife that sprouted around Michael could be felt immediately. The air around him felt lighter and less dense, lacking the contamination of the smog-filled Earth cities he had grown accustomed to. The air was so pure and unfiltered; it was irritable, stinging, and singeing the inside of his nose.

Upon getting acclimated to the unfamiliar environment, a crisp aroma of nature occupied his senses. The minty freshness of pine trees, a wafting breeze that exuded the moisture of the nearby lake, a hint of citrus, and the smell of neighboring rocks and boulders lingered in his nostrils. The combination of aromatic scents vanquished the stabbing sensation that had existed moments prior, reminding him of the overbearing fragrances of a candle shop around Christmas time.

Michael took a deep breath and took in the ethereal world that engulfed him, taking close notice to how glinting the sun in place was. After being trapped in a veil of darkness, the intense sunlight glared mercifully upon his eyes leaving them to need a few minutes to adapt.

Once adjusted, he could see the root of the scalding and intense heat. His current world, wherever that was, was sandwiched between two suns, one of which was much closer than the sun back home on Earth. The other sun was further away, but he could only assume that the planet traveled back and forth between the two as the year went on. Both growing and shrinking in size, ebbing and flowing like the tide.

Seven moons clogged the flaming orange and yellow horizon. The largest moon being so close it seemed destined to collide and crater into the realm, colossal enough that it could swallow a hundred different Earth-sized moons and still have room for more. The other moons ranged from large to almost indiscernible in the daytime sky.

Michael overlooked the nearby lake. Its calmness and serenity somewhat reducing the rapid drumming of his heart. His surroundings were quiet, the only sounds being that of the soothing whistling of the winds and the hushed chirpings of birds.

Pine trees encircled the lake, stretching as far back as he could see, blending into the beautiful mountains that surged into the distance. To his right, he could see a castle encrusted into one of the mountain tops, embodying itself so snugly and comfortably that it appeared as if nature had done the deed on its own. Even miles into the distance, the enormous castle thwarted everything else around it.

It wasn't the same castle Michael had visited as a child, but he was impressed nonetheless, enraptured by the beauty and magnificence of the planet. He was equally filled with angst and terror at the idea of venturing into an unknown world.

Any place with two suns and seven moons was galaxies away from Earth. And that thought terrified him. Anxiety immersed upon him uncontrollably, swaddling his every thought. Where the hell was he? How was he going to get home? Could he even survive here long enough to get home? What was he going to eat? Where was he going to stay? He didn't know how to camp. What about Darrius and Peter? Where were they?

Michael's crippling thoughts and fears submerged over him, leaving his chest heavy. His lungs struggled for air as he gasped in hyperventilating breaths. He hurled his hands to his face, cupping them around his mouth, trying his best to breathe as deeply as he could into them, attempting to feel the air expand into his lungs and chest , all the way down to his stomach.

He envisioned the anxiety that latched onto him leave his body with each breath that he exhaled. After years of extensive practice and breathing techniques, he learned to rid himself of the chronic anxiety attacks that plagued him.

He managed his anxiety some, but no matter how hard he tried, he couldn't stop the overwhelming distress that afflicted his mind when he thought about his cousin, Peter. If this was where Peter had ventured off to, he could be anywhere by now. Michael needed to find him fast; it had already been damn near three days.

Time was of the essence, and Michael had the slightest idea where to begin looking for him. He surveyed his surroundings, ultimately deciding that the best place to investigate would be an area of civilization, leading him on a path towards the castle.

On second thought, maybe it was best to avoid civilization. If racism and bigotry existed on his planet, he could only imagine an outsider such as himself wouldn't be well received here. What if the people here spoke a different language? How the hell would he translate that he was searching for his lost cousin?

Before his mind could dwell into another rabbit hole of paranoia and anxiety, a deep-bellowing voice greeted him. A voice that sounded as if the speaker had stones for vocal cords.

"Hello," said the gravelly voice, sending tiny ripples along the surface of the lake.

Michael turned around, startled by the booming and echoing voice. He looked up and immediately regretted making eye contact with the titan that lurched a comfortable thirty feet above him. His entire body quivered, billowing with fear to the likes he'd never experienced before.

The giant's lips curled and twisted mischievously, augmenting Michael's paralyzing fear. The beast had tusks that sprouted from the top of its head. One pair arched like a parabola out of the temples of his forehead while the other pair stood upright, erecting like a field goal post. His nose was a disgusting and pimply monstrosity, the size of a small child. His teeth proliferated out of his mouth like that of a snaggle-toothed bulldog.

"What you do on my lake?" the giant asked.

Michael, noticeably trembling, clasped his shotgun with dear life. "I'm h . . . I'm h-here for a young boy," he said shakily. "His n-name is Peter. I'm here to return him home."

"Young boy? You pedophile or sumtn?"

"No, sir, he's my cousin," Michael stuttered once more.

"Tiny gun don't hurt me," said the giant, pointing at Michael's shotgun.

"I'm sure it doesn't, and I have no intention of using it. You simply startled me, that's all." Michael gently placed the shotgun on the ground, slowly regaining his composure, trying his hardest to control his aggressive shivering. "I've never encountered someone of your magnitude before. I come here in peace. I only wish to seek my cousin and return home."

"No, you no return home. I eat you, instead," said the giant, flashing a malevolent grin. His teeth were grimy with slime and a remarkable amount of plaque.

Before Michael could reason with the giant or plead his case, he was met with a fist the size of himself. He dodged the exorbitant fist by mere inches, feeling the visceral force created by it glide across his face. The impact of the fist striking land created a small fissure in the Earth, sending Michael catapulting into the air, tumbling and sailing through the wind as if he had been on the receiving end of a double bounce on the trampoline.

He watched helplessly as Darrius's shotgun sailed into the lake, leaving him defenseless from any future giant attacks. His body crashed into a nearby boulder, knocking the breath out of him. He hunched together on all fours, harrowing and gasping for air.

An arrow zipped through the sky, its direction unknown, drilling the giant in the chest and digging into his callused skin. The giant let out a weak, disgruntled moan and pulled the arrow out of his sternum. His eyebrows tensed, revealing the fiery rage within. If he wasn't pissed off by the new intruder, he was definitely irate now. While discarding the arrow, it detonated in his hands, riling the giant up even more. He scanned the battlefield angrily, in search of his assailant.

Michael made it to his feet, still groggy from his collision. If he was ever going to make a break for it, this would be the time. Never mind, too late, he thought as he instinctively dived out of the way of a large boulder that had been hurled at him. Then the giant turned his attention back to his mystery assailant, examining across the lake once more.

Michael spotted the archer sheltered behind a pine tree, hoisting a bow and arrow at the heart of the giant. The bow master was a woman, arrayed in full body armor from head-to-toe, dressed nothing like the cliché, scantily clad fantasy armor Michael had grown accustomed to seeing in his childhood video games. The armor covered her legs and torso completely.

She sported a mask, similar to that of a masquerade mask, leaving her chin open to injury, but otherwise, it covered the rest of her face. She fired another arrow at the giant, but this time he backhanded it away with his rugged and stony hand, shattering the arrow into pieces.

The giant grabbed another boulder, this one larger than Michael, and tossed it at the warrior with ease. She swiftly shot another arrow into the hurrying boulder, exploding it into thousands of tiny meteorite chunks.

"We don't have to do this, Ortr," said the woman. "Let the man go, and we will leave you be."

"We?" the titan queried. "Who else with Steina? Show your face or die," he shouted, shaking the ground with fierce, thunderous stomps.

Hidden from behind another tree, a gentleman emerged. He lacked the full body armor of his comrade. Instead, he sported a very outdated eighties-esque jumpsuit with overly baggy, aqua-colored sweatpants. A similarly colored t-shirt with splotches of purple and pink draped over his torso. The shirt was also loose and baggy but tight enough to reveal the frame of broad shoulder pads underneath. The pads, whether they were full armor or not, nestled atop his shoulders, personifying the existence of large trap muscles.

Along his wrists and forearms ran an alloy enforced shielding of some sort that extended over his hands like gloves. His hair was a silky colored gray, a stylish gray as opposed to an aged, dingy-looking white-ish gray. To match his eccentric clothing, his hair slicked and pulled back like a ponytail, but instead of falling to his shoulders, the hair stood tall, almost like a hi-top fade that curled fashionably at its end.

"Ugh," belched Ortr. "Elf scum, Reynir. I kill you now. That make me happy."

"Elf scum?" replied Reynir with a roguish, wisecracking smile. "That's no way to treat an old friend, Ortr. Your old man would be disappointed in that type of behavior."

"Friends? Ortr have no friends. I teach you lesson."

"How about we hold on any lessons for the time being and bargain instead?" asked Steina.

"No bargain. I just eat you," said Ortr, snarling his funky, snaggle-toothed smile. He barreled forward, charging at the duo of Steina and Reynir.

"Be my guest," quirked Reynir.

Blinding purple and white lightning bolts began to dance between Reynir's hands and fingers. Michael could hear the electrical crackling from lengths away as Reynir's power began to intensify. The bolts buzzed and whirred, spreading from his hands to his entire body.

As Ortr surged closer, Reynir harnessed the energy together, suctioning it back to his hands. The energy swelled in size, spherical in shape, larger than an exercise ball. He thrust his right hand forward fiercely, powering the orb at Ortr.

Ortr drove forward without fear or hesitation. He backhanded the orb as if it was a mere tennis ball, propelling it back into Steina and Reynir's direction. The duo quickly dived out of the way to safety. The orb crashed into the turf, missing them narrowly and indenting a large crater in its landing place.

Ortr attacked relentlessly, taking full advantage of his dizzied opponents. He leapt in the air and smashed the ground next to them, vaulting them through the atmosphere. Reynir careened through the skies unsteadily, stabling himself by discharging more energy from his hands, this time more rapidly, creating a jet pack like approach. He spawned a large, oval-shaped disc that hovered below Steina and escorted her to the ground safely.

Ortr retaliated by chunking another monstrous boulder at them, this one larger than the last. Reynir stood tall in front of Steina, erecting a force field and shielding them from danger. The boulder collided into the force field and fragmented into tiny, obsolete pebbles.

"Now," yelled Reynir.

Steina wielded her bow and arrow once more, this time casting two arrows at Ortr. As the arrows zipped through the air, Reynir harnessed his energy once more. This time in the form of two bustling lassos that he fired at Ortr's wrists. The energetic ropes connected, cuffing Ortr momentarily, searing and flaying his skin.

Reynir etched his feet firmly into the dirt. He tugged at the ropes strenuously, trying his hardest to keep Ortr from breaking free. The more that Ortr jerked and pulled away, the more the ropes carved into him, burning and tormenting him, filleting away at his hands slowly.

Reynir's teeth clenched tightly as he pulled. His arms spasmed and shook involuntarily as he fought against the giant's strength. Reynir's arms gave way to Ortr's almighty power. Ortr's right wrist burst free from the lasso entangled around it. He flung his left arm forward, whipping Reynir into the air along with it.

Reynir held on for dear life, like a kid on the playground who lost their grip on the roundabout. He crashed into the ground forcefully, but he managed to maintain his death grip on Ortr's left wrist.

The arrows that Steina had expelled connected with Ortr, piercing through his chest. Ortr scowled in pain, each moan coming in muffled chokes. He attempted to remove the arrows with his free hand, but Reynir corralled his right arm once more, denying him the opportunity.

Reynir tugged mightily, restraining Ortr long enough for the arrows to erupt simultaneously, each one pulverizing a hole into Ortr's chest. Ortr's eyes rolled to the back of his head as he collapsed to the Earth with a thunderous plummet, causing the ground to tremor with the force of a minor earthquake.

Michael cowered behind the boulder in a daze. No. No, no, no. None of this was really happening right now, he told himself. None of this was real. He probably got knocked unconscious again, and when he awakes, he will find Darrius looking after him. This was all some horrible nightmare concocted by his subconscious that he couldn't wait to forget all about.

Fear lurked over him at every corner, but Michael pushed it away, slowly getting his grip back on the world in front of him. That fear had quelled and migrated into a mixture of bewilderment and fascination. Before today he would've never believed magic existed, but here he was in the midst of an epic battle between a giant and two magicians.

Sure, he did have a brief encounter with what he believed to be a magical realm, but he was a kid then, and prior to this morning, even he didn't believe that outlandish story. If Reynir had appeared on Earth and yielded the same level of magic that Michael had just witnessed, he would be revered as God, the second coming of Christ.

Steina and Reynir approached him from the battlefield, greeting him as they came within a social distance of one another. "Greetings and salutations," said the sorcerer, outstretching his hand towards Michael. "I am Reynir." His warrior façade now gone, replaced by a goofy and quirky smile. "This is my comrade, Steina."

Michael extended his hand and greeted both of them. He hadn't noticed how pale and fair-skinned either of them were until they had gotten closer to him. They both exuded a glamourous greyish skin tone that glinted exquisitely in the sunlight.

"Nice to meet the both of you," said Michael. "It's a pleasure. I suppose thanks are in order for saving my ass back there."

"Ahh, don't mention it, pal," replied Reynir. "That is part of my job as a glorious council representative of Alfheim. To protect and serve," he said, saluting overzealously.

"Well, thank you. I couldn't be more appreciative. What did you call this place exactly? Alfheim?"

"Alfheim, indeed. One of the nine glorious realms interconnected by the beauty of Yggdrasil."

Steina scoffed at Reynir and rolled her eyes. "He doesn't know what any of that means, dweeb."

"Yee-dra-seal?" questioned Michael. "What is that? A *Pokémon* or something?"

"Yggdrasil is the world tree," said Steina. "The tree of life. It is what connects the nine realms and separates them. Without it, there would be no harmony or unification. The worlds would be overrun and ravaged by chaos and war to the likes we have never seen."

"I'm sorry, please bear with me, but what?"

"You are on Alfheim, one of the nine realms of the universe. Home of the light elves."

"You two are elves?" Michael asked, his eyes widening at the remark.

"That we are," said Reynir. "Extravagant things we are, aye?"

Michael looked them over in the least menacing way possible. His face fairer than theirs, white with shock. Amid the battle with Ortr, he hadn't gotten the opportunity to pay close attention to Steina's appearance. But now that she was closer and without her mask, he gawked at her beauty, simply unable to get in a blink.

Her masquerade-less face accentuated her ears. They were much larger than the average pair of human ears and were pointed in style, similar to how fantasy lore portrayed them. She was very slender, petite almost, but maybe it only appeared that way because of her height. Michael was a solid 6'2, and she stood toe-to-toe with him, slightly taller if he were to count the tips of her ears.

But it wasn't her skin tone or ears that grasped Michael's attention. It was her eyes. They were the most radiating eyes he had ever encountered. They enchanted him, reminding him of a crystal-clear blue that could only be found on an ocean's shore. Light shades of green encircled her pupils, magnetizing him even more, compelling and hypnotizing him to her supernal beauty.

Michael broke their uncomfortable gaze after realizing Steina had noticed him checking her out. He began to ramble nervously, blurting out the first thing that came to his mind in an attempt to coax over the sudden awkwardness.

"Soooo," stammered Michael. "Uh . . . I was doing some research before I arrived here—on the internet—I don't know if you guys know what that is, it's this thing that, I'm sorry, disregard that, I'm rambling. But anyways, I came across a place called Faerieland. Is that a real place? Because I obviously see now that elves are real. And . . . I don't know. I was kind of wondering about the existence of fairies now."

"Elves, fairies—same thing essentially," said Steina. "Somewhere lost between translation and time, they became two separate entities to your kind. Midgardians, that is, but ultimately that's wrong. The fairies that come to the mind of humans are often sprites or pixies. To answer your question, Faerieland, you are looking at it, kid. The correct term is Alfheim."

Michael was awestruck with the absurdity of it all. He couldn't believe it. Emma had actually been right. Well, partially since fairies were technically elves and didn't exist, but whatever, he didn't have time to argue the semantics of it all. Alfheim, elves, fairies, magic. His brain was on fire, revving RPM's at a speed too fast for him to calculate.

"Let's get you to safety so we can work on getting you back home," said Reynir disrupting Michael's latest train of thought.

Michael cleared his head and brought his attention back to Reynir. "No, I can't. Not yet. I appreciate your help, but I can't leave here until I find my partner."

"Partner? Is there another traveling with you?"

"I don't know. He was accompanying me on Earth, but I haven't seen him since then. I arrived here via some portal, but he never made it through with me. I can't leave here until I know he's safe."

"You entered through converging points of Yggdrasil," said Steina. "Every time that meddlesome squirrel, Ratatosk, runs and scurries away from the dragon, Nidhogg, he rattles and sways the branches of Yggdrasil, converging worlds upon each other momentarily, for very brief periods. When they fold upon each other like this, portals appear at the convergence site. These convergence sites are heavily enchanted back on Midgard. Typically, only kids or returning adults can see them. I assume this isn't your first rodeo in interdimensional realm travel?"

"Correct, I suppose," Michael answered reluctantly. "Prior to today, I was skeptical of that visit, but it's beginning to feel more and more real. I don't know where it was that I wound up, though."

"Could have been anywhere," said Reynir. "No way of telling. Realms converge and collapse at random. Depends on what branches that pesky ol' Ratatosk ruffles. Fickle little tree that Yggdrasil is. Midgard lies at the heart of it, so it happens to be the most common convergence point."

"With that being said, your pal should be safe," said Steina. "Chances are he's back home on Midgard safe and sound. More than likely freaked out and worried sick about you, but safe nonetheless."

Michael breathed a sigh of relief. "What about a boy? He's my cousin, Peter, and he's been missing for over two days now. Any chance that he arrived here?"

Reynir gulped and swallowed hard, his uppity, happy-go-lucky demeanor shifting into that of a grim, dispiriting manner. He turned to Steina, his lips curved, expressing a grimace of pain and discomfort. "Not again. Not another one."

CHAPTER FIVE

THE COUNCIL OF ALFHEIM

"Another what?" Michael asked with flecks of fear in his voice.

"Every twenty or so years, Midgard time, the convergence of realms becomes more prevalent due to Ratatosk's travels," answered Reynir. "It seems to take twenty years to scale the enormity and beauty of Yggdrasil. At times of high convergence, kids are known to venture into the nine realms, never to be seen again. Only Odin knows their whereabouts, seeing as he can see everything from his high seat of Hlidskjálf."

Steina did her best to provide Michael with a look of encouragement, but Reynir's grave expression said it all. It was the same grim expression he and Darrius had shared on the job too many times to count.

"That's why we were guarding Skirnir's Cove today," said Steina. "To defend against any converging threats and to protect those who wander into Alfheim accidentally, like yourself."

A lump grew in Michael's throat. His stomach dropped for the umpteenth time this week. The thought of Ortr greeting Peter rather than Steina and Reynir supplied him with overwhelming grief. "How can I find Peter? He needs me . . . or you. He needs someone. He's been lost for nearly three days now. I have to find him before it's too late."

"We shall take you to the council," said Reynir. "They will be able to tell us more information on the matter. We have rescued a few children already. Let's hope that Peter is one of them."

Reynir led the infantry, walking at a brisk pace. Michael tagged behind, his mind still racing with thoughts. By the time one question formed, another emerged right behind it. Where the hell was Alfheim even located? Sure, Yggdrasil or whatever that was, but how the hell would he get home from here?

Michael questioned whether he could trust Steina and Reynir, but he reminded himself that they did just save him from a thirty-foot giant. For now, they were the closest thing he had to allies on Alfheim, so he followed behind them willfully with caution. At least he had the comfort of knowing that Darrius was back home, safe on Earth.

The walk to the council was quiet outside of some small chatter between Steina and Reynir. Michael, too enamored with his thoughts, chose to keep to himself. He did his best not to annoy them with questions and had done a pretty good job at it until they came across a hideous, nightmarish elf slain in the heart of the forest, discarded to the side like roadkill.

Michael studied the ominous being in-depth; by its looks, the creature was a different race of elf. Either that or it had been dead for a while now, and its skin had lost its luster, transforming it into a dehydrated form of leather in the intense heat of Alfheim.

Steina and Reynir's skin was radiant and moisturized. The elf before them had a rougher, courser exterior that reminded him of dried-out modeling clay. Its skin was a darker and shadier gray compared to that of their light gray. Even as the elf laid deceased, Michael could see the blood-red, demonic eyes that faded into its sockets.

"Uhm . . . what the hell is that?" asked Michael.

"That would be a dark elf, part of the Dökkálfar lineage," said Steina.

"As opposed to what? A light elf?"

"Precisely," exclaimed Reynir with glee. "See, I told you he would get the hang of things around here, Steina."

"No, seriously, what the hell is the difference between a light elf and a dark elf? Is it similar to skin color, like white or black or something? And why does this one have creepy-ass red eyes?"

"No, silly," said Reynir. "You Midgardians and your heavy emphasis on race. The Dökkálfar and the Ljósálfar—Ljósálfar meaning light elf—were once one of the same. There were no differences between the two; only light elves roamed the realms then. Alfheim was our home.

"Because of our close ancestry to dwarves, the elves of that period rendezvoused on Svartalfheim with regularity. In those days, Svartalfheim was a glorious realm, only known as Nidavellir back then. The words can be used interchangeably for the realm. Svartalfheim, Nidavellir, depends on who you are talking to. Sadly, thousands of years ago, the realm was ravaged by war, caught in the teeth of the Æsir-Vanir war."

"And what intergalactic war is that? They must have skimmed right by it in my World History class."

"The Æsir-Vanir war? Have you really never heard of it?"

"Nope," said Michael, exaggerating the sound of the letter p as it left his puckered-up lips.

"Oooh, you are in for a treat. Thor and Odin, you have at least heard of them, right? *The Avengers* are mightily popular on

Midgard, I believe. Although it has been some time since I last visited. I'm not as up on the trends as I would like to be."

"Yes, extremely popular. What does that have to do with whatever war you're talking about?"

"Oh, yes. It's all—as you Midgardians say—Norse mythology. The Æsir-Vanir war can be found there. Unfortunately, the details of that war are scarce across the realms. I'm sure deep in Asgard, a library exists with extended knowledge, but I, for one, have not voyaged there in my lifetime."

"So, you mean to tell me Thor and Loki are real?"

"Precisely so. Still with me?"

Michael shook his head in dismay, "Yeah, I guess so." He wished he had paid more attention to his history and mythology classes or watched more conspiracy theory videos on the internet. He felt overloaded with information and overwhelmed by the short amount of time he had to process it all, still half-heartedly believing that he would wake up from this dream with Darrius at his side.

"Good, I'm glad to hear it. You would be surprised by the number of Midgardians who lose their minds out here, even the well-tempered ones. Now, where was I?"

"Nidavellir, a realm ravaged by war," said Steina behind rolling eyes.

"Ahh yes," said Reynir. "Thank you, Steina. Dwarves are master craftsmen, known for the most powerful weapons the nine realms have to offer. Because of that, either the Æsir or the Vanir cursed the realm to keep any future alliances in balance. They concealed Nidavellir's sun, entrapping it in the realms' core. Once their sun disappeared, the elves that remained on Nidavellir went dark with it, like a plague sweeping in the middle of the night, with no warning.

"The curse afflicted both the elven race and the dwarven race. From that day forth, the light elves could not prosper without the sun, and with it, in the face of sunlight, dwarves would forever turn to stone. The dwarven community buried themselves deep underground in the realm of Nidavellir while the dark elves harvested above.

"The curse is believed to be broken when the sun returns above Nidavellir. The dark elves you see today were remnants of that time. Constantly evolving into the now brainless, ever-breeding zombies they are today. No matter how hard we try to turn them back or heal them, they will forever remain rabid until the curse is lifted."

"That's pretty dark," replied Michael. "To curse an entire realm, that is."

"Please, as if you Midgardians are any better with your religions of power burning 'so-called' witches at the stake," said Steina.

"Valid point," said Michael. "So . . . how much further until we get to the council?"

"Not too much longer. It's just beyond the Bridge of Frey," said Reynir.

They walked ahead a few more miles before arriving at the largest bridge Michael had ever witnessed. It could have easily fit twenty lanes of traffic on it. He questioned the purpose of such a large bridge when he hadn't seen any vehicles, but he chose to keep that question to himself.

Large tree trunks blossomed throughout, covering the bridge, jerking and walloping about reminding Michael of Galloping Gertie. He strode over to one of the wild, unruly branches, his curiosity tugging at him to touch it, although he was quite uncertain as to why he felt so compelled to do so. Even if he had never seen a tree move by itself, it was quite unlike him, but something about it captivated him.

"Don't touch that!" Steina shouted after him.

Michael halted in his footsteps. "What? The tree?"

"Yes, the tree," stressed Steina. "What else would I be referring to?"

"I don't know," said Michael, shrugging his shoulders.

"That's a branch of Yggdrasil. One touch will transport you to another realm at random, and Odin knows you don't want to wind up in Muspelheim with Surtr. We won't be saving you there."

"Well . . . that's good to know. Thank you." Michael looked at his hand like it was going to betray him again.

Along the bridge were beautiful, busting statues carved in bronze and gold. They depicted warriors who yielded magic and warriors equipped with shields, spears, swords, arrows, and any other weapon known to man or elf. Some were portrayed as gods, others as elves, and even a select few as humans, it appeared. Michael didn't recognize any of them, but he could only assume that they were heroes of Alfheim and shared a rich history with the realm.

Towards the bridge's end was a jagged, fluorescent crystal chiseled into the ground, towering over twenty feet in height. The bluish, transparent crystal sparked and flickered, protruding constant waves of energy and power towards the city.

"What's that thing do?" asked Michael, referencing the bewitching crystal.

"That's the crystal of Alfheim, made from the souls of our ancestors," stated Steina. "It grows by the day. As another life passes here, a part of their soul cements itself to the crystal, protecting the Castle of Dain from any danger at the hands of dark elves. Any dark elf that attempts to enter the city is eviscerated by the crystal instantaneously. You won't find any remnants of the elven war past its veil."

Michael nodded his head and followed their lead, unable to come up with an adequate response, his mind still spinning in amazement at the wonders of the realm. The three of them walked through the surges of energy provided by the crystal of Alfheim. The waves flowed in and out of Michael sending shock waves throughout his nervous system, raising the hairs along his neck. The waves didn't cause any pain, more so tickled and pricked his insides, feeling like tiny insects crawling around inside his skin.

Michael now stood toe-to-toe with the magnificent castle, close enough to admire the intricate details that had escaped his eyesight from Skirnir's Cove. The mountain was no ordinary stone mountain. It conjoined with the castle, making one large and massive dwelling. Windows and doors carved themselves into the terrain, daring for him to turn away from its memorizing beauty.

The castle had a historic look to it; the décor and exterior had a Victorian-era feel sprinkled with a light mix of modern architecture, most likely attributed to maintenance. And as beautiful as the antique castle was, it paled in comparison to the other buildings and skyscrapers that surrounded it.

The encircling buildings lacked the Victorian era feel and were constructed with a futuristic design. The architecture bowed and arched, spiraling beautifully, weaving and interlocking together rhythmically like a puzzle. Buildings flourished side by side, some of them curved intensely, shaped like the arches of a half-pipe, while others were sleek and circular, resembling that of a UFO from the set of a science-fiction blockbuster.

Spacecrafts paraded the sky, none of which were actual airplanes. They were some sort of car-plane hybrid, no larger than the average-sized sedan. They flew effortlessly, gliding through the air as casually as vehicles routed the roads back home on Earth.

Nature flourished alongside the city, sprouting at its side harmoniously. Each of the buildings had layers of solar panels attached to them. Michael couldn't find any of the pollution or harmful emissions that bombarded the American cities, nor could he spot any of the massive billboards or digital screens that lurked every corner. It was a futuristic world run on clean, renewable energy. A world that he could only hope Earth would be able to replicate someday.

The historic castle doors opened towards them, welcoming them inside. The walls were overrun with portraits, scrolls, treaties, and other memorabilia exhibiting the rich history of Alfheim. The images moved in gif form, as did the scrolls, showing the calligraphy and penmanship at work as if they were currently being written in present time.

There were three large portraits, embellished in gold, each with its own nameplate, displayed at the end of the hall. Michael could make out both Skirnir and Dáin to be light elves. Skirnir's portrait was positioned to the left of the middle picture, which was of a gentleman named Frey, leaving Dáin's photograph mounted to Frey's right.

"Who are they?" asked Michael, pointing towards the paintings.

"Skirnir's my father," said Steina with a tinge of sadness built into her tone. "He died twenty years ago. He was Frey's most trusted companion. Frey gifted him his sword in exchange for the giantess, Gerd's hand in marriage."

"Gerd? There's actually a giant running around named after heartburn?"

"To replicate the burning heartache that Frey experienced when he was without her. Midgardians borrow a lot of words from other realms. Even some that still stand in place today. Tuesday derived from Tyr's day. Wednesday was Wodan's day or better known as the Allfather, Odin. Thursday is Thor's day, and Friday is Frigga's day. All as you would say, Norse gods.

"The middle portrait is Frey, a Vanir god from the realm of Vanaheim. The gods gifted him Alfheim as a teething present for cutting his first tooth."

"Wait a minute," said Michael. "You're telling me the gods gifted him an entire realm for getting a tooth? Seriously? There's nothing like some good ol' fashioned colonialism, I suppose," said Michael with specks of sarcasm laced across his tongue.

"Yes . . . the old elves were not happy about the decision, but this was long ago before any of us were born. We have never experienced leadership outside of Frey. Besides, Alfheim and its beauty descend from Frey. Flowers spring from his footsteps. He is a god of nature, peace, and fertility. He is good-hearted and compassionate. He hardly ever visits as it is. As the prophecy foretold, he shall die at the hands of his own sword—the sword he gifted my father—during his infamous bout with Surtr during Ragnarök."

"Where's the sword at now?"

"Nobody knows. My father hid it so well amongst the realms that he lost the sword. It was his best attempt to keep it from Surtr."

"Why not give it back to Frey?"

"The sword of Frey is not your typical sword; it can fight on its own with no help whatsoever from its yielder. After Frey gifted the sword away, the sword would never return to him. They tried. Slighted by the heartbreak and betrayal of Frey, the sword shall strike him down with a vengeance, seeking the payback that it desires."

"So, the sword is alive then, I take it?"

"As alive as you or me."

"What of the elven prophecy? What happens to Alfheim during Ragnarök?" Michael didn't know much about Norse mythology, but even he had heard of the mighty tales of Ragnarök.

Angst and sorrow spread across the face of Steina as Michael questioned the realm's destiny. Michael immediately felt terrible for asking. He hadn't realized the distress his intrigue would cause her.

"The elven prophecy is to fall at the hands of Loki," stated Reynir with remorse. "As the ever-impending Ragnarök slowly descends upon us, it is predestined to start with the fall of Alfheim. The suns of Alfheim are to be devoured whole by the wolf, Sköll, and the moons devoured by his sister, Hati. Alfheim is fated to be the first realm to fall, and when it does, Heimdall will blow into Gjallarhorn, warning the other realms of Ragnarök's arrival, but by then, it will be too late. Sköll and Hati will have already begun their journey, feasting on the remaining suns and moons of Yggdrasil."

"A wolf eating the sun? And another wolf eating the moon?" questioned Michael dumbfoundedly. "You know what? As crazy as all that sounds, I still find it more believable than Jonah and the Whale," he joked.

Michael was overwhelmed with the fascination of it all. The prophecies of the realms had undoubtedly piqued his interest. He could've sat around forever picking their brains about the ins and outs of the universe, but he'd rather not upset Steina any more than he already had, so he quickly shifted the conversation back to the gentlemen commemorated on the wall. "What about Dáin?"

"Dáin is the appointed leader by Frey," said Reynir. "He introduced the runes to the elves of Alfheim long ago. Runes are a magical language, the language of the universe, only understood by a select few. They consist of all the magic in the nine realms. Thousands of years ago, runic magic was used as frequently as we talk or sleep. Unfortunately for us, and most realms, the old elven language and native tongues of that time are undecipherable. The majority of our history has been lost or damaged beyond repair. The recorded tablets have long been destroyed. Dáin disappeared millennia's ago, and since, Alfheim has run on a council. One of which I am an elite part of. Have I ever mentioned that I am the youngest elf in council history?" said Reynir with an obnoxious, cocksure grin.

"No, you hadn't but speaking of, aren't we headed that way, to the council?" asked Michael.

"Of course, of course. I get so lost in our transcendent history that I tend to babble at times. Follow me."

Reynir proceeded to take them both through a journey of mazes, one that led into another, until Michael's head spun with confusion once more. A feeling that had become all too familiar during his short stint on Alfheim. He had no doubt that without Reynir's assistance, he would've never been able to navigate through the complexity of them.

They arrived at the maze's end, leading them into a circular room with long columns and archways. The chamber was filled with old decaying bricks that were caked with dust and debris. Atop the room were large stoops that circled every twenty-five feet or so. The tower extended a few hundred feet, at least twenty stories. It reminded Michael of a lighthouse, but it lacked the narrowness of one and furthermore lacked stairs of any sort.

They were suddenly greeted with a large gust of wind. As a result of the gust, small rock chunks thrust into the air around them. Massive huffs of air trickled down Michael's face causing his neck to curl and scrunch into his shoulders like a tortoise seeking safety. He slowly arched his head upwards into the direction of the violent breaths of air.

Greeted before him was a monolithic dragon, its head the size of a three-ton truck. Rows of sharp, prodigious teeth lined the inside of its mouth as it unfurled a death-curdling shriek. The dragon stamped the ground causing it to rumble some more.

Michael fell to his back, encapsulated with fear. He crawled backward on all fours in a deathly panic. The dragon hovered above him, mouth still agape, sizing Michael up. With another terrifying screech, the dragon outstretched its mouth even larger. Michael trembled on the floor and huddled into a tiny ball, his lower extremities paralyzed and glued to the surface.

"Hi, there buddy," squealed Reynir in a high-pitched baby talk voice. "Who's a good boy? Are you a good boy?" he squealed some more, scratching and petting the side of the dragon's enormous head.

The dragon's ferocious gaze turned to that of delight as Reynir pampered it with love. The dragon licked Reynir repeatedly, the sheer weight of its tongue knocking Reynir to the floor. The dragon scampered atop him gracefully, careful enough to not stomp all over him and crush him, continuing his barrage of wet and slobbery kisses.

"Okay, Inon," Reynir pleaded behind laughter. "Okay. Okay. Stop it. Stop, Inon. Look, here's a bone."

Reynir gravitated a large bone from one of the stoops above and summoned it to the floor next to Inon. The bone was bigger than the average tree, yet it still paled in comparison to Inon. Inon galloped and frolicked around, his tail ablaze. He moved his focus from Reynir to that of Steina, greeting her with a mouthful of slobbery dragon kisses as well.

Michael, still trembling, stood up and greeted the dragon tensely. Inon embraced the affection and allowed Michael to stroke his face gently. Inon's tenderheartedness was no different than that of a family Pitbull. He greeted Michael with wet, powerful kisses after Reynir's introduction. Eventually, Inon's excitement wore down, and he snatched the bone from the ground and flew to one of the stoops overhead.

"Nice seeing you, Inon," said Reynir. "We will be back soon, buddy."

The dragon mustered a few playful growls but mostly ignored them, too entertained with his bone to usher them any more attention.

They walked through a wide, iron-wrought door which led them through another hallway and into the heart of the council room. The room was formal, reminiscent of a courtroom. A tenseness filled the air as the three of them entered. There were four council members seated before them wrapped in a semicircle, waiting as if they had been expecting them for some time now. A fifth seat was left vacant for Reynir, although he chose to stand with Steina and Michael at his sides.

Reynir turned to Michael and gestured towards him with his arm. "Council of Alfheim, this is Michael. Michael, the council of Alfheim." He turned to Michael and proceeded to introduce him to the council members individually, speaking softly enough that the others wouldn't be able to hear him. "The two in the center are Solfrid and Ólafur, the oldest elves on Alfheim. You won't find a soul on this realm that is wiser than the two."

Michael looked at Solfrid and Ólafur with amazement. Neither one of them looked a day over thirty. Well, he was uncertain what a thirty-year-old elf might look like, but both of them looked no older than Steina or Reynir. He couldn't spot any of the wrinkles or hair loss that was usually attributed to the elderly back on Earth.

The only difference between their hair and Steina's and Reynir's was that it was an older, dingier looking gray compared to that of a gleaming white. The closer Michael studied them, the more he noticed the crow's feet wrinkles that surrounded their eyes.

"Over there is Dafilrog," interrupted Reynir. "Half-elf, half-dwarf. By all means never . . . ever . . . leave a nice bottle of scotch around him. Somehow it always goes missing," he said, turning his back on Dafilrog and mimicking the art of chugging.

Dafilrog appeared to be very unamused with the council meeting at hand as if it interfered with something more important. On second thought, he looked kind of drunk. His eyes drooped and glossed over. His head rolled on his shoulders as if he was fighting sleep.

He had a much tougher exterior than the light elves. His hardened skin was like that of a rhino, similar in texture to the dark elves they had passed on their journey here. Reynir did not share his age, for it was unknown, but he sure seemed a hell of a lot older than Solfrid or Ólafur. His stony, unwelcoming gaze was enough for Michael to move on and hope to never look into it again.

"This is Ezra. She's a pixie. She has the shortest of tempers. Do not piss her off and by any means, do not, I repeat, do not, step on an ant in her presence. She will blow you up. Believe me, I have seen it. If you have any plans of harming nature, I advise you do it as far away from her as possible."

"Yes, sir." Michael nodded. "I hear that loud and clear."

Ezra's appearance was noticeably different from that of the elves. She was much shorter, maybe only three feet in height, similar in stature to a small child. She was also the only council member without gray or white hair; instead, her hair was a gleaming blonde.

Her body radiated and glowed as if she was a beacon of light. She apparently had a displeasure for clothes because she didn't seem to be wearing any, just a few leaves here and there to cover her private areas. Michael had the feeling that she wouldn't be wearing any at all if an essential council meeting hadn't been at hand.

After Reynir had introduced Michael to the council and gave him a brief profile of each member, he wasted no time getting to business. "As I have stated, this is Michael. Steina and I found him at a convergence point on the shore of Skirnir's Cove. We defended him from an attack by the jotun, Ortr. If not for us, he would have been killed."

"Yes," Dafilrog responded with glee. "Yes, tell me you killed that giant, Ortr. Fuckin' pest he is. I never liked him," he stammered as he took a large swig out of his flask, confirming Michael's suspicion of him being drunk.

"Sadly, we did. He left us no other option. We attempted to bargain, but he had other thoughts in mind."

"He left us no other option," Ezra cackled loudly as she mocked Reynir. "You couldn't have stunned him instead? It's always killing with you all. Every one of you has little value for life and the beauty surrounding it, from the smallest insect to that of the largest jotun. Each life form should be honored and respected. Adhered to by the peace treaty of Alfheim."

"That's unfair now, isn't it?" muttered Dafilrog. "Mighty presumptuous of you to think we don't value life. We just value all life forms over jotun scums," said Dafilrog, erupting with laughter and taking another swig from his flask.

Ezra's body began to flush blood-red, transforming her body from a gleaming yellow into a fiery shade of crimson. So far, Reynir's scouting report was to a tee; no lies detected thus far, thought Michael.

"Ezra, with respect, we did adhere to the peace treaty of Alfheim," interjected Reynir. "As article XIV is written, we did not administer physical contact unless physical contact had already been administered, and at that point, Ortr had already attacked Michael. From there, we attempted to negotiate, and he attacked us. His destiny lied in his own hands from that point forth."

Ezra stewed and boiled some more, seething with displeasure.

"Back to the matter at hand," said Reynir. "Michael arrived here in search of a young boy named Peter. I was hoping the council might know of his whereabouts so we can send them both back to Midgard to be reunited with their family."

"Hmm," hummed Solfrid. "Convergence points prevalent of late. No guarantee that Peter is with us but rescued a few kids, Alfheim has. Dafilrog," she muttered.

Dafilrog stumbled beside her, cane in hand, unraveling an ancient-looking scroll filled with a long list of names. Solfrid carefully eyed the parchment up and down, straining and squinting to get a better look at the writing.

"Lucky, you are," stated Solfrid. "We intercepted a gentleman named Peter a few nightfall's ago. Coincidence, doubtful. Reynir, retrieve Peter from the cellar. You and Steina guide Midgardians home. Shelter at Dagrún Village for nightfall. Come cockcrow, send visitors back to Midgard."

"Yes, madam. As you wish," said Reynir.

Michael sighed with relief, trying his best to temper his emotions, but he couldn't help it. The thought of Peter being here, safe and sound, swelled his heart with joy. He couldn't wait to return him home to Emma and alleviate her heartache and distress. Excitement pulsed through him like a child on their birthday.

"Thank you," Michael said to the council. "You have no idea how much this means to me. I thank you all for your hospitality." He bowed in their direction and followed Steina and Reynir as they exited the room.

Chapter Six

Dagrún Village

Michael followed Steina and Reynir through the castle, wandering down a vast array of corridors until they arrived at an antique elevator consisting of traditional pulleys and gears. It reminded him of a dumbwaiter, which he'd never actually seen in person, only in movies. Regardless, he didn't trust the thing enough to carry him, let alone the three of them. The gears were aged and rusted, corroding and fragmenting apart; the ropes were frayed and tattered. The word hazard screamed at him as he eyeballed the elevator warily.

"This?" asked Michael. "You expect me to get on this piece of junk? No way. Not a chance in hell I get on this thing."

"History is very important to the elven culture," explained Steina. "It must be protected at all costs. This piece of junk has all sorts of magic spelled to it. It has carried jotuns bigger than Ortr. I assure you it can handle someone of your stature," she winked.

Michael winced with displeasure, muttering a silent prayer as he boarded the elevator behind them. At this point, he was unsure as to whom he was even praying to; the act had simply become a force of habit for him over the years.

His only hope was that Peter was here safely on Alfheim rather than one of the many other realms Steina had mentioned during their walk here. It would be a shame to come this far and die over some stupid, outdated elevator, Michael thought as the gears churned and cranked slowly, sounding like broken and crackling bones.

"Really, guys, stairs are fine with me," said Michael nervously, somewhere between joking and serious.

"Be careful what you wish for," said Reynir. "That's over a hundred floors that you would have to navigate. Plus, we will be there in no time. This bad boy has—what do they call it on Midgard—ahh yes, this bad boy has some serious giddy-up to it."

To Michael's surprise, Reynir had been telling the truth. Somehow the elevator traveled a hundred floors in less than a minute. Michael had no idea how something that appeared to be moving so exceedingly slow could operate with such speed and efficiency. He was quickly learning that life was different on Alfheim. A lot of things were possible here that seemed inconceivable back home. Had he not had to take Peter back, he would have seriously considered an extended stay. The place was beautiful, minus the raging thirty-foot giants. He could certainly do without those on his next visit, he thought.

The cellar was old and musty, encrusted with cobwebs and dust bunnies. They walked through the narrow, grungy hallway, surrounded by rickety barrels and glasses. To each side of them were rows of gated rooms, resembling very little difference to a jail cell.

"What the hell is this place?" Michael questioned furiously at the sight of the hazardous, unkempt condition of the cellar.

"The cellar of Alfheim is one the safest places on this realm, mind you," stated Reynir.

"Relax," said Steina. "It is far more accommodating than you would imagine. And Reynir is right. It is for Peter's safety, after all."

"How is this old busted-up place safe?" asked Michael. "There's gotta be a shit ton of mold or something in here. Why couldn't you have just sent him home? You know, like to his family?"

"And send him where to, exactly?"

"Where he came from? What do you mean send him where?"

"Yes, I understand the question, but you must understand that time works differently across realms," stressed Steina. "By transporting Peter home, he could have wound up in present time, a few years past, or hundreds of years into the future, there's no telling. Besides, he is a child. We would not merely drop a child off on Midgard and evacuate. We would have to assure his safety. Sadly, most kids that arrive here stay here. Alfheim is not only home to elves but humans, dwarves, pixies, jotuns, gnomes, and many other elementals as well."

"How are me and Peter getting home then?"

"A device known as Fölsun Tíma," stated Reynir. "Crafted by the dwarves themselves. It tracks converging points nearby; that's why we were there waiting when you arrived. We were warned of an upcoming convergence. The device locks the coordinates of said convergence and tracks the time of that convergence as well. When the next convergence happens, we will use Fölsun Tíma to intercept it and lock your time and coordinates into place so that you and Peter will return to the exact moment in which you left."

"Sounds like time travel."

"Not exactly, the device merely intercepts a converging point and allows the user to manipulate said convergence. I would not be able to go back a thousand years if that's what you are asking."

"How far can you go back?"

"We refrain from going back a full day, Alfheim time. For instance, I could not go back to yesterday without the device having tracked a convergence there first. There would simply be no data to return to."

"So, without this device, had me and Peter tried to go home, we could have arrived hundreds of years into the future? Is that what you're telling me?"

"Precisely. Converging points of Yggdrasil are tricky. They are time periods and realms connected by the tree of life that fold upon each other interchangeably. The period could be that of the distant past or that of the distant future. The best that we can do is try to control them to the best of our ability."

"Kind of like a wormhole, I take it?"

"More or less."

Michael's heart dropped to his stomach when they arrived at Peter's cell. Not of sadness, but this time of relief, like all the weight in the world had been lifted off his shoulders. Peter was here, alive and well. Michael half-heartedly believed it when Solfrid mentioned Peter's name, but it was one thing to hear something and another thing entirely for him to see it for himself.

Michael watched from afar, latched onto the cell's gate. Peter was having a blast, far too intrigued by his video game to notice the three of them sneak up behind him. From inside the cell, Peter played some sort of virtual reality baseball game with astonishingly lifelike trolls and ogres, far more advanced and realistic than any of the technology back home on Earth.

The figures before him paraded the field in holographic form, as real looking as Peter himself. The cell was no bigger than a dorm room, but somehow, thanks to a three-dimensional projection system of sorts, it extended further. Far enough that Peter had no problem canvasing the entirety of the simulated baseball field to his liking. He reared back and threw the baseball into the projected force field where a hideous, green, snot-filled troll stood at bat anxiously awaiting the pitch. There must have been some noise-canceling effects at work because Peter couldn't hear anything outside of his game.

Michael studied the game intently, fascinated by the technological advancements of Alfheim. Even more amused at the fact that they had baseball video games on the realm. After everything that he had discovered today, he wouldn't be shocked if baseball had originated here. Nothing would surprise him anymore, he thought.

The more he evaluated the gaming system, the more bewildered he became. There weren't any projection screens, televisions, consoles, or controllers. Nothing. It was as if the game was running on magic itself. Then again, he thought about how hard it would be to explain how the internet worked to someone who had never experienced it before. He briefly imagined himself trying to explain Wi-Fi to someone from the 18th century and could only fathom how difficult that conversation would be. Even he didn't know how it functioned, he only knew how to use it.

Reynir opened the cell gate, disabling the video game in the process.

Peter turned around swiftly, agitation speckling across his face. "Aww, c'mon, I was just bout to whoop that ugly butt ogre."

"Maybe next time, buddy," replied Michael, from behind Reynir.

Pure elation exuded from Peter at the sound of Michael's voice. He sprinted towards him and greeted him with the tightest bear hug he could offer, wrapping his arms snuggly around Michael's legs. "Mikey, I knew it. I knew you were gonna come n' get me."

Michael kneeled down to Peter's height and hugged him, latching onto him tightly, knowing that he needed the embrace far more than Peter. "Of course, buddy," he said chokingly, overwhelmed with emotions. Peter's head rested gently against his chest, warming his heart in the process. "There was no way I wasn't going to find you," said Michael, hugging him even tighter. "I'm just so glad you're safe."

"Oh, I'm fine, Mikey. This place is awesome. After I eat my chicken nuggets, there's always more chicken nuggets. Will and Cam would love it. We gotta bring 'em here sometime."

"I don't know about all that. I have to get you home. Your mom is worried sick about you. But I tell you what, when we get back, I will make sure you get all the chicken nuggets you could ever imagine. Speaking of, some of those chicken nuggets sound pretty damn good right about now. I'm starving."

It hadn't occurred to Michael how hungry he had been until Peter mentioned food. He had been far too distracted and worried to even think about it, but now that he knew Peter was safe, his hunger struck with a vengeance, collapsing upon him at once. As far as he could tell, it had to have been well over twelve hours since his last meal.

He had completely lost track of time while here on Alfheim. Transitioning from nighttime on Midgard to a bright and sunny day on Alfheim had left him with the slightest idea of how long he had been away from Earth. He felt like he had trekked to

Narnia and back by now, and it was still daylight somehow, which in part made sense due to the realm's two suns.

"I haven't eaten in ages," said Michael. "Is there anything to eat around here? Lunch or dinner? I'm not sure what time it is on Alfheim."

"We can eat on the ride to Dagrún Village," said Reynir. "There is food in the car. It's almost nightfall; we need to get moving."

They took the elevator once more, this time stopping on a floor with a massive car garage that was home to a slew of the airplane-car hybrids that Michael had seen roaming the sky earlier. The vehicles had four tires like a car yet had the wings and stabilizers of a plane. They got inside one of the parked vehicles, this one lacking a set of wings. It was rather large and comfy in space, about the size of a standard SUV.

Reynir ignited the engine, and the car throttled to life without noise, as quiet as the calming silence of snow. He toggled with a few buttons on the dashboard, resulting in the vehicle's wings and stabilizers extending outwards, similar to an RV expanding. He entered in a set of coordinates and operated more switches and controls.

The plane took off on autopilot, accelerating gracefully. Through the window, Michael could see the car become invisible, blending in with the surrounding air. He and Peter stared out the window in amazement, awestruck at the beautiful realm beneath them.

Reynir exited the cabin and joined the others in the back. "Auto-pilot, a thing of beauty."

"You should consider letting me take this back home," said Michael. "After all, I will need a believable explanation to go home to."

"The last Midgardian that we let borrow one crashed it in Roswell," said Steina.

"Wait? Are you for real? Were you even alive then?"

"Were you even alive then?" Steina quipped playfully.

"No, but it was a widely famous phenomenon. It still is back home, on Midgard, as you Alfgardians like to say."

"Hey, he finally said Midgard," said Reynir with a smile.

"Alfgardians?" chuckled Steina.

"Yeah, Alfgardians. Is that a problem?"

"I suppose I can allow it this one time."

"What's Roswell?" asked Peter, injecting himself into the conversation.

"I guess the time someone from Earth borrowed one of these planes and crashed it, resulting in the frenzied alien enthusiasts you see today," said Michael with a lighthearted chuckle. He was somewhat unsure of whether Steina was pulling his leg, but at this point, he didn't know what to believe anymore.

"I believe in aliens," said Peter.

"Oh, you do?"

"Yeah."

"I suppose after everything I've seen the past couple of days, I do as well."

"Can we go look for aliens when we get home?"

"I'm not letting you near anything otherworldly when we get home. Not for a long time. How about we go fishing like normal people instead?"

"Yay, I love fishing. I can't wait."

Trays of succulent meat and vegetables emerged from hidden compartments of the vehicle at Reynir's touch of buttons.

"Aw, yay!" exclaimed Peter bouncing up and down in his seat with excitement. "Is this the lamb again?"

"That it is," said Reynir.

"You like lamb?" Michael questioned. "Since when?"

"Since I got here," said Peter. "It's delicious."

Michael had never tried lamb before, but he was famished, and it smelled and looked amazing. Peter wasted no time devouring into his food, attesting over and over again how good it tasted. Michael followed in his footsteps and found the food to be marvelous. He ate his meal as he overlooked Alfheim and its beautiful mountains. He couldn't help but think about how much he would miss this place. It was so ahead of Earth's time. It seemed so peaceful here, even during a never-ending war.

It was going to be hard to return home to the tedious tasks of his day-to-day life, knowing that other worlds like this existed. Not only other worlds but magic, raw and physical magic was real and accessible. He proceeded to eat, trying his hardest to drown out his thoughts and enjoy his last remaining hours on Alfheim.

They arrived at Dagrún Village in roughly half an hour, much shorter than their walk to the castle earlier that day. It was the perfect amount of time for them to enjoy their supper and let their stomachs settle. They exited the plane and were greeted by a couple of smaller, uglier looking individuals, about two-three feet in size. Steina and Reynir shook hands with the lot of them and introduced them to Michael and Peter.

The tiny troll-ish looking creatures turned out to be forest gnomes. They had the same pointed ears as elves but desperately lacked the beauty. They all had large, bulgy noses, and all the men in the village had long, scraggly beards. Michael doubted that clippers had ever been introduced to them before. Most of the gnomes lacked shoes; only a few here and there adorned any kind of footwear.

One gnome, in particular, a gentleman named Nillbeck, guided them throughout the village. Despite the lack of beauty, they were all extremely friendly, especially Nillbeck as he spoke of the village's ancient history. From what Michael could gather, the gnomes were beings of peace and benevolence. They took great pride in helping and fostering others in their village, a safe zone for all he called it.

The village consisted of tiny huts, some of which Michael was taller than. The cabins were perfectly suited for Peter and someone of his size, but there was no way the others would be able to fit inside one of them. As they strolled through the village, they passed by rows of nut and potato farms. Gnomes passed by tipping their caps as they carted loads of vegetables, potatoes, and just about every other nut known to man.

After a small trek through the settlement, they arrived at a few larger huts near the village's rear. The huts were still tinier than the average-sized dwelling back home on Earth but large enough for one or two to bunker in snuggly.

Nillbeck tipped his cap one last time. Reynir bowed slightly. He untied the sack of coins tied to his belt loop and tossed it to Nillbeck. After the exchange, the gnome disappeared promptly, and it was just the four of them again. Twilight had slowly set upon them during their stroll to the housing.

"This ought to do for the night," said Reynir, enabling a fire for them to gather around.

"Nillbeck said this place was a safe zone?" asked Michael.

"Safe for a thousand years and counting."

"If war exists in this realm, how is this place safe, exactly?"

"It was agreed upon in the treaty of Alfheim. Gnomes are arguably the most kind-hearted creatures in all the realms. Most afflictions concern gods and are related to their quarrels. But strike down a gnome, and Surtr and Odin would team up to deliver the vengeance. Most people are not ignorant enough to testify against that, at least over the last thousand years, that is."

"I guess I understand. The countries of Earth are constantly at war, yet they can all miraculously agree not to colonize Antarctica, which I find peculiar but whatever."

"That's because it is inhabited by the frost jotuns," said Steina. "Surely, you know that? You don't actually believe that a realm ravaged by war over ninety percent of its existence would actually agree upon peace, do you?"

"Hell no," exclaimed Michael. "I knew something fishy was going on over there. Humans are terrible. I mean, individually, maybe not, but as a whole—well, you said it best—we've been at war for over ninety percent of our existence. You know, I don't even think humans are bad people. It's the people in power that control everything. If you took two world leaders who disagreed and put them in a Roman coliseum to battle to death rather than send millions of the innocent, there would never be another war. It's much more believable that giants roam Antarctica than Earth's countries ever being peaceful."

"I like this guy," said Reynir to Steina. "You have a lot of spirit and life kicking inside you," he said, returning his attention back to Michael. "We could use more people like you around here."

"I wish. This place is amazing. It truly is. I would love to be able to spend more time here . . . but I have other obligations back home," said Michael with a wholehearted smile, patting Peter on the back gently.

"I understand. We look forward to getting you back to a lifetime of happiness."

"Thank you," said Michael with a nod of his head. "What's the plan for tomorrow?"

"We will rise at daybreak and wait for a convergence. Hopefully, an early one."

"You will come to find that nights here are not as long as they are back on Midgard," said Steina. "They are hardly nights at all in comparison. More like one long sunset as one sun rises and the other falls."

"I feel like that's a hard thing to get used to," said Michael.

"Not when you are from here. Besides, elves cannot be without sunlight for long. We need the sun to replenish and give us life after long and laboring days."

"Can you leave Alfheim to journey to another realm?"

"Yes, as long as there is adequate sun there to support us. I spent a summer on Midgard during my elder year of schooling. To pass our final assessment, we had to spend our summer at a location within the Arctic Circle. For my class, it was Norway. It is easiest for us to adapt to the climate there with the wealth of daylight that is offered."

"What about you, Reynir? Have you ever visited Midgard?"

"That I have," said Reynir. "For me, it was Iceland. Ahh, what I would do to go back to those days and see Katrin again. She was a beauty."

"Why can't you go back and spend some time with her?"

"Sadly, she passed away," he said behind a sorrowful expression.

"I'm sorry to hear that. How did she pass, if you don't mind me asking?"

"Not at all. She died shortly after we made love for the first time. I was unaware of the fragility of the Midgardian immune system. Elves carry certain viruses that Midgardians simply do not. I caught quite the lashing from the university upon my return."

"Oh, what rubbish," said Steina. "The schooling system explicitly prohibits—Steina glanced at Peter, bringing his presence to her attention—that sort of intercourse, and you know it."

"Duh. Why do you think they prohibit it?" he asked, pointing at himself emphatically. "Because of me."

"You are so full of it. The elven universities have been in place for thousands of years, and you just happened to be the first person to engage in that sort of behavior. I sincerely doubt that."

"Ask my cousin, Skirnir. He would tell you."

Steina glared at him, singeing with annoyance. "Skirnir's dead, asshole."

"Well, he would certainly vouch on my behalf."

"Whatever," she said, rolling her eyes.

"You two are related?" asked Michael.

"Cousins, unfortunately," said Steina.

"Aww, you don't mean that," said Reynir, sporting a pesky and nagging smile. "You would have no idea what to do without me and my shenanigans."

"I would certainly have more time on my hands rather than dealing with you and all of your mind-numbing escapades. That's for sure."

After some more lighthearted conversation and bantering between the cousins, Michael escorted Peter to their hut to get some much-needed sleep.

Peter climbed aboard the tiny cot-sized bed and threw the blanket over him, waiting zealously for Michael to tuck him in nice and snug. "Tell me a story," he chimed, struggling to keep his eyelids open.

"A story about what?" asked Michael.

"Chicken nuggets."

"A story about chicken nuggets, huh?"

"Yeah, chicken nuggets."

"Okay," said Michael. "There once was a chicken nugget named Peter."

"Hey, that's my name."

"Did I say Peter? I meant Peterson the third. Well, Peterson the third was a chicken nugget but not any chicken nugget. He was the golden chicken nugget, fried and crisped to perfection. Bound for greatness. One day while he was with his chicken nugget brothers Sam and Bill, he accidentally ventured into a whole other world called Alfheim. There he waited for his chicken nugget cousin, Mikey the Great, Mikey the Outstanding, to come and save him."

"C'mon, Mikey," said Peter, yawning and rubbing his eyes. "I know you're s'posed to be Mikey the Outstanding."

"Me? Oh no. I could never be Mikey the Outstanding. See, this chicken nugget was a champion. Mikey the Outstanding fought gallantly. He watched time and time again as his fellow soldiers had been eaten on the battlefield, but Mikey, no, Mikey was a trooper. He battled hard. He trekked and trekked through giants and other vicious magical beings until he found his cousin Peterson, and when he found his chicken nugget cousin, he gave him the biggest bear hug he could muster and delivered him home safely to his mother, and they lived happily ever. The end," he said, peering down at a now sleeping Peter.

Michael caressed Peter's head gently, his heart swelling with joy at the sight of Peter safe and sound. He exited the hut and returned to the campfire where Steina sat alone as the sparks flickered and flared around her, reinforcing her beauty. He moseyed over next to her, close enough to keep an endearing conversation but far enough to allow her space. "Where's Reynir?" he asked.

"He went to get some shuteye. I advise you do the same. You have a big day ahead of you tomorrow."

"Nah, I doubt I'll be getting much sleep tonight if I'm being honest."

"Why is that?"

"There's just too much on my mind right now. I won't be able to rest until Peter gets home safely. I must say though, I'm going to miss this place. How does one go back to a normal life knowing that all of this exists?"

"Most don't."

"Yeah, I can imagine. How could I ever forget a place like this?"

"No, really. When I say most don't, I mean most people never return home. Consider yourself lucky, Michael. You and Peter both. I can count on one hand the number of humans I have ever seen return to Midgard after entering Alfheim. It's incredibly rare."

"I don't understand. Why us then? What makes us so special?"

"The council trusts you. They must see something special in you. Most humans that wander here never leave, unfortunately. If a kid does find his way back home, they hardly ever find this place again. It is unheard of that you have accessed two different convergent points in your lifetime. That is a feat I don't know of any other Midgardian accomplishing . . . If you don't mind my asking, what happened during your first visit amongst realms?"

"My first visit . . . I lost my little sister. My cousins and I ventured to an alternate world, somewhere with a castle, and in our excitement, we left my sister behind. I don't know who it was, but the gentleman who guided us there took her away, and we never saw her again. I failed her . . . that's why I couldn't fail him," said Michael, motioning to the hut where Peter was sleeping soundly. "From the moment he disappeared, I knew I had to find him and return him home safely."

"How long ago did you *lose* your sister?"

"Twenty years ago, Midgard time."

"I am sorry to hear that. Twenty years ago, my father died. We share that time of difficulty and grievance together. Even spread across Yggdrasil, our pain had been connected . . . We should mention your sister to the council. Twenty years is a long time, but surely, if anyone has information on her whereabouts, it would be them."

"I'm okay. I appreciate the offer, but I will respectfully pass. I know what happened that day. I have come to terms with it, and quite frankly, I don't wanna relive that day again."

"I understand. No need to dig up old wounds . . . I'm going to go get some rest before I wind up with an episode of insomnia. It truly has been a pleasure, Michael."

Steina waltzed to her hut, leaving Michael behind with the tranquility of the sun-setting nighttime sky. He stared into the horizon, mesmerized by its beauty, alone with his thoughts. He remained by the campfire for about an hour, keeping patrol, eventually moving his stakeout to the outside of the hut where Peter slept.

His eyes began to weigh down on him like anchors. His exhaustion had reached a point in which it felt less like fatigue and more like inebriation. He staggered inside the hut, flopping onto the all too small mattress positioned beside Peter's. He looked at Peter, sound asleep, before allowing the weight of his eyelids to close on him for good.

A few hours of sleep wouldn't hurt, he told himself between a cascade of dreamy thoughts. The village's rich history of benevolence and Steina and Reynir protecting them next door allowed the re-assuredness needed for Michael to sink into bed and enter a never-ending bliss, a freefall into some much-needed sleep.

Michael's dream that night was bizarre. It was unlike any he had ever experienced before. In the past, he would occasionally awake from a dream that felt so real he would find himself waking up in despair, clutching at himself for dear life, only to be reminded the dream was only that, a dream and nothing more. But here he was once again, dreaming or experiencing memories from the perspective of his sister, Skye.

His latest vision appeared to have come moments after Skye had vanished. She was being dragged by her hair through a dark and grungy hallway until she reached a tiny dungeon in which she got heaved into with no remorse. Her body slammed against the brick floor forcefully. She screamed in pain, her young voice wavering in terror.

"A thousand years have come and gone, none of it mattering but this moment here," said the gentleman who had just hurled Skye to the floor.

The man seemed different from the one that had guided them to the castle, but at the moment, he was the last standing connection Michael had to Skye's whereabouts. The gentleman's body was shredded; he had herculean arms the size of tree trunks. Every ounce of his torso was littered with gruesome and savaging scars.

"I have battled against the finest jotuns, gods of old, gods of new," continued the gentleman. "None of which have bested me, and yet, Mimir states that my inevitable downfall will come at the hands of a mortal Midgardian girl. That is no longer. Skye Leitner, together destiny shall be ours. Fate shall be mine, and nothing will stop me from that."

The man slammed the dungeon gate shut, locking Skye inside. He turned around and walked away, ignoring Skye's desperate pleas for help.

Skye wailed tirelessly. "Mike? Michael, where are you? Somebody help. Please, somebody, help me."

Her cries and sobs eventually became muffled by the deathly shrills of another woman in a nearby room. No, the shrilling that Michael was hearing was coming from that of present-day Alfheim. The cries were so loud and horrifying that they intertwined into his subconscious, latching and connecting onto his nightmarish dream.

Michael awoke in terror, panicked by the palpitating screams. He burst through the hut door to find Steina shrieking in horror. Reynir followed closely behind, waking up to her startling cries as well. Before either of them could console her, they were left speechless by the source of her anguish. Michael hoisted his hand to his mouth in shock, gazing over the village with widened eyes of despair.

It was a massacre, dead skeletal remains scattered across the village in every direction. The rocky, bricked road was layered with flesh and bones, deluged with the village gnomes' blood. Rows of them laid slaughtered and dismantled, their carcasses garbled along the gravel like roadkill. The gnomes that hadn't been disassembled were instead fried and flayed, electrocuted to crisps.

Michael felt his stomach turn sour, turning violently and repulsively, in a manner that it hadn't since he rode the *Mind Buckler 3000* repeatedly on a slow, drizzly day at the fair when he was a child. His stomach twisted in knots like the day he lost his sister. He did his best to hold in the lamb from the day before, refraining from adding any more wretched bodily fluids to the crime scene.

"Who would do such a thing?" cried Steina. Her knees buckled beneath her as her gravity lost its balance.

Michael overlooked the onslaught, enraptured with grief. His job had exposed him too many things over the years, including an assortment of dead bodies but never to the likes of this. This was genocide, an act of savagery and barbarism.

"This is the work of some severely dark magic," stated Reynir. "The darkest I have ever seen."

Michael was unaware of the others, but he felt incredibly groggy. He knew he had been tired from his lack of sleep, but this was a different feeling. It felt as if he had been drugged. He was dazed and lethargic, fighting against bouts of vertigo and overwhelming nausea. Far worse than any hangover he had ever experienced. Something wasn't right, he told himself.

"How could we all have slept through this?" Michael asked the group, struggling to remain on his feet. The world around him was dizzying. He felt sea-sick, or more so land sick. The wobbliness of his body reminded him of the sensation he would experience after a long cruise. He was physically on land, but his mind was offshore, rocking and swaying with the ocean.

"It appears as if we were under the influence of some very heavy enchantments," said Reynir. "I just don't understand who would do such a thing. For none of us to awake during a massacre of this size, it would require a sorcerer of impeccable magnitude.

It is simply impossible. Only a few could yield the power to sedate us to that nature."

A sound of minor grunting could be heard from across the ravaged, soulless village. The three of them hustled over to the sound as quickly as possible. Lying before them, hardly recognizable, was Nillbeck. He was in desperate need of medical attention. His face was battered and bruised to the extent that it had become a different shade of purple. It was now oblong, obtruding from different angles unsymmetrically.

"We have to get him to the council asap," Steina emphasized to Reynir desperately. She grasped Nillbeck's hand and clutched it tenderly. "You are going to be okay, Nillbeck. We will get you to safety."

"N-n-no," muttered Nillbeck, hacking up blood. "It is time. I g-g-go with m-my village."

"Let us save you, Nillbeck," stressed Reynir. "We can get you back to the council in no time. Just hang in there a little longer, pal."

Nillbeck mustered the little amount of remaining strength he had left to offer and shook his head no. He was adamant about dying alongside his village, with the other gnomes who had fought valiantly at his side.

"Who did this?" asked Reynir. "Who could do such a thing?"

"Loki," responded Nillbeck before closing his eyes and resting his head peacefully on the dirt beneath him. The spark left his brutally purple eyes, glimmering for the last time, leaving him and the world to become one.

Steina turned an even ghastlier shade of white, one that Michael didn't think was possible. She trembled with fear upon hearing Loki's name. "He can't be back," she clamored. "No, no, no. Not even Loki would do something this evil. He couldn't have. Not Loki."

Reynir stared back at her blankly and expressionless. The gravity of the moment left him rattled and unable to speak until finally he found his bearings and stammered unnervingly. "We must get back to the council at once and warn them. I pray that Loki has not already beaten us there. Michael, gather Peter. We must hurry."

Michael had been so engrossed by the terror Loki had inflicted he'd forgotten about Peter, still asleep in their hut. He sprinted back to the cabin to wake him so they could return to the council immediately. He darted through the open door that he had busted ajar earlier, only to find Peter lying there lifeless, drenched in puddles of his own blood.

Michael dropped to his knees, falling face-to-face with Peter. He hoisted him up and hugged him, squeezing him as tightly as possible as if that would somehow bring him back to life. Square in the middle of Peter's forehead was a gashing hole, excavated cleanly and precisely through as if the act had been done methodically with joy.

In the middle of the night, Loki had murdered Peter and slaughtered the village of Dagrún. A village that took pride in their peace. Michael didn't understand how a person could be so vile and evil. He longed for the opportunity to go back in time and remain awake throughout the night.

He would do anything to stop Loki. Even if it meant he would have been one of the dead soldiers littered across the battlefield because he'd rather be dead than have to live with the remorse that followed. He desperately wished to trade places with Peter. It should be him lying there, not Peter. It wasn't fair.

Warm and salty tears rolled down his cheek as he carried Peter's dead, limp body outside for Steina and Reynir to see. He gently placed Peter's body on the dirt. The guilt and grief that he felt transformed into an uncontrollable rage. He could feel his temperature rise as his ears flared blood-red. He got to his feet and shoved Reynir as hard as could, unconcerned with the repercussions that might follow. If he was lucky, Reynir would strike him down and kill him. At least then, he wouldn't have to deal with the overwhelming guilt and heartache.

"You said this place was a safe zone," screamed Michael, shoving Reynir once more. "This is all your fault. I trusted you! I fucking trusted you!"

"My fault?" Reynir rebutted. "Look who's talking."

"What do you mean look who's talking? You're the most powerful one in the village. How do we know it wasn't you who did this?" said Michael, shoving Reynir as hard as he could this time.

"I could say the same for you," Reynir shouted, pushing him back. "Dagrún Village has been a safe zone for eons, and now you appear, and Loki returns. You do the math, trickster."

Tension filled the air as they stood face-to-face, nose-to-nose, so close they could feel each other's breath snarling down their face after every exchanging insult. Michael knew he didn't stand a chance against Reynir, but he didn't care. Michael was consumed with a white-hot rage. He wanted nothing more than to harness that rage and energy and bombard Reynir with it until Reynir felt the same immeasurable amount of pain and guilt that he felt himself.

Before either of them could lay another hand on the other, Steina inserted herself between them with her arms up, separating the two. To Michael's surprise, she was very powerful. She pushed them back with force, using her body as a barrier between them.

"Enough!" she shouted. "This is exactly what Loki wants. Odin knows how he escaped or why, but he wants this dissension among us. He wants a civil war. If anybody knows that . . . it is me. We have to be strong and remain a team."

Both Michael and Reynir continued their death stares, relentlessly glaring at the other, waiting for the other to back down.

"Cool it, Reynir," said Steina calmly. "We need to retreat back to the council. There is more at stake than your stubborn arrogance. We will guide Michael back to Midgard another time. Alfheim's safety is our number one priority. I need you calm and level-headed."

"To hell with Midgard," snapped Michael. "I won't be going back there for a long time. This is my war now. That bastard Loki will be sorry he ever crossed my path." Determination seared across his face filling his words with a brash assertiveness.

"You are right," stated Reynir, turning his attention to Steina. "We need to return to the council this instant and warn them of Loki's return."

"I'm not leaving here until I bury my cousin," said Michael. "He deserves a proper burial."

Reynir scowled with annoyance, grumbling profanities amongst himself. With the flick of his wrist, he hollowed a hole into the soil, a hole with ample enough room for Peter to fit inside.

"No!" exclaimed Michael. "I can do this myself . . . without magic." He snapped a sturdy branch off of a nearby tree and began digging into the Earth. Slowly but surely, the hole widened and deepened with every stroke.

"We don't have time for this," said Reynir, whispering to Steina. "Take the keys and take him back when he finishes. I can teleport close enough to the castle to walk the rest. I must get back and warn the others. If there is even a council to return to, that is," he said uneasily. He summoned a portal and vanished into it, leaving Michael and Steina behind.

Steina overlooked Michael as he stabbed his branch violently into Alfheim's crust. Each thrust, more and more violent. She offered her assistance but was only met with restraint each time. After an hour of digging with his makeshift shovel, the hole was more than big enough for Peter to fit inside, but Michael kept shoveling away with passion.

"I think the grave is ready," said Steina.

"No, not yet," said Michael, digging some more.

"It should suffice for now," she said, placing her hand on Michael's shoulder. "We can come back and do a proper burial after we meet with the council. You have my word."

"You don't understand. If I stop digging," he said as a knot built into his throat. "If I stop digging, then this all becomes real, and I can't have this become real. Not yet," he said as tears began to burst from his eyes like a fire hydrant.

Michael couldn't control his tears, nor did he care that Steina was there to see them either. All that he cared about was the guilt that weighed heavily on his chest. The same guilt that he would use and harness to execute Loki. He didn't know how but one way or another, he would get the vengeance that he desired.

Steina grabbed the branch from his hand and tossed it aside. She hugged Michael, clenching her arms around him tightly. Michael cried into her arms like he had never cried before, not since he was a young boy. A full-bodied, hyperventilating cry consumed him as he cried into her chest.

Michael could feel the warmth and compassion radiate from her soul and transfer to his, allowing his vulnerability to meld into the melting feeling of his heart as he hugged her. Ordinarily, he wouldn't have allowed her to see him in such a weakened and susceptible state, for his pride wouldn't allow it, but at this moment, he needed Steina's affection. His agony far too unbearable to tackle by himself, and for the first time, maybe ever, he was okay admitting that. He didn't want to be alone with his grief any longer, so he held onto her until his red, teary eyes could cry no longer, not even the smallest of whimpers.

Chapter Seven

The Fall of Alfheim

Michael knelt before Peter and cradled him in his arms. Peter's limp, cold body hung loosely, feeling as if he was in a weightless sleep, but Michael knew that his death was permanent. He rested his head against Peter's, uncaring of his nasty, hollowed flesh wound. They were forehead-to-forehead, just like when Peter was a baby fighting his sleep.

With one last gentle embrace, Michael placed Peter inside the informal grave. He dumped the soil onto Peter's barren body. Each clod of dirt weighing more than the last, both on Michael's heart and Peter's corpse. Steina and Michael shared a moment of silence as they overlooked the plodded area of dirt that concealed him.

After a moment alone with his grief, Michael followed Steina back to the vehicle. Steina helmed the pilot's seat this go around. She plugged in the coordinates back to Dain's Castle, accelerating much faster than their arrival there. From the aerial view above, the city seemed to be just fine. The bustling, futuristic town looked as alive as ever. From what they could gather, and only hope, is that Loki had only plagued Dagrún Village in the nighttime and nothing more. The rest of the realm appeared to be safe from his wrath, at least for now.

Michael couldn't help but wonder, why Dagrún Village of all places? Maybe it was Loki's plan all along to attack a historic safe zone such as Dagrún. The idea of a historical relic with such beautiful and rich history of peace and benevolence destroyed in one night ought to bring angst and terror amongst the nine realms. Was that what Loki wanted, to be feared amongst the universe? Maybe he wanted nothing more than to announce his return in the most horrifying way imaginable.

Regardless of Loki's intentions, Michael couldn't get over the fact that somehow, he had been in the epicenter of it all. There were nine realms, seven of which Michael had never stepped foot on, and he just so happened to wind up in the crosshairs of Loki's heinous return on his one and only night on Alfheim. It didn't make any sense.

Why strike now of all times? And why kill Peter? Peter had absolutely nothing to do with whatever Loki had planned. Why murder a young boy but let the three adults live? The detective in Michael was rousing, but he was confident that Loki's homecoming was not coincidental. Nothing ever was.

They pulled into the hangar, parked the vehicle, and took the rickety old elevator all the way to the top. The council must have been waiting on their return because all the standard security protocols that were typically in place had been dismantled.

Initially, it struck Michael and Steina as suspicious. They feared that Loki had already beaten them there and decimated their friends. They tiptoed the perimeter with caution until Inon greeted them with claws and paws of playfulness, filling them with relief that things were, in fact, okay. They briefly pampered the dragon with love and just as quickly made their way into the hallway beyond Inon's chamber.

They could hear some chatter and discord coming from inside the council room. "We ain't need no more stinkin' humans polluting our airspace, now do we?" said a raspy voice. Michael couldn't quite pick up on who was behind the gruffy accent with all the muffled bantering taking place inside.

"I surely don't see why not, Dafilrog," another voice replied, a voice Michael believed to be Ezra's. "If his heart is inclined on staying, who are we to tell him no? He could become a valuable asset to the council."

"How can one with no experience of magic help us in our wars against Loki and Nidavellir?" asked the unmistakable voice of Reynir. "If he desires to stay here on Alfheim, he has my vote. I truly like him, and his spirit is genuine, but he is filled with nothing but pain and torment right now. He would be nothing more than a nuisance. A damsel in distress that would only get in our way in the presence of war and other interdimensional threats."

Michael had to agree with Reynir on that aspect. What would he be able to offer when it came to magical combat? Ultimately, as much as he hated to admit it, he would only get in their way, but that didn't change his mind. This war was personal now. He was etched into its history, and he would rather die than head back to Earth like a coward. Loki would pay for what he did to Peter, and if it meant that Michael would die in the process, then so be it.

"Cause his own demise, he will," said an aging voice. "Hellbent on revenge. He would only hinder our plans."

"We can teach him," said the voice believed to be Ezra. "Just as we were all taught once a moon ago." She was the only voice that had any remnants of belief in Michael thus far. "We will teach him the art of magic."

"We simply lack the time or patience to do so," stated Reynir.

"With all due respect to each of you," a familiar voice interrupted, a voice near and dear to Michael's heart. "If I get an opportunity alone with him, I believe I can ch—"

"Darrius," Michael shouted, cutting him off and rushing inside the council quarters to greet him. He couldn't believe his eyes. It was actually Darrius. Here on Alfheim, somehow, he had made it. Michael wrapped his arms around him for an embracing hug.

Darrius gripped him tightly. "I'm so sorry, Mike. I just got the rundown on everything. I should have been there for you and Peter," he said, his voice sobering and sincere.

"It's not your fault, you know that," said Michael. Pain still etched tightly in his chest, but he'd be lying if he said seeing Darrius alive and safe on Alfheim didn't brighten his day. "I know you would have been here if you could have. I'm just so damn happy to see you again. How the hell did you even get here?"

"Root of Yin-and-Yang-seal or something. I don't know. Some magic tree they said," said Darrius referencing the council. "I guess you were right about that magic tree shit."

"Yggdrasil."

"Yeah, whatever. That thing. I touched it and voilà! After you disappeared, I spent the next four days on Earth looking for you around the clock. I was like a madman trying to find you. I barely slept, barely ate. I spent every waking moment in those woods searching for you. I wasn't gonna leave until I found out what happened. I even camped out there one night. Can you believe that? My scared ass camping out there? Fuck that. I never wanna do that shit again. That damn raven wouldn't shut up, but finally, while I was out there hiking, I gripped a tree branch and got transported here somewhere. Ezra found me and brought me to the council."

Wow, no way it had already been four days since he had disappeared, Michael thought. He'd only been here on Alfheim for, at most, twenty-four hours. Time really did operate on different frequencies across realms; Reynir and Steina weren't kidding.

"I had to tell Emma about your disappearance," said Darrius. "Which was a disheartening conversation, to say the least."

Hearing Emma's name out loud for the first time since Peter's death daunted Michael. All that he could think about on the flight in was the heartbreaking conversation he would have to have with her, but suddenly it felt that much more real at the sound of her name.

At some point, he would have to go back to Earth and explain to Emma what happened. What really happened, not the typical cotton candy riddled bullshit military officials regurgitated to the public after rather convincible UFO sightings or Alfheim vehicle landings as he'd recently come to discover.

Emma deserved the truth. Peter died on his watch, and he would never be able to forgive himself for that, and if she never forgave him as well, he wouldn't blame her one bit. All Michael could hope is that Emma was somehow more forgiving of him than he was of himself.

Michael focused his attention back on the ongoing dispute at hand, the never-ending debate about Michael's future on Alfheim. Between all the disagreement amongst them, it was hard for him to focus. From what he could gather, the council was divided.

Ólafur and Dafilrog adamantly disagreed with Michael's request to stay on Alfheim and fight at their side in war. At the same time, Ezra and Reynir argued in favor of him, even if Reynir believed training him in the art of magic was a waste of time. The deciding factor would be that of Solfrid. The final vote was in her hands. After much confusion and bickering, Solfrid got the council's attention and ushered order and civility amongst them.

The room was tense; all eyes were rested on Michael. He felt his skin crawl, his face flush red upon becoming the center of attention. Before Solfrid could cast her vote, she was interrupted by a bright and scintillating rainbow. The rainbow sparkled and danced in the middle of the room, gyrating slowly like sparklers in the night, far too captivating and mesmerizing to look away from, and then with no warning, the rainbow disappeared and, in its place, stood three men with the physique of gods.

It didn't take rocket science to understand that the trio was revered highly. Two of the gentlemen stood tall, supporting a third individual who was on his knees in handcuffs. From across the room, a shriek escaped from the outstretched mouth of Steina. Her hand spasmed as she attempted to cover her lips. Her face shrouded with fear. Her eyebrows vaulted upwards and widened with terror as her pupils swallowed the once vibrant shades of green.

Michael's eyes darted across the room, scanning the reactions of the council members. Their responses varied from panicked to terrified to that of relief, a whole spectrum of emotions elicited amongst them, and one by one, each member slowly began to kneel, bowing before the gentlemen.

Darrius nudged Michael in his leg, gesturing for him to kneel beside him. "Psst, get down," he whispered. "I don't know who these dudes are, but if they're kneeling, we're kneeling."

Michael slowly knelt beside Darrius, trying his best to get his bearings back after the sudden shock of their arrival. He studied each of the newest arrivals with rigor. Michael recognized the gentleman to the left of the handcuffed individual as Frey.

Although his beauty resonated through the portrait he had seen yesterday, it paled in comparison to the real thing.

Frey had glistening, goldish-blonde hair with perfectly manicured facial hair to match. His locks of hair hung elegantly, shimmering as if the sun orbited him at all times. Michael was sure of it; his power must come from his hair like the biblical character Samson. Frey's clothing was flushed so tightly to his skin that you could see every chiseled muscle of his body bulging from underneath.

The gentleman to the right of the bonded man was less muscular but far bigger and burlier. Michael was unsure of who this god was, but he reminded him of the traditional Viking he was accustomed to seeing on television. The god had the stereotypical big and strong like an ox look to him. Around his head was a helmet with rams' horns tightly wrapped and woven around it, and hanging from his neck was a horn the size of a small guitar.

And the last of the newcomers was the prisoner in bonds. An androgynous, soft-featured gentleman with fiery, vermillion hair. He was rather pale, but it was a pale that was closer in nature to humans rather than the greyish pale of elves. Between his eyes, on his forehead was a gaping flesh wound that bubbled profusely with flesh-eating bacteria, and although Michael was positive, he had never seen the man before, some intuition in his gut suspected differently.

"My lord, Frey," Solfrid stated delightedly. "A pleasure it is."

"The pleasure is all mine," said Frey. "Albeit I wish it were under better circumstances. Heimdall and I reacted promptly to your warning where we found Loki in his cave, still in his bonds."

"Precisely," said Loki behind a wry and sinister smile. "How could I have possibly eradicated your precious, stupid gnomes if I was bonded in my cave? Riddle me that, please. I'll wait."

There he was, the man that had caused Michael so much pain and torment. The man that had murdered Peter in cold blood. Michael felt his heart pulse inside his chest, his face and body flushed hot with rage. His jaw and fists clenched in unison. His heartbeat pounded so violently it was the only thing he could hear as the drumming berated his ears.

"Have you not escaped your bonds before?" asked Frey. "Or let me guess, that was not you either, I suppose."

"I escaped one time," responded Loki. "Once and only once, and in doing so, I found the love of my life," he said, glaring at Steina with admiration. "And now you have returned me to her, so if you would please release me from my bonds, that would be much appreciated. That way, I can be reunited with my lover once more."

"Tell that to Odin," said Steina, bristling with disgust. Her cheeks turned crimson as she slowly began to get color back to her face.

"Steina, you must believe me, honey. I never got the opportunity to apologize to you before . . . but I'm sorry. I'm sorry for pretending to be someone I am not, but I only did that because the gods fear my true nature. The feelings, the emotions, it was all genuine. So, the name was different, who cares? I love and adore you. You know that I would never slaughter and attack Dagrún Village as they have claimed. I know it doesn't make sense right now, but in due time, the truth will see the light of day. If you believe nothing else, believe that, for me. Please, I beg you."

"I believe you, alright. I believe you are a liar. A traitor and a thief. I believe you are the most repugnant, despicable piece of shit to ever live. We saw Nillbeck as he died, as he trembled to his death, claiming that it was you who murdered those innocent lives. You are a monster, and I wish you the most unspeakable of deaths."

"I never killed that village, nor did I kill the young boy. I swear that much, Steina. I swear that on my children. On Jörmungandr, on Fenris, on Hel. I am not the man they portray me to be but rather the man you know me to be in your heart. The tales that you have heard are false."

"Ahem," Heimdall coughed. "So, it is us who have presumed you to be evil and not your own sinister doings? Is that correct?"

"Correct," said Loki.

"Hmm, that's mighty peculiar. I seem to recall you murdering Balder. I have this vision of you doing so. I see it as clear as day."

"Well, technically, it was Hod who murdered Balder."

"Get him up," Heimdall barked to Frey. His nostrils flared as tension ignited between his brows. "I have had more than enough of my share of you today. It is off to Odin, you go. It is clear that your bonds are too weak if you can escape with such ease. Now the Allfather shall decide your fate."

"No, you don't understand," pleaded Loki. "Yes, I was behind the death of Balder. He was a pompous, braggadocious asshole with his look at me 'I cannot die' masquerade. Quite frankly, it got on my every last nerve, so yes, I engineered a plan to kill him, but that's the thing, we all die, just as we have thousands of times before. Ragnarök occurs and reoccurs endlessly. It is as timeless as we are. Ragnarök wipes the slate clean, we reincarnate, and the Norns weave new stories. Life goes on for us gods as it always has, and every cycle brings forth a new god in command.

"Once, it was me. Once Frey. Once you, Heimdall. We have all had our share at becoming the Allfather, and after years of exile, I finally see what I could not before. It is Odin. It always has been. An all too powerful ruler, hellbent on ruling the throne for eternity. He has cursed you all into not remembering our true nature. If I did not believe Balder would not reincarnate, I would have never had a hand in killing him. It is Odin who we must stop so we can return to our natural order. If you do not believe me, find the Norns and ask them. They know the truth. We need Ragnarök, Heimdall."

"Spare me your lies, Loki," said Frey. "Your deceitful tongue has betrayed us one too many times.

"Once a trickster, always a trickster," Heimdall snorted.

"We would be foolish to ever believe your words again," said Frey. "Ever since Odin invited you to the halls of Asgard, you have done nothing but plot against him, and now you seek to do the same. Your retribution knows no bounds. Now, if you have run out of slander, it is time for you to face the damnation you deserve."

"Fine," replied Loki. "If you must take me away, so be it, but first, I have a surprise." A wrathful smirk emerged from behind his lips, and on cue, green misty clouds of smoke began to permeate throughout the room.

The air was toxic and left them in coughing fits, engorging their lungs and overflowing their eyes with tears. A silhouette had emerged from the settling haze. The newcomer was a female swaddled with a tight jawline and a bony face. Her smile was as sinister and dark as Loki's. Her eyes were darting and venomous like a snake, a hazel-ish green with slits at the pupils.

Even the mighty Heimdall cringed at the sight of her. "G-G-Gullveig?" he shuddered with a face whiter than snow. "H-how is that possible?"

"Anything is possible, my dear," cackled Gullveig, her shrill devilish and ear-piercing.

"I thought you were dead. We killed you."

"Oh, pish posh. Your sad attempt to murder me, well darling, just consider it water under the bridge. Besides, who's counting the three times you tried to burn my corpse alive?"

"How could I have not foreseen your return unfolding?"

"There are ways around your all-seeing eye, Heimdall. Some to the likes you would never imagine," she smiled.

"We can do this the easy way or the hard way," stated Loki. "I never did the deeds that you have claimed against me, but nonetheless, I appreciate you releasing me from my bonds. Now it is up to you to decide where we go from here."

"Where you go, will be Odin," said Frey, his voice unwavering.

"So be it," Loki responded, ripping free from his handcuffs. The remains of his bonds erupted from his wrists, showering across the room like confetti.

Gullveig fired a green, energy blast at the council, catching them off guard and brushing them to the floor. Michael, safe from the explosion, scanned the room for a weapon. His ears still pumped madly, synchronized to the rage in his heart. He should have been fearful, should have been petrified like his peers, but he wasn't. Maybe it was the adrenaline fueling him, perhaps it was his bloodlust for revenge, but all he could feel was the fury that had been pent up inside him for too long now, just waiting for the opportunity to be unleashed.

There was no way he could allow Loki to escape without consequence. He had to do something, anything, to get the justice that Peter deserved. He couldn't be left with the same regret he had felt this morning when he was left incapable of helping, not again, he told himself.

In one swift motion, he unsheathed the sword hanging from Reynir's waist and joisted it forward with precision. A quick jab that pierced Loki in his rib cage. With both hands gripped around the blade, he vaulted it upward, thrusting high and hard until he heard the sound of Loki's bones crackling.

Loki screamed in agony, squawking a deathly howl. He blasted Michael backward to the ground with a furor. The blow was quick and powerful, the energy hot and excruciating, leaving Michael feeling as if he had just been singed with boiling water. Loki violently tugged at the sword prodded into his rib cage and swiftly propelled it through the air as far away from him as possible.

The sword rattled and clanked to the floor, landing at the feet of Gullveig. She clutched control of it and quickly bludgeoned Ólafur in the chest, impaling through his aged and brittle sternum. He fell to the ground and garbled, choking on the fleeting breaths that escaped his lungs.

Dafilrog reacted promptly, fastening his hands together and harnessing his energy at Gullveig, expelling an assortment of squealing and smoldering skulls that streamlined towards her.

Gullveig chuckled lightheartedly as if Dafilrog's attack was nothing more than that of a mere chihuahua. She lifted her hand upright, in a stop position, halting the skulls in midair. They scowled and convulsed scathingly, and with the roll and flick of her pointer finger, she directed the skulls back at Dafilrog. The skeletons followed her command, engulfing him in flames, consuming his body, and beelining him to an alternate realm that reeked of death.

Ezra, in a fit of fury and passion, lasered bright and blistering hot energy beams from her eyes at Gullveig. Gullveig reacted promptly, intercepting Ezra's lasers and freezing them in place, shattering Ezra's eyes into broken, frozen-glass pieces that dazzled across the floor like diamonds, sparkling the room to life like a chandelier.

A full battle had emerged inside the cramped and compact corridor. Energy blasted and radiated left and right, glass exploded from the windows, smoke and flames flooded the room, and cries from every direction could be heard with little idea of who was behind them. The sound of metal could be heard as swords and arrows clanked and chinked amongst armor.

Heimdall had been relatively quiet during the skirmish, subdued by the shocking re-emergence of Gullveig. Slowly, the strength gathered back into his legs, and the courage he lacked restored into his heart. He targeted Loki, barreling through Michael like a poor offensive lineman in the process, and tackled Loki through the broken window.

Michael somersaulted to the window's edge, watching the two of them as they catapulted through the air, free-falling thousands of feet to the rocky terrain beneath. They barreled and rolled, clinging together tightly, each throwing punches and kicks at one another tirelessly. Energy danced between their hands as they attempted to generate spells, but neither would allow the other the luxury of doing so.

A few hundred feet before plummeting into the soil, the two of them stopped midair and levitated above the surface as their fight continued. The ground began to tremble beneath them, splitting the landscape into tiny cracks and enormous crevices, like a dry and barren desert spider-webbing Alfheim's core. Seismic waves tore apart layers of Alfheim until finally, their fury and energy grew strong and intense enough to splinter the city into two, leaving a gap the size of the Grand Canyon underneath them.

As a result of their volatile clash, the ground beneath the castle grew unstable. With each powerful surge of Loki and Heimdall, the canyon widened, vacuuming the castle's base and collapsing its infrastructure.

The castle tilted, toppling like a *Jenga* tower, sending everyone barreling across the room towards the open windows as if they were a crew out at sea caught amid an unforgiven storm. The council and Gullveig alike clawed at the floor desperately, trying to maintain any sense of stability. The manor gave way to the tremors, and each subsequent floor followed suit, tumbling into the great abyss that had been forged in battle.

Frey levitated out of the window. His hands and face tightened, both tense with pressure as he strained enough energy onto the castle to support it momentarily. He held it upright just long enough for Inon to flap his mighty wings and soar to the council's rescue, scooping each member upon his wide and monolithic spine.

Inon danced through the air, dodging the flying debris that caromed the sky. The council held on to his bony and rigid spine for dear life. Inon thrusted higher and higher until they were free from the cyclone of rubble and destruction below.

The council rested safely upon the dragon's broad shoulders, watching the murky, indistinct battlefield in despair where they could see Frey struggling tirelessly under the weight of the building. His hands and arms quivered intensely, but the god still managed to hold his grasp, keeping the castle and its civilians afloat. The council watched beneath as an outpour of elves marched out of the castle in herds, stomping over one another recklessly like ants fleeing a collapsing ant bed.

"Frey," screamed Steina trying to warn him, but her voice drowned and muffled in the chaos as if her face had been smothered with a pillow.

Gullveig stormed after Frey, caring little for the civilian's safety. Blinding green energy radiated in her right hand, and with it, she drove her fist hard into his gut, releasing Frey's grip on the castle. After thousands of years of war and immaculate architecture, Dain's Castle stood tall no longer, replaced by an atomic bomb of rubble and dust instead.

Inon vaulted upwards, zooming far and away from the ashes below. The council scanned the perimeter, their eyes darting for either Heimdall or Frey, but the scenery beneath them was far too enveloped with dense clouds of smoke.

"There, Inon," ushered Reynir, pointing in the direction of Loki and Heimdall, both of which were still locked in battle.

Inon darted below to allow them a closer look, all while managing to keep a safe distance. Loki and Heimdall's conflict had seemingly picked up steam as large chunks of mountains and boulders were now magnetizing around them. The debris orbited them like planets, acting as a battering ram as it crashed and walloped into the futuristic buildings of Alfheim that had managed to remain tall. Moments later, those same buildings nosedived into the soil, adding to the myriad of remains that already circulated the once fresh air.

Loki and Heimdall felt around one another with grips of death, stabbing and poking at each other's eyes, clawing and scratching away at whatever they could find. Both gods looking to gain whatever advantage they could as their eyes caked with blood and the dense rubble of the city.

The flying cars that usually ornamented the horizon streaked through the sky like comets darting into the ground beneath them. Alarms and sirens wailed throughout the city, filling the town with a purging, apocalyptic horror.

Spectators emerged from the blinding haze in a panic, trying their best to watch the battle above while dodging the fleeting ruins of the castle. They disappeared as quickly as they had appeared, getting lost and entrenched in the soot below.

Heimdall, still gripping around Loki's throat, channeled the Bifröst, summoning the rainbow bridge before them. Heimdall swiftly elbowed Loki in the gut and proceeded to uppercut him with that same elbow in one rapid succession. He latched onto Loki's head with his other hand and forcefully dragged it across the scorching Bifröst, simmering and charring Loki's face into a sizzling blob leaving Loki's skin to drip and melt like candle wax.

He wedged Loki's face against the Bifröst like cheese against the grater until Loki had only half a face left; the other half disintegrated into oblivion. Heimdall thrusted harder, his hands and forearms quivering from the strain. Loki jerked his body, trying to writhe himself free, but the pressure was so immense that even he could not escape Heimdall's stranglehold. Now in control, Heimdall calmly but powerfully held Loki steady, driving what was left of his chargrilled face deeper into the Bifröst.

Loki's one and only remaining pupil widened to the point that they could no longer see the white. Loki struggled once more against Heimdall's grip, his legs somersaulting frenetically, bouncing up and down, thrashing relentlessly. His body began to pulse and vibrate in a fight-or-flight response.

Loki's veins illuminated a fiery-red, and with it, his health regenerated. His body had restored to its original form, only this time it was stronger, like a reptile re-growing an appendage. His face reemerged, fully revitalized, even removing the nasty flesh wound, completely ridding him of the snake poison that had tormented him for years.

Reynir guided Inon closer, surging to the relief of Heimdall. Inon shrieked, the pit of his stomach rumbled, rattling the council above. His lungs filled, and out he exhaled a torrid burst of flames. The heat emitted from Inon emanated across the faces of the council, leaving them to brace for cover.

Loki invoked a shield before him, catapulting the fearsome flames back into the direction of Inon and the council. Inon swerved right, veering out of the way, but in his drifting, Loki expelled two daggers, crafted from his energy, aimed at the eyes of Inon. They hit Loki's target, and Inon plundered. His wings flailed, losing altitude like a helicopter spinning out of control, leaving the council to clutch their nails deep into his skin as they clasped onto him in horror.

Heimdall blasted Loki once more, thrusting his head back into the Bifröst, but this time the Bifröst only grazed his hair, leaving it frayed at its tips. With a quick sleight of hands, Loki ejected a switchblade from his wrist and thrust it across Heimdall's gullet, lacerating him cleanly.

The council shrieked in horror, but Inon had descended too far for any of them to be of assistance.

Heimdall garbled and choked on his own blood, his windpipe slashed, leaving him breathless. Loki shifted, rolling into a one-eighty, flinging Heimdall's head against the scolding hot Bifröst and engulfing it into flames.

A fully healthy Loki, now in advantage, blasted Heimdall with all his might driving Heimdall's body flush against the Bifröst, searing it in half just like Loki's face only moments before. Every one of Heimdall's attempts to escape was matched against the strength of Loki.

Heimdall cried in pain; whatever was left of his body convulsed against the Bifröst. Loki was too powerful, free of injury, and fully healed; he was simply too much for an exhausted Heimdall incapable of regeneration.

"I'm sorry, brother," said Loki. "I wish there was another way, but you will be reborn again, soon enough. I promise."

Heimdall pursed what was left of his lips around his horn and blew with all his might. The horn's powerful tune sang majestically across Alfheim and all the nine realms until it stopped abruptly because Heimdall's body was no more. The Bifröst enclosed around him and consumed him, burning him into a nothing left crisp and eviscerating his body. The melody of his horn echoed eerily across the mountains, ushering the era of Ragnarök amongst them.

CHAPTER EIGHT

GJALLARHORN

Inon swiveled rampantly, still blinded by the daggers of Loki. Reynir pulled and guided his neck to the best of his ability, trying desperately to stabilize the dragon. Alerted by the agonizing screams of Frey, Reynir steered the shaky dragon in that direction to find Gullveig wailing mercifully upon Frey.

Trees snapped from their roots, circling Gullveig with ferocity. She used nature to her advantage, ironically, against the god of nature himself. She walloped Frey with boulders and trees and anything else that entered her orbit that could be used as a weapon. Her power surged; wind gusts swirled around her like a powerful tornado. With her magic, she bonded Frey's hands together using the branches of the rampant, unruly trees that shadowed her.

Gullveig floated to the restrained body of Frey. She placed her right hand, flickering with green flames, atop his chest, directly on his sternum. With her hand over his beating heart, she siphoned the life from out of him, withdrawing the power within him. A scream escaped from the flaccid lips of Frey, a cry so raw and primeval, it forced its way from the depths of his stomach like an infant in a scourged panic.

Inon surged at Gullveig, Reynir as his guide, his mouth drooling globs of molten hot lava as he dived near the ground next to her. His teeth unfurled, showing their massive size. His snout huffed steam, emitting singeing heat. With the council still draped tightly across his back Inon unleashed a sizzling hot stream of fire at Gullveig.

Gullveig released her grip from Frey, letting him fall limply to the ground, fifteen or so feet beneath them. She closed her eyes as if she was sunbathing, enjoying a nice summer day on the beach, basking in the flames discharged from Inon, letting them absorb upon her skin.

"Please, darling," said Gullveig. "Haven't any of you learned by now that fire cannot kill me?" Her devilish laugh filled the air with terror once more. She scrunched her left hand together slowly as if she was crushing an invisible soda can.

Inon's wings compressed to his spine, vaulting the council from his shoulders and hurtling them to the ground. Inon's limbs sandwiched to his torso, confining him to the fetal position, plummeting him to the soil beside them. The dragon tumbled vehemently. His large body striking the ground with such ferocity that it rumbled lightly.

Gullveig wasted little time returning her attention back to Frey. With his body still weak and gutted, Gullveig raised Frey by his collar. She placed her hand back on his sternum, continuing to spigot the life from him. Frey jolted, his body jerking in the form of cadaveric spasms, squirming like a dying insect.

Gullveig clubbed his chest forcefully, straining his remaining power. Frey's skin and flesh shriveled to his bones. The once muscular god now resembled that of a malnourished stray dog who hadn't had a hearty meal in weeks. His body was frail and decrepit, appearing as if one touch would collapse him into ash and dust.

Gullveig fell to dirt abruptly, landing beside Frey. Her body writhed and spasmed with convulsions, overloaded with power. Her body bent and rolled unnaturally, turning in manners that seemed impossible, stirring like a bad exorcist movie. The tremoring stopped, leaving her gasping for air. Her breath rolled loud and heavy in undulating waves.

She glared at the council with a look of menacing pleasure. "With the power of Frey, I can now control nature at will. Not even the almighty Odin can stop us now." She peered to the sky, her eyes sparkling with joy. "I know you heard the sound of Gjallarhorn. Ragnarök is before us, darlings. I suggest you choose your sides wisely and maybe you will live to tell the tale. Loki has a soft spot for you," she said, her attention on Steina. "I advise you to keep it that way."

Gullveig turned to the sky once more. "Skoll and Hati. No longer is Frey here to control and enslave you. Your powers no longer limited. I give them back to you in full. The time is now that you fulfill your destiny and venture across the realms of Yggdrasil, consuming every star in the sky until every sun and moon has been vanquished. Be free, my wolves."

At her beck and call, the sky opened, unveiling a black hole that spiraled like a hurricane being viewed from outer space. Within the vortex were the stars of other galaxies, displaying a vivid portrait of the nighttime sky alongside the everyday, sun-soaked horizon of Alfheim. Two enormous and daunting wolves, the size of large clouds, erupted through the abyss, flying and roaming the sky as effortlessly as birds.

One of the wolves was white and lighter than snow, the other dark and blacker than coal. Like greyhounds at the racetrack, they zipped seamlessly with beauty, devouring the suns and moons of Alfheim with one large gulp, absorbing all the light the realm had to offer, entrenching it in darkness.

Only one source of light and heat remained, the Bifröst. In a world so impenetrably dark, the rainbow bridge burned like fire in the nighttime sky, and in the blink of an eye, the bridge extinguished with Loki and Gullveig mounting it, leaving the council alone on the desolate realm.

In thirty minutes, the realm of Alfheim had been altered forever. The council had been gutted, their god, Frey, executed, and their home ransacked with only the stars above to illuminate them, leaving them all to wonder how much longer they had to enjoy them before Skoll and Hati would feast on them too.

The air chilled drastically as the temperature on the realm dropped tens of degrees without both suns in place. A frantic game of Marco Polo occurred as the council members hollered at one another while searching through the ravaging darkness. Wisps of flames illuminated the dark night as Inon huffed fire to life. With the help from Inon, the council members regrouped, building lanterns from the bulkier tree branches.

"What now?" asked Michael.

"I . . . I don't know," stated Reynir, looking to Solfrid for resolve.

"Must restore Alfheim," replied Solfrid. "Prepared we are, for, the prophecies have warned of this day."

"Indeed, but the prophecies also predicted that Heimdall shall slay Loki during Ragnarök, and now he is dead. And what of Frey and Surtr?"

"Unsure, I am. For now, we must find remains of vault. Fornviska, Heimsstrengur, and Meginórsól will be needed for journey ahead."

"What of the council? We only have three remaining members," said Reynir, fighting against the overwhelming grief lodged between his words.

"Council proceeds with new members, just as centuries before have done. Steina—Michael—Darrius—acceptance amongst council granted."

"Huh?" said Darrius, taken aback. "Me?"

"I don't understand," said Michael. "We just got here. Ten seconds ago, everyone was arguing whether or not I even belonged here."

"What of the trials?" blurted Steina.

"Surely, it would make more sense to add more experienced replacements?" asked Reynir.

"For their fates have been written," responded Solfrid. "Fight at the side of Alfheim, they will. Upon finding possessions of vault, to Konungr you four quest. Needed Konungr is to restore our realm. Ezra and I journey to Mimir in hopes that he has answers to lift the curse of Nidavellir."

"Who is Konungr?" asked Michael.

"He's one of the few magicians left to have scholared in the art of runic magic," said Reynir. "Or so it is rumored. He is a demi-god, a descendant of Heimdall."

"No offense to this Konungr guy, but shouldn't we get some of the heavy hitters involved? Like Thor or Odin, maybe?"

"Only runic magic can save this place now, hence the need for Konungr. That or the curse being lifted. Gods like Thor and Odin mostly focus on war and protection. After a realm lies in ruin, they typically show very little interest. Just look at how many times Midgard has been decimated to the likes of floods, asteroids, plagues, you name it."

"And what about Konungr? Where is he?"

"Whereabouts unknown," said Solfrid. "Fornviska needed to find him."

Michael nodded his head. Part of him was excited. He had been admitted to the council and entrusted to go on a quest. Not just any quest at that, but a quest to save Alfheim, potentially the world.

Ever since Skye disappeared, he had this clutching feeling, a premonition almost, that he was destined for more. At times his detective work filled him with relief, a false sense of a higher calling, but it was nothing more than a ruse. Maybe this is what he had been missing for so long. If he could contribute to saving Alfheim, he might finally feel worthy. He would get that feeling of belonging that he had been yearning for his entire life.

The other half of him was terrified, less of the likely death that accompanied his quest and more so with the shrouding possibility of failure. That part of him coveted to return to Earth, have his memory erased, and go back to solving cases with Darrius where the stakes weren't nearly as high as saving an entire realm. Not to mention he was massively unprepared for another encounter with the likes of Loki and Gullveig. He was way over his head, and this war was far more than he'd bargained for.

Before self-doubt could absorb him, he was reminded of Peter. Reminded of how he had failed him. The guilt of Peter's death still weighed heavily on his heart. This was his chance at redemption. His opportunity to get Peter the justice he deserved. He may not have been able to save him, but he was bound and determined to save Alfheim, and he wouldn't stop until Loki laid before him with a knife in his heart. This time he wouldn't miss his mark, he told himself.

Solfrid led the crusade through the once glorious realm, guided by an internal compass she had cast after multiple failed attempts. The task proved to be dizzying for her as Alfheim had been shifted off its axis. Her heart heavy, her focus scattered. With no sun in place, and in Alfheim's case, two suns, her mental control proved feeble and disoriented. Nevertheless, she pushed through her heartache, following the compass as it propelled them forward, directing them to the desires of Solfrid's heart.

In a way, it reminded Michael of his journey to Alfheim, when he and Darrius voyaged through the eerie forest of Earth with nothing but a flashlight and the unknown ahead. The stillness made the vast darkness of the once lively city that much more daunting.

What was once the majestic Castle of Dain was now nothing more than a dusty heap of rocks and rubble that proved difficult to navigate around in the night sky. They couldn't be too far as both battles never left the vicinity of the castle, but it was impossible to know where Dain's Castle had once stood with the crevices and valleys that now preserved the area.

"Here," said Solfrid, stopping before a tower of rubble and boulder chunks. "One of the artifacts lies beneath. Too weak, I am. Reynir, would you?"

"Of course, madam," said Reynir.

Reynir's magic was wary and disconcerted yet still strong enough to disperse the large, cracked in half columns out of their way as well as any other remaining clumps of the castle that piled underneath. Snuggled into the debris was Fornviska, encased inside the rubble like a pearl protected by the shells of an oyster.

Reynir palmed the orb in one hand and admired it. It gleamed and shined, as slick and smooth as marble. Activated by Reynir's touch, the sphere came to life, filling with misty smoke.

"So, what, it's like a crystal ball or something?" asked Darrius. "What does it do?"

"Fornviska," said Solfrid. "Artifact of ancient wisdom. Knowledge comes at price. To obtain wisdom, sacrifice is needed."

"What kind of price are we talking about?" asked Michael.

"Something near to heart. Sacrifice must be of honor, for it leaves and travels Yggdrasil if offended."

"Sounds like a lot of pressure."

"Nothing equals free, most of all wisdom. Its value immeasurable. Money, goods, equal different value across realms. Priceless are knowledge and wisdom."

Reynir and Ezra proceeded forward at Solfrid's guidance, dismantling rocks and boulders that intruded upon their path. Each of them hoisted remnants of the city into the air and discarded them safely. In the strenuous labor process, their respective energies began to dwindle under the befallen realm's weight.

If their magic gave way, all that would be left was Steina, and Michael knew, based on her brief encounters in battle, that her knowledge of magic was only a few shades more than that of himself or Darrius. She wasn't nearly strong enough to man the rest of the journey alone.

Sure, those fluent enough with magic could recharge as they regained their energy, but with no sun in place, that could take weeks. As the magic withered from their grasps, Inon surged forward, taking on the brunt of the workload before weariness and lethargy eventually grabbed hold of him too.

Michael and Darrius could use their brawn to try to lift some slabs, but neither were strong enough for that task, nor were they capable of administering any spells such as the one Solfrid had cast to obtain Fornviska.

They lugged through more scraps in search of the remaining artifacts hidden beneath the city's havoc until Solfrid stopped them once more. It took a collaborative team effort to excavate through all the detritus, but as a team, they were able to slug through it. The last piece of masonry proved backbreaking, but it wasn't nearly as heavy as what came after.

Beneath them laid Ólafur, lying there lifeless with Reynir's sword still etched firmly into his chest. Solfrid's internal compass had led them to her greatest desire of all, her partner and lover. A desire that none of them were ready to encounter quite yet.

More guilt tinged inside of Michael, piercing and stabbing away at his insides. His body burned with remorse, a sensation that had become all too familiar during his short tenure on Alfheim. Had he not stolen Reynir's sword and stabbed Loki with it, Ólafur might still be alive.

He had only been here for two days, and he was already responsible for the death of Peter and Ólafur. Even if he knew the others would tell him otherwise, the guilt that resided within him said differently.

His heart dropped even further into the pit of his stomach, plunging to depths unknown after he managed to sneak a glance at Solfrid. Her face wrenched in pain, scrunching together and revealing the wrinkles that otherwise remained hidden. It was the only time Michael had ever seen any emotion slip from her impassive exterior. Even she could not hold back the tears that plagued her after seeing her loved one deceased in such a horrifying fashion.

She placed her left foot firmly onto his chest and tugged at the sword lodged tightly into his sternum. The sword released its way from Ólafur's heart only to transfer that pain to Solfrid. She paused and stared at the sword with dejection before handing it back to Reynir. Reynir extended his hand slowly as if an internal battle was present on whether he should accept the sword from her.

"Please," said Solfrid behind tears. "I insist . . . Ólafur would insist."

Reynir retrieved the sword back into his possession and sheathed it into place. Before Reynir could speak on the matter, Steina emerged between them and wrapped her arms around

Solfrid, clutching her tightly as she wept into Steina's chest. Their exchange of tears rolled gracefully from their cheeks to their armor plating like a waterfall.

Ezra wrapped her arms around Solfrid and Steina, followed by Reynir, followed by Michael and Darrius as they shared an embracing hug. Even Inon joined, nuzzling his head into Solfrid's leg and wrapping his large body and tail around them, closing the circle.

The council took all the time they needed to regain their composure before continuing their journey through the remains of the castle. After sifting through more rubble, they came across another artifact; this time, it was Meginórsól. A spherical globe of heat shaped like the sun, far too hot to touch and could only be yielded with magic. The combination of Solfrid, Ezra, and Reynir used their remaining energy to harness the artifact into the air.

Meginórsól erupted open like a bottle of pop that had been shaken profusely and through its explosion emerged a sun. A sun much smaller than the second sun of Alfheim but the false sun was more than large enough to brighten the realm and offer its heat. The darkness around them descended, and rays of sunshine returned upon their faces just as they would after a Florida rainstorm in the summer.

"Well, that feels nice," said Darrius.

"A sight for sore eyes," joked Ezra, having lost her eyes in her battle with Gullveig, but only she laughed at her spell of dark humor.

"Is that sun capable of withholding all of Alfheim's needs?" asked Michael.

"For now," replied Steina. "Its power will diminish. Its life span, maybe only a couple of years, but it should bide us enough time to restore things back to some level of normalcy."

"And when it falls?"

"I . . . I don't know. I don't think any of us do."

"Have the prophecies ever been wrong before?"

"Not until today, when Loki killed Heimdall and Gullveig slaughtered Frey. Heimdall was prophesized to kill Loki and Surtr to kill Frey. Nowhere in the oracles is Gullveig ever mentioned."

"How is that possible?"

"Ahh, the age-old question?" said Reynir. "Can what that has been written be rewritten?"

"Without a doubt," said Darrius. "There's no such thing as fate. I am in charge of my life. Myself, and God. Free will and the choices I have made have led me here. Not fate, not destiny. Only myself. Fate, religion, all just a means of control told by those in power to enslave us. Why else would the bible forbid against gays or women? Unless, of course, the men who wrote it used it as a force of entrapment. A force of power, so to speak."

"God?" replied Steina. "Yggdrasil is filled with them. There is only one god that is almighty with power, the Allfather, Odin."

"You have your beliefs, and I have mine, but I choose to believe in free will."

"Fate itself, the only thing that exists," stated Solfrid.

"Alright now," said Michael. "You know what they say about politics and religion. How about we all cool down and recharge? I know a lot of us could use the sunlight. We can pick back up after everyone feels rejuvenated. Sound good to everyone?"

"Sounds like a plan," said Reynir. "I'm beat. I could use some rest."

The council disassembled momentarily, allowing the sorcerers the opportunity to recharge and let the sunlight work its way back into their emaciated bodies and replenish them.

Michael and Darrius took the opportunity to scour the city for more artifacts or valuables, neither entirely sure what they were looking for. This was their first time alone together since the moment Michael had disappeared. However long ago that was now, the difference between the times on Alfheim and Earth was far too headache-inducing to keep up with.

"You really think we should go through with all of this?" asked Darrius.

"I mean, we kind of have to, right?" asked Michael. "We're members of the council now. It's our obligation to help restore this place, isn't it?"

"But we never asked to be a part of the council, Michael. You heard them arguing at the castle before everything happened. This isn't our war; they said it themselves. I came here for you and Peter. Not some ancient war of the realms between Nordic gods. I mean, these are gods I didn't even know existed a day or two ago, and now I'm supposed to fight beside them? Give me one good reason why we should do such a thing?"

"Because Peter deserves justice, and this is how we provide that for him. Look, I don't blame you if you leave. If I was in your position, I would probably do the same thing. You've done more than enough for me. You owe this place nothing, but whether we stay or leave, Loki is out there, and we both know that he's gonna strike again. We can pretend that ignorance is bliss, but if shit hits the fan, then this war is coming to us whether we like it or not. At least with the council, we have a fighting chance in all of this."

"I've seen war. I've been there, and I vowed to myself to never get involved with it again. It's not right. It's always the guys like us who have to pay the price, not those in power who started it. We might have a fighting chance here, but only because they intend to fight. How do we even know that Loki would come to Earth? For all we know, he might leave us alone. No one's bothering him there."

"Look around you, Darrius. This place, these people, none of them were bothering Loki either, and look at what he did."

"Alfheim got caught in the aftermath of a fight between gods. Heimdall has just as much fault as Loki does in Alfheim's destruction."

"You're right. That's fair, but that doesn't change the fact that Heimdall and Frey only came here because Loki murdered a village of gnomes. He murdered Peter, Darrius. I want revenge! And damn it. I'm going to get it. Yeah, so what? We're dealing with some gods. All I see is a bunch of murders on our hands that require justice. This is right down our avenue. This is what we do best, and we do this shit better than anyone so let's solve this case and give this place the justice that it deserves. The justice that Peter deserves."

Darrius nodded his head but kept whatever thoughts he had to himself. The two of them searched some more in silence but came up empty-handed. When they arrived back, they found everyone awake and revitalized. Reynir had even retrieved the last remaining artifact that they needed while Michael and Darrius had been away. The most recent artifact was, Heimsstrengur, an item resembling an elaborate, double-doored gate.

"Nice, good work, guys," said Michael, marveling at the artifact. "What does this one do?"

"Heimsstrengur, an entrance to all realms," said Solfrid.

136

"None of us are capable of traveling between realms," Reynir explained. "With convergences out of whack thanks to Skoll and Hati and with roots of Yggdrasil being so unruly, this allows us to be precise in our travels. It can only be used once. We have had it saved in the vault for centuries, waiting for a time like this to use it."

"So, what are we waiting for?"

"Two brave souls to offer sacrifices to Fornviska," said Steina. "One sacrifice is needed to find Heimdall's horn, Gjallarhorn. The other will be used to find Konungr's location. Without Gjallarhorn, Fornviska is incapable of extending its wisdom across the realms. It requires the blood or possession of a relative to navigate across such vast distances."

Michael grabbed Fornviska from the soil and felt the orb begin to pulsate in the palm of his hands. "Fine. I'll go first. No need to waste any more time, right?" The artifact surged to life in his fingertips as misty smoke began to settle inside. "How does this work? I just speak into it and make a sacrifice or . . . what?"

"Speak as normal," stated Solfrid. "Offer sincere sacrifice. Hope Fornviska accepts."

"No pressure, right?" Michael joked uncomfortably. "Only the world, no big deal." Michael took a deep breath and stared into the orb. "Fornviska, in exchange for the location of Gjallarhorn, I sacrifice my loyalty and allegiance to Alfheim. I pledge to never return to my home of Midgard while Alfheim is in danger, except when an excursion as such is needed. I vow my life to this place, and I will spend every waking moment here rebuilding, doing whatever it takes to bring Alfheim back to prosperity."

Michael had the slightest idea of what the repercussions would be if he backed out of said arrangement. He had forgotten to ask the council before making his sacrifice, but it didn't matter. He meant every word he uttered, and he would die protecting this realm if that's what it came down to, but he would make sure that Loki died first. He vowed that much.

Fornviska began to rumble, shaking violently in Michael's hands, seemingly accepting the terms and conditions of his sacrifice. The orb convulsed, guiding him by rolling in his hands, tugging and pulling him in different directions. It steered him forward, left, right, left again, further ahead, through the rubble, and over it, until it rolled backward with ardor, signaling Michael to look above. Crested above him was Gjallarhorn, laid atop a mountain of rubble looking regal and elegant like the sword in the stone.

It occurred to Michael that one of his fellow councilmen could have easily levitated the horn out of the air, but this was his mission. After all, it was he who made the sacrifice. He would be the one that would have to deal with consequences if he tried to weasel out of his promise. Therefore, it was only right for him to retrieve Gjallarhorn himself.

He scurried atop the rubble before anyone could stop him, like a squirrel climbing a tree, and with that thought, he couldn't get the vision of Ratatosk climbing up and down Yggdrasil out of his mind. With each hand that etched into the rubble, he thought of himself as Ratatosk. How big could that damn squirrel be, anyway, he questioned.

He thought about that all the way until he reached the top. It was the only thing keeping his mind off the thirty or forty feet he had just climbed. An overwhelming feeling of success surged through him as he grabbed Gjallarhorn. He'd begun to feel useless during his time here. The council had done everything meaningful, thus far, and he had little to show for his efforts.

One stupid horn had never felt so good. Sure, it wasn't as noble as relaunching a sun, but it counted for something. After a long list of failures, this felt like a lottery ticket in his hand. He felt triumphant, at least for a moment, and for now, that was all that he needed, a small victory of some sort. He emerged from the rocks victorious, on cloud nine, but as he got back to ground level, he soon realized that nobody else matched his eagerness in offering their sacrifice.

He looked around as Reynir, Steina, and Darrius shared looks of uncertainty, each playing hot potato with the orb, avoiding it at all costs. Awkward tension built up between them, each standing their ground firmly, hoping that another would courageously step forward. Michael's victory felt short-lived. He felt foolish. He wished he had confirmed with the others prior to making such a monumental and life-altering decision.

Steina was the first to budge. She scoffed at the others and grabbed Gjallarhorn and Fornviska from Michael with reluctance. With the horn cradled in her arms like a newborn and the orb nestled between her palms, she offered her sacrifice. "Fornviska, in exchange for the coordinates of Konungr, I choose to sacrifice my bow and arrow. No longer will I wield it in battle."

The orb willingly accepted, leaving Michael dumbfounded. He felt slighted. Here he had offered his life to Alfheim, and all Steina had to sacrifice was a damn bow and arrow. It didn't make any sense, but likewise, it didn't matter either. All it meant was they were one step closer to embarking on their quest to find Konungr.

Fornviska jolted out of Steina's hands and nudged the feet of Reynir repeatedly.

"What?" asked Reynir. "What does this thing want? I'm not making any sacrifices. Get it away from me," he said, kicking at it.

Fornviska buzzed and hummed incessantly, growing more aggravating and insistent, tapping at Reynir's shoes to get his attention.

"Not you that it wants," said Solfrid. "Heimsstrengur it desires. For your journey begins."

Reynir pulled Heimsstrengur, the double-doored gate, from out of his pocket. He ushered a spell and watched it sprout in size, blooming like a plant until the artifact had become large enough for his peers to fit inside.

The gated door gleamed of gold, looking elegant, reeking of remnants of the lost city of El Dorado. The gate doors swung open, and now standing before them was a connecting flight to another realm. They gazed inside the newly assembled gate, marveling at the beautiful white sand that bordered the body of water.

Reynir turned to Solfrid and Ezra. "Are you sure you do not wish to accompany us? The more, the merrier."

"No," said Solfrid. "Needed here, I am. Ezra too. Together we bury Ólafur. Afterward, I locate Mimir."

"Let us help you with Ólafur," Steina begged. "We can do this together, Solfrid. You don't need to take on that burden alone."

"I do. Never alone is a heart full of love. See you soon," she said behind teary eyes and a soft and trembling smile.

Michael and Darrius said their goodbyes out loud and waited by the gate while Reynir and Steina exchanged more intimate farewells with Solfrid and Ezra.

"I guess this means you're staying a little longer then, I take it?" asked Michael.

"Who else is gonna keep you out of trouble?" said Darrius.

"Thank you," said Michael.

Steina shared a longer embrace with Solfrid than any of the others. It was hard to watch as the two of them wept together. The war had barely started, and it had already taken so much from them. Alfheim had lost its god, Frey, Michael had lost Peter, Ezra her eyes, Darrius his life back home on Earth, and the council lost three members today with Solfrid losing her soulmate and lifelong companion in Ólafur.

Worst of all, none of them were granted the time needed to grieve and process it all. Their journeys were urgent and required their immediate attention, likely for the best. None of them were ready to come face-to-face with everything they had lost. If they took the time to stop and pick up the pieces around them, they might never get back up to continue their fight. They had each other to lean on, and for now, that was all they needed to keep pushing forward.

CHAPTER NINE

RIVER OF THE REALMS

Steina held one last longing gaze with Solfrid and Ezra before following the others, leaving Alfheim and its peril behind. The gates shut behind her, displaying the marvelous doors of Alfheim, both crested in gold with immaculate art embroidered across it.

Painted on the door was Frey and beside him was the elf, Dain. Together they held a scroll in their outstretched hands, both conversing and pointing at the document. The Castle of Dain and the mountains that entwined it gleamed elegantly in the skyline with the now-defunct suns and moons of Alfheim.

Their latest landscape was small, its horizon scooped and bubbly, giving Michael the impression that they were trapped inside a snow globe, but what it lacked in size it made up for in magnificence. The white sand sunk beneath their feet, caving in before leaving footprints in its place. They edged towards the shore where the water broke calmly, slushing lightly along an old majestic, wooden ship.

They loaded into the vessel, where Steina and Reynir took the helm and led the way. They directed Michael and Darrius with different tasks when needed, telling them what to hoist or lift but mostly only instructed them to keep out of their way.

The body of water was a river, a river that bent in a circle, and in its center lied an island with a strange and eerie ambiance to it. No matter which direction the vessel rowed, the island stood there ominously. Like a painting with eyes that followed one's every direction, there was no escaping the vast territory of hopelessness. Emanating around the island was a filmy white haze of dense, impenetrable fog. No trees nor bushes existed. No signs of anything related to life inhabited the dismal region, only fog as if a storm of clouds made themselves at home and resided atop the lake.

"That's the island of Ginnungagap," said Reynir as if he could read minds. "Here, it exists as an island, but in actuality, it is the great abyss that was here before any of the cosmos or realms were created. It will remain tall after Ragnarök and consume the cosmos around it like a black hole. In its northern end lies Niflheim and its fierce cold. Its southern end consists of Muspelheim and its intense heat. The cosmos were created when the two realms forged together and intertwined in the middle creating a combustion of energy throughout."

"So, like . . . the big bang theory essentially?" asked Michael.

"More or less."

"Has anyone ever been there, to Ginny-nunya-gap? Or whatever the hell you called it."

"Ginnungagap," said Reynir, correcting Michael teasingly, annunciating the word with ease. "None that I am aware of. The rumor is that if one's soul does not go to the pearly gates of Valhalla, Fólkvangr, or Helheim upon their death, they wind up there, in a netherworld of emptiness. It is the most powerful and magical place there is, but no one in their right mind would dare enter into it willingly."

Surrounding the river were eight other gates, all embellished in gold like the gates of Alfheim. With each passing entrance,

Reynir described the corresponding realm in detail. The first gate they passed was Svartalfheim, which both Michael and Darrius had already been briefed upon, leaving no further explanation needed from Reynir.

Steina and Reynir rowed by the gate speedily, both tense and uneasy. Judging by their reaction, Michael assumed them to have the same worrying thought as himself, a fear that in their absence, the dark elves would seek ruin and demolish whatever else was left of Alfheim.

"Next up, Asgard," said Reynir.

"Hey, I know that one," Darrius rejoiced.

"Home to the Æsir and their gods. It is also home to Valhalla, where those who die in combat go and become einherjar where they prepare every day for the battles and endeavors of Ragnarök."

"That doesn't sound like much of a heaven," said Michael.

"Would you prefer Helheim with Loki's daughter?" asked Reynir.

"I'd prefer Gingygap over there over either of those two options," joked Michael.

All these different afterlives had Michael questioning his own thoughts and beliefs. Were they all interconnected like continents on Earth, different afterlives for different religions? All sharing the same planet or living space?

Growing up, Michael never conformed to a religion, and to this day, he still hadn't committed to one. He didn't really believe in any of them. How could he? In a world filled with thousands of them, how would he know which one was the right one to pick? Instead, he studied them all to varying degrees. Well, he researched most of them, he thought. He may have skimmed past that Pastafarianism religion he had heard about somewhere.

Right or wrong? Heaven or hell? Who decided it all? Instead, he just believed in his god. Whoever that was. Man, woman, or deity, who knew? He just felt that being a good person was all that mattered, and when one's heart was put to the scale, it would be more beneficial to be a wholesome and kind-hearted person who didn't believe than a good for nothing shitbag who happened to ask for forgiveness on their deathbed.

He did know one thing with certainty; if it came down to him choosing Valhalla or the heaven he had grown up learning about, he'd pick heaven every time. No chance in hell did he want to die, only to find out that he was forced to fight to his death every single day after. In no way, shape, or form did that sound appealing to him.

"And speaking of Helheim . . . there she is," said Reynir, pointing to its gates.

"But it's not like any of that fire and brimstone, demon-infested Hell that the Midgardians believe in," said Steina. "That would be Muspelheim where the fire giant Surtr reigns. That would be the closest to your prototypical Midgardian Hell accompanied by fire giants and fire demons, but Surtr doesn't house the dead. The realm is more of a living hell. I would advise not to go there altogether if you can avoid it."

"Noted," said Darrius. "You don't have to tell me twice."

"So, what is Helheim exactly?" asked Michael.

"A cold, clammy place where the dead roam," said Reynir. "They just do dead people stuff, which is mostly normal people stuff except well . . . they're dead. It is a realm for those who did not die nobly in war or for those who died of old age and other natural causes."

"That doesn't . . . sound too bad, I guess," said Darrius.

"Doesn't sound too great either," said Michael. "That place gives me the heebie-jeebies. Let's keep it moving."

They paddled past Helheim and unanimously agreed to skedaddle on past Muspelheim just as quickly, landing them upon the gates of Jotunheim.

"Jotunheim is the land of the giants," said Reynir. "It is also the realm that is closest to Midgard on the tree of Yggdrasil. Most of Midgard's convergences happen to be with that of Jotunheim due to the proximity of the two."

"Giants, roaming Earth?" asked Darrius.

"David and Goliath, of course," said Steina. "Jotuns used to try to invade back in the primitive days of Midgard, but they wouldn't dare cross Thor and risk meeting the path of Mjölnir."

"Thank God or Odin or whoever the hell for that cause I don't ever want to meet someone like Ortr again," said Michael.

"Thank Thor," said Reynir. "That's who you need to thank."

"Well, thanks, pal. And thank you again for destroying my beautiful Hyundai Accent, you, asshole."

"Oh great, here we go again," sighed Darrius. "Get over it. That was forever ago, man."

"Yeah, well, I'm still in debt over it. I had just put three grand into that car only for it to be struck by lightning. I mean, seriously, what are the odds? It still pisses me off."

"Luckily for you, Midgardian debt does not transfer across realms," quipped Reynir. "Unless it's for your life," he said, his tone slightly glummer than before.

"Not to mention, you won't ever have to go back," said Steina. "Not for good at least, you know after vowing your life to Alfheim and all."

"That's right," said Michael. "Nevermind, Thunder God. We're good, bro. But like . . . I'm still a little mad about it," he said, overly exaggerating the teensy-weensy, pinched hand gesture.

"Whatever." Darrius rolled his eyes. "We've passed by a lot of, how should I put this, not so fun places to go. Is there anywhere besides Alfheim and Midgard that are worth a shit?"

"Vanaheim," said Reynir as he twirled his oar around like a baton, pointing into the direction of a crumbled gate in the distance.

Whatever Vanaheim had once been, it was no longer. The gate was nothing but a scrap of heaps now, reminiscent of the destroyed Alfheim. The only difference was that the gates of Vanaheim just so happened to be a golden scrap of heaps but a scrap, nonetheless. Enough gold to drive a sane man mad, but it was no entrance to another realm, that much was certain.

"Why is it destroyed?" asked Darrius.

Reynir shrugged his shoulders. "I don't know. It has been that way for centuries. I think it was destroyed by the Vanir themselves during the Æsir-Vanir war. That way, the realm could remain hidden. No one knows of its whereabouts besides the Vanir gods. Even Frey would not offer its location."

They rowed by Niflheim, the coldest region of the nine realms, which gusted a waft of freezing cold air towards them. They swiftly oared past it, trying their hardest to avoid the bone-chilling cold that seethed from its shore.

Their next destination was their last and final stop of Midgard, its door consisting of a large, gigantic snake looking creature that made Inon the dragon look like a tiny Pomeranian.

"What the hell is that thing?" asked Darrius behind widened eyes.

"Oh, that's just Jörmungandr, the world serpent," said Steina, sporting a quirky smile, clearly getting enjoyment out of toying with him. "Don't worry, he's a good wittle boy. I'll make sure we pay him a visit during our time here."

"Oh, hell nah. Ain't nothing little about that thing. Seriously? Y'all aren't fucking with me? That thing is really on Earth?

"That thing is Loki's son," said Reynir.

"He resides in the ocean," said Steina. "So big that he wraps around the world clenching his own tail. Prophesied to battle Thor in Ragnarök, killing one another in the process. When he releases his tail, it signifies the beginning of Ragnarök."

"Now had I known that thing had existed, maybe I would've believed in Jonah and the whale growing up," said Michael.

"I doubt many things have gone into Jörmungandr's mouth and lived to tell the tale," said Reynir. "To tell the tail," he chuckled. "You get it, Steina, because you said tail."

Steina made a point to ignore him and shook her head.

"And all this time, I was afraid of sharks," Michael laughed.

"Haha, real funny," said Darrius. "But no, like for real, isn't Ragnarök before us now? Cause I'm really not trying to greet that thing."

"Maybe," said Steina. "No one really knows. That's why Solfrid went to visit Mimir. To find answers. This is the first time any of us can recall the prophecy being wrong. None of us know what to believe when it pertains to Ragnarok."

They approached the shores of Midgard and anchored the ship on the slope of the sand, each gawking at the beautiful intricacies carved into the marvelous gate, minus Darrius, who avoided any eye contact with the sculpture of Jörmungandr.

"Ah, good ol' Midgard," said Reynir, patting the door. "It's nice to be back. Oh, how I long to see Katrin again."

"Oh my gosh, whatever," cried Steina, rolling her eyes. "Try keeping it in your pants this time."

"So . . . hypothetically speaking, if I, ya know, wanted to do certain things with an elf, would I die too?" asked Michael.

"Really?" asked Darrius. "Cause now of all times is the time for this?"

"What? It's a logical question if I'm to spend the rest of my life on Alfheim."

"All things considered, you would be fine on Alfheim," said Reynir. "We have cures for those kinds of infections there. We can get you vaccinated upon our return but here on Midgard . . . I might suggest abstinence."

"Well, that's good to know. That shouldn't be a problem. I mean, the only elf on Midgard would be you," said Michael, gesturing towards Steina, oblivious to the awkwardness that would follow. "And that would have to mean that me and you, you know, did something of that nature. Which we both know would never happen. I'm just a friend. So . . . I don't want you . . . like thinking I would make that sort of move or anything."

"Do you not find me to be pretty?" asked Steina.

"No . . . No. No. No. That's not how I meant it."

"Wow. One simple no would have sufficed just fine, let alone four of them. Ouch."

"No, that's not what I meant. I meant no, no, no, like as in, no, no, no, of course, you're gorgeous. But like, like I said, I wouldn't just insinuate that because of your exterior beauty, that would sleep with me. You know? Does that make sense?"

"Oh my god, just stop talking already," blurted Darrius.

"So, because of my interior beauty, you would not sleep with me, is that what you are insinuating?" asked Steina.

"No, your interior beauty is well . . . beautiful too," said Michael, grimacing. "So much that it makes you more attractive and . . . even better suited to sleep with."

"Even better suited to sleep with?"

"No . . . I mean, well, yeah. I don't know. I'm sorry. I was only trying to say that any man would be lucky to have you."

"In bed? But not as a significant other, I see. The truth stings with you Midgardians."

"Not at all. I'd love to have you as a significant other."

"You would?" said Steina with raised eyebrows.

"I mean . . . not right now, per se, but maybe after we get to know each other a little better?"

Steina smiled, biting her lip to conceal the layers of laughter hidden within. Reynir and Darrius didn't care to hide their emotions. Both of them erupted with laughter at Michael's awkwardness and catastrophic fumble of words.

"I'm clearly only fucking with you," laughed Steina.

"Oh," Michael replied, wide-eyed. His face hot, flushing red with embarrassment. "That's . . . That's good to know."

"I must say, I'm feeling a little disrespected here," said Reynir.

"I'm sorry," said Michael squeamishly. "I didn't mean to offend either one of you."

"It is only me that you offended. You said that Steina would be the only elf on Midgard, but here I am," he said, glaring at Michael with googly eyes. "Am I not beautiful to you?"

"No, you are. You're very beautiful . . . in your own kind of way. I just don't roll like that if that's what you mean? I thought . . . I thought you liked girls. You know, cause you mentioned Katrin and stuff."

"Maybe I like both," winked Reynir.

"And nothing's wrong with that. I commend you. Power to you."

Steina and Reynir burst with more laughter.

"Oh, I can't," squealed Reynir. "I just can't."

"That was great," said Steina, wiping the tears from her eyes. She let out a deep breath. "My stomach hurts from laughing so much. I needed that. Thanks for the laugh, Michael."

"Yeah," said Michael with a forced smile, like that of a fourth grader forced to take family photos. "I'm glad I could be of service."

"So . . . where will this gate lead us?" asked Darrius, changing the subject on Michael's behalf, and for that, Michael was appreciative.

"Not sure," said Reynir. "Usually, we arrive via convergence portals and go from there. I have never traveled through the lake realms before."

"Only one way to find out, I guess."

Reynir placed Heimsstrengur into the keyhole of the gate. The gates opened, immersing them into the vast wilderness of a forest, its exact location unknown. The skies were riddled with clouds, the day overcast and gloomy. Luckily, before they could question where they needed to go, Fornviska began to rattle in Steina's hands, guiding them to their next destination, hopefully, that destination being Konungr.

As they walked, they naturally split up, Steina and Reynir in the front, leading and guiding the way while Michael and Darrius sagged off behind them.

"What was that?" asked Darrius. "Seriously, what in the hell was that?"

"What?" asked Michael, scanning the perimeter defensively. "Did you see a bear or something out there?"

Darrius smacked the back of Michael's neck. "No, idiot. I'm talking about whatever the hell kind of flirting you attempted back there."

"Oh, yeah." Michael looked down sheepishly. "I don't know. It just got me thinking if I'm gonna be on Alfheim for good. Eventually, I'll have to find a connection with someone, right? And I didn't want to die in the process. That seemed like an appropriate question to ask."

"Appropriate, sure. The incoherent babbling that followed, not so much. That was pitiful. I don't even know if I can be your friend anymore. I'm embarrassed by association."

"That bad, huh?" Michael winced.

"I've seen dogs with more game than you. Like actual baby puppies, bro."

Michael sighed. "Welp. It's a long journey. Let's hope I can redeem myself."

"You better hope so, for your sake."

They trailed along the forest straight ahead with Fornviska as their guide. Nothing seemingly stood out to any of them, no landmarks or trails, only trees until they ran into a stream. They followed the creek for what felt like a couple of miles, anxious energy consuming them all as Fornviska began to vibrate uncontrollably, signaling to them that they were getting closer to Konungr's whereabouts.

"Who is this guy supposed to be again?" asked Darrius. "And if he's that big of a deal, why hasn't anyone from Alfheim ever contacted him before?"

"Heimdall's grandson," said Reynir. "Konungr is one of few who can actually utilize and harness runic magic. Even Solfrid herself understands very little in comparison. None of us do. Most of our knowledge was lost. The older artifacts having been destroyed through war or time. Our remains consist of a dead language that time forgot. As far as contacting him goes, we have never had a reason to. Until now."

"Speaking of Solfrid, how old is she?" asked Michael.

"Hmm . . . I don't know," responded Reynir. "Do you know her age, Steina?"

"I'm not sure either," said Steina. "No one knows, to be exact. She and Ólafur were close to the thousands, maybe even older."

"Thousands?" Michael questioned shockingly. "How does that work out? I take it elves live longer than humans?"

"Sort of; it's complicated," explained Steina. "Magic exists as a whole throughout the universe. It flows inside each and every realm just as it flows through every living individual, flowing as smoothly as air. There are microcosms to magic, including you, me, and everyone around you, and then there is a macrocosm, which would include the nine realms, all the way up to the mecca in Yggdrasil.

"Some people are more sensitive to magic than others, just as some realms are more sensitive as well. Midgard is the least sensitive of all, and because of that, Midgardians tend to be the least sensitive to magic. Long story short, yes, elves do naturally tend to live longer than Midgardians, but for instance, the average human life on Alfheim can be upwards of five hundred years. An elven life on Alfheim is on average nine hundred, give or take. If an elf were to live their entire life on Midgard, I would guess the average would be somewhere closer to a hundred and fifty or so. It is not an exact science."

"You're telling me that by living on Alfheim, I could potentially live to be five hundred years old?"

"Maybe," replied Steina. "How old are you?"

"Twenty-six."

"Let's see, barring anything catastrophic, you have more than likely already lived at least a third of your life. Simple math would say that a third of a Midgardian lifetime on Alfheim would be approximately one sixty, meaning that you have a good chance of living to maybe three hundred and fifty on Alfheim."

"That's not too bad. I think I can live with that."

"And that's not even countering in the idea that you might learn magic one day. Add that in, and who knows that three-fifty could easily turn into five-fifty, maybe more. A few of Idunn's Apples and you might just live forever."

"What are those?"

"Apples that keep all the gods immortal," said Reynir. "Those bad boys are priceless. Good luck getting your hands on some of those."

"Maybe that will be my next goal," said Michael. "You know, after trying to stop that whole Ragnarök thing from destroying the universe, that is. So how old are the two of you?"

"I am one hundred and ten," answered Reynir. "This year was actually my fiftieth anniversary of becoming a member of the council. The youngest one in history too," he said with a cocksure grin.

"Was the youngest," Steina smirked, nudging Reynir in the arm. "The bar's been set at fifty-eight now."

"Whatever doesn't count. You are the youngest based on a technicality."

"Technicality, oh really?"

"Yeah, I would say the suns getting swallowed by Skoll and Hati and half of Alfheim dying in the process is a technicality. Wouldn't you?"

"I was going to get in regardless, and you know it."

"Sure. Maybe so, but not at fifty-eight. Not before my record of sixty either. That is some stretch-a-roo you have concocted up there in your head if you think you would have actually taken my record fair and square."

"Still the youngest council member," she said in an antagonizing tone. The same tone Michael would see Cam and Will share with one another all the time.

"All thanks to your precious technicality, princess."

"Someone's just jealous," said Steina, winking at him obnoxiously.

"Whatever." Reynir scoffed, flaring his chest.

Between the back and forth bickering of Steina and Reynir, the four of them had arrived upon a cave without realizing it. Fornviska powered off and turned pitch black. The four of them exchanged anxious and hesitant expressions, none of them knowing what to expect next.

"I think this is it," said Steina nervously.

"Nose goes on going in first," said Michael, touching his nose. He removed his hand just as quickly after realizing how silly he must have looked because no one else followed suit.

"It is only fair that one of you two go," said Steina, pointing at Darrius and Reynir. "Michael and I sacrificed something to get here. You guys did not, so one of you two should have to step up this time."

"Looks like you're up," said Darrius, looking Reynir's way.

"Why me?" Reynir asked.

"I would think it would be a job for the youngest council member ever, am I right?"

"Was the youngest," said Reynir, correcting him.

"Oh, now he admits it," said Steina.

"We're here to save your home," argued Darrius. "Plus, you have the whole back story on this guy. It makes more sense for you to greet him."

"But," stammered Reynir. "And hear me out on this . . . You are less threatening. You don't know magic, whereas I could be seen as a threat."

"Should we be afraid? Is this dude dangerous or something?"

"No. I don't believe so, but war makes people do crazy things. He might think I'm a shapeshifter."

"How many people can shapeshift in this godforsaken universe?" Michael interrupted. "I see Loki can. Now Konungr. Who else? My middle school bus driver?"

"To be fair, the jury is still out on Konungr," said Reynir. "I'm unsure of whether or not he can, but to answer your question, the only known shapeshifters are Loki, Odin, and Freyja. Typically, only select gods can master the craft. The old Norse literature is lined with tales of Odin and Loki in disguise. Unfortunately, we have seen Loki's illusions up close and personal.

"Just wait until I tell you of the time that Odin traveled in disguise as the wanderer, Bolverk, all for a taste of Suttung's luxurious mead. From giant to snake to an eagle. That Odin is a brilliant one. Ooh, even better, wait until you hear about the time Loki mated with a horse and birthed the beautiful, eight-legged horse, Sleipnir."

"Okay, knock it off," said Michael. "You're just making shit up now."

"Reynir," said Steina, letting out an exasperated sigh. "Konungr. The cave. Can we please proceed now?"

"Fine, if we must," bickered Reynir, mocking Steina. "But yes, Darrius, it would be wisest if you went forth into the cave. That way, Konungr has no suspicions of me being a shapeshifter."

"He could think I'm a shapeshifter then too," said Darrius. "What's your point?"

"My point is you have no magic. You are non-threatening. I have magic dripping off me from miles away. Therefore, I could be viewed as a potential life-threatening shapeshifter. See the difference?"

"That doesn't even make sense. If you're afraid, just say it. You don't have to start making shit up about eight-legged horses and stuff. I just figured, you know, with you being the most experienced council member and all, that you would relish an opportunity like this but if you're not man enough—"

"Man enough? Psh. Fine. I will go inside first seeing as, I am the most fit to do so, as you eloquently stated yourself." Reynir turned around and walked towards the cave conservatively, energy radiating around his hands as a precaution.

As Reynir was about to enter, a hooded man emerged before him, adorned in an aged and worn-down cloak that appeared to be made from the old burlap used in gunnysacks. A pair of white, marbleized, and glossy eyes stared at Reynir. The man's pupils were undecipherable. His eyes were old and withered as if they suffered from a severe case of glaucoma.

He levitated above the ground casually as visible white energy danced between his fingertips. Smaller items such as rocks and twigs orbited him, never straying from his side like a loyal puppy. Reynir surrendered the energy that ignited between his palms and kneeled at the gentleman's feet.

"Konungr, my liege," said Reynir. "A pleasure it is. I am Reynir of Alfheim. Behind me are my fellow council members."

This time Darrius didn't have to nudge Michael to get his attention. The three of them bowed in unison behind Reynir, offering their respects to the demi-god.

"Our home in Alfheim has been destroyed, decimated by the likes of Loki and Gullveig," continued Reynir. "Our suns and moons gone, devoured by Skoll and Hati. Our head of council, Solfrid, sent us to find you in hopes that you would be able to assist us in restoring our homeland."

Konungr didn't respond. He remained in the air, his energy still bustling. If he cared in the slightest, he didn't show it. Not a glimmer of emotion dripped out from underneath the veil of his hood.

"Please," repeated Reynir. "Alfheim needs you. Our god, Frey, has been killed. We turn to you in a time of desperation. You are our only hope, Konungr."

"I am sorry to hear of Frey," responded Konungr, finally cutting into the budding tension between them. His voice, soft and raspy. His vocal cords had clearly seen better days, whatever left of them, down to their last thread. "And equally sorry to hear of your home, but I have no desire to enter your war nor will I. I fear you have wasted your time."

CHAPTER TEN

KONUNGR

"But sir, you don't understand," pleaded Reynir. "We need you. Loki is back and free from his bonds."

"No longer do I intervene with the affairs of gods," said Konungr. "My time as a conqueror, as a fighter of war, have come and gone. That part of me is dead now."

"And we humbly accept your wishes, sir. We do not wish to reinvoke that inside of you. We only ask for your help. We ask that you use your knowledge of runic magic to assist in the restoration of Alfheim. Something that we cannot do without Frey."

"I wish nothing more than for my remaining years to be lived out here on Midgard in peace. In the solemnness of this beautiful forest. Never to be disturbed by such matters again," he said, his stare fierce and unrelenting. "By stepping foot on your realm, by restoring it in the slightest means, I have chosen an alliance. That I will not do."

"Your grandfather, Heimdall . . . he has been slain at the hands of Loki."

"Heimdall?" Konungr asked, his voice wavering faintly, but his face remained placid and cold, lacking emotions. His glossy eyes remained impossible to read.

"Sadly so. I am sorry to be the bearer of such unfortunate news . . . The prophecies have been altered. We mustn't let Heimdall's death be in vain."

"I told you, I am through with the blights and afflictions of gods. Heimdall's death does not change that. The gods care for themselves and themselves only. They are selfish and repugnant beings. However, it is not fair that innocent lives have died as a result of their egos. I shall teach you and your fellow council members' magic. Real magic, and with it, you can save Alfheim."

"With all due respect, we don't have the time for such a prolonged task. It would take us years to train in the rites and passages of true magic. Alfheim needs our assistance now. It needs you now. It needs a hero. Otherwise, I would be more than flattered to learn from someone of your magnitude and intelligence."

"Then, a few years, it will be. You four save Alfheim. You four become the heroes that it needs. Or don't and watch everything you love die. I don't care. It affects me none, for I am old and likely to be dead soon. The fate of Alfheim is on your shoulders, not mine. The decision is yours."

Konungr removed his hood, revealing a wizened old man with scars scattered across his face and neck. His skin was wrinkly, hanging loosely from his body, smothered with age spots and damaged blood vessels. His hair was thin and grey, yet it still covered his head full of aging hair, fighting against any male pattern baldness.

The council gazed one another over as if they were telekinetic, each of them knowing that time was of the essence, but Konungr had been firm in his response. This wasn't his war, and he was intent on keeping it that way. It was apparent that the only way for them to save Alfheim would be to train with him and learn the secrets of magic. If Alfheim was going to get saved, it wouldn't be Konungr who did it. It would have to be them.

"I suppose we have no other choice but to humbly accept your offer," stated Reynir.

"You always have an option," said Konungr. "No matter the circumstances."

"My only fear is that there will be no Alfheim to return to upon our arrival home after training with you."

"The realms have stood since the dawn of creation. They will not falter. Not even Ragnarök can consume them. They will remain tall—reborn again after Ragnarök's grasp has come and gone. Your cities, your buildings, your people, all that may not remain but Alfheim itself will be fine. And what is left of your home will be up to you to rebuild."

Reynir remained silent, his expression deflated, but he nodded his head in agreement.

"Since we are short on time, we shall proceed forthwith our first lesson," said Konungr.

"Like right now, now?" asked Michael.

"No better time than the present."

"What do you have in store for our first lesson?" asked Steina somewhat apprehensively.

"A battle to the death. The last one standing will become my apprentice and learn the magic of the runes. A bold sacrifice indeed, but a sacrifice that I am willing to make," said Konungr, flashing a disgustingly, vile grin, one that was reminiscent of Loki's.

The group stared at one another in dismay. What the hell had Solfrid signed them up for, Michael thought. A battle to the death? Seriously? This dude was insane. He and Darrius wouldn't stand a chance. The council had already lost so much today, they couldn't afford to lose three more members.

Konungr erupted into a light-hearted laugh. "Am I not allowed to joke? Some good-natured ribbing does the soul wonders. You should try it sometime."

They each forced out a chuckle as if their lives depended on it.

"That's a sick sense of humor you got there," said Darrius.

"Yeah, you really got us with that one," said Michael, still chuckling somewhat nervously.

"I'm glad to see that I could force some laughter because I fear that fun time is over," said Konungr. "It is time that we begin our extensive training into the art of meditation."

"With all due respect," said Reynir. "I fail to see what meditation has to do with magic, the magic we need, at least. How can it possibly assist us in restoring Alfheim or defeating Loki and Gullveig?"

"It has everything to do with magic. Meditation holds the key to your entire universe, and through it, you will find that nearly anything is possible. We are learning from the ground up. Everyone will start with the basics, no matter how advanced or novice you are. If you do not like that, you can leave," he said, pausing to see if anyone might take him up on the offer. "I want each of you to concentrate on your thoughts for a few moments, paying particularly close attention in remembering them. You may begin."

The council stared at one another, each of them equally dumbfounded as the other.

"We . . . just begin meditating?" asked Michael.

"Correct," stated Konungr. "Now, no further interruptions."

Michael closed his eyes and felt his mind go blank. It felt as if his brain had turned into a spaceless void, lacking all thoughts, numb to the ability to think freely. Until finally, his first thought emerged, bursting through the metaphorical dam that had been blockading inside him, overwhelming him with incoming ideas.

Three or four days ago, none of this existed, he thought. He was a normal Midgardian, as Steina and Reynir liked to say, unaware of the expansive universe around him. So far during his brief tenure with them, he had been introduced to an entirely new world consisting of giants, cosmic wolves who feasted on stars and moons, and wizards who yielded magic, and now here he was about to become one of those wizards.

All this time, magic had existed, only it had been unattainable to him, and now he was going to be trained by one of the most powerful sorcerers in the nine realms. A sorcerer who held the secrets to the runes, whatever that meant. None of it felt real. It felt like one long, eternal dream that he was bound to wake up from at any time. But Michael knew otherwise. Peter's cold dead body reminded him how very real this was.

The thought of learning magic was exciting, but with that excitement came anxiety. How long was this going to take? If his schooling took tens of years to learn, would he have enough life left to enjoy his newfound powers? What if he was incapable of learning magic? Had his years on Midgard tainted his ability to do so?

What if Loki and Gullveig had already destroyed more planets or realms by now? And say he could harness said magic, how the hell would they be able to stop Loki and Gullveig with it? The two of them killed Frey and Heimdall with relative ease and simplicity, and now two elves and two humans, mostly devoid of magic, were going to take on two of the most powerful beings in existence, one of which couldn't even be killed apparently, at least not by fire.

There's a difference between a good underdog story and suicide, and this felt like the latter. Even with the secrets of runic magic, even if Konungr chose to help them, it still seemed highly unrealistic that they would ever be able to defeat one of Loki or Gullveig, let alone both of them.

Michael was reminded of the fact that he offered his life to Alfheim. If he managed to come out of all this alive, there was no guarantee that he would ever set foot on Midgard's soil again, which would prevent him from seeing Emma and provide her with the truth and closure that she deserved.

He could only imagine that she and his colleagues at work were searching tooth and nail for him by now, Darrius as well. News outlets had to be buzzing at their disappearances. Two detectives and a child gone missing in the same week. That would no longer be a local story anymore. That would be receiving nationwide coverage by now. As hard as it was for him, he had to rid himself of those thoughts and concerns.

That wasn't his world anymore. More important matters were at hand. His disappearance would be forgotten about over the next couple of days or weeks, recycled and refreshed by hotter and trendier news stories. At some point, the president would probably make another jab about the size of his nuclear weapons, and Michael and his little town would cease to exist.

In hindsight, Michael preferred that. It would be easier for the mind to accept that he had been kidnapped or killed over the fact that he had entered a different universe. That was a can of worms best left unopened amongst the public mind.

Thoughts flowed together seamlessly, transitioning as smoothly as scenes in a well-crafted movie. He questioned what he would be able to learn under Konungr? Would he be able to teleport when this was all said and done? Would he learn to fly? Or breath underwater? Maybe even master the art of shape-shifting?

Exciting thoughts of magic exuded throughout his brain, swarming like bees fleeing their hive. But no matter how excited he got, it was always short-lived. His mind always retreated to Peter and Emma and how he had failed them.

He tried to quell his guilt and insecurities by focusing on happier thoughts, such as going out and watching football on the weekends with his buddies, but even that brought back the inevitable feeling of failure that seemed to harvest in his mind rent-free.

The simple thought of football transformed into something more, the memory of his senior year, where he played wide receiver at Garden Shore High. Against all odds, his team made the state 5A championship game that year, and with four minutes left, he caught a touchdown pass that gave them the lead.

He could recall the memory in pristine, picture-perfect detail. He could remember the exhilaration that he felt as he walked to the sideline after scoring. It was an unforgettable sensation, a feeling of widespread euphoria that he could still feel at the thought of that memory.

He sat on the sidelines, counting down the clock with the rest of his teammates. All of them waiting for the clock to strike zero, and when that moment happened, he would become the hero of the game. He'd go down in history for catching the game-winning touchdown, but fate never writes the same story that one envisions.

He tried not to relive that memory once more, tried not to recall what happened after his touchdown catch, but he couldn't stop it. The guilt of that moment weighed too heavily. With a minute left, the opposing team scored, bumping their lead to four.

His teammate and quarterback, Jordan Neely, responded under pressure. He was miraculous on that last drive. He carved through the opponent's defense, executing their two-minute offense perfectly with poise and precision, throwing first down after first down, utilizing the sidelines to his advantage.

Neely was unstoppable. He darted a pass to the nineteen-yard line and called their last timeout with twenty-four seconds left on the clock. The stadium was boisterous, so loud that it was damn near impossible to hear the incoming play call. With his eyes closed, Michael could still hear the deafening roar of the stadium that night.

The coach called a post route in the middle of the field, a designed play, just for Michael, their star receiver. If he was open, the ball was coming his way. All he had to do was catch it, and time would stop after the first down. They would rush to the line and spike it, leaving them roughly anywhere from eight to thirteen seconds, a chance for two or three plays at the end zone.

The defense was playing man coverage; all he had to do was get by his man, and he would deliver. Michael did just, planting his foot firmly into the ground and faking a cut right, then left, then back right again until he had the defender turned around, leaving Michael able to skate past him. He made his cut to the middle of the field, and Neely delivered the ball on a dime. A perfect pass. There was no pressure around him. The safety had picked up the go route and was at least fifteen yards away.

The football spiraled tightly, a heat-seeking missile, directly to him. He could still remember his thoughts as the ball sailed through the air. Time slowed as every negative thought suffocated his mind. What if he dropped it? When should he close his hands to catch it? Should he use his hands or his body to catch the football?

He felt the pressure mount over him, a pressure that was only possible when he was left wide open. There was no time to think with a defender draped over him but alone with his thoughts, without a soul around him, the pressure was insurmountable. The ball ricocheted off his hands and into the air. Time moved even slower than before as he watched helplessly as the football landed in the hands of the closest defender. Like a scene from a movie, he saw it all frame by frame, in slow motion.

He had the game in his hands, an easy walk-in touchdown had been delivered to him on a dime, and he dropped it. He let down his team, his coaches, his quarterback, all the seniors who had fought so hard to get there over the years.

His only thought was to run, run as far away from it all as he could. Leave his team, his school, and his city behind him. The following Monday after the game, he transferred to adult high and finished his schooling online, leaving his Division 1 scholarships in the dust. He couldn't bear the thought of failing anybody else the way he had failed his team.

He recalled the moments that transpired after as a result of that guilt. He packed his bags and took a bus out of town as far away as he could think, landing him in Seattle, Washington, eventually leading him to Tacoma. He became a part of law enforcement there. He thought about how that guilt had stayed with him, etching itself onto him with its vice-like grip.

Needless to say, that guilt didn't include Skye's disappearance, but her kidnapping had been engraved deep inside him at a young age, to the point that he didn't really know how to live life without it. He had grown so accustomed to it that it became a scar. That was the best part about childhood trauma. Most don't remember it. Growing up, his mind glossed over it without a second thought unless his mother berated him about the event, which happened far more frequently than he would've liked.

It wasn't until a year and a half ago that he returned to the hometown that he thought to have left behind for good. His mom had become ill, so he moved back to help, only to find out that she had only wanted money from him to enable her everlasting pill addiction instead. At times he thought about her and how she was doing, but he learned long ago not to attach his happiness to the well-being of others.

Some good did manage to come from his mother's blatant cry of wolf. In his move home, he met Darrius, his one and only true friend in life. In part, he was somewhat thankful for that game. Had it not turned out the way it did, he would have never up and moved to Washington like he had. He would've never joined law enforcement and likewise never have met Darrius.

Occasionally, he did stop to think about how life might have been had he attended UCF or FSU like he had planned, but none of that mattered anymore. He gave up on living in the past and sorrowing over the coulda, shoulda, woulda's of life a long time ago. The inevitable butterfly effect that spiderwebbed his life, molting its hands onto the many different outcomes of what life could have been, was nothing more than the product of his very own imagination.

"Time's up," said Konungr. From thin air, he christened together four long scrolls of parchment. "It is time to record your thoughts. Every single thought that came to mind. Record it. If you can do so in the order in which they were contrived, even better. Begin."

Time fascinated Michael. It was amazing how three or four minutes felt like an eternity to him during his meditation exercise. He was able to accomplish so much in such a short span, and in retrospect, it was incredible how the same three or four minutes flew by during other tasks. It reminded him how time had slowed down during his dropped pass, where a couple of seconds felt like hours.

Being in his mind and conscious thought for so long slowed time down. Maybe that was the point of this exercise. Perhaps that was the first step in controlling time. After all, time was man-made. Clearly, it existed, but man was the one who emphasized it. Maybe without that emphasis, he could structure time however he saw fit. He could stop it, alter it, potentially even go back in time, or forward. Perhaps Konungr was going to teach them time travel, and that would be their means of saving Alfheim.

Shit, he thought. He'd been so enraptured with his thoughts he had completely forgotten about the assignment at hand. His mind was full tilt, revving with carryover thoughts from his mediation. It wasn't until he heard quills scribbling fiercely that he realized he was the only one not writing anything.

Reynir and Steina were jotting so intensely they were surely in competition with one another. Considering their latest quibble about who was the youngest council member, it didn't surprise Michael in the slightest. Even Darrius was attacking his scroll, albeit much slower than the other two.

Michael closed his eyes once more, trying his hardest to recollect his most recent thoughts. He could remember fragments. Little bits and pieces appeared but disappeared just as quickly. It was like a standardized test where the answer was on the tip of his tongue, but for the life of him, he couldn't remember it. The jotting and scrawling of his peers ringing inside his ears didn't help either. He felt like he was the only one struggling to grasp the exercise at hand.

All he had to do was remember what he was just thinking about, but it was as if it was a dream. It was like a vivid and tantalizing dream that he could see with perfection while experiencing it, but by the time he got his morning coffee, that same dream had already dissipated into the abyss of his subconsciousness. Gone forever only to return on the occasional clutch of déjà vu, leaving him to wonder whether his dream had been a dream or remnant of something more.

He racked and scoured his brain for details and could only come up with football. Something about guilt and football, but he couldn't piece together the thoughts that preceded them. Watching football with friends brought back his high school memory, he recalled. Yes, and before that was how he would miss his friends and family. Which led him to thinking about how news outlets would be buzzing over his disappearance.

Thoughts began to come back to him, piece by piece, trickling in slowly. Konungr made rounds behind them, peering over everyone's shoulder to check their progress. Michael felt good about his work until he gazed at Steina and Reynir's parchment, which looked like the *Old Testament* compared to his few lines of incoherent chicken scratch.

"Stop," said Konungr. He picked up the scrolls and discarded them to the side. "Now start again from the top. This time longer than before."

Nobody argued with him. They proceeded forth with their mediations. Michael was determined to do better than last time. Determined to focus on every thought with the goal of remembering each and every one of them.

CHAPTER ELEVEN

MEAD, MEDITATION, AND HANGOVERS

Their meditation exercises were repeated for days. Days slogged into weeks, and weeks churned slowly into months. A few minutes of meditation grew into ten minutes, ten minutes turned to thirty minutes, and those same half-hour sessions evolved into hours. They practiced nonstop every day, with small breaks in between only to eat and sleep. They did this until every one of them could recollect their thoughts for hours on end.

After harnessing the ability to recall their thoughts for hours at a time, they went back to smaller time increments. This time, instead of writing them, they had to revisit their thoughts in the same exact synchronization in which they occurred. Any failed thought would lead them to a full restart, or any new idea that emerged and interrupted them required them to restart as well.

This practice proved to be much more intricate and frustrating. During their first exercise, the thoughts did not have to be in chronological order. Also, other thoughts could emanate within them without it being an issue. This exercise didn't allow that liberty. There were multiple times over the ensuing months where they would be hours into recalling their thoughts only for new ones to arise, culminating in a complete do-over from the top.

There was no fooling Konungr either; initially, they tried. None of them saw the harm in a new thought emerging as long as they could still recall every other subsequent one. Nobody except Konungr, that was. He quickly nipped it in the bud anytime someone wasn't up forth with him about their failings. New thoughts tinged his ears like high-frequency whistles pestered dogs.

Eventually, they all learned to be honest with Konungr and more so with themselves. They practiced this exercise repeatedly until they could master it for hours at a time. Their days consisted of a grueling three-hour session, a thirty-minute break, and another three-hour session. Tedious never-ending intervals, over and over, as if they were experiencing their life in the form of the movie *Groundhog's Day*. It was as if they were entrapped inside of an inescapable, never-ending time loop.

Konungr spoke in riddles about how these pieces of training would allow access to their brain's full potential, giving it the power to browse memories long forgotten. A few hours wading through the thoughts of their mind felt like days. As sessions grew longer, one five-hour meditation felt like a full day back home when life had a level of normalcy to it.

In their passing breaks and few and far between lake excursions, they collectively wondered what the hell any of this had to do with magic. Reynir deduced that Konungr was enhancing the concentration of their mind. Focus and attention to detail were critical in spell casting, but even Reynir agreed that this was somewhat overkill. Regardless, they went through with Konungr's practices in stride, embracing whatever unique exercise he sprang upon them.

Reynir and Steina's experience in magic was quite apparent early into their education with Konungr. They would complete practices weeks ahead of Michael and Darrius, but Konungr only urged them to practice some more, encouraging them that it would only make them stronger and wiser magicians. If they had any problems with his educating, they never mentioned it out loud.

Upon completing the last exercise of each new workout, they were granted a day off to relax and ease the tension of their minds. This time Konungr supplied them with a barrel of mead for their lake visit, claiming that they deserved it after all their hard work. Nobody obliged; they happily accepted his gracious gift, each of them looking forward to the buzz that would accompany it.

They invited him to come along, but to their relief, the old man stayed behind. Not that they didn't like Konungr, but after a long and strenuous tenure of training, the last person they wanted to be around was their teacher. It would only provide a constant reminder of everything that they were escaping.

They spent their time swimming and drinking, enjoying each other's company, engaging heavily on the drinking part. It was refreshing getting their minds off of the stress they had endured during their conditioning. They were mentally exhausted, their brains fried and running on fumes. They were enrolled in an accelerated boot camp for sorcerers and magicians, learning things five times the speed as average.

The day was a much-needed release for all of them. The mead certainly did its part in loosening them up, but they'd all be lying if they said it tasted any good. The taste of it reminded Michael of some sweetened garbage he would find at the gas station, like one of those nasty alcopop malt beverages that only college kids would drink, but it was all the council had, so he drank it with little complaints.

After a healthy buzz, Michael approached a sunbathing Steina, hoping to continue upon the subtle flirty relationship they had developed over the last few months. The attraction between them was apparent, but due to the strenuous nature of their exercises, most of their conversations were light, kept to a minimum of playful quips and remarks between whatever break time Konungr had allotted for them.

"Mind if I join?" asked Michael.

"Be my guest," said Steina, patting the ground next to her.

Michael accepted her invitation, laying down a few feet away from her. "How are you liking it here? Midgard, that is?" It still felt weird for him to refer to Earth as Midgard, but that seemed to be the appropriate term used amongst them.

"It's nice. It's relaxing to get away from everything. My anxiety has been a little on edge as of late. Not knowing how long our training will be surely doesn't help either, but I trust that Solfrid was well prepared for our lengthy departure. She always knows more than she puts on. I just worry about everyone back home."

"If she knew how long it would take us, why didn't she say so up front?"

"Probably afraid that if we knew the truth, we would have never agreed to have come here, which is true. But I trust her judgment. I only hope that our temporary sun is holding up. Even this sun here doesn't nourish Reynir and I as much as we need, so I can only imagine what they are going through but who knows . . . they say you need a full eight hours of sleep and eight glasses of water, and who in their right mind gets that?"

"Not me, but who needs water when you have this succulent mead," said Michael, raising his glass to Steina and taking a sip, trying his hardest to fight the bitter expression scourged across his face. "Next vacation day, we can plan a trip to Florida. You can get all the sunshine you need there."

"What is Florida?"

"You don't know Florida?"

"No, I suppose I do not."

"How do you know so much about this realm, so much about the ways of human life, but you don't know Florida?"

"You can't expect me to know everything about Midgard."

"That's fair. Florida's a place where people ride alligators to amusement parks, and powerful sorcerers exist that go by the name of Florida Man."

"Really? Real sorcerer's on Midgard?"

"Sorcerer Mickey, duh. But nah, I'm only kidding. Florida Man is more of a cracked out, face biting, bath salt junkie. Never mind that, though. It was an ill attempt at humor, but the place is like a thousand degrees. You would love it there."

"Is that where you are from, Florida?"

"Yeah. I'm not sure where we're at now, though. I couldn't tell you what continent this is even. I'd have to imagine somewhere in the Arctic Circle due to all the daylight, but hell, I have no idea. I haven't seen any other humans here besides us, so I imagine we're pretty deep into this forest."

"That's because it is enchanted. Konungr peppered this place with them. Unless you have an affinity to magic, you would never find him."

"That makes sense. Do you know how long we've been here for? I lost track a while back."

"A hundred and sixty-four days. There's a tree near camp where I have been keeping count."

"Damn. It feels longer than that but at the same time, not at all if that makes sense."

"It does. I feel the same way as if we have been here anywhere from a couple months to a few years. It has all seemed to run together."

"That's good to know. I'm glad I'm not the only one who feels that way . . . How do you feel about everything? I mean, I'm still new to all of this. Do you feel magical? Like, have you learned anything since being here?"

"I am unsure, honestly. I wasn't very affluent in magic back on Alfheim. I had yet to truly learn it. Usually, it is something taught by the council upon initiation. My mind feels sharper now, sharper than it ever has, but I don't feel any stronger yet."

"Do you think we're wasting our time here?"

"No, I don't believe so. Reynir is the lone council member to truly understand varying levels of magic, and he has kept the same resounding confidence in Konungr that he had on day one. He tells me he feels mentally stronger than ever before, so I see no reason not to trust our training."

"I agree. I just . . . I don't know. I feel like there's more we should be doing."

"Such as?"

"Anything besides this. Lift the curse. Defeat Loki. Restore Alfheim. There has to be more productive things for us to do than sit around twiddling our thumbs with King Chakra. Armageddon is looming, and the man responsible for killing my cousin is roaming scot-free, and instead of doing anything about it, we're camping in the woods seeking holistic self-validation and mental health evaluations." Michael paused, reading Steina's expression. "I'm sorry . . . I'm just venting. I know we are on the path that Solfrid deemed best. I just find it hard to remain patient while Loki's still out there."

"I assure you that nobody wishes for the capture of Loki more than I, but the only way for us to accomplish the things you have stated is by trusting and completing our training."

"I know." The silence caused by Michael's outburst vexed him. He silently wondered if he had turned Steina off with his recent comments. Not knowing where to take the conversation next, he struck up the courage to ask her a question that had been plaguing him since they had left Alfheim. "Can I ask you something?"

"Only if I get to ask you something after."

"Deal. So, the bow and arrow, what's up with that? How did you get away with only sacrificing archery?"

"Ahh, are you having second thoughts about vowing your life to Alfheim?"

"No, not necessarily. Just curious as to why my dumbass sacrificed so much when all I had to do was sacrifice a bow and arrow," chuckled Michael.

"It's deeper than that, of course. That bow and arrow used to belong to my father. Before the sword of Frey, my father's weapon of choice was his bow. He was a masterful bowman, the greatest of Alfheim, and that is a skill that he passed along to me, so it wasn't necessarily the bow and arrow but what it represented."

"And what of Solfrid and Ólafur? You seemed to have had a rather close relationship with them."

"That's two questions, Midgardian," Steina teased. "When my father passed, I went to live with his best friends, Solfrid and Ólafur, and they have cared for me ever since," she said with a tinge of sadness etched into her words. "I suppose it is my turn now, yes?"

"That is only fair, yes."

"Before . . . at the campfire at Dagrún, I mentioned bringing up your sisters' whereabouts to the council? Why would you refuse that? Even if you know the odds are slim, wouldn't you like to know the truth about what happened that day?"

"Not really. At least in my scenario, I can envision a better life for her. A life where she made it to another family or something, and they looked after her. Before I knew that Alfheim and other worlds existed, I always assumed she had been kidnapped, but I still held onto the tiny glimmer of hope that maybe she hadn't been, that maybe she got saved instead. Sometimes ignorance is bliss. I've learned that even the mightiest of superheroes have secrets that would ruin their illusion. By finding out the truth, I'm robbed of the fantasies I've created, robbed of the hope that she is still alive somewhere."

"And if she is still alive, you would rather not know?"

"I'd rather not know and believe that she was than come to find out that she's dead. It was that way with my mother's addiction too. I'd rather be far away and believe that she was okay than be up close and personal and know the truth that she wasn't. I don't know. That's just how I'm wired. We are nothing without hope, and if that's all I have left, then I need to keep it intact. It's not to say that I don't think about that day or think about my sister. I'd just like to think the events that followed were good rather than that of grotesque nature if that makes sense."

"No, I get it. I truly do understand. I guess I'm just different. If there was any possibility that she was still alive, I don't think I could stop until I found out the truth. No matter how painful."

"You know the old saying—well, maybe you don't—but don't ask questions you don't want to know the answer to. Sometimes you have experienced so much pain that you would rather shut the door that leads to happiness in order to not experience the inevitable feeling of sadness and disappointment that always follows it."

"But is that living? Don't you feel numb, living your life that way?"

"Kind of, but in doing so, I'm numb to pain too . . . It works for me."

"But are you really numb to pain? You still grieved for Peter. You still feel immense pain. Instead, you are only closed off to true happiness by guarding your heart with such high, impenetrable walls."

"I don't know. Maybe. Enough about me," said Michael, diverting the conversation. "What about you and Loki? Obviously, something happened there."

Steina paused, her face tightened. "This isn't the first time Loki has escaped his bonds. I'm sure he's done it on numerous occasions, but the last time he escaped, he masqueraded as a man named Lifthrasir. Lifthrasir is, in fact, a real person, but he's not the man that Loki pretended to be. The real Lifthrasir is destined to survive the events of Ragnarök with his wife, Lif, where they hide away in Hoddmímis Holt and return after Ragnarök has subsided and together, they repopulate the Midgardian species. The Norse version of Adam and Eve."

"So . . . let me get this straight, you fell in love with a dude prophesized to repopulate the world with another woman? Why?"

"Lifthrasir," said Steina, pausing, recognizing her mistake. "Loki was charming. Cunning, in a way, I didn't think existed. He had a way with words. He told me he had yet to meet Lif, and even when he did, she would pale in comparison to my beauty. I was young and naïve, so I believed him. I believed what I wanted to believe. I knew the risks and overlooked them. Ragnarök was supposed to be eons away. I thought I would be dead before it happened, so what did it matter that he would eventually move on from my dead corpse? I wasn't willing to look past a love like ours just because some stupid prophecy said otherwise, but I have long learned that prophecies cannot be changed, even when we think that they can be."

"Then what of Loki and Gullveig putting fate into their own hands? You said so yourself that they changed their destiny."

"Perhaps they did. Perhaps the prophecy was recorded incorrectly or misinterpreted. No one is ever truly dead here, depending on who you are. Frey and Heimdall could return to fulfill their destinies after all. They could be in Valhalla right now as we speak, cheers-ing and laughing it up with Odin for all we know."

"I guess if we're lucky, we will get to find out one day . . . So, what happened after, with you and Loki?"

"Long story short, it was revealed to me that Lifthrasir was not who we thought him to be. Loki shapeshifted before us and was carried away back to his bonds. Obviously, more detail happened in between, but that is the gist of it."

"Doesn't that scare you away from ever loving someone like that again? From ever trusting someone again?"

"At first, it did, yeah, but not anymore. Loki robbed me of my trust and happiness for too long, but you have to let go at some point. By holding that grudge, it only affected me, not him. I can't go on living my life with Loki in charge of my trust and happiness. Only I can decide that."

"Aren't you scared that you will get hurt again?"

"Maybe I will get hurt again, but that's for me to decide. Not someone else. Aren't you afraid that you will never be truly happy again?"

"I guess . . . I guess I never thought of that. I only thought of the pain. I never thought of the happiness that I could be missing out on."

"Well, you're young, and if all goes according to plan . . . you still have roughly three hundred and fifty years left on Alfheim, so you have plenty of time to rid yourself of such silly fears."

Steina's lips curled into a close-lipped, lopsided smile. A smile that was non-threatening and at the very same time the most threatening thing Michael had ever encountered because one kiss from those lips, and he would be spellbound to her. A smile that was intoxicating and full of magic. Not the magic he had yet to learn but the magic that melted the heart and captivated it, filling Michael with a sense of optimism, that even in times of war and heartbreak, life couldn't be all that bad when a smile like Steina's existed.

Michael smiled back at her, lost in the beauty of her eyes. "Enough with all of this sad stuff. What do you say to more mead?" He stood up and offered his hand to her.

"Finally," she rolled her eyes and tilted her head back obnoxiously. She grabbed his hand and vaulted herself up with his help. "I thought you would never ask. Boy, can you talk. I thought it would never end," she joked, nudging him playfully.

"Is that right?"

"Oh my gosh, yes. Put me out of my misery now," she said, pretending to impale herself with an imaginary sword.

"Okay, it's like that. I see you," said Michael, swiftly grappling her knees and hoisting her over his shoulders. She rolled and kicked playfully, attempting to escape, but Michael gently tossed her into the lake before she could do so.

"Better hurry to the mead before I drink it all," said Michael, racing away from her.

"Oh, you are definitely going to get it now," said Steina, wiping away the water from her eyes. She chased after him, the both of them giggling and grappling their way to the barrel of mead.

"Sheesh, knock it off, lovebirds," said Reynir, with his feet hoisted in the air, enjoying a nice cup of mead himself.

"Not fair, he started it," rebutted Steina.

"Me?" questioned Michael. "You were talking all that noise. I had to put you in your place."

"In my place?"

"Yeah, your place. Surely, you understand that there are repercussions for all of your bad-mouthing back there."

"Uh-huh, well, I am not afraid of whatever little repercussions you have planned," she said, pouring her glass of mead over Michael's head. Her smile smug and devious.

Michael tossed his wet, wavy hair out of his eyes. His hair having grown substantially during the few months that they had been on Midgard. "Alright. It's on now."

"You have to catch me first," said Steina, darting back to the water with Michael nipping at her heels.

The four of them spent the rest of the day enjoying the sunlight, none of them eager to get back to work the following day, or were they enthusiastic about carrying the heavy, half-filled barrel back to camp. Instead, they decided to drink its remains to lighten their load, a decision they would live to regret.

The next day they awoke with hangovers meant for the gods, each of them swearing that they would never drink again. Konungr took little pity in their slothfulness, requiring their immediate attention to the lesson at hand.

Their next exercise involved another form of mediation. This time their only goal was to eradicate any thoughts from entering, to turn their brain off entirely. The activity proved to be more challenging than their previous workouts, resulting in a never-ending cycle of each exercise becoming increasingly more complicated than the last.

The skill proved to be damn near impossible for Michael and his peers to grasp. Even thirty seconds without thoughts felt inconceivable. It required a supreme level of attentiveness and self-control. The more Michael tried to suppress any of the outside noises around him, the louder they became. The same went for the voice inside his head. Whether he ignored it or gave it attention, the voice festered inside of him. Either way, he failed in his attempts to stifle his thoughts, and the more flustered he became, the more problematic his exercises became.

To clear his mind completely, he would have to harness and control his emotions. It was a journey of self that could only be completed individually. Things that worked for Steina failed miserably for Michael, and vice versa. With every passing day, the tasks at hand proceeded to become more challenging than the day prior, as Konungr would raise the stakes and time limits in which they had to control their thoughts and emotions.

Each member of the council was beginning to know exactly who they were in every facet of life. They learned unique insights into what made them tick and what made them the way they were. It was a cleansing of their aura, a true insight into their mind, flushing and stripping away the outside bias and opinions of the world that surrounded them. They were diving deep into the depths of their souls, discovering who they were on every fundamental level.

This included every aspect and variation of themselves, the five-year-old within them, all the way to the oldest part of them that had yet to be seen. Michael couldn't decide if it was easiest for him since he was the youngest and had the least amount of time to reflect upon or if it was more challenging because he had the least amount of time to have learned about himself.

All his worth lied within; nobody else could decide that for him. It sounded corny, like some inspirational quote on a poster in an elementary classroom, but it was true. And part of him had always known that, but the more the world around him perceived who he was, the more he began to believe it. Somewhere along the way, people lose themselves and conform to the world around them, becoming what society pushed them to be rather than transforming into the being that they desired.

In some form or another, everybody went through life wearing a mask, and through Konungr's practices, they were able to recognize that mask and reveal the truest parts of their inner selves. Whether or not they wanted to share the person underneath was up to them, but Konungr made it a point for them to find that person hidden deep within.

After mastering the art of vacating their thoughts for hours at a time, they were granted another day of relaxation. This time Michael had only finished six days behind Reynir, three days behind Steina, and one day behind Darrius. He was slowly beginning to catch up to them. They still hadn't gotten into any physical magic yet, but it felt good to finally show some progress.

The night before their next lesson, Michael laid in his cot, unable to fall asleep. His mind did cartwheels, thinking of any and everything possible. After locking his conscious mind in a cage over the past few months, it seemed to have taken back control of the steering wheel. Like a puppy that had been locked up all day in its kennel, his mind raced with the zoomies, releasing all the built-up energy it had stored.

Michael decided to go with it. He let his mind wander down whatever avenue it chose, from a pair of shoes he had stolen as a teenager to some zombie apocalypse, all the way to that damn pass he dropped in high school.

Then suddenly, as if a flip had been switched, he was no longer in his subconscious anymore. He was in Skye's. Once again, he found himself in her memories, just as he had the night before Peter was murdered.

Loki . . . the god who lurked in Michael's mind at all times, made an appearance once more. This time he stood before Skye, striking blow after blow with his spear. Technically, Michael couldn't see Skye to confirm whether or not it was her, but his intuition flared. Somehow, he knew this memory was from the perspective of his sister.

Based on her height and limbs, she was older. Michael was unaware of how old she was exactly, but her long, lengthy arms blocked each of Loki's powerful strikes. She had to have at least been a teenager, maybe older. Her voice sounded deeper, wiser than that of the average teen.

The spear that Loki hoisted and slugged through the air was a marvelous one. It gleamed of gold, pulsing with lightning and energy as it slashed in his hands. It had three heads to pierce with, the middle one being the largest of the three.

Loki spun acrobatically, twirling his spear around between his hands, attacking her with every opportunity that arose before him. Skye, too busy focused on the spear, failed to notice the strenuous kick that landed on her chest plate, knocking her to the ground. Michael felt the kick land upon his chest, jolting his sleeping body into a hypnogogic jerk. Skye looked up at Loki, but it was too late. She was met with another thunderous boot, this time to her face.

Everything went black. Michael couldn't see what had happened behind Skye's starry eyes, but he could feel the electrical, hot spear pierce through her right quadricep. The spear tore through her, searing through her flesh, barreling into her left hamstring, perforating it cleanly. Both legs remained tightly flushed, trapped together by the spear of Loki. The spear's tip staked through Skye's leg and clutched into the ground.

Skye screamed in agony. Excruciating pain flooded through her central nervous system as she sneaked a look at the spear that was carved into her. The pain was unlike any she had ever felt, and somehow the rage, the panic, the icy-hot sensations that shackled inside her were shared by Michael, connecting him to her pain.

"Father," she screamed in horror. "Save me." She squirmed and contorted her body in distress, but it only tightened the spear's clenching hold upon her flesh like a fish straining against the hook, only for it to drill itself deeper with every panicked convulsion. "Please, father, save me."

Loki stared over her in disgust, his wrinkled nose and deathly stare reeking of disappointment. "You disappoint me, daughter. The day will come when I won't be here to save you. You must learn to save yourself. You got yourself into this situation. Get yourself out."

Loki held his hand in the air, his fingers tightening as if they were gripping an invisible object. The sharpening blades of the spear torpedoed out of Skye's flesh and returned to Loki. The blades devoured and ripped her skin apart, fileting her leg muscles.

Skye laid in torment, wailing at the top of her lungs. Sweltering tears singed upon her face as she looked up at her father for relief. Loki gave her one last look of disgust before turning his back on her. He opened a large wooden door and proceeded not to turn around. "Be back before dinner, or do not come back at all," he said, slamming the door shut behind him.

The sounds of Skye's howls for help filled Michael with such terror that he awoke screaming, his body drenched in sweat.

Darrius stood at his bedside with his hands on Michael's shoulders. "Mike. Mike, you're dreaming. Calm down, buddy. You're only dreaming."

Michael looked around in confusion. How was any of this possible? He could feel Skye's thoughts, feel her pain. He felt the searing hot metal puncture and cauterize her legs, to the point that his thighs ached with excruciating pain. His legs throbbed and trembled with fire as if he had just finished an intense leg workout. He stood up shakily, falling onto Darrius for support.

"I—I don't know what's wrong with me," Michael clamored shakily. "I keep having these visions . . . visions of Skye. Like into her psyche, but this time, I could . . . I could feel her pain. She was sparring with Loki, and he stabbed through her legs with his spear, and I don't know how but I could feel it," grunted Michael, massaging both of his legs.

"How are your legs now?" asked Darrius. "Can you walk?"

Michael leaned on Darrius a little more. He took a few hobbled steps with Darrius's guidance, attempting to regain control of his legs. He shook both of them vigorously, as if that would release all the pain that subsided within them.

"Yeah, I'm fine," said Michael behind long and slogging breaths. "I can—I can walk now."

"How long has this been going on for?" asked Darrius.

"It started the day I touched the tree, the day I traveled to Alfheim. I told you about it after. How I recalled my sister's disappearance, remember?"

Darrius nodded his head. "Yeah, I remember. That's what led our ass here in the first place."

"What I failed to leave out was that that vision came from Skye's perspective, not mine. I don't know. It doesn't make any sense. I had another one the night Peter got murdered. That one revealed Skye getting locked in some sort of dungeon. She was crying out for me. It was from the day she disappeared. Now this one. She was older and sparring with Loki. She called him father . . . She thinks that evil bastard is her dad. I think she's still alive, Darrius."

"We need to tell Konungr. He will have a much better understanding of how to handle this."

"No," said Michael strictly. "I don't know what any of this means, but I'd like to keep it between us for now. I don't want everyone finding out yet."

"Of course, whatever you want. But if it gets worse, we gotta tell him, Mike."

"Deal," said Michael, nodding his head reluctantly. "But I'll be fine."

CHAPTER TWELVE

STREAMING SERVICE
OF THE MIND

Michael awoke, having barely slept at all after his horrifying vision. His rage left him in stirring fits as he tossed and turned, trying to find any connection between Skye and Loki. He tried to convince himself that it had only been a dream, but unfortunately, he knew better.

It was a vision, just like the others before it. This one being the strongest of all, so powerful that it left him kneeling over his bedside, in need of Darrius's support. No dream had ever done that before. Skye was alive, and sadly, she was convinced that the man Michael despised most was her father. Michael didn't need any more ammunition to hate Loki, but he found one more reason to loathe the vile and despicable trickster.

"How are you feeling?" asked Darrius upon waking.

"A little groggy," replied Michael. "My head's still kind of spinning a bit. You?"

"I feel fine, but I'm not the one having visions."

"I'm good, don't worry," said Michael sternly, hoping to end the conversation before eavesdropping ears overhead.

They proceeded to have their usual morning breakfast, and afterward, they met Konungr outside of the cave to go over their routine for the day.

"Today, we begin our journey into the subconscious," said Konungr.

After last night, Michael certainly had some trepidation about moving forward into his subconscious. But his had to be better than Skye's, he thought, erasing his doubt and insecurities.

"I have a vial for each of you," said Konungr, handing them one each. "In it is a medicine that will administer you to sleep with ease. After this initial dose, we will shift our dream mediations into the nighttime and proceed with other lessons during the day. It will become a twenty-four-hour workweek from here on out while we begin our dream training."

"What's in this thing?" asked Darrius, examining the vial suspiciously.

"Passionflower, Valerian root, a sprinkle of other natural ingredients. Enough to put you back to sleep. I wanted to start our sleep training with a fresh mind."

"I don't know about this, chief."

"If I wanted to kill you, I would have done it the moment you trespassed along my cave."

"True. Bottoms up, I guess," said Darrius, opening the vial and chugging its remains.

The others followed suit, none of them fond of the elixir's taste.

"Within the hour, you will fall back into a state of a deep sleep," said Konungr. "I need you to try to recognize that you are sleeping. It will be difficult at first. Some of you might not be able to recognize it, and that's okay. It takes time. If you happen to recognize that you are dreaming, then I want you to visually record your dream, the same as our meditation practices. Study it with intricate detail and when you awake, recall the dream to the best of your capabilities."

Sounds easy enough, Michael thought, but he knew better than to believe that anything that Konungr had prepared for them would be easy.

They all awoke around the same time, somewhere within the hour of one another, each one of them struggling to evoke the dreams that their subconscious had elegantly constructed moments before.

They spent the next few months elaborating on dream practices and studies. As much as Michael wanted to sleuth for the truth behind Loki and Skye's horrifying relationship, he had to put the vision behind him, or risk being surpassed even more by his fellow council members. The task, just like the many that came before it, required his utmost attention. Surprisingly, the council grasped a hold of the training a lot quicker than their initial practices with Konungr, but they were also mentally stronger now compared to then.

After a few months of intense training, they were able to write entire novels detailing their dreams. Their sessions were aided by some magic Konungr had administered that allowed their thoughts to transfer to paper instantly. With his help, they could finish pages as quickly as they could think; that way, ideas never got left behind by the heavy hands that wrote them.

They started to spend their nights around a campfire reading the novels that replicated their dreams. They weren't exactly good novels, seeing as each of them lacked any sort of structuring or formatting. Characters would jump from place to place without warning and just as quickly disappear. New characters would emerge from out of nowhere and interrupt the story's climax. Locations shifted in the middle of scenes, chapters overlapped, and conversations would stop mid-sentence as new worlds appeared from nothing. It was an utterly chaotic mess, but it provided for great entertainment and comradery amongst them, helping ease their stress.

After mastering the art of recalling their dream in vivid detail, they quickly moved onto controlling their dreams. This proved to be a more strenuous and challenging task, but that much they were used to.

Dreams moved at alarmingly quick speeds, shifting from one to another effortlessly, requiring an impeccable amount of attention to detail to be able to grasp. The trick that Michael learned was to start with something small in the dream. If he could learn to control the lamp or the door or some other small insignificant object, he could slowly move onto more important things as he got stronger.

Pretty soon, that practice turned into controlling the car that the characters of his dream were driving. He would drive the car off a cliff to alter the dream and see the character's reactions. He couldn't control their emotions yet, but he could control the substances that elicited their emotions.

He practiced until he became the artist behind the masterpiece with the ability to control every aspect. Once his subconscious took over, but with his guidance and supervision, it was like fireworks. He could feel his brain tingle as if tiny ants were crawling atop it, tickling him with their vibrating tarsal claws. After harnessing the ability to control his dreams, it unlocked gateways to his subconscious that he didn't know existed, launching a streaming service of himself, the *Netflix* of his mind, he liked to call it.

He could now recall every single dream he had ever had, some of them from his infant years, and man, were those things weird to watch. He could stream his memories now, too, every last one of them as simple as he would watch something on a streaming platform. He could categorize every thought, memory, and dream by category, alphabetical order, characters, guest appearances, etc.

On their last day, when Michael had fully mastered the art, they shared another campfire. This time he had only finished two days behind Steina and Reynir and one day behind Darrius. Konungr projected a film of some sort before them, displaying as clearly as HD or Blu-ray.

"I want us all to reveal a memory, a dream, or even an eloquent piece of fiction that you have crafted together recently with your newfound skill set. Something that you would consider monumental or life changing. I know how private or intimate this might be, so it is only fair that I start."

The screen came to life, playing whatever it was that Konungr wanted to show them, none of them knowing whether it was fictional or not. Konungr was running full sprint in a panic, his breath loud and heavy. He was in a forest, hustling through branches and brush, speeding by everything in sight.

He kept looking up repeatedly, following the blaze of smoke that blistered through the canopy of the forest. He arrived at a village littered with small wooden cabins, all of them set ablaze besides two or three of them. An army of elven soldiers gathered the village people up in ropes and bonds.

"Stop," shouted Konungr. "Leave them be. It's me that you want." They couldn't see Konungr but judging by his youthful, exuberant voice, he was much younger.

A gentleman with long, golden locks of hair turned around, revealing himself to be a younger-looking Frey.

"Konungr, it's so nice of you to join us," said Frey. "And which one of these lovely women would be your wife?"

Konungr didn't answer.

"I see that you would prefer this the hard way," continued Frey. "Talven, let's make this simpler for him, shall we?"

Talven, a light elf with a scythe in hand, nodded his head. He walked to the nearest bonded person, a female. He raised her chin, rubbing the blade of his scythe gently across her neck. "Konungr's wife, where is she?"

Tears ran down the female's face. "I'm sorry, Konungr." With her hands tied behind her back, she pointed with her head, directing Talven to a woman who was shielding herself in front of a young girl, maybe five or six in age.

Talven walked over to the woman believed to be Konungr's wife.

"No, stop," Konungr pleaded. "Take me, instead," he said, dropping to his knees, relinquishing his wrists forward to be cuffed.

"Wise decision," said Frey. He pulled out a pair of cuffs, heavily engraved with runes, from his satchel. He tightened them around Konungr's wrists. "Now, where is Heimdall?" he asked Konungr.

"Like I told Skirnir before, I do not know."

"You're lying." He looked to Talven and nodded his head. "Make him talk. I don't have time for manners."

Talven brought his scythe to Konungr's wife's throat. The small girl, assumed to be Konungr's daughter, stepped in front of Talven.

"Honey, get back behind me," Konungr's wife begged behind tears of distress. "Please, Ragna. Behind me."

"I said I don't know," screamed Konungr. "Please, stop. I beg you."

Frey nodded once more at Talven.

Talven backhanded Ragna in the face, brushing her to the side like a ragdoll. He grabbed a fistful of Konungr's wife's hair and thrust her into the dirt, proceeding to place his foot forcefully atop one of her knees. He raised his scythe into the air.

"Stop," mumbled Frey lackadaisically. "Not yet." He looked at Konungr once more. "Last chance. Where is he?"

"I don't know. I haven't seen him in months. Last he told me was that he was off to Svartalfheim. That is all I know, I swear it. Now please let everyone go. Take me if you must."

Frey nodded at Talven once more. Talven raised his scythe again, this time striking it downwards with force shearing through the ankle of Konungr's wife, chopping her right foot off the bone.

"Eerika," Konungr screamed. "Let her be," he said, rising to his feet. His body began to tremble with anger; flares of white-hot energy danced around him.

"Sit down," commanded Frey. "There is no use trying to get past those cuffs, so don't bother."

Konungr proceeded forth in a rage, running awkwardly with his hands cuffed behind his back.

Frey swiped his left hand in the air, vaulting Konungr across the village into one of the few cabins that remained unburned. Konungr looked up shakily, still raging with anger, his energy increasing.

"Her head this time, Talven," said Frey.

"No," screamed Konungr.

Talven slashed his scythe through the air aiming for Eerika's head. The scythe was intercepted by Ragna as she stepped forward to shield her mother, cutting through Ragna's neck and severing across her shoulder blade.

Ragna's head and right arm fell limply to the floor, her body dropping next to her upper torso, landing in the puddles of blood that divulged from her corpse.

Konungr unleashed a blood-curdling scream. His rage intensified, exploding the cuffs from his wrists. He surged forward and blasted Frey with blistering heaps of energy. One surging disc after another, only to be evaded by the elusive acts of Frey.

Frey grabbed hold of Eerika and escaped into a portal behind him, leaving Konungr alone with his rage. In Frey's escape, he left behind his army of ten or so elven soldiers, none of which appeared to be affluent in magic.

Konungr went from one to the other beating them mercifully with his bloody hands until only three remained, one of them being Talven. With his hands clenched, Konungr dropped two of the soldiers to the floor, crippling them with pain. He shifted his attention to Talven and lifted the scythe he had commandeered from him. Talven desperately crawled on all fours beneath him, and with one mighty blow, Konungr sliced through the center of Talven's head, sawing him symmetrically in half from his head to his genitals.

He turned to one of the elves attempting to flee for an escape. He clenched his hand in the air, raising the elf in place, paralyzing him in midair. He reared back and threw the scythe sidearm, airmailing it like a boomerang, connecting it upon the neck of the elf, beheading him.

Konungr turned his attention to the last remaining elf, who laid sprawled across the floor. He summoned the scythe back to him. With two precise swings, he cut off the elf's hands. Konungr placed the scythe to the elf's throat, piercing it lightly. "Tell me where Frey ran off to."

The elf shuddered, trembling in fear. "H-h-he's r-returning to Vanaheim."

Konungr gripped the elf by his neck and brought him to his feet. The blood from the elf's hands dripped profusely from his severed wrists. Konungr kicked the elf hard in the sternum, barreling him backward.

"For your sake, you better not be lying," said Konungr slashing across the elf's rib cage, leaving a scythe-sized cut in its place. "Get up and lead the way," Konungr barked.

The projection faded to black, and the council left in dismay, all of them in stunned silence.

"I—I take it that was a memory?" Michael gulped, unsure of whether Konungr's answer or the awkward and tense silence that filled the air would be more comforting at the moment.

"It was," said Konungr, refusing eye contact with the lot of them.

"I'm sorry," said Steina.

"Don't be," he said, turning his focus back to his pupils. "There's no reason for you to be sorry. This was long before your time."

"I know, but Frey . . . that was our leader . . . Our god. Skinir was my father. I'm embarrassed to have any association with either of them after seeing the horror they have afflicted upon you. I'm sorry that they would do that to you, Konungr."

"Don't apologize for the actions of others, for it is not your responsibility, nor is it your burden to carry. What is done is done."

"I don't understand," said Michael. "I thought Frey was benevolent," he said, looking to Reynir and Steina. "How could he do all of this and then show up to Alfheim with Heimdall, all buddy-buddy like none of this ever happened."

"That memory was from the Æsir-Vanir war, thousands of years ago," said Konungr. "Everyone affected by that war had parts in doing unspeakable things they aren't proud of. Myself included. Time goes on, and people change. Wounds heal. Friendships and alliances blossom from conflict, but the blood of those hands can never be washed. The lives that were lost too heavy for forgiveness. All those lives simply because gods couldn't control their egos—all of that for nothing. There was no winner, only an alliance formed between the two realms. The losers were the poor that were feasted on and ravaged during a war that they had no part in starting, no part of controlling, and no part of wanting, but it was them who paid the most."

"It always is," said Darrius. "The powerful wage war knowing they have nothing to lose but pride."

"Indeed. Even if they know it is a war they will lose, they have no problem risking others' lives for their foolish pride. I fell for their propaganda then. I was foolish. Compounded by such a vengeance that I was blind and willingly followed them into battle. I show you this not to reminisce on my pain but to ask yourselves, when the time comes, what is it that you are truly fighting for? If it's revenge you seek, you will never win," said Konungr, staring at Michael as if those words were articulately delivered for him to digest. "Good and evil are never as black and white as it seems."

"What are you saying?" asked Reynir. "Are you suggesting that Loki and Gullveig are not evil? That they did not destroy our home? I don't understand."

"No one is wholeheartedly evil, nor is anyone wholeheartedly good. Propaganda is used as a weapon for war. Be careful who you choose to follow. I am merely asking that you take a hard look within and ask yourself what it is that you are fighting for. If it is not worth losing everything over, save yourself the trouble. Let the gods battle without you, just as they have done their entire lives."

"If you know more about this war, why not tell us?" asked Michael.

"Because whatever I show you, whatever I tell you, you will believe. I do not wish to alter your opinion of others. That truth is for you to find."

Michael nodded his head, not entirely sure how to respond. It seemed the others did not either because they remained silent as well.

"Time for someone else to present now," said Konungr. "As stated before, you do not have to display a memory. You can present something entirely fiction or a mixture of both. Whatever you present, make sure it elicits a burning passion inside of you."

They each stared at one another, none of them eager to follow up on Konungr's presentation.

"I guess I'll go," said Darrius, stepping up to the occasion.

It was a story Michael knew all too well, but seeing it first-hand was gut-wrenching. From the moment the first scene opened, he knew it was a flashback of the night Darrius's father had been murdered.

On the projection, Darrius's father, gun in hand, guided his wife and a younger Darrius into the closet, ushering them to keep quiet. Darrius was seven at the time, something the others wouldn't have known or been able to tell, but Michael knew the story by heart.

Darrius's father stealthily tiptoed downstairs to greet the intruders, he turned the corner, and that was the last they ever saw him. Deafening gunshots flared loudly as Darrius's mother covered Darrius's ears, cradling him tightly. They heard the sound of broken glass from the window, followed by an ear-ringing silence.

Muffled, hyperventilating sobs escaped between Darrius and his mother as she did her best to control their breathing. A quiet so loud, like hornets buzzing inside their ears. She waited about five minutes in the silence, those five minutes feeling like a full-length feature presentation.

Each second dragged by, filling the air with impalpable tension like a volcano on the brink of eruption. Michael knew the outcome, but still, he hoped that somehow he could change it and sift through fates pages as if it were a Choose Your Own Adventure book.

Darrius's mother called out for her husband to no answer. "I need you to stay right here, baby," said his mother. "Whatever you do, don't leave until I come and get you," she stressed, leaving Darrius alone curdled in the corner of the closet.

"No, Mama," Darrius cried through struggling breaths. "Please don't leave me."

"I'll be right back, baby. Don't you come downstairs, okay?"

Darrius nodded his head as the tears erupted some more. He tucked his head into his lap and scrunched tightly into a ball.

His mother crept down the stairs to a living room stained with so much blood that Michael could smell the metallic scent of rust and copper as if it ebbed through the projection. Michael knew that Darrius never saw his father's body that night. His mother forbade him from seeing it, sheltering him from the horrifying images that he would later find as an adult in case files.

The remaining projection must have been pieces fragmented together by a combination of his imagination and the crime scene photos that Darrius had analyzed routinely before their venture to Alfheim.

The lamp was broken, glass shattered across the floor, lining along the rug. The door was kicked in off its hinges and there on the ground was Darrius's father, lying in blood with a gaping hole in his head the size of a bullet. The wound still fresh as blood pooled slowly from it, oozing softly.

Darrius's mother's horrifying squalls synced to his creation. They were cries that only trauma could create. Cries that Darrius likely heard in his sleep more than he wanted to admit. It was hard to watch, even harder knowing that there was nothing that any of them could do to change it.

Bloodstains littered across the couch and up and out of the window, leaving a trail of evidence behind for the crime scene investigators, but they ultimately came up with nothing. They could tell from the footprints that it was two men, but it wasn't enough to find the perpetrators. It took a rare breed to become a detective, and it rarely came from someone without a horrifying backstory of their own; this was Darrius's.

From there, Darrius's presentation transformed into a younger version of himself growing up through grade school in search of a father figure. He later found that relationship by becoming a psychic medium with the ability to communicate with the dead. Through it, he was able to build the relationship with his father that he was robbed of.

This was where Darrius's projection became a clear act of fiction, creating the happy ending life never gave him. His story ended with him finding his father's killers. Darrius was a teen at this point, a well-known psychic who exchanged a favor with a detective. He offered his services to the detective, help him crack one of the most prominent cases in town, which would catapult the detective's chances at becoming mayor.

In return, the detective would accompany Darrius on his psychic quest to capture the men who murdered his father. It was the epitome of a buddy-buddy cop movie, only it involved a psychic teenager instead.

Darrius's father, in the form of a ghost, haunted along at Darrius's side. Together, they navigated through all leads until they found the people who assassinated him. It was a heartfelt program, showing the man Darrius remembered his father to be, a fun-loving and kind-hearted yet stern man full of passion.

In the end, after they apprehended the killers, his dad's soul was put at rest. They shared one long embrace, both crying together before Darrius's father disappeared for good. The reception was met with applause and prolonged droughts of silence, nobody knowing exactly what to say.

Michael placed his hand gently on Darrius's shoulder and patted his back. "He'd be proud of you," he said quietly, for only Darrius to hear. "I'm proud of you."

"It looks as if we all share a wealth of pain together," said Steina out loud.

"No, only you guys," chimed Reynir. "My parents are absolutely fantastic. Remarkable, you could say."

"Seriously? Not now. Read the room, Reynir."

"What? Is it so wrong that we used to pick flowers and berries together in the majestic fields of Alfheim when I was a young boy? And then after the flower picking, we would—"

"Zip it," said Steina, clearly biting her tongue. "Just hurry up and go already and present your exuberant flower picking youth."

"Hey now, you picked flowers with me once or twice. Remember that time my mom took us to—"

"Reynir," said Steina once more, motioning to the glum atmosphere that was present in the room.

"Okay, fine. I will go. Sheesh."

Reynir proceeded with his presentation. As predicted, his projection was the opposite of Darrius's, which was for the best because after Konungr and Darrius's heart-wrenching stories, the council needed a breath of fresh air. Whether by design, to lighten the suffocating mood, or simply just a product of Reynir's personality, his projection was a comedy, transferring the solemn atmosphere to one of silliness that only Reynir could provide.

The screen before them displayed a circus, apparently one from Reynir's first visit to Midgard. Reynir entered the arena, his face hidden, cloaked like a Jedi. The boisterous crowd hushed at his arrival.

Reynir unsheathed his sword slowly and turned his attention to the ringmaster. He attacked him with fury, toying with the gentleman's fear, making a mockery of him in front of the audience. He summoned ropes and cast them to the audience's wrists, leaving behind a long line of shackled Midgardians. He freed the imprisoned animals and marched his Midgardian prisoners through a portal that led to Alfheim, letting the lions and bears chomp at the feet of anyone who dared to toe out of line.

One too many montages later, Reynir led his own circus filled with the humans of Midgard, his audience consisting of the lions, elephants, bears, and monkeys that he saved back on Earth. Each of the animals howling and cackling at the displeasure of humans.

Reynir's story never gained traction, nor did it have much of a plot, just show after show for tens of years with the human performers humiliating themselves for the sake of the audience's entertainment. Furthermore, it ended with Reynir as the ringmaster, where he bowed as the circus lights dimmed to his story's completion. It was undoubtedly bizarre, but nonetheless, they all applauded his efforts upon its ending.

Reynir, catching the awkward, wide-eyed gazes amongst them, spoke out about his eccentric creation. "Look, I am certainly no Ezra, but I don't believe in animal cruelty, and something about that circus back on Midgard rubbed me the wrong way."

"It was," said Darrius, struggling to put the words together. "It was very good, profoundly put together. A very nice piece of art, Reynir."

"Thank you," said Reynir, beaming with pride as if his kid had just won student of the year or earned valedictorian of their class.

Steina's projection followed along the lines of Konungr's and Darrius's, tugging at the heart and never letting go, encompassing the story of her and Loki and his inevitable betrayal.

Her story journeyed across many of their dates, conveying the beautiful sceneries and architecture of what Alfheim used to be. Atop one of the many glorious mountains, they were sharing wine and discussing their future together.

Loki, disguised as Lifthrasir, was handsome. A gentleman with curly hair and masculine features. A man much more attractive than the vermillion-haired, scar-adorned Loki that Michael had seen back on Alfheim.

"I've never seen a person as beautiful as you," said Loki, his eyes glimmering in the radiant sunlight of the realm. "Inside and out. Your eyes are beyond captivating. They have their own gravity, pulling me in every time. The cosmos exist within them, and inside, I can see the stars of our realm. They hold the windows to our souls, and through yours, I see pure enlightenment. And one day, if I'm lucky enough, I will have your hand in marriage, making me the luckiest man to ever wander along Yggdrasil."

"You know why that will never be," said Steina, her voice fighting against the wave of despair that those words held.

"I know, and I know that we have talked about it before, but I assure you that I could never love anyone the way that I love you."

"And I believe you, but we already know your fate, and nowhere am I in it."

Loki stroked her face gently and placed his forehead upon hers. He tilted her chin, falling victim to her lips. He kissed her with rigor, with the passion of a man who knew the world was going to end, kissing her until she pushed back to catch her breath. He tilted her chin once more and stared into her eyes, mesmerized by their beauty.

"To hell with fate," said Loki. "You are my fate. You are my right now. You are my forever, and if I ever let a day go by without you, I would never live to see tomorrow because I couldn't bear to see a day filled with that much agony and despair."

"I want to believe you . . . I do, but . . ."

"But what? Fate? Fate is nothing more than a lie that is used to control the masses. It brainwashes people into believing they are or are not rather than being. Only I can control my fortunes. And I couldn't imagine a better way to spend my life than with you by my side as my wife." He grabbed her hand. "What do you say?"

Steina paused, staring longingly at Loki. "What do I say to what, babe?"

"My proposal? Your hand in marriage, making me the happiest man to walk the nine realms?"

"I say yes," she said, clutching his face and kissing him passionately.

Loki pulled away. "I didn't expect this to happen today, so I still have to get you a ring, but I will, I promise. It will be the most gorgeous ring the realms have to offer, as pretty as Brísingamen."

"I don't care for a ring or any exterior beauty," said Steina. "I only care about you . . . but I'll hold you to that."

They began to kiss with more lust and passion than before, and wisely Steina glossed over their romance, fast-forwarding to the two of them returning to the corridors of Dain's Castle where they were greeted by the gods, Thor and Tyr.

Thor was big and muscular, just as he was portrayed in Hollywood, except unlike the movies, he had red, mangy hair rather than the golden, heaven-like blonde. He held Mjölnir in hand, gripping it tightly. His body filled with scars from his years of battle, same as Tyr.

Tyr was smaller but chiseled with more muscles than the human body could hold. Both gods stood there waiting for Steina and Loki to return. The council of Alfheim stood behind them, Reynir included.

"Save the charades and make this easy on all of us by revealing yourself now, Loki," said Thor.

"Me?" asked Loki in confusion.

"I'm not talking to your beautiful little sidepiece, now am I?"

"Excuse me?" questioned Steina.

"Sit this one out, darling. It's a matter for men," said Thor.

"I don't care who you are. You are not going to disrespect me like that."

"Save yourself the embarrassment," said Tyr.

"Steina," said Reynir, desperately shaking his head no. His eyes wide, gesturing for her to stop.

"Enough of the games, Loki," said Thor. "Reveal yourself or allow me the pleasure of having Mjölnir reveal you for me," he said, swirling his hammer with the broadest of smiles.

"Surely, you must be mistaken," said Loki.

"I only wish that were the case. Mind helping me here, Tyr?"

"I thought you would never ask," smiled Tyr.

Tyr gripped Loki and punched him in the gut, dropping him to his knees. He got behind Loki, one hand gripping his hair tightly, the other firmly pressed down on his shoulder, not allowing for Loki to return to his feet. Thor reared back, ready to throw Mjölnir through Loki's skull.

"Stop," cried Steina, rushing to grab ahold of Thor's arm.

Reynir intercepted her and held her tightly in his arms as she tried to writhe herself free.

"Okay, okay," said Loki, cowering his head in shame. "It is me, Loki." His nose scrunched and wrinkled, growing smaller before their eyes. His bones cracked, and his back arched and popped. The curly, well-manicured hair atop his head shed into longer, unkempt, vermillion-red hair. Scars emerged on his once fresh, model-esque face.

All of this came from Steina's point of view, so her expression remained hidden to them, but Michael could only imagine it replicated the look of pure shock and horror that was exhibited across every member of the council's face.

"Steina, listen," said Loki. "I'm so very sorry, dear. I meant every word I ever said to you."

"Save it for the jury, snake," said Thor, whacking Loki across the face with Mjölnir and knocking him out cold.

The Bifröst emerged from nothing and consumed the gods of Asgard, leaving the council alone, paralyzed from the shock of it all.

Seeing this made Michael's blood boil, consuming him with even more hatred and resentment for Loki. What he had done to Steina, to Peter, to Skye, to Alfheim, could never be forgiven. Michael's whole life going forward would be committed to making Loki pay dreadfully.

Steina's projection transitioned into one last agonizing scene, one made of fiction, rooted in her darkest fears. She battled against Loki alone in a chamber or cellar of some sorts. Surrounding them were the skeletal remains of other elves and allies. Amongst those remains were Michael, Darrius, Reynir, Solfrid, and Ezra. The council of Alfheim lay dead, encircled around her. She was all alone, destined to face off with Loki by herself.

She thrust her sword at him, fury and concentration built into each of her menacing thrusts. The two battled back and forth, reminding Michael of his vision a few months prior, where Loki had severely injured his sister and left her for dead.

With Steina's free hand, she blasted magic at Loki, but he blocked each blow with energy of his own. This continued until they both huffed and puffed and were depleted of energy.

Loki transformed before her back into the Lifthrasir that she had known and loved, changing into the man she had fallen in love with on the mountaintops of Alfheim. The man she shared wine and laughs with, the man that she committed her future to, and with that one transformation, she was powerless.

Loki spoke softly in her ear, speaking of her eyes and her beauty, claiming to have missed her unbearably. He marveled over her power and rage, declaring that it made his desire for her even stronger. He confessed that he still loved her and that he still wanted to marry her one day.

He sweet-talked her and caressed her, kissing her up and down her neck, slithering upon her like the snake that he was. He lifted her chin as he used to do and kissed her, leaving her gasping for air. She kissed him with the same passion, the same lust that she had from the day he had proposed.

She traded her fury and hatred for her desire and lust for Loki. He picked her up gently off her knees and assured her that everything would be okay. He placed her on her feet and grabbed her hand, guiding her out of the chamber into a new life together, walking past the bodies of her old friends.

The group was left flabbergasted, in utter disbelief, even more than they were with Konungr's revelation. Steina wouldn't dare make eye contact with anyone. Her shame would not allow it, but Michael respected her more after what she had shown them. She could've chosen any dream, yet she chose the one that invaded her intimacy the most.

She let everyone into her spirit and sacredness, laying out her biggest fear for everyone to see. When the time came, she feared she wouldn't be strong enough to defeat Loki because, deep down, a part of her still loved him. There was bravery in what she showed them, even if it was riddled with fear, a level of courage that Michael could only hope to exhibit one day.

The group turned to Michael, all eyes on him. It was his turn to present. It was one of those moments where he regretted not going first and setting the bar. Now he had to follow after Steina and Darrius and even Konungr and live up to the unreasonable expectations that they had set.

His dream felt corny compared to the extravagant art displayed, but then he was reminded of Reynir's kooky piece of work and felt a little better about himself. Surely, his presentation couldn't be any worse than that, he thought.

Had he had the courage to go first, he probably would've copped out, playing the memory from his last football game, but now after everyone else's presentations, it was rather apparent what he needed to present, the day that Skye disappeared.

A memory that haunted him for so long. A memory that had long since been forgotten until it miraculously reemerged from the perspective of Skye. He hadn't viewed this memory since gaining his most recent skill set. It wasn't necessarily something that he wanted to dig up quite yet, but everyone else had shared intimate accounts of their past. It was only right that Michael did the same.

It felt like an out-of-body experience watching the memory project before him. The ability to watch as if it were television was like reading something on paper compared to on-screen. Details emerged that he had missed entirely when he experienced the memory from Skye's perspective.

One noticeable thing was glaringly obvious to him and the rest of the group. Had he taken the time to access this memory before presenting, he would've noticed it instantly. The sly, charming individual who led him and his family astray twenty years ago was none other than Loki.

CHAPTER THIRTEEN

CLAIRVOYANCE

"Loki?" Steina blurted in disbelief. "You were led here by Loki, and you didn't tell us?"

"I didn't know," said Michael. "I swear. This is the first time I've recalled that memory since gaining these powers . . . I can't believe it's been him all along. How did I not realize this on Alfheim? I'm so stupid."

"Don't be too hard on yourself. I dated the guy. I was with him every night and never knew."

"Because you were blinded by all the mind-numbing sex, eh?" chirped Reynir.

"Seriously, Reynir?" said Steina.

"What? Sex with a god? Riddle me with jealousy. I can only imagine how fiery and intense it must have been. And he's a shapeshifter. I bet that came in handy making certain things bigger, eh? Or what about role-playing? Did he ever transform into Thor for you? Tell me did," said Reynir, taking pride in the pestering of his cousin.

"Shut up," said Steina, her face flushing red with embarrassment.

"I'm just saying, consider yourself lucky. Maybe one day, I will be lucky enough to seduce the beautiful Freyja. What a fox she is."

"You and half of Nidavellir," Steina jabbed.

"Hey, that was uncalled for."

"You started it."

"Enough," interrupted Konungr. "Proceed forward with your memory, Michael. Not your revised interpretation, but the original."

Michael nodded his head and continued with the memory from that day. He studied everything imaginable, eyeballing the details closely for any leads on their whereabouts, but ultimately wound up with nothing. His vision ended with him and his cousins sprinting home, leaving Skye behind without a trace of where she may have disappeared to.

"Do you know where I wound up that day?" Michael asked Konungr.

"Sadly, I do not," replied Konungr. "I have never seen that castle before. I'm sorry."

Michael nodded his head. "I guess this would be a good time to tell you all that I've been having visions . . . I was planning on keeping it to myself a little while longer, but with this latest revelation of Loki, it only seemed right to come forth now."

"Visions?" asked Konungr.

"Yeah. They're few and far between, but I've had a couple of them now."

"And these visions, what are they about?"

"All of them revolve around Skye. The latest one was of her and Loki sparring together. She was older, maybe a teenager, maybe my age. I don't know. I couldn't see her. All my visions have come from her perspective, but he messed her up pretty badly in the last one. He left her legs all carved up from his spear. It was gruesome. He sliced through her without an ounce of remorse in him. She thinks . . . she thinks Loki is her father. I think she might still be alive, Konungr."

"When did your first vision occur?"

"When I touched that root of Yggdrasil or whatever in the woods, back on Midgard. Well, my part of Midgard, I should say. I'm unsure exactly as to what happened, but I could see the memory from the day she disappeared, all of it coming from her perspective, though. I had another the night that Peter was murdered . . . and the last one came sometime before our dream studies. What does all of this mean? Is any of it real?"

"As I expected . . . but yes, I do believe that these visions are connected with those of Skye. You and her are bound to Loki. Those who guide others into a virgin realm become forever connected. Your consciousness intertwined together like the stars of Yggdrasil."

"So, what does that mean for me and Loki?"

"It means that you and Loki can share thoughts. He has access to them. He always has, and by leading you and Skye into whatever realm he did—it was done by no accident. He wanted access to one of you. By the looks of it, Skye."

"I don't understand what Loki would want from Skye. She was only a kid. What good could she have been to him?"

"That I do not know."

The group sat around silently, everyone's mind buzzing, trying to put together the pieces of Loki's ingenious plan. Konungr dismissed them for the night and told them to be prepared for tomorrow's lesson, stating that it would require their utmost attention. One by one, they made their way to their cots to try to get some sleep, but Michael stayed behind, nestled by the fire, enamored with his thoughts.

His mind was doing somersaults once more, as it frequently did. No longer did he feel like he had any control over his life. Did any of this even matter if it had already been written? Loki had been controlling his and Skye's life since youth, stamping his signature across it, fiddling their lives on a string like a puppet. All of that, for what? What was his motive for Skye? It didn't make any sense. He'd been so enraptured with his thoughts that he hadn't heard Steina sneak up behind him.

"How are you holding up?" she asked.

"Shocked mostly," said Michael. "My whole life just feels like a lie. If Loki's playing god, then what's the point in even trying anymore?"

"I understand, more so than anyone else here. I don't know what he has planned, nor do I know his intentions for Skye, but you can't let him hold that power over you. Believe me, I know."

"I'm sorry . . . about everything. Everything you've had to go through and endure. I know it's not my fault, and I know Konungr said not to apologize for the actions of others, but we have to have empathy, right? I know we've only known each other for, shit, how long have we known each other now? I know you're still keeping count somewhere."

"Three hundred and four days."

"No way. We've almost been here a year now?"

"Yeah, almost."

"It's kind of weird. I mean, everything is weird. My whole life changed ten, eleven months ago, but besides the jotuns and the gods, it's weird being away from technology for so long. I mean, back home or back before Alfheim, I guess, that was a staple of life. There wasn't a moment I spent away from my phone, and now here we are slumming it out in the woods, camping, hunting, and fishing, doing things that I never thought I would be able to do, but it's refreshing being away from it all. Free from the constant feeling of always needing to check your phone, ya know? Well, maybe not. I'm not sure if you have phones on Alfheim but anyways, what was I saying originally? Oh, yeah . . . what you showed back there, that took a lot of courage. You didn't have to show that, but you did. I'm proud of you."

"Thank you, and likewise, I'm proud of you as well. I know the last time that we spoke about your sister, you weren't interested in exploring her disappearance."

"All thanks to you. I wouldn't have shown that day if I had gone first. But after everyone else's projection, it only felt right."

"I hope my future projection didn't scare everyone into thinking that I would choose Loki over the council."

"I don't think anyone thought that. I think everyone was more or less shocked by the suddenness of it. Nobody expected the ending to unfold the way it did, I should say."

"I just fear that when the time comes, I will not be strong enough to defeat him. That I will succumb to his charm like I have in the past."

"You're plenty strong enough, and besides, when that day comes, we will be fighting at your side and if for some reason we are unable, just know that I believe in you."

"Thank you, and I believe in you too, Michael," said Steina, her voice fading as if her mind had drifted elsewhere. "Are you tired?"

"Not really. I don't think I could go to sleep if I tried. What's up?"

"Let's go to the lake."

"Right now?" asked Michael, taken aback. "Just the two of us?"

"Yes, unless you are too afraid." Her smile daring, like gravity amongst the ocean waves, inhaling him in.

"I mean, kind of. I don't know magic yet. What if there's a shark or something out there?"

"The odds of that are one in however many million."

"And do tell, what are the odds of one's sister getting kidnapped by Loki? Or the odds of a Midgardian venturing across the realms of Yggdrasil as if it were no different than a road trip along some county road?"

"Oh, hush," she said, turning around on the balls of her feet. "You coming or what?"

Michael jumped to his feet and followed behind her. "I guess so. Lead the way."

They followed along the path forged across the forest floor, only the moonlight guiding them. After five or so minutes of scurrying through the ominous darkness, they arrived at the lake. The water was blissful as the moonlight danced atop it serenely.

"It's even prettier out here at night," said Michael.

"Agreed," said Steina. "I come here some nights when I can't sleep. Something about the stillness of the water soothes me. With all the war amongst us, it's refreshing to see something larger than you remain so calm and tranquil. The realms may be unraveling into chaos as we speak, but for now, this large entity of water remains unphased, its pulse still composed, still peaceful."

"I used to do the same back when I was younger, and the world seemed to be spiraling out of control," said Michael, scoffing at himself. "The world spiraling out of control. Get a load of that guy. If only he knew what I know now. But yeah, something about the waves crashing onto the shores of the gulf. There's not a better sound in the world."

"Do you miss being back home?"

"Sometimes. I miss my cousin, Emma. She's Peter's mom. I hate that she's living a life without the slightest idea of what happened to Peter or me. I have all this guilt inside of me. If she's never going to have her son back, she at least deserves to know the truth about what happened to him."

"None of that is your fault. I hope you know that. There's nothing you or Reynir or I could have done to stop Loki. You shouldn't harvest that much guilt inside you. Especially for something completely out of your control."

"I shouldn't, but I do. I was a superhero to Peter. He looked up to me in a way I didn't think was possible, and I let him down. The one he counted on to save him wasn't there for him, and that stings. Whether or I could've changed something or not, it hurts."

Steina didn't say anything; instead, she nuzzled herself alongside Michael's arm, falling in place perfectly like a puzzle piece. Michael jolted at her soft touch, startled like a finicky cat, but he quickly gave way to her embrace, letting his guards down and relishing her head against his arm.

He extended his arm around her, forming a sort of side armed hug. Steina wrapped both her arms around his waist, her head falling against his chest, leaving Michael to wonder if she could hear the beating of his heart. Without realizing it, his head fell onto hers, breathing in the intoxicating fragrance of her hair.

The hair on his neck raised, his neck curling. His body loosened, weightless in her arms, melting in her presence. His hand gripped tighter along her hip, inching, grazing further along her lower back. She cozied into him tighter, savoring his touch.

He wrapped his other arm around her, closing them together. Their breathing heavy and relaxed, rolling in waves, their chests cresting in and out harmoniously in a rhythmic manner with one another. The tension mounted between them. Surely it couldn't just be him, Michael thought. She had to have felt the connection between them, but before Michael could act on it, Steina pulled herself away slowly.

"There," she said. "Do you feel any better?"

"What?" asked Michael, visibly confused.

"Hugs, they make everything better."

"Oh. I see. Um . . . yeah, I actually do feel a little better. Thank you," he said somewhat dejectedly, believing that the exchange they had just shared was more intimate than that of friends.

"What do you say to a nighttime swim? Or are you too afraid of the sharks?"

"You think you're funny, don't you?" Michael asked playfully, taking off his shirt and shorts, leaving only his briefs.

"A little bit, yeah," said Steina, stripping down to her undergarments.

Her body was mesmerizing, leaving Michael to gawk at her stupidly, but he simply couldn't take his eyes off of her. Her waist was slender, her stomach tight and trimmed, but her hips were calling his name, and he had to fight every last urge not to think about grasping onto them while he thrusted deep inside her.

The cool water around Michael's waistline temporarily cleansed the lust he had to taste her flesh against his lips. He took a deep breath, his hands quivering, fighting against the nippy temperature. He dove underneath, submerging himself, like ripping off a bandage. The quickest way to do it was all at once rather than tiptoe in.

He waded around, swimming in circles, trying to get the blood circulating in his body. The exercise helped some, but his lips still trembled when he stopped to talk to Steina.

"Do we need to get out?" asked Steina. "You are shivering an awful lot."

"N-N-No," stuttered Michael, his lips shaking. "No, I'm good. How are you not cold?"

"I know a little bit of magic."

"I thought you said you didn't know any magic?" asked Michael, stammering.

"No, I said I wasn't very affluent in magic, but I do know some of the basics," she said, swimming alongside Michael, brushing her body against his.

"What the hell, you're like a furnace. How?"

"Just a simple heating spell. Nothing too fancy."

"Simple, my ass. I wish I could do that. Scooch on over and help me warm up some," said Michael, hamming up his performance, pretending to be colder than he was. Anything to feel the heat of Steina's body against his.

"Like this?" she asked with her chest flushed upon his and her hands along his waist.

"A little closer."

"This better?" asked Steina, inching even closer to him, their bodies pressing even tighter together.

"Eh, a little closer. I'm still a little cold," said Michael, gently pulling her legs upwards and wrapping them around his waist.

"Close enough yet?"

"Almost," he said as his forehead rested upon hers. "My lips are a little cold still. You think you could fix that?"

JOHN STOETER

"Maybe," she said, her lips curling into that hypnotic smile of hers.

Her lips pressed close to his, yet they fleeted, tempting him as if she was daring him to kiss her first. Michael wanted nothing more than to fall into her lips, giving in to his carnal desire. Wanted nothing more than to be trapped inside an infinite loop with this moment playing over repeatedly.

The tension, the butterflies, the infatuation, the look of her eyes, an explosive mixture of lust and passion. A look he thought he would never forget. He embraced the tension between them, letting it build until it could build no longer. His body took over, diving into her lips, but they exuded him at the startling voice of another.

"Mike," hollered Darrius from the shore. "What are you doing in there? Are you alright?"

Mike's back was to Darrius, shielding Steina from view. He must not have seen her, thought Michael. Had he seen her, he would've walked away as quiet as a mouse, pretending to have seen nothing.

Steina unclenched her legs that had woven so perfectly around him and slithered into sight.

"Ah . . . yes," said Michael.

"Oh," said Darrius apologetically. "I'm—that's my bad, I'm sorry. I noticed you weren't asleep and came wandering to make sure you were okay. You know, after your vision and everything. But my bad, y'all carry on. I'm headed back up."

"No, wait up," said Steina. "We should head back too," she said to Michael quietly. "It's getting late. We don't want to be out too long. We will surely regret it in the morning with Konungr being the early riser that he is."

"Yeah," said Michael, the words struggling to escape like he'd just been punched in the gut. "Good point."

220

The three of them walked back to camp, mostly in silence, Michael's head throbbing. Why? Why now? Of all the times for Darrius to interrupt. His body pulsed, pent up, and sexually frustrated to the likes he hadn't experienced since his teenage years.

Darrius slipped off inside the cave, leaving them alone together once more, but the moment had slipped away, a transient bubble of time that popped to the disappointment of both of them.

"Well, I guess it's good night then?" Michael asked, unsure.

"I guess so," said Steina, holding her gaze, her hand lingering in Michael's.

If Michael could read through her eyes, he would guess they still longed to be close to his, wishing to be shut as he kissed her with the passion that only a first kiss could elicit, but he folded. He let her hand go, telling himself the moment had passed and whether it had or hadn't. He didn't want to run the risk of coming on too strong.

He escorted her to her cot, and while he laid in his, his mind did circles, exhausting him. He couldn't sleep with the thought of her body grinding against his. Konungr's powers coming together in the form of a gift and a curse. His past, future, and present colliding into one, kaleidoscoping together.

His past clenched onto him, recalling a memory from his younger years. He was at the pool with Julia Green, a high school crush of his. His subconscious merged with his newfound streaming service, accessing the memory in pristine detail. Her legs swaddled around his waist, just as Steina's had been moments before. He guided Julia through the pool in circles, kissing her, leaving her out of breath as his hands fondled inside her bikini, and then he reimagined that moment, but this time with Steina.

He was infuriated with himself, infuriated with Darrius. He knew his emergence was an accident, but that didn't stop the frustration boiling inside him. His mind was overwhelmed with images of what could have been. He couldn't get the vision of Steina's lustful eyes out of his mind.

He craved her lips, lusting to place his along her navel and work his way down until she begged for him to stop. He laid there envisioning fantasy after fantasy, wondering if Steina was still awake, left with the same hungering desire as him. He let his subconscious take over, surrendering to the heaviness of his eyes. His subconscious left him with a flurry of memories but mostly only fantasies of Steina, leaving him not wanting to wake up when the time came.

Michael awoke the next morning in a mist of confusion and anxiousness, reminiscent of the awkwardness that kindled after a one-night stand. Should he talk to Steina about everything? Was it best to act as if nothing had happened? His mind tormented him with anxiety, wishing that it would just shut up and leave him alone for a moment.

Darrius interrupted Michael's train of thought upon seeing him awake. "Hey man, look. About last night, had I known she was with you, you know I wouldn't have bothered you. I was just worried about you with everything going on with Loki."

"I know, man, I know," said Michael. "But fuck what unfortunate timing. God damn. Motherfucking fuck. You know how long it's been since I've had sex?"

"About as long as me, I'm assuming."

"Exactly. We've been here almost a year. Which makes it over a year for me, dude."

"If that's the case, then I did you a solid."

"How could you cockblocking me ever be solid?"

"Cause if it's been a year, you would've shot faster than me on an iso. And you know how quick I am to shoot a jumper one-on-one. You probably wanna hold off until you learn some magic or some shit. Just saying, as a friend."

"I'm going to punch you."

"Hey man, I'm only trying to help."

"What are we fellas talking about here?" interrupted Reynir with his usual, perky morning charisma.

"Uh . . . baseball," said Michael.

"Yeah, just how we miss the Yankees and shit," said Darrius.

"Ahh, well carry on," said Reynir. "I'm more of a badminton guy myself."

"You owe me, bro," said Michael once Reynir was out of earshot. "I hope you know that."

"Yeah, whatever," replied Darrius. "I was doing you a solid. A blessing in disguise. Let's go get some food."

Their morning routine was normal, consisting of breakfast and yoga until it came time for Konungr's latest lesson.

Steina greeted Michael as if nothing had happened the night before, her poker face on par with that of a world-class poker player. Her presumed disinterest, her ability to turn off her emotions with such ease, as if it were nothing more than a light switch, corroded inside Michael's mind, eating away at him. He kept having to remind himself to focus on the lessons at hand. He'd come too far to get sidetracked as a result of his carnal desires.

"Magic is the universal language in which Yggdrasil operates," stated Konungr. "It's roots infiltrate and nourish across the realms, waiting to blossom inside each and every one of us. Bits and pieces of magic have been practiced all throughout recorded time. Different religions have grasped certain parts of magic—none of them having harnessed it to its fullest.

"Hinduism, Hermeticism, Paganism, Judaism, as well as Native American beliefs, a plethora of religions grasping pieces of magic like straws, worshipping it as a god yet never fully understanding the intricate process of it. And in ways, some of these ancient beliefs are correct.

"As above, so below. As below, so above. Every aspect of Yggdrasil exists as the macrocosm of the universe. The macrocosm of magic. And within that macrocosm lies an infinite number of microcosms. Every existing being is a microcosm of Yggdrasil, just as every being is a macrocosm with endless amounts of microcosms inside, seamlessly working together to keep said being alive.

"To understand the magic of Yggdrasil, one must understand the magic within themselves first. You have only walked along the shore of your subconscious mind. For you to become a magician of extraordinary power, you must tap into that subconscious and grasp ahold of the fear and insecurities that remain hidden inside you.

"I say this because I can read each of your minds as if it were a book, and today Loki presides over all of you," said Konungr, stopping, making eye contact with Michael. "Surprisingly, Loki has not clouded your presence as much as I anticipated, Michael. I expected your mind to be tormented after your alarming discovery, but nevertheless, you seem to be the least preoccupied with Loki."

"Ah . . . yeah," said Michael. "I've been trying to think about other things to distract me."

Konungr stared hard at Michael as if his gaze could pierce his soul. "I see. Your mind is bemused amongst other things," he said, putting emphasis on the word things. "Indeed, it is. Best of luck with your endeavors. I do hope that I have your full undivided attention for today's lesson, yes?"

"Yes, uh . . . yes, sir. Absolutely." Michael's cheeks turned rosy; his face beet red with embarrassment. He felt the eyes of everyone else bearing on his neck. He made it a point to stare forward at Konungr, certainly not making eye contact with Steina.

"As I was saying," continued Konungr. "You must rid yourself from Loki's bond over you, or he has already won before the war has even begun. Likewise, you must rid yourselves of all fears and insecurities, or else you risk them manifesting into the macrocosm, emanating from your thoughts into the physical world before you.

"That's why the mental plane holds such extreme value. Inside it lies your thoughts, your beliefs, your knowledge and wisdom, and within that lies your power. When the concerted efforts of your mind believe that you can defeat Loki and save Alfheim, then you will be capable of such heroic feats.

"If you cannot envision that future or see yourself accomplishing those obstacles, then Loki is already victorious. That goes for anything in life, as well as magic. If you have preconceived notions that a spell is too difficult or that you are not powerful enough to yield it, you are correct, and if the person beside you believes the opposite, they are equally correct.

"It's not to say that a simple can-do attitude means that all is possible. You must work extremely hard on your craft, but any lack of confidence will lead to shortcomings both physically and mentally. I say this because today, we begin our transcendent journey into the art of clairvoyance. A task many of you will fail at. Some of you may never pick up this skill, but if you get discouraged and start to believe that you can't, then ultimately, that will prevail to be true.

"Clairvoyance is the ability to see and perceive past your physical limitations. The awakening of your third eye. An art that none have mastered better than my grandfather, Heimdall. It can be classified into many categorizations—psychometry, astral projection, telepathy. My focus will be on retrocognition—the ability to manifest your or another's past. Precognition—the ability to manifest your or another's future. Telesthesia—the ability to perceive with your third eye rather than your sense organs."

"Wait a minute?" questioned Darrius. "Telesthesia? I've heard of that before. I read about it online one time, but it was classified as remote viewing. You're telling me that's real?"

"Correct."

"What were you doing looking up remote viewing?" asked Michael.

"Bro, I displayed a projection before y'all showing me running around with a psychic. I'd done a little research before."

"So, you were giving me grief on fairies, but you believed in psychics the whole time?"

"Turns out psychics are real, though. What about fairies?"

"Really? That's a technicality. Elves, giants, and gods, that's not good enough for you?"

"But was it fairies?"

"He's got a point," said Steina.

"Okay, I see how it is," said Michael in a tongue-in-cheek manner. "All of you are just gonna gang up on me today. Okay . . . Okay."

"As I was saying," said Konungr, clearing his throat. "In a way, each of you has already experienced a form of retrocognition. You each have access to your memories—

therefore, your past as well. Retrocognition can be dangerous. You cannot change your past or anyone else's. Many magicians have succumbed to the temptation that retrocognition presents. Same as precognition. The old Norse men and women were fascinated with their destinies—the gods as well. You mustn't fall prisoner to your past or your future. Neither can be changed.

"For that matter, I will be focusing on telesthesia or, as Darrius stated, remote viewing. Like everything else, it requires your utmost focus. Any distracting thoughts will result in failure. I have buried three different destinations into the earth—a picture of each lies somewhere beneath. It is your job to find out what these destinations represent by using your second sight."

"How are we supposed to do that?" asked Michael.

"Concentrate on the destinations. Focus solely on these destinations and nothing else. If successful, you will begin to see your intended target—begin to feel that target. When you find said targets—write them down, and we will compare. Begin."

Michael closed his eyes, and like his first practice with Konungr, thoughts swarmed him at once, but now he was stronger and more experienced. He quickly closed his mind, flushing out those thoughts and quieting the mental noise that surrounded him.

Flashes of black and white washed over him, compounding together like the static interference of an old analog television. A blinding white submerged over the static, panning across his mental sight until that subsided and transitioned into the grainy sand beneath him. His physical eyes remained closed, but his inner eye had awoken, burying its way into the dirt like a hedgehog, the grainy sand sending tickles along his spine.

The first picture was blurry and distorted, as if he'd rubbed his eyes for too long. Michael did his best to centralize on the target. His mental nozzles rotating into focus, transforming the hazy outline into a photograph of Alfheim. The photo was taken at the foot of the bridge, before the apocalyptic ruins of Loki and Gullveig. The golden statues that once stood tall gleamed and blended in with the futuristic city. A sorrowing reminder of everything that they were fighting for.

Michael turned his attention to his second target. This time the cloudiness from before had subsided substantially. A crisp picture emerged almost instantly, requiring him with no need to wiggle his figurative antenna bunny ears.

This target was a desert, a typical desert accompanied by barren sand, rolling hills, and cactuses that extended for miles. Michael had never seen the place before, but he could envision it as easily as his childhood home.

He set his vision on the third target, finding it with relative ease. It was another place unfamiliar to him but equally beautiful as Alfheim and the desert before. Large clouds hovered above even larger mountains. A snowy terrain that spanned across the horizon endlessly.

Michael opened his eyes, immersing him back into his physical senses. He felt invigoration flowing inside him, just as he had felt upon mastering the skill of replaying his past memories. He still couldn't cast any spells yet, but it felt incredible to see all of his hard work and training amount to something.

He had the slightest idea of what to expect when Konungr announced they would be practicing telesthesia, but never in his wildest dreams did he expect to excel at the art so quickly, let alone see each target with such a resounding clarity. Sure, he could've been wrong. Those targets could've been an elaborate work of some mental imagery he concocted, but he felt it, like the release of a perfect jump shot or the beautiful *ping* that was heard after an excellent swing of his driver.

When you know, you know, and Michael felt the magic pulsating inside of him. He was absolutely positive that what he had seen had been accurate, and he couldn't wait to dig into the Earth and verify that truth.

He took the quill beneath him, writing brief descriptions of each of the three targets. He finished, laying the quill to rest beside him, expecting everyone to be waiting on him as usual, but to his surprise, he had completed the activity first.

Steina, Darrius, and Reynir were still deep in concentration, deep enough that Michael doubted they had heard him scribbling fiercely onto his parchment. Michael looked up at Konungr for some kind of affirmation, but his teacher remained silent. Konungr stared back with a look of mild amusement, as if to say *good job.*

Michael always felt like somehow Konungr knew who would excel at what categories and seemingly knew which order they would finish as well. He was equally confident that Konungr had been aware of Michael's visions long before Michael divulged them, especially after his latest reading minds tidbit.

Michael sat in silence, awaiting the others. His surroundings were mind-numbingly quiet, but his mind remained ear piercingly loud, boasting his recent successes. Steina and Reynir finished almost simultaneously, within seconds of one another, while Darrius finished a few minutes behind them.

Each of them emerged with the same shocked expression that Michael had finished first, but they were all overjoyed for their fellow companion. Michael would be lying if he said he didn't love every minute of the attention. For once, he was the first to finish a task, something that had yet to happen during their training.

They proceeded to explain the three targets in detail. Michael's descriptions being the most accurate of the three, with

Reynir trailing closely behind him. The pictures were exact replicas of what Michael had envisioned. It was incredible; even Michael couldn't believe the accuracy of them.

Darrius got the targets correct but lacked any of the intricate details that Reynir and Michael had provided. No matter how hard he focused, the photos remained blurry for him, he explained.

Steina struggled the most, missing one of the objectives entirely, but Konungr encouraged her not to harp on the matter, explaining that each member would have varying strengths and weaknesses.

"Again, stated Konungr. "But this time, I have left coordinates. Once obtained, you shall follow them. Let the trail be your guide."

Michael closed his eyes once more; he quickly scoured through the dirt for the coordinates and found them with relative ease. The static that had bombarded him moments prior transitioned into overwhelming darkness, but a magnetic pull attracted Michael towards it.

He followed the pull instinctively, believing it to be the trail that Konungr had spoken of. Remnants of blinding white speckled past his line of vision, blurring like the white lines painted on the pavement of the interstate. He was unable to see the force, but he was able to feel it like the friction created from repelling magnets.

He rode the gravitational pull and gripped onto it as it accelerated wildly. The pressure from the centrifugal forces hunkered atop his shoulders, condensing him against his will. How he was able to grip hold of the invisible force that guided him was beyond him. He didn't even know how to navigate a map, let alone a compass, so the idea of linking on to some foreign space coordinates seemed implausible, but he learned that it was best not to apply logic when it came to magic.

Shit, he thought, he lost concentration. Stars sailed by much faster now, like comets streaking across the night sky. He was skyrocketing out of control, hydroplaning through time and space, unsure of where he was headed, but he knew that he had accidentally abandoned his original coordinates.

He plummeted viciously, hurdling for what felt like miles at a time. He was aviating blind with no steering wheel or guidance, nosediving until he thundered violently into the asphalt. Not his physical self, but the spiritual vessel within him had crashed. He was unsure of how to describe it, but he knew he had to go with it.

Once majestic, beautiful towers and ruins enamored with golden architecture laid crumbled. Dirt clumps and weeds filled and lined the splintered marble slabbed interior. Dead skeletal remains filled the cold and dingy hallway.

Michael ventured forward, grasping the walls and barreling ahead. Eventually, he found a corridor that led him to a much grander and civilized-looking ballroom. There was a feast on display accompanied by large tables that lined across the extravagant hall. Shadowy figures flocked together, conversing and dancing. Most of them were pitch black, the only white being the ominous glow of their empty, filled eyes as if the toddler that drew them forgot to detail their pupils.

None of the beings seemed to have noticed Michael, but he made it a point to skate past them before testing his luck. The dark, hollowed-out silhouettes were humanoid but held no form, lacking anything concrete to hold on to. They were gaseous figures, the things nightmares were made of.

Michael thought the blank white stares were terrifying until he was confronted with the demonic, blood-red eyes of the other shadow figures. Michael refused to make eye contact with any of them. Instead, he focused on things much prettier to the eye, which was few and far between in the desolate and ransacked hall.

More figures existed. These were white and grey rather than the terrifying red-eyed, pitch-black beings from the hall before. Michael hurried by them, refusing to acknowledge their presence. Whatever they were, Michael thought it best to leave them be and mind his own business.

A loud moan was heard straight ahead, a scream plagued with agony. He was unsure of who was behind it or why he would ever voluntarily follow anything so ghastly and horrific, but he knew that he had to.

Michael arrived at the gold-plated door that concealed the harrowing cries. To his surprise, he didn't need to open it. He simply sifted on through to the scream on the other side. There were two gentlemen, one standing tall over the other. A clear battle had taken place between them. Unlike the terrifying shadow figures that he had previously encountered, these beings were both human in shape and stature.

The gentleman who stood tall and victorious was none other than Loki. He held his spear in hand, the same spear he had impaled Skye with. He had the tip of it placed gently against Thor's throat. Michael recognized him from Steina's shared memories.

With a last-ditch effort, Thor reached for his infamous weapon. "Mjölnir," he shouted in desperation. His beautifully crafted hammer soared through the room towards him, barreling through anything that dared to stand in its way.

With his free hand, Loki caught Mjölnir. His wicked smirk spread like wildfire across his face. "Fine. You leave me no other choice but to kill you with your own weapon."

Loki struck the hammer before Thor could plead for forgiveness. He attacked with such force that Thor's head bounced along the tiled surface, spewing blood from his battered skull. He did so until Thor laid unconscious, and then he hoisted his spear high into the air and thrust it forcefully through Thor's sternum.

Michael violently gasped for air, hyperventilating. He opened his eyes to find himself back on Midgard in the comfort of his friends. The group huddled around him, worried for his well-being. Darrius and Steina each rested a hand on his shoulders, doing their best to help him regain his composure.

"Another vision?" Steina asked with distress.

"What's wrong, Mike?" asked Darrius. "What happened?"

"Th-Thor," Reynir stressed behind deep, hobbling breaths. "He killed Thor. Loki killed Thor."

CHAPTER FOURTEEN

RUNIC MAGIC

"You," said Michael, compressing the gigantic knot etched inside his throat. "You saw it too?"

"Yeah," said Reynir. "I saw your silhouette and followed you to Valhalla. That spear . . . that's Odin's spear, Gungnir. I don't understand how it could have fallen in the hands of Loki. You don't think—"

"No, I suspect not," said Konungr, answering Reynir's question before he had the opportunity of asking it. "If Odin were dead, the realms would be in chaos. Surtr would have set Midgard ablaze by now if that were the case. As to how Loki retrieved Gungnir, that I do not know. Are you sure that it was Gungnir and not another spear perhaps?"

"Positive."

Konungr nodded his head quietly, mumbling snippets of words together under his breath. "And Michael, how did you arrive at Valhalla?"

"I don't know," said Michael. "I was following the trail as you said, and I guess I got distracted."

"And this was Loki's first appearance without your sister, am I correct?"

"It was, yes, sir."

"With no connection to your sister, I believe you may have targeted Loki's subconscious without his knowledge. Your bond with him is stronger than I anticipated. As hard as it may be, you must try to tune these visions out. Even if they do involve your sister."

Michael nodded his head dismissively. "I'll try . . . but it's not easy."

"Thor, you said? That was Loki's latest victim?"

"Yes."

"And what about Gullveig? Was she accompanied by Loki's side?"

"No, sir."

"Peculiar, indeed," said Konungr. "Might I suggest some rest for you all. Take the day off and relax. We will pick back up on our efforts tomorrow," he said, leaving them behind and exiting to whereabouts unknown.

They continued their practices in the art of clairvoyance the next day, which in turn transitioned into more strenuous weeks of repetitions until Konungr felt that each of them had mastered the craft to his liking.

Finally, one day they awoke, around the anniversary of them arriving on Midgard, and Konungr instructed them that their time had come to practice physical magic, kick-starting a lesson before any of them could fully relish the excitement of his words.

"Orka," stated Konungr. "That's the energy you feel surging inside of you when you navigate via telesthesia, and it's the same energy you will feel when you correctly cast a spell. The more powerful you become, the stronger the orka inside you becomes.

Every spell has varying degrees of difficulty, and every wizard is unique—having sensitivities that others might not.

"Through different languages and periods of time, spells have an assortment of names attributed to them. Therefore, these spells' names are irrelevant other than the categorization in one's head used for memorization purposes. Incantations can be uttered if you choose, but they are otherwise unneeded unless they help aid in your ability to focus. I will grant you each a wand. At some point, you will no longer need this wand, but for now, I want each of you to use it until I state otherwise," said Konungr, glaring at Reynir, upending any future rebuttals from him.

"There are many reasons for a wand," continued Konungr. "For one, it acts as a barrier, shielding you from the exerting forces of orka. You will find the wielding of orka to be both exhausting and draining, physically, mentally, and spiritually. Your wand acts as a conductor—a form of shock absorption. This way, you can practice for hours on end without overexerting yourself. And second, a wand is needed until you can summon orka at will.

"Let us start with a simple task. With your wand, take a nearby pebble or rock and levitate it off the ground. If you complete that task while others are still working, move along to larger objects until I say otherwise. Envision the act before you and let it manifest into reality. Begin."

Michael cleared his mind or attempted his best effort to do so. Even with all his practice and meditations, he was still a human, vulnerable to the emotions that jostled inside him, and when they did, his thoughts permeated from them, and at this moment, all that Michael could feel was excitement.

The moment that he had been waiting patiently for was emanating before him. Raw, physical magic was at the end of his fingertips, begging to be explored, and he couldn't wait to colonize it and make it his own. His excitement was impossible to eradicate as it etched away at his insides like hydrofluoric acid on the skin.

He focused his attention on the teensiest of pebbles, trying to simmer his excitement while at the same time dislodging the rock in the slightest. He held out his wand as if it were a sword and fenced in the direction of the pebble, attempting to make it move or leap or wiggle, and when that didn't work, he held it as still as can be, not allowing it to slip or waver. He held it with two hands, and then he held it with his less coordinated left hand and even carried it like a pool stick, all in a culmination of failed efforts to make the tiny pebble before him frolic to the slightest degree.

He watched as Reynir juggled tens of rocks, waving his wand flamboyantly like a baton in the hands of a conductor. Not too long after that, Steina's rock danced marvelously in the air, requiring much more strain and focus than that of Reynir. Her rock swayed and bobbed with each fiddle of her hand. Almost simultaneously, Darrius's did the same, leaving Michael as the only one left to have not accomplished the task.

Michael couldn't help but let his infuriation get the best of him. Just weeks ago, he was a master in the art of telesthesia, something undoubtedly harder than moving a stupid little rock, and now here he stood, glaring at the rock, praying that it would move the faintest of centimeters. The hope and excitement that he generated moments before had dissipated, transforming into anger and agitation.

He took a deep breath and cleared his mind, focusing on nothing else besides making the rock move. He closed his eyes and began to envision the rock dancing elegantly in the air, as if it were dangling from an invisible line attached to his wand. He imagined himself waving his wand and the rock obeying his beck and call, flowing up and down with each flick of his wrist.

And then no longer was he imagining it; he could feel it. He could feel the orka inside of him radiate as his body smoldered with power. He felt his wand flex a smidge as if it were a fishing pole with a tiny fish attached to the other end of it. He felt the minuscule weight of the rock pulling at the tip of his wand. He opened his eyes, and there it was, his rock floating four feet in the air, and whichever way Michael whipped his wand, the rock followed with precision.

He reared back and cast the rock tens of feet into the distance. He did that repeatedly until his arms grew tired, and his body swelled from the orka that he had elicited, providing him with the same satisfaction he would get after an intense workout that left his body numb.

Michael had produced magic. Real and honest magic, and prior to that moment, there wasn't a sensation in the world that he could compare it to. It was the highest of highs, a feeling of euphoria and overwhelming pride that could only be understood by the select few that had procured magic. And now he was one of the members of that extraordinary community.

They practiced levitation for weeks, moving onto larger objects as their skills grew stronger. One day, while Michael was attempting to move a rock much heavier than he could physically lift, he stumbled upon something exceptional.

Michael strained and flexed, his wand torquing from the invisible friction created from the large boulder, and then the friction snapped. His wand leaped from his hands, catapulting away from him, and almost instinctively, Michael thought to himself, *oh shit, my wand*, and there it came flying back to him, summoned perfectly to his hand. A wand he no longer needed because he could now hoist magic from within.

After they mastered levitation, each of them no longer required the aid of a wand, which ensured Konungr that they were ready to proceed forth with more challenging lessons. He gathered them around the lake early one morning, detailing their exercises for the following week.

"I'm proud of each and every one of you and the progress that you have all made thus far," said Konungr. "Today, we focus on the element of water and what you will need to harness this element and other elements alike," he said, clenching his hands apart from one another, forming a spherical globe of water between his palms.

"Water can take the form of nearly anything if you will it," he continued, transforming the globe of water into a cube and then into the form of a triangle. "Just as I have done, I want you to summon the element of water and will it into whatever you see fit."

As expected, Reynir did the act in mere seconds, flashing water droplets between his fingers with bravado, making sure that everyone around him was aware of his theatrics.

Fittingly, Steina performed the spell after Reynir, albeit with much less grace. The water between her hands trembled, lacking the concrete form of Konungr's and Reynir's. Her hands wilted beneath the blob of water, fumbling and lacking coordination.

Michael focused, his concentration razor-sharp, but no matter how hard he attempted to summon the element, he was ultimately left short-handed. Darrius appeared to be struggling with the task as well, seemingly unable to materialize any water before him.

"Darrius," stated Konungr. "Why do you believe that you are struggling to summon the element of water?"

Darrius shrugged. "Uh . . . I'm not entirely sure. I'm not doing anything different from our levitation practices."

"And what about you, Michael?" asked Konungr.

"I don't know either," said Michael with a bewildered expression shrouded across his face. "Do you think it's because we need our wands again?" He asked somewhat discouragingly.

"No, I do not believe that will be necessary. I was simply inquiring to see if either of you recognized the reasoning behind your failures. Would you like to inform them, Reynir?"

"It would be my honor, sir," said Reynir, bowing obnoxiously. "Water must come from somewhere—you cannot christen it from thin air."

"Splendid, Reynir," Konungr applauded. "Whether or not you were aware of it, when practicing levitation, you were generating orka internally, from within yourself. Orka exists throughout Yggdrasil, and at times when you are not strong enough to summon that orka from within, you can harvest it from the tree of life itself. When summoning an element, you must have that element present to draw from."

"Like a gigantic lake nearby," Steina teased.

Michael gave her a menacing glare. His eyes connected with hers, both of them holding their gaze. Michael was tantalized by her stare, infatuated with the way her eyes radiated behind her smile.

It had been a few months now since their moment at the lake, and not a day went by that Michael didn't think about that night. He tried to get her alone again, he really did, but between all their lessons and the fatigue that followed those practices, he hadn't had the opportunity. At least that's what he told himself, but gnawing inside his head was the idea that he'd missed his window, yet he made it a point to remind himself that she wouldn't still be flirting with him daily if she wasn't interested.

"And when water isn't present nearby, how can you summon it, Michael?" asked Konungr.

The sound of Michael's name startled him. His attention drifted from Steina and back to Konungr. "I'm . . . I'm assuming that if you are strong enough, you can summon it from a place where you know it resides."

"That is correct, and if you are unable to summon that element across a certain length or distance, what would be an alternative option?"

"You could remote view to survey your surroundings," said Darrius. "Check and see if that element happens to be somewhere nearby."

"Correct, again. Great job, Darrius. Now that both of you have the knowledge on how to attain it, would you be so kind as to demonstrate the spell again?"

Michael closed his eyes, one hand atop the other as if he were gripping an invisible soccer ball. He imagined his top hand as a faucet, a source of power, infiltrating water from the lake and siphoning it between his fingertips. He felt the water swell between his grasp. His hands grew shaky; the water began to kilter off-balance, as if he were holding a glob of jello and expecting it to maintain form.

The water eventually dissipated, like sand dispersing between the cracks of clenched hands, but he had done it at long last. He had summoned water, achieving another form of magic that seemed impossible only a few weeks prior. Michael looked over at Darrius just as his oblong globe of water burst, serenading the ground beneath him, but he had achieved the feat as well. They all had, and Konungr was left brimming with pride because of it.

They spent the next few months bolstering their repertoire of spells. It seemed to Michael that if he could do one, he could do them all. Obviously, there were exceptions. Certain spells required a level of strength he had yet to attain or a level of power typically attributed to gods, but the understanding and administering of each spell had become apparent.

Like everything else involving magic, the key to spellcasting was concentration, reaffirming Konungr's year and a half of tedious, painstaking meditation practices, and thanks to those lessons, his mind had become a concentrated and well-oiled machine.

Michael could now usher his orka however he saw fit, configuring it into whatever fashion he desired. He could propel orka from his hands and levitate for moments at a time, just as Reynir had done in his battle with Ortr. He could generate shields from his orka, fire orka in the form of a blast, using it as a weapon of destruction, even use his orka to heal others. The difficulty was no longer producing spells but holding them.

Initially, Michael and his peers, with the exception of Reynir, could only sustain their spells for a few seconds before succumbing to fatigue. Each spell felt like that last push-up. Michael's hands and arms trembled under the exerting forces until he could hold no longer, releasing whatever magic he had just produced moments before. A few seconds of spellcasting felt like a day's worth of excruciating standardized testing.

As a result of the mental fatigue and exhaustion attributed to spellcasting, Konungr supplied them with ample time for recuperation. With his brain fried to crisps, Michael could only think of mead as an alleviation. That, and Steina, but even the thought of her was far too exhausting to act upon. He mostly found that he wanted solace and a good old-fashioned buzz to quell the anguish of his mind.

He found himself craving those ten seconds of silence. Ten seconds of solitude, of everyone shutting the fuck up, including his own thoughts. It reminded him of those long drives home, where he drove absent-mindedly without even realizing he had been driving in silence.

As they each became stronger, struggling to retain small and minuscule spells became a thing of the past, with each of them now able to hold spells for minutes on end without wearying. They began to master increasingly more difficult spells as well, maturing into their magical sensitivities.

Michael was naturally receptive to clairvoyant and telekinetic qualities. He wasn't powerful enough to read minds like Konungr or communicate with his thoughts, but his susceptibility to ESP was apparent early on, and the more he practiced, the stronger he became in that department. He began to get glimpses of random precognitive and retrocognitive events.

Sometimes, he would be in mid-conversation with his peers, and without intending to, he would get a vision of their past. He tried to control it, understanding that what he had seen was a dire invasion of their privacy, but the images were as involuntary as a yawn or sneeze. Suppressing them only seemed to make matters worse.

Darrius showed a remarkable aptitude for teleportation. Michael could teleport, but the accuracy in which he could do so was as unruly a form of travel as the roots of Yggdrasil. Reynir and Steina were a little better than Michael, but only Darrius could navigate to and from different realms with pinpoint accuracy. The precision with which Darrius could teleport was a rarity that even Konungr was astonished by.

Steina became a maestro of time itself. She spent her free time wielding it to her pleasure, spinning it like the webs of a spider, speeding it up and slowing it down, grasping the intricacy of it, and when she wasn't weaving time, she was practicing shapeshifting. A feat that none of the others were able to accomplish.

Reynir had no outstanding strengths and equally no notable weaknesses either. He was a natural mime, a symbiote that emulated the powers of those who surrounded him. In his peers' presence, he could teleport with the likes of Darrius, access telekinetic qualities as well as Michael, and distort time on par with Steina, but without them, those talents ceased to exist. He was a master of none, and yet a master of all. He was their joker, their wild card in the deck.

They spent months crafting their skills and honing them to perfection. Together the four of them encompassed a full spectrum of magic, utilizing their magical properties collectively as a team. There was only one thing left for Konungr to teach them, and that was the art of ancient runic magic. The thing that they had traveled to Midgard for in the first place. Hopefully, it was the magic that would piece Alfheim back together.

One morning like many others that preceded it, Konungr gathered them around in a semicircle. Beneath him lied an old, beat-up leather bag. He emptied the bags belongings onto the dirt, revealing an array of marbleized and polished stones about the size of one's palm.

Each stone was engraved with letters from the old Nordic alphabet, some of the inscriptions looking more like hieroglyphics than alphabetic characters. All the rocks were asymmetrical. None of them consisted of the same shape. Some protruded more than others, some oval and some more circular. Each stone was uniquely different from the one lying next to it.

Reynir's eyes widened, his jaw dropping slightly. "I've never seen so many runes before in my life. How long did it take you to collect all of these?"

"A few hundred or so years," said Konungr. "But who's counting?" His signature crooked smile hid behind his cracked lips. "Because of that, we must be diligent in our use of them.

For those who don't know, runes are the most magical and powerful tokens the realms have to offer. They were made from the gods and giants themselves. The original runes were crafted from the bones of Ymir, created by the Norns. Once used, they disappear—returned to the Norns to be prepared once again, keeping supply and demand strict and in order.

"You will find the act of casting runes to be relatively simple. That is because you are now powerful magicians. Each rune has varying levels of difficulty. It goes without saying, but the more difficult a rune, the rarer it is. Because of this, you will only practice casting simple and remedial runes, saving the more arduous ones for when they are needed."

Konungr picked up a rune from the pile. He ran his fingers along it, inspecting it carefully before chucking it into the air. The rune dispersed into a cloud of dust and ash, settling into a torch that blazed with fire. The torch levitated, floating into the hand of Konungr. He showed them each the torch before extinguishing it, transforming it back into the rune he held moments prior.

"The rune of Kaun," said Konungr. "Very basic and simplistic. It is a common rune that is as expendable as it is replaceable. This rune allows for multiple uses, whereas the scarcer runes can only be used once before they are returned. Any rune can be carved into the dirt or a tree or even yourself and be cast in that manner, but without the physical rune in hand, it proves to be much more difficult and strenuous."

"So, theoretically, it's possible to cast the most powerful rune that exists without ever having contact with it?" asked Michael.

"Theoretically, yes," replied Konungr. "Pragmatically, no. That would exceed a power far beyond me, or even Odin, for that matter. Typically, the carving of runes is used for common runes such as the rune of Kaun or the rune of Úr. In all likelihood, neither of you will ever cast a rune in this manner because the rune itself will be insignificant to your power or far exceed your limitations."

"Then what's the point of these things ultimately? It seems as if they will be little use to us or too powerful to perform?"

"The carving of runes is a more intricate and challenging process. Having the physical rune in hand can temporarily grant you the wisdom of Odin or the fertility of Frey. As stated, the rarer the rune, the more difficult it will be to cast. As for the importance of a rune, that depends on the person yielding it.

"Before you leave, you will each be granted a powerful rune that at some point or another may be needed. A power that would be unattainable by spells. While the rune of Kaun and the torch it blazes may be insignificant to you, imagine the primitive being who wandered upon it in the harsh winter only to find that his wish for fire had been fulfilled by that ancient piece of magic."

"I get it," chimed Darrius. "Runes are like steroids."

"Precisely. They are shortcuts to magic that may be inconceivable otherwise. Steroids anyone?" asked Konungr with a rune stone in hand.

They proceeded to cast the rune of Kaun, each of them achieving the task with relative ease. After producing the rune of Kaun, they launched the rune of Úr, which manifested the element of water. They released a few more of the easier runes, the rune of Yr, which created an orka shield for protection, and the rune of Isa, which produced ice.

As Konungr had stated, most of the runes that they composed would realistically never be used by them, considering they could summon the desired result by spellcasting. Still, Konungr wanted to implement the process of casting runes upon them for when that day might occur.

After casting the physical runes, they yielded the same runes by sculpting them into their nearby surroundings. This process proved to be more difficult, but overall, it was still relatively easy for them. The remaining runes were too rare to waste, so Konungr spent the remaining lesson explaining them in detail as well as documenting runes that he had yet to accumulate that might come in handy if ever attained.

"The rune of Óss," said Konungr, holding the rune in hand. "Will momentarily provide one with the power and wisdom of Odin and in severe cases may even usher the lord upon your presence. Arguably the most powerful rune in existence."

Konungr picked up another rune, this one embossed with the symbol of a backward 'Z'. "The rune of Eihwaz. A rune that will provide a direct route to Yggdrasil, imparting an entrance to all realms."

"Aye, that's like the little golden gate thingy that got us here," said Darrius.

"Indeed," said Konungr. "Except it leads to Yggdrasil, which is as vast as the cosmos. One can get lost wandering inside, consumed by the enormity of the World Tree."

"Yeah, no thanks. I'll just stick to teleportation."

"Perhaps that is wise. Now . . . onto the rune of Ár," said Konungr, with a different rune in hand. "This rune will emit the power of Frey, soliciting bountiful harvests across the land. It will be essential to the re-harvesting of Alfheim. Nature will blossom as if Frey had flourished the realm himself." Konungr set the rune down, palming another in its place. "And last, the rune of Sól. The rune that will be needed to restore your suns and replenish the malnourished elves of Alfheim. I advise that you wait to use these runes until you are absolutely sure that Loki and Gullveig are not around to extirpate your goodwill."

Konungr proceeded to place an assortment of runes into tiny drawstring bags, handing a bag to each of them. Michael opened his bag and peered inside. The thrill reminded him of opening a pack of baseball cards as a young boy. He reached inside and felt two marble stones in his hand. He pulled them out, recognizing one as the rune of Óss. However, the other rune was unfamiliar to him.

"Damn," said Darrius. "I got that stupid Yggdrasil one. What a waste. I can already teleport to other realms. What'd you get?"

Michael showed him the rune of Óss as well as the rune he had no knowledge of. Steina and Reynir joined them in sharing their runes. Steina had received the rune of Sól and Reynir the rune of Ár, all four having the same mysterious rune that Konungr had failed to mention.

"As you can see, I have provided you each with an additional runestone," said Konungr, interjecting himself amongst their confusion. "This rune is the rune of Mannaz. A rune that can be used to see inside others, but most importantly to see inside yourself. It is the rune you will use tomorrow to journey into the depths of your soul. The last lesson that I have in store for you before returning you to your home in Alfheim. I advise you each get a good night's rest, for it will be needed."

CHAPTER FIFTEEN

THE DEATH OF BALDER

They awoke the next morning jazzed up, each of them excited to see what they might find during their expedition into the depths of their soul. Konungr wasted little time, advising them to cast the rune of Mannaz.

Michael did as he was told and cast the rune, imagining nothing else but the interior of his subconscious, whatever that might look like. Unlike the other runes he had cast, which typically resulted in a loud *pop* and explosion of smoke, the rune of Mannaz remained stationary, levitating above the ground.

Its sleek, brandished white exterior transformed into impenetrable darkness. A black hole that quietly consumed all remaining light, expanding slowly yet articulately like a fire spreading its hands across cardboard. This happened until Michael was shrouded in nothing but darkness, and that's when panic began to absorb him.

He sought ideas quickly, thinking of the element of fire to soothe him, but without any idea of where to pull it from, he ultimately wound up unable. Before another concept could emerge, he was thrust forward with urgency. The wind brushed against his face as if he were accelerating expeditiously, yet his feet remained fixed to what he believed to be the floor.

Light began to trickle past him at alarming speeds until he entered a tunnel of surrounding pictures and videos. Everywhere he looked solicited a different memory from his past, and just as quickly as he acknowledged a memory, it jettisoned past him even faster. It was like catching the blade of a fan while in rotation, for glimpses his eyes could fixate on an upcoming moment only to slip away into another memory that he desperately attempted to grasp onto.

No longer was Michael ascending forward. He was now plundering into a rapid descent, still encircled by the memories of his past. Eventually, the speed of his freefall began to cease, slowing into something more palpable.

Random memories played sporadically about; the lack of organization reminded him of a dream. Things that had relative importance or memories he might expect to see were instead replaced with the time he and his cousin Reed found a go-kart in the woods or the memory of him faking sick in the first grade resulting in him having to eat lunch in the nurse's office, but because he didn't want to be alone, his buddy, Bryan, offered to join him.

The damndest, most obscure memories populated before him, leaving him to wonder why? Even with his newfound ability to recollect his past, these were things he wouldn't dare dream to recall because they lacked any sort of significance whatsoever. Surrounding him were long forgotten inklings of his past; things that in no way, shape, or form defined him or developed him into the man he was today, yet here they were, plastered across his very own *Sistine Chapel*.

His speed decelerated once more, now to a seething water-based boat ride pace, but instead of memories orbiting him, it was a slew of eccentric objects from his youth. All of them maximized to the size of a recliner. He slogged past a cartooned themed baseball, the hand gripper his uncle had given him when he was six, the peculiar bobblehead of a man holding a beer mug that had sat in his grandfather's kitchen all those years, and his handheld digital pet that his mother failed to keep alive while he was in elementary school.

A plethora of outliers that Michael hadn't seen or thought of since grade school paraded past him in droves, forming a surreal display, as if they had been nabbed from the pages of an *I Spy* book until finally, he arrived at a halt, bumping into Steina.

"Excuse me," said Steina playfully. "You better watch it, mister."

"I'm . . . I'm sorry," said Michael, somewhat distractedly.

"What's up with you? You seem tense."

"Nothing. I'm good. That was just weird. Did you just have to relive some of the most random assortment of objects and memories of your past?"

"Somewhat. I mostly traveled by places and memories of Alfheim. What Alfheim was, I should say, not what it currently is."

Beneath them, memories began to illuminate upon the ground like a roll of film. They followed their respective memories, slowly distancing apart but still close enough to communicate with one another.

"Are you thinking of any of this?" asked Michael as he stepped on a frame revealing a memory from his elementary years that consisted of him dropping his cheeseburger on a much older patron's skateboard. A memory in which he shortly thereafter curtailed it out of the skatepark, calling his ride to pick him up, only to leave in the nick of time as heard the older skateboarder seething about the pile of ketchup oozing atop his grip tape. "The memories, that is? They just appear. Randomly. On a whim of their own. I haven't thought of these things in ages."

"No," replied Steina. "I have not recalled any of these on my own volition. They appear to be volatile and undeterminable, but do tell. What did end up happening with the cheeseburger and that skateboarder? That seems like quite the story," she winked.

"Shut up," said Michael, lifting his head and neck to get a better glimpse of Steina's trail of memories. "What is that? Do explain the . . . memory of you reading by the lake with Reynir. Okay, whatever. It appears to just be a memory of you reading at the lake with Reynir. It's not like I can control these things. I haven't thought of that cheeseburger incident in fifteen years. I swear."

"And what of that memory there?" asked Steina, teasingly.

"What memory?" asked Michael, peering down below his feet to see himself kissing Julia in the pool. "Oh, that? I think it's from a movie I saw back on Midgard when I was younger."

"You don't have to hide the fact that you have been intimate with others," scoffed Steina. "Quite frankly, I find it as a relief. I was beginning to think you were more interested in Reynir, you see."

"What? Reynir is . . . he's . . . ?"

"Reynir is what?"

"He likes men?"

"Reynir is attracted to other souls. Men. Women. Jotuns. Elves. Midgardians. Gods. Dwarves. I have seen it all. He is quite the free spirit, and I doubt there will ever be a being that can contain him. Although, he really does have the hots for Freyja for some reason."

"That's weird. I would think it would be the opposite. I would think that someone like him would be willing to settle down."

"Someone like him?" Steina objected.

"No . . . no. Not like that. I couldn't care less that Reynir is into men or jotuns or that he has quite an array of lovers. I'm just saying he's different from us. From me and you and Darrius. He hasn't been hurt like us, has he?"

Steina shook her head no.

"That's what I gathered," continued Michael. "I would think that he would admire the idea of settling down. The rest of us, in some shape or another, have had walls put up at some point in time or still do. He doesn't. To tell you the truth, I envy him. I wish I knew what it was like to live a happy-go-lucky life like that."

Steina remained silent. Her expression was one of someone deep in thought. Michael argued with himself internally on whether he should keep the conversation heavy or lighten the load. He chose the latter. "Anyways, back to that whole into Reynir thing," said Michael. "You find it a relief that I'm into girls?"

"Huh?" replied Steina, her cheeks rosy, flushing with embarrassment.

It wasn't often that Michael caught her off her toes. Come to think of it, he wasn't quite sure that he ever had. This may have been a first.

"I'm just saying," pressed Michael, continuing his assault. "Why would that be a relief, me liking girls?"

"Well, you see, I have this cousin," said Steina, clearly back to her perky self, taking pride and joy in volleying against Michael. "And once this is all said and done, she might be interested in you."

"Maybe you'll have to set me up with her . . . but on second thought, I don't know. If she looks anything like you, then maybe not," smirked Michael.

"Oh, okay. I will be sure to remember that," said Steina, stepping off her memory guide and onto Michael's, pushing him off his trail.

"And what are you gonna do?" asked Michael, wrapping his arms around her from behind.

They tousled and vied for control, enjoying the other's touch until Steina stopped abruptly. "Michael, your trail's gone."

Michael looked down shockingly, finding Steina's words to bear the truth. In the joy of flirting with Steina, he hadn't noticed that his trail of memories had disappeared. "Hmm," he mused. "That's weird. Look," he said, pointing at Steina's track. "Yours seems to still be going strong. We should follow it."

"We? And risk you invading my privacy?"

"Oh, right. I'll look up the entire time. Pinky swear," said Michael, extending his pinky outwards.

"Pinky swear? What is that?"

"It's like an unbreakable swear. It holds the highest of honors."

"And if one breaks that swear, will they lose their pinky?"

"Well . . . no, not exactly."

"Then I'm not sure I see the point if I am honest."

"Yeah, I'm not sure the origin of it, and now that you say it, it does seem kind of stupid. But it holds a lot of weight on Midgard, and besides, you wouldn't want to leave me all alone in the dark, would you?"

"I should. It would certainly serve you right, but I suppose I will allow you to follow me this one time since your cheeseburger memories seem to have disappeared," said Steina.

"My savior. I'll be sure to tell your cousin how generous and noble you are."

Steina rolled her eyes. They followed along her trail, the only light coming from the video clips beneath them. Michael made it a point to stare forward, making sure his eyes didn't wander aimlessly onto her memories. They journeyed in the dark, huddled together closely, for what felt like twenty or so minutes until the memories dissipated, leaving a dark and sinister cave in the trail's absence.

"I guess this is it," said Michael, releasing her hand.

"I guess so," said Steina. "Care to accompany me?"

"Really? Whatever is in there could be intimate."

"It could be dangerous as well. I would enjoy the company."

Michael nodded his head. He held her hand as she led the way to the entrance of the cave. After a deep breath, Steina marched inside cautiously. Michael followed behind her, but the ease that allowed Steina to venture through ceased to exist for him. Their hands separated as Steina entered. Michael pushed forward, but it was as if an invisible force field had been constructed after Steina had passed.

He and Steina both fired orka into the invisible field, but the blasts seemingly degenerated at the touch of the invisible barricade. Steina stepped back through to the other side with the same ease as she did before.

"I suppose this is my journey and my journey only," said Steina.

"It appears to look that way . . . but I'm sure that whatever you encounter in there, you'll handle in stride," said Michael.

Steina looked at Michael as if she were going to respond, but before she was able to, Michael was suctioned into the air, absorbed into the darkness. He ascended back the same way he had come, through his trail of memories, past the inanimate objects, all the way back to where he had cast the rune of Mannaz.

The ferocity and suddenness of his return left him with bouts of vertigo. His equilibrium surely having seen better days. It felt as if he'd just been spit out of the dryer. His stomach twisted in knots, his vision danced with stars, and his knees trembled weakly beneath him.

He looked around at his peers, all of whom seemed to be in the deepest of trances. They each bobbed and swayed on their feet, eyes closed as if they had been possessed. There Steina was, wholly bewitched, whereas moments before, she was as alert and conscious as ever. Michael couldn't help but think that Konungr must have gotten a kick out of watching them eerily mumble and sway while their minds were away, transfixed on the inner part of their soul.

Thinking of Konungr, Michael turned to him for answers. "What happened back there? I didn't see anything. My trail of memories or whatever it is you want to call it just vanished on me."

"The cave only opens for those who are prepared for what they might find," stated Konungr, his voice calm, like waves lulling onto the shore.

"That's bullshit. I am prepared. Do you have another rune? I need to try again. I can't be the only one who doesn't get to visit."

"I regret to inform you that I do not, but now is not the time to brood, Michael. The cave will call to you when you are ready and when it does, be sure to answer. You can cast the rune of Mannaz into the dirt as I am about to do myself. Now come along, there is something that I would like to show you," said Konungr, carving the rune of Mannaz into the arid and gritty sand.

"Did you know that this would happen?"

"I know a lot of things, and even still, there is more to be learned than what I have discovered thus far. Perhaps that was something I did know but, now is not the time to worry." Konungr stuck out his elbow, indicating to Michael to interlock with his arm. "Now, this will be disorienting, I must warn. Consecutive travels to the cave of self can be strenuous, but I have faith that you can handle the vigor's."

Michael nodded his head, not entirely excited to journey back to the dizzying cave in which he had just departed from, but it'd be a cold day in Muspelheim before he denied any wisdom that Konungr wished to impart upon him.

"Off we go," said Konungr with a smile, as if their commute was no different than a brisk walk to the corner store down the street.

Michael grimaced and closed his eyes. His body clenched, hugging the arm of Konungr tightly as they voluted into the depths of Konungr's soul. The stochastic items from Michael's upbringing had been replaced with magic that Michael could only imagine to be revered highly.

Elixirs, talismans, runes, and other valuables sparkled and gleamed on neat and organized shelves. Michael tried to focus on each one individually, but it was as if he was drunk. Their vertiginous arrival had left him seeing double. He was so disheveled that he had to keel onto Konungr for support, but his superior seemed to not mind in the slightest.

Even in his drunken stupor, Michael had the wherewithal to notice that Konungr's subconscious was undoubtedly tidier than his. They trudged past Konungr's collections into his very own trail of memories, stopping at one memory in particular.

"Here it is," said Konungr, fiddling his hand and casting the memory overhead. "I thought this might come in handy at some point."

The memory came to life, surrounding them from every angle as if they were viewing it from the inside of a planetarium. The contrasting brightness mixed with the golden hall of Asgard blinded them temporarily.

Once their vision reemerged, they watched as gods drank and partied, laughing and rejoicing because the god, Balder, was now immortal thanks to his mother, Frigg, who got every element, material, and living thing imaginable to swear an oath not to endanger her son.

Thor swung his mighty hammer, Mjölnir, in the direction of Balder, but each mighty swing missed as if the hammer grew too heavy mid-strike, leaving Thor's tiresome arms flanking along the ground. Heimdall unleashed his beautiful sword, Hofud, upon Balder, but the sword seemingly became dull with every strike.

Gods wielded fire only for it to dance away from Balder any time it neared. Every proceeding element did the same, avoiding Balder at all costs. Arrows flew across Gladsheim, encircling around Balder with precision, but none of them searing upon his flesh.

Balder grew cocky, begging and pleading for a god to so much as give him a papercut. The party ensued as the gods drank more and more, growing more rambunctious with each sip of mead. Likewise, the memory grew hazier with each drunken gulp.

And then the hall grew silent because Balder's blind brother, Hod, with the assistance of Loki, had pierced through Balder's chest with a dart made from mistletoe. The victorious roars of laughter now replaced with a tormenting silence. All eyes laid upon Hod and Loki.

"W-w-what happened?" asked Hod, his voice shaky and strained under the silence.

Loki did not respond. His face turned faint and pallid. His body shook in a convulsing manner as terror began to spread over him rapidly.

"What have you done?" asked a teary-eyed Thor.

Other gods emerged around them, all sharing the same crestfallen expression.

"I—I only did what everyone else was trying to do," said Loki, visibly shaken and on the verge of tears.

Hod began to cry in uncontrollable heaps. A couple of the other gods attempted to console him while the remaining gods glared at Loki with a bristling disgust.

"It's okay," pleaded Loki, desperation knotted into every word. "Everything will be fine. We will all die, and when we do, Balder will be reborn. Better than ever," he said, but the outpour of sinister stares seemed to think otherwise. "Right, Odin?"

Odin emerged from his chair, his face seemingly expressionless, but even as Michael watched from afar, he could see the calm before the storm exhibiting inside of him. A searing hatred was etched into Odin's eyes as he stared at Loki. "There is no reincarnation, Loki. You are a murderer, and for your sinister deed, you will be bonded until Ragnarök rips your soul apart or until the day I grow impatient and seek revenge upon you for murdering my beloved son. Take him away!"

Arms gripped around Loki, dragging his trembling body across the golden hall. "No," screamed Loki. "Release me. You don't understand. Balder will be reborn. How do none of you remember? We die during Ragnarök and reincarnate afterward, breeding a new Allfather every time. I can't be the only one who remembers. Hod! Hod, you have to know I wouldn't do this if I knew it was permanent."

Loki's screams began to drown out the further Thor and Tyr dragged his body across Gladsheim. The remaining gods consoled Hod and Frigg. Odin returned to his chair. His expression remained stoic in a sea of sorrowing and grieving faces.

The vision collapsed, ascending Konungr and Michael back into darkness.

"You were there when Loki killed Balder?" asked Michael.

"No," said Konungr. "This memory long precedes me. I siphoned it from Heimdall some time ago. He willingly parted with the memory."

"Why would he part with it rather than sharing it?

"To forget. To be at peace just as I am about to do myself," said Konungr, motioning his finger into a tight spiral. On his command, his trail of memories coiled together like an old roll of film. "Here, take this. When the time comes that you must cast the rune of Mannaz, take it with you. You may find some of these memories to be of use."

Michael reached out shakily, his hand proving to be impossible to steady. "No, Konungr. I can't. These are yours."

"I insist. The only way to move on is to let go. I have been hindered by these long enough. By accepting my gift, you will be doing me a great service."

Michael nodded his head, unsure how to respond or why Konungr would give him a vial of memories of all people. "Why? Why take me here and show me all of this?"

"Because to see is to believe."

"And what do you believe?"

"I believe in a lot of things. I believe that good and bad can be flipped on its axis based on the perceiver."

"Okay," said Michael, far too perturbed to try to unravel Konungr's cryptic messages. "And what do you believe about Loki?"

"Did Loki intend to kill Hod? Is that what you are asking?"

"I suppose so, yes."

"I believe full and well that Loki intended on killing Hod. I also fully believe that Loki truly was under the belief that gods are reborn upon their deaths. The question is, why does he believe that? If that is true, why does no one else seem to remember? And if it is not true, why does he full-heartedly believe it? There also remains the possibility that he had been bewitched by another god into believing the idea of reincarnation. There is a lot to unfold in that memory."

"And which of those particular scenarios do you believe?"

"I believe that biases can be so detrimental to one's growth that I am unwilling to provide you with my beliefs. After all, it is only an opinion, but by providing you with my opinion, it will grow inside of you and harvest life. That is something that I do not wish to take responsibility for. One must find the truth themselves, or else they have only adopted the opinion of another. Typically, the victor. But I shall say, time is of the essence, and you must get going. Your friends are likely to wake soon, and you shouldn't miss out on their return."

"What are you about to do?"

"I have a little left that I must visit before returning."

Michael felt annoyance bubbling inside him. He was appreciative of Konungr, but it didn't make his riddle-laced tongue any less irritating. He felt like he was being treated with kid's gloves. Surely, even if Konungr revealed his opinion of Loki, Michael was self-conscious enough to form his own opinion on the matter. Then again, maybe not considering he couldn't even access his very own cave of self, said the nagging sliver of self-doubt that nestled inside of him.

"Ready?" asked Konungr, interrupting Michael's inner thoughts.

"Not really, but I guess it's now or never," replied Michael begrudgingly, praying that he could stomach a fourth kinetically disorienting journey.

Before Michael had the opportunity of psyching himself out, Konungr sent him whirling past the collective spells and elixirs, landing him back onto the soil of Midgard to find his peers awake and energized about their discoveries. His stomach churned as if he'd devoured too many sweets. He laid there for a moment, eyes closed, but as a result of the spins, he opened them to avoid getting sick.

Steina kneeled at his side. After revisiting the cave with Konungr, it felt as if his shared memory with Steina was eons ago.

"How are you feeling?" asked Steina. "With you not being able to get inside, I expected you to be back earlier," she said quietly so the others wouldn't overhear.

"I feel like . . . I feel like I do after a long night of drinking where I promise the next morning to never drink again," said Michael.

"That bad?"

"Yeah," he groaned. "I don't think it would've been so bad had Konungr not dragged me back there."

"He brought you back to find your cave?"

"No. I don't know when I'll have the luxury of seeing that. He took me to his own personal cave to show me a memory."

"A memory?"

"Yeah. I think he only did it because he felt bad for me."

Reynir and Darrius ventured over to Michael, who was still curdled into a ball like a drunk person wrapped around a toilet.

"How'd it go?" asked Darrius.

"Not great," said Michael. "I was just telling Steina how I couldn't get in. I hit a certain point and got vaulted back here against my will."

"What the hell took you so long? We were beginning to worry about you."

"After I got back, Konungr insisted that I travel with him to his cave of self," said Michael, keeping his newfound memory of Balder's death a secret for the time being. He felt far too nauseated to strike up that conversation at the moment. "I think he felt bad. I'm pretty sure he knew that I would fail."

"I'm sorry, bro. If it makes you feel any better, you weren't missing out on anything too special," said Darrius rather coyly.

Even though Michael knew that he was lying, he appreciated the effort. "Thanks," said Michael, reaching his hand up to Darrius for assistance to his feet.

"Speak for yourself," said Reynir. "It was incredible. I feel so utterly delightful. The orka that is orchestrating within me is upper echelon. I could fly to Alfheim and back a hundred times right now."

"Somebody has a complete lack of awareness," said Darrius as he glared at Reynir and shook his head. "Let's go to the lake, Reynir, or better yet, we can fly there since you feel so fantastically remarkable."

"Oh, what an extraordinarily splendid idea," said Reynir, placing his arm around Darrius.

"Yeah, yeah, yeah. Just knock it off with the big words, *Webster*," said Darrius, as his voice began to fade the further that he and Reynir trekked.

Michael knew that Darrius was only leaving to give him and Steina a moment alone, another act that didn't go unnoticed and was equally appreciated.

"Man, your cousin is the worst sometimes, you know that?" said Michael.

"Yeah, I'm sorry," said Steina. "He seems to be entirely oblivious to empathy."

"That . . . and he completely lacks the wherewithal of when to shut the hell up," Michael chuckled light-heartedly.

"He certainly has the temperament of a five-year-old, but that's why you have to love him. After everything that has happened, he always finds a way to remain positive."

"Oh, I love him alright. He's just a pain in my ass. He reminds me of the twins . . . my other cousins that live here. He's a pest just like them, but he's our pest."

"That he is. At least you didn't have to grow up with him. Can you imagine how obnoxious a younger aged Reynir was?"

"I don't even want to imagine how unequivocally and extraordinarily splendid a youthful Reynir happened to be. My brain has been through enough already today. Just using Reynir's vocabulary makes my head tingle."

"What did Konungr want to show you?" asked Steina, somewhat hesitantly.

"He showed me the memory of Balder's death. All from the viewpoint of Heimdall."

"Why would he want to show you that?"

"He seems to believe that there is more to that death than history seems to tell. He wouldn't tell me his opinion on the matter, but I think I'm starting to believe that Loki would not have had his part in killing Balder had he known the death to be irreversible."

"I wouldn't be so sure. Balder had an opportunity to live again. If everything in the nine realms loved him and mourned his death, that is . . . and every living and breathing thing did just that except a giantess named Thokk. A giantess long rumored to be the shape-shifting, deceitful Loki."

"But we don't know for a fact that he was Thokk, do we?"

"No. That we do not. Do I sense a growing feeling of remorse for Loki?"

"Fuck no," said Michael, his eyes searing red with hatred. "I will kill him if it's the last thing I do. For what he did to Peter. For what he did to you. To Alfheim. I saw him with my own eyes tear down Alfheim and kill Heimdall. And I fail to believe that on his dying breath, Nillbeck chose to lie to us. He's gonna pay, and when he does, I will have him beg for forgiveness only to take his head clean off before he has the opportunity to do so. I mean every word of that.

"I also mean it when I say that something isn't adding up with this story. Maybe Loki is just a phenomenal actor worthy of Oscar's galore. But the three times I've seen him plead his innocence, I have believed him. The memory you shared, his plead to Heimdall and Frey on Alfheim, and now Konungr's memory. He truly does seem to believe in reincarnation, and I think that's reason enough for us to try to find out why."

"I agree. I believe that is something worthy of our attention, but I wouldn't bother putting too much stock into Loki."

"What do you mean you wouldn't put too much stock into Loki? He's supervillain galore. He's the stuff comics books are made of. He's responsible for the ruins of Alfheim."

"Yes, in that regard, he is worth every ounce of caution and vigilance that we have to offer, but he isn't worth your every waking thought. Trust me, I have been there and done that. You can't let him consume you. It is a poison better left alone."

Michael felt his blood begin to boil. It seemed that no one understood his searing hatred for Loki. Then again, no one else saw the visions of Loki that plagued his mind at night, the dreams of Loki tormenting his sister. It's not that he enjoyed pondering about Loki. He simply couldn't help it with the god invading his mind every couple of months.

"You have a point," grumbled Michael, trying his hardest to contort his face, not to reveal the disdain he convincingly held in his heart. "So, what did you end up seeing back there?"

"A lot about myself that I had never been aware of. Rather, a lot of things I had not been honest with myself about."

"At least you had the opportunity to see those things."

"I have faith that you will find yourself soon enough. You are far too hardheaded not to."

"Yeah, I guess. It just sucks being the only loser out here unable to do it."

"I don't think you are a loser."

"I feel like one, that's for sure."

"Perhaps I could help ease your mind," said Steina, nuzzling tightly into Michael's chest.

"I think," said Michael, losing his train of thought as Steina grazed her hands along his ribs and waistline. "I think I would welcome that."

"Yeah?"

Her eyes felt like magnets, embroidering themselves into Michael's soul. "Yeah. I think it's about time," said Michael, leaning into her smoothly, placing his left hand on her right hip and pulling her towards him gently.

His right hand grazed upon her left cheek as he inched closer to her lips. The same lips that had eluded him for so long. They were close enough to feel each other's breath, hot and heavy, upon one another, and as smooth as Michael felt in that moment, Steina was smoother. She froze time in place, utilizing her signature ability to perfection.

"Speaking of time," she smiled, complimenting her radiating beauty and confidence. Her eyes danced in the sunlight, sparkling like fireflies in the night. "Catch me if you can." She turned on her heel and waltzed ahead to the lake, leaving Michael to marvel behind.

Michael stood frozen in place moments longer than needed. He was free from her grasp yet, still captivated by her charm. He followed her to the lake where he found the rest of his companions, and it was there that they enjoyed the day together.

After their morning expedition to the lake, they strolled back to camp where Konungr awaited them. The day was still young. The sun shined high overhead, peaking through the branches of trees, casting elegant shadows upon the forest floor.

Konungr bore a bittersweet grin, a grin that none of them had ever seen from him before. A grin that didn't need any level of mind reading to comprehend. Their time with him was finished. There were no more lessons, no more early routines or practices. This was it—their last day of school.

And just like that last day of school, that bittersweet feeling swelled inside of Michael's chest. Happy to be done but sad to have finished intertwined into one singular emotion, and at that moment, Michael knew just how much he would miss his time here.

It was something that he was blinded to at the time but now, seeing it all being stripped away seemed to provide clarity to just how important his time had been here, how vital Konungr had been to him. It was just short of two years since they had arrived on Midgard, and in that time, they learned ancient thousand-year-old magic, and without realizing it, they each grieved and healed from the losses that they had suffered on Alfheim.

Friendships had blossomed into beautiful, budding relationships, making them stronger than ever, and it was in that regard that their strength lied and now their reprieve was over. It was time for them to get back to the real world. The idea of enjoying the ride rather than the destination never resonated more with Michael.

"Let's not make it hard on the old man," smiled Konungr, his eyes wet and his arms outstretched wide.

They each cuddled into his grasp, everyone bear-hugging one another tightly. After a long embrace, Konungr turned to them and steadied his final goodbyes.

"Care to lead the way, Darrius?" asked Konungr. His eyes were still on the verge of overflowing, but the exuberant joy he exhibited could still be found inside the held-back tears of his.

"I thought you'd never ask," Darrius responded. A look of fury and concentration built across his brows as he navigated across realms until he found the broken frontier of Alfheim. A bright and emanate portal now stood before them. The dusky twilight of Alfheim appeared inside, looking ghastly and unwelcoming. "We have room for one more, sir. If you'd like to accompany us? We could sure use the help. Even if you wanted to retire . . . we would always welcome your company."

"I'm afraid not," said Konungr. "I belong here. This is your battle. You each be the hero I know you to be. Alfheim is in good hands."

Darrius nodded. "We're gonna miss you. When it's all said and done, we will come back and retire here and drink the rest of your nasty ass mead."

"I look forward to it," said Konungr, his smile proud and trembling. He gestured them forward and watched them as they ascended into the portal, becoming entrenched into the remains of Alfheim.

Chapter Sixteen

Date with Surtr

The once exquisite vacation destination of Alfheim looked much worse than when they had left it. The false sun had waned almost entirely, leaving Alfheim with bone-chilling temperatures. The departure from Midgard to Alfheim felt like leaving the coziness of one's home during a harsh winter storm.

Their exact location was unfamiliar. It appeared as if it had once been a populated and habitable area, but now it was nothing more than piles of brick debris and ash. Mountains of infrastructure and rubble lined the landform. They walked mindlessly with no sense of direction, taking in the leftover destruction that had yet to be cleaned or renovated. None of them expected Alfheim to be restored when they returned, but none of them remembered it being quite this devastating either.

It was tempting not to unleash the rune of Sól immediately, but they heeded Konungr's advice to wait. They only had one opportunity of restoring Alfheim's sun. They needed to be precise with their timing, making sure that Loki and Gullveig could not come and decimate it as quickly as it had been assembled. A miscalculation on their end would result in a failure of catastrophic proportions.

"All personnel is stationed near Skirnir," said Reynir, breaking the silence. "Ezra and Solfrid included."

Steina let out a long sigh of relief. "I'm so happy to hear they're still alive."

"Me too. I know the terrain best. Let me guide us there," said Reynir, crafting a portal leading them to the shores of Skirnir's Cove.

They stepped through to the place where it had all started for Michael, but this time instead of being greeted by the enrapturing beauty of Skirnir's Cove, he found himself face-to-face with an army of hurricane relief-style tents. The area looked like a biohazard experiment gone wrong, now in the midst of a full-level quarantine.

Lined along the perimeter of their settlement were rows of the dead, repugnant dark elves that Alfheim was prophesized to become. By the looks of it, Alfheim had certainly had their hands full while Michael and his peers had been away on Midgard.

They entered the largest tent there, immersing themselves in the loud coughing and hacking of the elves inside. The overwhelming majority of elves were bedridden, too weak and frail to do anything else. Ezra spotted them at the entrance and hurried to greet them. A cheerful greeting was in order. After all, it had been close two years since they had last seen her, but Ezra was in no mood for such an exchange of pleasantries.

"This way," said Ezra, stern-faced and tight-lipped. "Solfrid is in unwell."

She guided them through the large tent into a smaller tent that was isolated in the back-right corner. Ezra unzipped the zipper of the compartmented tent and quietly ushered them inside. Solfrid looked as if she'd aged hundreds of years.

Her face spread with aged and pruney wrinkles, reminiscent of a dried-up raisin. She laid there lethargic, unable to move her body, but she was able to motion the council to her bedside by using her eyes. "Launch sun," she muttered softly under her breath.

Steina sat at the beside of Solfrid, gently grasping her veiny, arthritic hand. She looked at her with both a mixture of admiration and grief.

"We must break the curse of Nidavellir by launching its sun," said Ezra. "That is what Solfrid saw as she drank from Mimir's well."

"What did it cost her?" asked Steina worryingly. "Drinking from the well?"

"That she did not say, but she has been persistent in the fact that the only way to save Alfheim for good is by resurrecting the sun. In doing so, we will eradicate Loki's army of dark elves and save two realms. Alfheim and Nidavellir."

"Loki has an army of dark elves?" asked Darrius. "Since when?"

"That I am unsure, but allies have informed us that he and Gullveig are stationed on Nidavellir. It is there that they have gathered their army and are plotting their attack on Odin."

"Are you sure they're on Nidavellir?" asked Michael. "My visions have shown Loki in the halls of Asgard."

"Visions?" asked Ezra.

"Yeah, I've been having them since I arrived here. They've become more prominent as of late, and they only feature Loki or my sister, but my latest vision showed Loki on Asgard."

"That may be well and true, but our intel explicitly stated that Loki and Gullveig have made base on Nidavellir."

"What do you suppose we do with Loki and Gullveig conveniently located at the one place we need to be at? I'm sure that's a coincidence," said Michael sarcastically.

"Whatever we decide to do, it must be done fast," said Reynir. "Our people won't make it here much longer. I took for granted the severity and spread of this curse."

"We can take them all to Midgard," replied Darrius. "I can teleport them to Konungr. They'll be safe there. There's a sun in place to replenish them. If we need an army to invade Nidavellir, then we're gonna need them healthy. It's our only choice."

"The elves are too weak. They wouldn't be able to withstand the rigors of portal travel in their current state. They wouldn't make it."

"How long have we been gone for?" asked Steina, still nurturing Solfrid at her bedside.

"Four months," said Ezra. "That is all it took for things to unravel to the nature that you see now. What of Konungr? We expected him to accompany you back and help us."

"That was the plan," said Reynir. "Instead, he trained us. I am stronger than I have ever been before, Ezra."

"I certainly hope so. We could use your assistance in healing."

"Absolutely," said Darrius. "Where would you like us to start?"

"We can go help the others," said Ezra. "Steina, that will leave you alone to heal Solfrid. We will revisit our plan in the AM."

"No," Solfrid whispered faintly. "Must help others."

"No," said Steina, caressing Solfrid's face. "We are helping you. End of discussion. You are going to make it, Solfrid. I promise," she said, resting her head gently onto Solfrid's chest.

Solfrid gave the weakest of nods and closed her eyes. Steina nodded as well, silently expressing her appreciation to the council for the alone time with her mother figure.

Despite much resistance, Reynir convinced Ezra to get some rest, insisting that they could manage the load for the night. One by one, they went to the sick elves, exerting their orka upon them and replenishing them, alleviating the elves just enough to buy them some additional time before they turned.

After aiding all the elves in the shelter, Michael was mentally and physically depleted. He thrust himself into a nearby cot, succumbing to the exhaustion that vanquished him, orienting him to another visit from Loki.

This time, just as every vision prior, Skye was older than the last time Michael had seen her, and for the first time, Michael got the opportunity to see his sister's face again as she stood before a mirror.

Her appearance was maybe that of her early twenties. Potentially this was the present-day her, he thought. She was stunning, her beauty resembling that of their mother in her younger years. However, her beauty was not appreciated by Skye herself.

Michael could tell by the way she looked into her reflection that Skye only noticed one thing about herself, and that was the scars that tormented her. Her hands felt along their jagged, uneven spines. Her face wilted from years of battle and abuse at the hands of Loki, but even then, she hid the trauma well.

The hall in which she resided was unfamiliar. It gleamed and glimmered of the shiniest silver one could imagine. Loki emerged between two large, silver-plated doors and Skye turned around swiftly to greet him.

"Father, what shall we do with Konungr now that the others are gone?" asked Skye.

Loki sat in an extravagant chair, chiseled in glistening gold. He sharpened Gungnir, his beloved weapon of destruction. The spear that he impaled Skye with, the one he used to kill Thor. The same spear that Michael vowed to kill him with in the future. Beneath Loki were two behemoth-sized wolves. The monstrosities were bigger than any wolf Michael had ever seen, whether on television or in real life.

"We shall assemble the finest army of fire demons from Muspelheim and have Surtr lead the masses," said Loki. "Maybe even, I will be so enticed to join in on the fun," he said, as a sinister smirk spread across his face. "Konungr will be extinct soon enough, daughter."

"What of his disciples?" she asked.

"What of them?" Loki asked dismissively. "They are of no challenge to me. Not in the slightest. Besides . . . let's just say that we desire the same thing. We lust after the same affair, whether they know it or not."

"Can I journey with you to Midgard? Please, father. I've been locked up here for ages. I only wish to make you proud, and that is something that I cannot do as a prisoner locked away."

"And one day you will, darling, but for now, you wait."

"This is so unfair," groaned Skye. "I do nothing here. I'm a prisoner! I'm ready to fight at your side. Please let me prove my worth to you, father."

"Watch your tone," shouted Loki, backhanding Skye across her face.

Skye immediately brought her hand to her face to comfort the swelling. "I'm sorry, father. Please, forgive me," she said in a soft, dejected whisper. She stared at her feet, unable to meet Loki's gaze.

Loki snatched her by the hair, forcefully lifting her head high enough to maintain eye contact with him. "Look at me when you speak to me, child."

"I said I'm sorry, father. Please, forgive me."

"That's better," said Loki cheerfully. "What's the only rule while I'm away?"

"Don't sit in your throne. You are the only one worthy of Hlidskjálf, father."

"Yes, dear. I believe that I am," said Loki patting Skye on her head delicately.

Michael awoke in a fit of vehemence, a fervor for bloodlust. The whole vision left him seething. Loki's demeaning manner in which he treated Skye. The audacity to put his hands on her only multiplied Michael's lust for revenge.

He replayed it over and over that night, unable to sleep, and every time he repeated his vision, he was met with more infuriation of the event. He stirred in his wrath until he couldn't see straight. From there, he set the vision aside, trying his best to cool down and focus.

What could he and Loki possibly have in common? There is nothing in any of the nine realms that he and Loki could mutually desire together. Unless Loki himself wanted to be slain by Michael, that is. Michael was at a loss. What on Midgard was he talking about? And Gungnir, Renynir had been explicit in the fact that the spear was Gungnir and not another.

How could Loki have retrieved the spear from Odin? If Odin was dead, surely the realms would know it. Was Loki keeping him prisoner, along with Skye? Insomnia plagued Michael the rest of the night, but he knew two things for sure, he was going to save Skye, and Loki would pay for his latest acts of vileness.

Michael rose from his cot at the earliest sign of sunlight, desperately hoping to find another early riser like himself, but Michael appeared to be the first person up. Like a child on Christmas morning, he spent his time anxiously waiting for the others to wake.

One by one, his fellow council members slowly awakened. Peculiarly enough, the order in which they woke seemed to match their stamina and vitality levels. Ezra stirred first, appearing to be significantly sharper than the day before. Michael was sure that their arrival had something to do with that. Last night was more than likely the first night she hadn't spent cowered over Solfrid, nourishing her back to health.

Darrius awoke next. He seemed a little more fatigued than usual, but nothing a morning cup of coffee couldn't fix. Reynir looked the worst that Michael had ever seen him. He clearly lacked his familiar flamboyant and charming personality, but all in all, he seemed to be okay, just a little more tired than usual. On second thought, a morning without Reynir's chirpy routine of karaoke was surely appreciated.

Steina looked the roughest of them all. Michael wondered if she had been able to get any sleep last night. Her eyes were puffy, drooping with dark, baggy circles underneath. It looked as if she spent her entire night mourning as she watched over Solfrid. Her skin was paler than usual. Her energy was noticeably languid, and her body sluggish.

Michael waited for everyone to eat breakfast and sober up from their grogginess before breaking the news. "I had another vision last night," he said, wasting little time cutting to the chase. "Loki plans on sending Surtr and an army of fire demons to attack Konungr. He even claimed that he might pay a visit as well. We need to get back to Midgard asap and warn Konungr."

"Any sign of Gullveig this time?" asked Darrius.

"No. I have still yet to see her in a vision. Only Skye or Loki."

"That makes sense considering your ties are to your sister and Loki, but I just find it weird you haven't seen her at least once."

"I agree," said Steina. "Surely, Gullveig wouldn't dare miss out on such festivities. A fight at the side of Surtr sounds like something she would beg to be a part of."

"And maybe she is a part of the plan," replied Michael. "All my visions between Skye and Loki have been intimate and solely between them, but I wouldn't put it past Loki to be hiding a child from her. It looks as if Skye has been locked away all of these years."

"Where were they this time? Do you know?"

"I don't know. Some hall made of silver. Skye said something about some throne called Hlidskjálf. I don't know if that rings a bell to anyone."

"Valaskjálf?" asked Reynir. "What would Loki be doing there? That is one of Odin's halls. First Gungnir, now Valaskjálf. What in Odin's name is happening on Asgard?"

"I don't know, but that's my second vision of Loki on Asgard, which is why we must warn Konungr immediately. We should gather our things now and leave."

"I agree, but somebody will have to stay behind to protect Alfheim," said Darrius. "It would be smart if two or three of us did."

"I will stay," said Steina, volunteering instantly. "I'm sorry. What I meant to say is that I would like to stay behind with Solfrid. If that is okay with everyone?"

"I will stay as well," said Reynir. "As it is, Steina and I are weaker than the three of you. Even just one day here with no sun has weakened us. We would do more harm than good in our current states, but together we can aid and replenish the elves here."

Steina nodded her head in agreement. She glanced at Michael briefly before gazing upon the rest of them. "Please be careful. Get in and out of there as quickly as possible. Don't be foolish and stick around longer than needed."

"I know," said Michael. "We will be back in no time. Hopefully, with that stubborn old man at our side."

"Then it is settled," said Reynir. "Michael, Darrius, and Ezra—you three retrieve Konungr and get him back here safely. Steina and I will keep guard in the meantime."

"Sounds like a plan," said Darrius, promptly deploying a portal before them. "All aboard. To Midgard and back."

The three of them entered the portal, journeying back to Midgard, not even twenty-four hours since their departure, and for all they knew, months could have passed during their check-in on Alfheim.

"Damn, I'm good," said Darrius boastfully after successfully teleporting them with pinpoint accuracy.

They arrived to find Konungr sitting in front of his cave with his legs crossed and his eyes closed, deep in meditation. He was damn near naked, leaving only animal pelts to cover bits and pieces of his torso and waistline.

He looked like a full-on berserker, the kind one would hear about in the Viking myths and legends. A gold-plated helmet covered his face, looking as if it were wearing him as opposed to the other way around. Their time on Alfheim must have been long enough because he now adorned a fully manicured and braided beard.

"You shouldn't have come," warned Konungr.

"You should know us better than that by now," said Michael.

"We've come to help, and we're not leaving here without you," said Darrius.

"I'm afraid you're too late," Konungr countered.

"Then we fight at your side. One team, one fight."

"I've lived more in my life than the three of you combined. My time has come and gone, and I accept that fate. Head back to Alfheim while you still can. The battle has only begun. Go home and win the war." Konungr closed his eyes, and when he reopened them, they were the color of a blinding blue and white that swallowed his pupils entirely. "They are here," he said, as electricity radiated around him.

On cue, fire demons began to encircle the forest in droves. The sight of them left Michael trembling in fits. Goosebumps crept along his back and arms as he eyed the creepy sleep-paralysis-looking demons of his nightmares. It was as if the gates of hell had opened before them, and out came hundreds of eight-footed lucifer's flying around, adorned with wingspans the size of the average sedan.

Konungr soared towards the demons, flying with radiance. He released an array of electrical energy from his hands that shocked the army of fire demons, chain linking them together with bolts of lightning that tangoed from one to the other until all the fire demons surrounding him had been vanquished.

The ease in which Konungr had dismantled his assailants helped loosen up some of Michael's nerves, but he still wasn't overly excited about battling against the ominous beings.

"Watch your six," yelled Darrius. "We've got company."

Too late to be scared now, thought Michael as the fire demons began to storm away from Konungr and into the council's direction. There were roughly twelve of them, but ultimately, they were moving too fast to count. Darrius swiftly teleported behind the incoming flock as Ezra flew to the sky above.

Michael waited front and center for the army's arrival. He summoned orka between his hands, preparing for their imminent attack. The adrenaline mixed with the orka pushed away any remaining thoughts of fear. His actions were too impulsive to have any thought behind them. His fight or flight giving way to his innate desire to fight for his and his companion's lives. "Now," Michael shouted to Darrius as the army drew closer.

Darrius created a portal directly behind the incoming army. Michael released his orka into one powerful blow, blasting the squadron through the portal for Darrius to close behind them.

"Nice work," Michael shouted. "Where'd you send them off to?"

"Florida," Darrius winced.

"Like Florida, Florida?"

"Yeah, it was the first place I could think of. I panicked, okay?"

"I can see the headlines now. *Florida man finds extraterrestrials while high on meth.*"

"Well, it looks like I'll be getting a do-over. Watch out," said Darrius motioning towards another swarm of demons that were emerging their way.

"Again," screamed Michael, blasting a trio of demons through another one of Darrius's portals.

This time the portal closed and reopened in front of Darrius, who promptly blasted them back at Michael. Michael discharged multiple orka blasts at the incoming demons, catapulting them into the ground violently.

Two more demons mounted upon Michael from the shadows. Michael thrust his hands apart, sending both fluttering through the air into a portal created for each of them. Darrius closed both portals meticulously, disemboweling them both at their waistlines, sending the bottom half to god knows where while the top half thudded across the ground like zombies.

"Happy now?" asked Darrius.

"Much better," said Michael. "Look, you even made some crawlers."

"Some . . . what?" Darrius asked, perplexed.

"Crawlers. Like *Call of Duty*. The zombies, you know?"

Darrius rolled his eyes, but their feel-good moment was only temporary.

Another wave of demons surged before them. This wave more immense than the last. There had to be hundreds of them. The onslaught seemed to have no end. The teamwork that the council had exhibited before was placed on halt as each member began to experience more demons than they could physically handle.

Michael blasted his orka at a surging group of demons. His attack proved to be successful as it barreled them backward. He turned around swiftly at the sound of another group emerging. Before Michael could initiate an attack, he had been flanked from all corners. Twenty to thirty demons circled around him like the minutes that surrounded a clock.

Michael swiveled around desperately in circles, firing blasts of orka rapidly like a sprinkler system at work attempting to nourish every blade of grass. For a moment, his attack kept the demons at bay, but his strength began to wane, and the army only doubled in numbers. Before Michael realized it, he was on the floor with his hands above his face, bracing for protection.

There were too many to count. The demon's piercing shrieks deafened him. Saliva and slime drenched along his body as they mounted atop of him. He felt carnivorous bites along his torso as the demons gnawed along the entirety of his body, in too many places for Michael to feel individually. He just felt a collective burning sensation as teeth and claws etched into his skin, flaying him alive.

The snarling breath of Surtr's demons was repugnant, leaving Michael nauseated. The combination of their putrid scent and his loss of blood left him concussed and seeing stars. His vision faded, forming into a vignette of black. With his eyes closed, he blasted orka in desperation, unsure of where his attacks were landing, but ultimately, it proved to be to no avail. He was outnumbered, on the brink of death, and without an escape.

An abrupt thought formed within, a desperate attempt to save his life. The rune of Óss remained nestled in his pocket securely. If he could just use his telekinetic ability to cast it, he would be safe. A flash of white panned before his eyes before he had the opportunity to do so. The blast was blinding, so much so that for a moment, Michael believed he had died and ascended to heaven or Valhalla. It didn't matter which one, anywhere that would get him away from his current, insufferable state.

He felt hands caress across his body soothingly, and suddenly it felt as if everything in life would be okay. His wounds had been healed. The excruciating pain he had felt before had dimmed to a mild and simmering pain. A pain that coincided more along the lines of a stubbed toe rather than the hundreds of menacing bites he had received.

Michael opened his eyes to find Konungr. The battlefield was plastered with the fire demons he had slain, but it appeared that Konungr had arrived at the council members in time to save them.

"There's too many," said Konungr. "You must leave."

"Then come with us," said Darrius. "We aren't leaving without you."

"We can go to Alfheim and regroup there," Michael pleaded. "It's the only way. Please, Konungr."

"They will only follow me," said Konungr, closing his eyes and meditating once more.

Konungr, with his palm outstretched, summoned Hofud, the sword of Heimdall. The blade landed in his hand with a sense of belonging, and just as quickly as it arrived, Konungr thrust it back through the air, letting it helicopter its way through every incoming demon, decapitating them with grace and harmony. The satanic heads fell to the floor, thunking to the surface in unison as their bodies fell shortly after.

"I advise you to leave before it is too late," said Konungr, retrieving Hofud back into his possession.

As if Konungr had spoken it into existence, a portal of incredible magnitude opened before them, and through it existed the harshest, most intense heat imaginable. The council, Konungr included, quickly displayed force fields, protecting them from the scalding heat of Muspelheim. Like solar flares, wisps of splashing heat and lava danced in between the portal, melting everything that encountered it. Trees went up in flames faster than a matchbook, transforming the forest into a conflagration.

Surtr stepped out of the portal and onto Midgard, vibrating the ground with every thunderous step he took. His footsteps left valleys along the battlefield. He towered hundreds of feet in the air, taller than ten Ortr's standing atop of one another. His body was engulfed in blistering hot flames, too bright for the eyes to withstand. He carried Frey's legendary sword in his enormous hand, making the blade look more like a toothpick rather than the fearsome weapon that it was. He dropped the sword, letting it go to battle on its own.

The sword targeted Konungr and began to attack him fiercely. Konungr dodged out of the way of the sword's strike, eluding the blade's skillful attacks. Konungr matched the blade's swordsmanship, etching closer to Surtr with each strike, trying his damndest to attack the fire giant.

Based on the legend, Michael knew the sword of Frey would fight forever, never growing tired until it was told to stop by its owner, or its owner had been slain. Konungr's only hope of outlasting the sword would be to defeat the all-powerful ruler of Muspelheim.

Surtr trudged forward, blazing his flames upon everything in sight, spreading fire with the same regard that trees dispersed pollen in the spring. What was once a beautiful forest was now a volcanic, molten pit of hell resembling the apocalyptic Armageddon Michael had grown up imagining.

Trees began to topple left and right. An immense tree collapsed before Ezra, but she managed to dodge it efficiently, flying quickly to her left, right into the path of Surtr. Surtr swatted his monolithic hand at her, striking Ezra across the battlefield hundreds of miles per hour into a tree that had yet to lose its roots. She dropped limply to the floor like a fly beaten by the swatter.

Darrius immediately teleported to her, with Michael trailing loosely behind him. He felt along her neck worryingly, frantically searching to find a pulse. "She's breathing," said Darrius.

"Good," said Michael. "Send her back to Alfheim."

Darrius urgently crafted a portal for Ezra. He picked her up gently with the assistance of Michael. Together, they delicately placed her limp body inside the portal, guiding her back to the safety of Alfheim.

"We need to go," said Darrius, restraint spreading across his face like the wildfire that consumed them.

"No," said Michael. "We gotta help Konungr. I'm not leaving here without him."

"We can't help him, Mike. There's nothing we can do to stop Surtr. We need to leave now before Loki arrives."

"Then I'll die trying. I can't live with myself knowing we fled for safety as Konungr died. I'm not leaving."

"It's suicide, Michael. We have to go, now," Darrius shouted assertively.

"Then go. I won't stop you . . . but I'm staying here," said Michael, turning his back on Darrius and focusing his attention back on the battle between Konungr and Surtr.

Konungr was still managing to hold his own in combat against Surtr and the sword of Frey. With every block of Frey's sword, Konungr rapidly attacked at the heel of Surtr, like a chihuahua nipping at one's feet.

"Surtr's heel," said Michael. "If we can take that out, we can beat him, Darrius. That's his weakness."

"Take it out? You say that like it'll be easy. His heel is larger than a damn Sequoia tree."

"It's three against one. We got this," said Michael rushing to the battlefield to assist Konungr.

"Fuck," muttered Darrius, hurrying behind Michael.

They sprinted in unison. Michael fled towards Konungr with Darrius's footsteps behind him until they smashed into an invisible brick wall. It was as if Michael had been halted outside of Steina's cave again. An impenetrable force had disrupted them, paralyzing them into place like trees rooted deeply into the Earth's core.

Konungr strained, using his left hand to wield the orka that inhibited Michael and Darrius while his right hand etched tightly around Hofud, attacking and defending against the blows of Frey's sword. "Leave," said Konungr. The words labored from behind his lips as his teeth ground together, sounding like rocks in a blender. "Now! You must go. C-Can't hold much—"

Konungr's words were cut short by the emergence of another portal, this one much smaller than the one Surtr had entered from. From inside the portal stepped Loki, enamored in more armor than the average Midgardian could bench press. He stepped onto the battlefield alone with Gungnir in hand, his sight set on Konungr.

The sword of Frey took advantage of the momentary distraction and penetrated deep into Konungr's left rib cage. Surtr had seen enough from his sword. He punted Konungr through the air with ferocity. With two large footsteps, Surtr covered a quarter-mile and picked up Konungr in the palm of his hand, squeezing him tightly. Konungr screamed, but the sound seemed to be thwarted from his punctured lungs.

Michael surged forward, seething with hatred. Orka exuded from his body without the slightest realization it had done so. All thoughts of logic had dissipated from his mind, replaced by the hatred and retribution that festered inside of him.

Darrius grabbed Michael's arm from behind, trying his hardest to retain him, but Michael slithered from his grasps, forcefully pushing Darrius's arm away. He continued his flurry towards Surtr and the impending death that awaited if he arrived there.

"Release him," shouted Loki. "It is time that I send him to Valhalla."

Surtr released Konungr, dropping him in the same disrespectful manner that one would exhibit with a mic drop. Konungr nosedived, colliding into the torrid and chargrilled soil. He attempted to crawl back to his feet but stumbled to his knees instead. His equilibrium reflected that of a boxer knocked to the mat. His body singed with burn marks from Surtr's death grip.

"Now, this will be fun," said Loki, flashing his signature heinous smirk.

Loki marveled at Gungnir before chucking it into the direction of Konungr. Konungr, too weak and feeble to stand, remained on his knees. He assembled a portal before him in hopes that it would protect him, but Gungnir spiraled through it. The spear connected with the skull of Konungr, excavating a perfectly shaped circle through his scalp.

Konungr dropped to the floor lifeless, his body flailing loosely as if he lacked any form or bone structure. The spear, drenched with Konungr's blood, returned to Loki on his command.

"Great job, my dear," said Loki, admiring his weapon. Loki marched to Konungr's corpse. He glowered over the dead body with a look of revolting infatuation and picked up Hofud from the ground. "Another piece to my bountiful collection. For good measure," he said, striking beneath the chin of Konungr, beheading him.

"Konungr," Michael screeched at the top of his lungs, piercing the air like a jet breaking the sound barrier. "You bastard, Loki! You will pay for this."

"We need to go, Michael," Darrius screamed, etching his nails deep into Michael's skin, clutching his torso with desperation. "Now!"

Enraptured by his animosity and disdain for Loki, Michael blasted Darrius as hard as he could, hard enough to send Darrius's body caroming off the collapsing timberland. Michael was hellbent on getting the vengeance he lusted after. A blistering hot rage built up inside him, a rage unlike any he had ever felt before. He was glowing, his orka spiking to astronomical levels, erupting from his soul, spurting for everyone to see.

He blasted Loki repeatedly, his left fist, his right fist, both filled with orka, smashing away at the face of Loki. He charged up an orka ray, larger than anyone he had ever crafted, and unleashed it at Loki, sure that it would severely injure the god.

Michael hunched over after its release, huffing and puffing, depleted of energy. The rage subsided, cresting over him like the afterthought of an orgasm. The raw and visceral emotions from before washed away, leaving him a prisoner of his thoughts and mistakes he had just made. The ash and debris created from his orka attack settled, and somehow through it all, Loki remained unscathed.

"W-what?" asked Michael in between breaths. "H-how are you still standing?"

Loki waltzed towards Michael nonchalantly, unphased by Michael's previous assault. "I'm a god, you petulant mortal. Did you actually think that you, a mere human of all people, could kill me? You're more foolish than you look, Midgardian."

Loki reared back and punched Michael, catapulting him rigorously off the ground. He picked Michael up, holding him in the air by his scalp just as he had done with Skye.

Michael looked down at Loki through bludgeoned eyes, and with no regard to the repercussions, he spat at the face of Loki. "Kill me, you coward," he screamed.

Loki jammed Gungnir softly but fiercely into Michael's throat beneath his Adam's apple. He applied more and more pressure until it became a strenuous task for Michael to breathe. "Perhaps, I will," said Loki thrusting Gungnir deeper into his throat, slowly sculpting its way into Michael's flesh.

"I think not," said Darrius, teleporting behind Loki. He fiercely kicked the back of Loki's calf, upending him to one knee. He gestured for Hofud and thrashed upon Loki with the sword. The blade whipped through the air slicing Loki's neck and ear, colliding into the steel armor that rested atop Loki's shoulder blades.

Darrius's connection with Loki left him with a gaping gash carved into the side of his neck, purging a river of blood onto Loki's armor. Darrius swiftly kicked the other knee of Loki leaving the god to bow before him. He swung the blade with all his might, aiming for the head of Loki, but Hofud stopped inches from his neck, so close to connecting that it trimmed locks of Loki's elegant hair.

Loki used his telekinetic powers to his favor, halting Darrius in place. He returned to his feet and rotated his jaw in circles, popping it back into socket, as the freshly chiseled piece of meat hung from his neck like a hangnail. "Great swordsmanship," said Loki. "That will do great in Valhalla. I will personally guarantee you a first-class ticket," he said, smirking, blasting orka into his neck and cauterizing his wound.

He punched Darrius, airmailing his body through the forest further than Ezra had traveled at the hands of Surtr. Darrius ricocheted and careened off of the surrounding trees like a game of pinball. Loki teleported to Darrius and proceeded to catapult him back to their original starting point.

Darrius's body somersaulted for tens of feet until he skidded to a halt. Loki picked him up by the neck and strangled him for dear life. He unloaded haymaker upon haymaker until Darrius's head laid limply. His body hung feebly in the hands of Loki, his head glued to his chest like an infant unable to support it.

With a last-ditch effort, adrenaline surged through Michael one last time. He focused on grasping Loki's hand and restraining it from the relentless wrath that he was issuing upon

Darrius. To his surprise, it worked; Loki's fist froze in place, his arm straining shakily next to Darrius's head.

Darrius's head perked up slightly, his face unrecognizable, beaten, and bruised abominably. Michael could see Darrius's hands tighten into a fist, grasping for every last ounce of orka his weakened state could generate.

"Don't!" Michael shouted, his voice wavering with tension from the bond he held over Loki. "Don't do it, Darrius. I deserve to die here with you."

"Like my father," Darrius whimpered in a low, barely audible whisper. "I'll die protecting those I love." He summoned a portal behind Michael with his left hand, and with his right, he cast his remaining orka at him, sending Michael barreling into the portal.

Michael flew through time and space uncontrollably, tumbling and gripping at the portal, hoping to grasp onto any part of it. His mind and consciousness existed in Midgard and Alfheim simultaneously, all at once. He watched helplessly as he was being tugged from one dimension into the other.

With Michael no longer able to hold his grasp upon Loki, Loki unfroze and called for Gungnir. His faithful spear arrived promptly at his beck and call. Loki etched the spear into Darrius's sternum. He pushed Gungnir slowly, deeper and deeper, drilling its way into Darrius's heart. Even from within the portal, Michael could hear the wails squalling from Darrius's lips. Michael fought powerlessly to escape and come back out on the other side, but the portal was closing too fast, and he was far too weak to vault himself through it.

Loki dislodged Gungnir from Darrius's chest. Darrius's eyes rolled to the back of his head, closing for the final time. Loki tossed the lifeless carcass to the ground, admiring his work as he watched Darrius's body hit the earth, rolling twice before coming to a complete stop.

Michael's body did the same, plunging into the unforgiven terrain of Alfheim. He quickly got to his feet and sprinted as fast as he could to the closing portal. "Darrius," he screamed, with tears searing across his cheeks. "Darrius, I'm coming. Hang on."

He dove into the air, contorting his body the best he could to fit into the narrow, diminishing portal, only for it to close moments before he could reach it. He was left with nothing more than the soil of Alfheim as he crashed into it once more.

He laid there in shock, almost emotionless, on the cold, harsh boulders, hoping that if he laid there long enough that he might die as well. He wanted to close his eyes and have the luxury of never opening them again. He envied the dead, forever yearning for a life without pain. Loki had taken everything from him, and Michael's one and only remaining wish were that Loki would reunite him with Darrius and Konungr by taking his life next.

CHAPTER SEVENTEEN

THE RUNE OF MANNAZ

After spotting Michael's body crash land onto Alfheim, Steina quickly hurried over to him to check on him, leaving Reynir alone to heal Ezra. Michael laid there defeated, anguishing in the pain of his losses. Steina placed her hand on his battered face, caressing across his abrasions lightly. Michael immediately brushed her hand away, firmly enough to express to her that he had no desire for an embrace of any kind.

"I'm glad you're okay," she said tentatively. Her stature caught somewhere between the restraint of not wanting to upset Michael more, but equally wishing to convey that she cared about him. "What . . . what happened?" Her voice slipped, catching somewhere in the middle of her throat. "Where are Konungr and Darrius?" she asked as tears began to fill her eyes.

Michael said nothing. His stare ice cold. His eyes hardened with rage and ire, refusing to make contact with Steina. "You're fucking boyfriend killed them. That's what happened to them," he said, turning his attention to her and meeting her gaze for the first time since returning.

The tears that swelled Steina's eyes filled over and began to roll down her cheeks. Her facial expression caught somewhere between disbelief and disappointment. "He's not my boyfriend, jackass."

"Whatever. I don't care anymore," said Michael, storming off, away from Steina.

Steina scurried after him, grasping his arm as she got within reach. "Where are you going?"

"Anywhere," Michael shouted. "Anywhere that's not this place because fuck this piece of shit ass realm. Nothing good has happened since I got here."

"You can't leave, Michael. We need you . . . I need you," she said, cupping his hand tenderly. "Alfheim needs you now more than ever."

"Well, I damn sure don't need it. There's nothing left here for me. I think it's best I go."

"Reynir and I mean nothing to you? Your oath to Alfheim means nothing?"

Michael stared at her, genuinely catching her eyes for the first time. Even without a sun, even while in so much pain, they still sparkled with life, filling him with hope, a hope that things would get better as long as they stuck together, but Michael didn't want hope. He wanted revenge. He wanted death. Either the death of him or Loki would suffice.

The only thing that would help him overcome his suffering would be killing Loki, quelling the pain inside him, or being killed by Loki, forever relinquishing the hurt that he bottled within. It no longer mattered to him which one happened. He just knew that he didn't want to feel anything ever again, so he turned away, unable to stare into Steina's eyes a moment longer. He turned away because he wasn't strong enough to fall into her arms and cry like he desired deep down.

"I guess not," he said, knowing that his words would break her heart, but he couldn't stick around and succumb to her tender touch. His wrath needed to be unwound, something that she would only get in the way of, so he turned around slowly and began to walk away, taking everything in him not to turn around and face her.

"If you leave, Darrius's death will only be in vain. Same for Konungr. Their sacrifice must mean something. You know Darrius wouldn't want you to do this."

Those words pinned him like needles. His one button and she dared to push it, but she was right. She was always right. If he walked away, then Darrius's death would be in vain, but he wasn't ready to have that conversation with himself yet. He turned around, still boiling, on the verge of erupting. "How do you know what Darrius would want?" Michael shouted. "You barely even knew him."

"Excuse me? We spent two years together on Midgard, Michael. Of course, I know Darrius. How could you even say that?"

"Whatever. If his sacrifice means so much to you, then you can go back to Midgard and gather his body from your little pal, Loki. I should be dead . . . Not him. Loki was supposed to kill me!"

"What the fuck is up with your infatuation with death?" she screamed back at him, shoving her hands hard into his sternum. "And he's not my lover. You're such an asshole," said Steina, walking away in disgust.

"You don't . . . you don't understand," said Michael, crumbling to his knees, halting Steina in her tracks. His head fell to the ground in sorrow as he pounded the ground with his fists. "It shouldn't have been him." He felt his chest get heavy, and his eyes begin to well up. "Darrius should be here with you. Not me. He's dead because of me, Steina. He's dead because of my failures . . . He was my hero. He was the only person who believed in me, and now he's gone."

"He's not the only person who believes in you, Michael. We all do," she said, lifting Michael's head gently. "Me, Reynir, Ezra, Solfrid. Everyone believes in you. And I'm so very sorry to hear about Darrius. The weight of it hasn't fully dawned on me yet, and I already miss him more than I can bear. We will miss him dearly—all of us. But you do yourself and Darrius no justice by running away. By abandoning Alfheim, you would only be doing him a disservice. We will get through this together. We will heal together, and when we do, it will be up to us to defeat Loki. It will be up to us to restore Alfheim, and it will be up to us to stop Ragnarök from taking away anything else that we love."

"What's the point?" asked Michael, his face flushed with defeat. "He's taken everything from me. Peter. Konungr. Darrius. I have nothing left to fight for. If I just stop caring, if I just stop giving a damn, then he can't take anything else away from me, and the only way I can do that is by removing him from that power."

"So, I mean nothing to you?" Steina repeated once more.

Michael stared at her, getting lost in her eyes one last time. He wanted nothing more than to give in to his flesh. He wanted to hold her, tell her how he truly felt about her. He wanted to kiss her now more than ever. Life was short; if there was ever a time to confess how he felt, this was it, but Loki had inflicted enough damage already, he couldn't risk Loki taking anything else from him, most of all, Steina.

Michael said nothing. His teary eyes told the story for him.

"The point is saving others, so they don't have to feel the same pain that we have suffered," said Steina with her hand in his. "We have to keep going because others weren't allowed that luxury, and it would be an injustice to them and all of Alfheim to give up now."

Michael looked away sharply, unable to stare into her suffocating gaze any longer. He stood up to his feet and dusted himself off. "Consider me an injustice then, Steina. I'm done."

Steina shook her head in disappointment. Michael could see her eyebrows tense as they did when she got upset. He knew her well enough to know that she was scanning her brain for every insult she could think of, searching for the one that would hit him the hardest, but to his surprise, she didn't.

"I'll be sure to let the others know," she said, walking back to the shelter, never turning around once.

Steina opted to take the high road, paining Michael even more. Misery flooded him as he watched her walk away because maybe that was the moment she had given up on him for good. She was the one person he had left, and he pushed her to walk away, but at least now he could plot his revenge against Loki with no remorse.

He turned around and began to walk, unknowing of where his feet would take him but knowing all the same that he needed to be somewhere else. His feet walked with a mind of their own as his current thoughts torpedoed inside him.

For the first time in a long time, he was truly alone, and he was the sole reason to blame for that. He had people who truly cared for him, and he chose to walk away from them, and that's when the stubbornness of his situation hit him. He had no way out of this godforsaken realm.

Michael swelled up at the thought of it all. Why did he have to be such an asshole? It wasn't Steina's fault that Darrius and Konungr died. He immediately wanted to retreat back to the shelter and apologize to her. He wanted nothing more than to change the hands of time, but it didn't work like that.

No amount of time or wishing would bring Darrius back, and no amount of hoping would erase the words that came out of his mouth during his argument with Steina. He was far too stubborn for his own good. Out of all his bad characteristics, that was arguably the worst one. He had little ability to swallow his pride and admit to his wrongdoings.

He stared long and hard at the shelter one last time, longing to go back and right his wrongs, but he couldn't. He may have been a powerful magician, but he wasn't strong enough to face his mistakes or the past that haunted him, so off he ventured into the forest alone.

He strolled through Alfheim with nothing but the shirt on his back, a broken heart, and a bruised ego. Alfheim was nothing but a desolate and barren wasteland now, something that Michael could not only appreciate but sympathize with.

The heart of the city had been destroyed, and without the landmarks that used to stand tall, Michael had no idea how to navigate through the broken realm. Just as he had no idea how to navigate his own life without the pillars that used to be Darrius and Konungr. Michael was wandering aimlessly, both physically and emotionally, lost at the wheel and flying blind, hoping to find sanity and resolve somewhere.

His walk reminded him of his first night here when they sheltered at Dagrún Village. He had to be close, he thought. His first night, they stayed there because it was the nearest safe zone to Skirnir's Cove.

He searched deep within, pulling on the memory of their arrival, and with that memory, he was able to extract the coordinates from the plane's dashboard. Michael analyzed them and plotted them into his mind. From there, he had his own personal GPS. Dagrún Village was a few miles south.

He had no idea what to expect upon arrival, but it was the only other place he knew of in this realm. He could've tried teleporting, but he wasn't nearly skilled enough to get that far, and he knew it. Not to mention, his energy levels were still vastly depleted from his bout with Loki. He was operating on pride entirely, pushing himself to get to a destination to collapse upon.

The walk was needed. He needed the fresh air and alone time to clear his mind. He tried his hardest to clear his thoughts and focus on nothing more than the journey before him, telling himself that his grief could come at another time. With his mental compass in place, he trekked in solace across the ravaged, plagued city, thankful that something could be more broken than the current version of himself.

The beautiful nature had begun to dissipate into oblivion. The trees no longer bustled about majestically. Instead, they were sunken, rotten, and decaying in place. The once breathtaking aroma now reeked of sulfur and mildew, sprinkled with hints of death.

After summiting through the ransacked realm, he finally made it to his destination. Surprisingly, Dagrún Village seemed to have made it out of the scuffle between gods mostly unscathed and in its preservation resided an eeriness. The tiny huts and the village itself looked the same way it had been left, but without the citizens who populated it, it was nothing more than a ghost town with a rich history that would never be remembered.

Michael strolled through the village, making his way towards the tail end, feeling as if he was on the movie set of a horror film where he was abandoned in an old town that was barely operational anymore. He didn't know why he had the urge to go back to where it started, but his heart tugged at him and told him that he needed to.

It would've been much easier staying at one of the tiny huts near the front of the village, somewhere far enough away that he didn't have to see the place where his cousin had been murdered, but his feet kept pushing him forward.

He had little concept of time and how it operated. Back on Midgard, he had spent a little over two years training with Konungr, but here on Alfheim, it had only been four months since the bloodbath had taken place.

He was quickly reminded of the horrors of that night as he passed by the housing quarters where he had stayed. The area was still littered with the remains and carcasses of gnomes. The sight of it sent shivers up his spine, causing him to fight and suppress the memories and post-traumatic stress that followed. He couldn't get the image out of his head, the image of Peter's limp body hanging dangly from his arms.

Michael didn't know what his future comprised of, but he knew that he had to make amends with this place. If there would ever be a future version of himself that was fixed and put back together, then he knew he needed to embrace his past and stitch the wounds still left agape. None of what happened here was his fault, and he had finally come to terms with that, but it was only right to give the village the proper burial it deserved.

One by one, he etched his way into the soil with his mind, carving out gnome-sized holes until every gnome rested in peace. He made his way to the woods and found a slew of boulders and sticks, making tombstones for each of the gnomes that bravely sacrificed their lives that day.

Michael walked to the center where he had buried Peter two long years ago. He kneeled down and stared at the gravesite long and hard until he found the right words to say. He spoke aloud and from his heart, knowing that Peter wasn't around to hear it but still longing and hoping that maybe, somehow, he was.

"I'm sorry, little buddy," said Michael. "You should be home right now, with your mom and your brothers. You should be in school hanging out with friends. Playing sports. Going fishing. Feeling the experience of your first crush. I'm sorry the world robbed you of that, and I'm even more sorry that I was unable to stop it. I should've been there for you. I failed you. I'll carry that weight with me until I die. I'm just so sorry, Peter . . . I just wanted to say that I love you and I miss you. Rest easy, champ," he said, patting the ground in which Peter laid.

He walked away from Peter's gravestone, back towards the front of the village. He stared once more at the graveyard he had created, giving one final look at the hut Peter had been murdered in. He didn't have the heart to stay there. He couldn't stomach the thought of staying in that same building. The bed was more than likely still stained in blood, and the walls were more than likely splattered with it.

It was all more than Michael could bear, so he found the hut furthest away from the incident and stayed there. The cabins near the entrance were cramped, to say the least. He took two of the beds and placed them beside one another so he would have something remotely long enough to lay down upon. He laid there, eyes closed, not thinking about much but at the same time thinking about everything that had transpired the past couple of years.

After Peter had died, his one and only desire had been fueled by his vengeance and bloodlust for Loki. Without even realizing it, Konungr had healed him from that pain. The seething hatred that he had shared for Loki had transformed into a feeling of belonging as he spent two years with his family. Konungr, Darrius, Steina, and Reynir, that was his family, and now half of that family was gone, and he didn't even get the chance to say farewell.

He had all the magic that one could desire, and yet it didn't fulfill him. There was no magic for happiness. It wasn't the end-all-be-all that he had hoped for. It was up to him to find that joy, something that Konungr had harped long ago, and the happiness that he had found was all for naught. He was back at square one, experiencing unbelievable grief once more at the hands of Loki.

All his healing meant nothing because, once again, his deepest desire in life was the death of Loki. The worst part about it was Michael now understood the importance of Loki's grasp over him. He knew that Loki's most significant victory thus far had been his victory over Michael's mind. Michael was smarter than he was before. He was wiser, stronger, and more emotionally connected to himself, but none of it mattered. He didn't care. He wasn't going to rest until Loki experienced the same agonizing pain he had put Michael through.

His mind was a rollercoaster, stopping and going, flipping and turning until it finally settled upon Darrius and the overwhelming grief that consumed him. His mind plagued him with memories of Darrius. It was fucked up that life would grant him the ability to recall and revisit his past with perfection, only for him to be stripped of the happiness that encompassed those memories.

The fragility of life ate away inside of his mind. Darrius was a superhero; his superhero and superheroes weren't supposed to die. They grow old, ride off into the sunset, and retire, which was the life he'd always envisioned for Darrius. Even when they were together solving cases, Darrius was invincible, impervious to pain and death.

Darrius couldn't really be gone. Michael wouldn't believe it until he found the body himself. If Darrius had really died, his soul would live on in Valhalla as an einherjar and fight at their side during Ragnarök. Michael was sure of it, and he would go to Asgard and back to prove it, bringing Darrius back with him.

His mind raced, and as it did, he felt the resounding need to cry and wash away the grief that tormented him, but he couldn't no matter how hard he tried. An overwhelming numbness shrouded inside of him, debilitating any ability to feel. He saw Darrius die with very own eyes, but he spent the remainder of the night telling himself otherwise until his eyes closed and his mind drifted into the abyss of his subconscious.

So seamlessly, so smoothly, just as dreams tend to do, his destination shifted to his cave of self just as Konungr told him it would. Shards of pain jostled inside him as he recalled his last conversation with Konungr.

The cave was finally ready for him, but Michael struggled on whether or not he was prepared for it. Fear etched at his insides, begging to be turned loose. He feared what he might find inside. Hell, what more did he have to lose? he thought.

He awoke in a state of excitement and trepidation, ridding himself of any lethargic energy that still lingered. He dragged his finger into the sand and traced out the rune of Mannaz, a rune resembling two flags facing one another. He focused on his destination and summoned the rune, ascending into the darkness once more, and just as before, he scurried past the tunnel of memories and strange objects, landing onto his very own trail of memories.

This time his trail of memories didn't vanish abruptly. They led to the cave that eluded him on his prior visit. Michael was bound and determined to get the answers that it eloquently hid from him before. He walked up to it with optimism, confident that this time would be different, but he still reached his hand out cautiously, feeling for any invisible force fields that may attempt to block him.

He sifted through the cave. It appeared that this time there would be no barricades obstructing him from entering. He took a deep breath and wandered inside the entrenching darkness, wondering what the cave might have in store for him. He walked for a few hundred feet, following a set of lights that appeared the further he trekked, revealing murals of Michael's life onto the walls.

"Hi there," said a squeaky voice, startling Michael.

Michael jumped at the sound of the voice and turned around quickly, his hands generating orka instinctively in case it would be needed. The speaker was a dry erase board level of white, not Caucasian. The being was short, something along the lines of four-foot nothing, and resembled a two-dimensional figure, reminding Michael of an old video game.

"Hi," said Michael, skittishly, still encumbered with orka. "If you don't mind my asking, who in the hell are you?"

"Oh, of course, I don't mind, silly," said the silhouette. "I am you, Michael. I'm the good in you. The you that you admire. The you that others love and enjoy being around."

Michael looked the being up and down, tilting his head sideways like a puppy to get a different perspective of the peculiar version of himself. "If that's the case, then I must be a pretty shitty person. Why are you so . . . small? And where is your face? Or the rest of your body?"

"You tell me," said the figure, shrugging its unformed shoulders. "You created me."

"Me?" asked Michael, pointing at himself. "You mean to tell me I created you? Do explain how, please."

"In every person, there's a good and bad side to them. Light and dark. Angel and demon. Some people even have more sides. I'm your good side."

A loud, thundering wallop could be heard reverberating from the furthest end of the cave.

Michael took a deep breath. "Why do I get the feeling that that's the bad version of me?"

"Always trust your gut," said the silhouette. "It's usually right."

"How is he? The bad me?"

"He used to be, well, not so bad. I was bigger than him then, ya know? I was more defined as well, but that was a long time ago. Now . . . let's just say I try my hardest to avoid him."

"I guess it's time we face our fears then, huh?" Michael walked towards the direction of the earsplitting clobbering. "You coming?"

"I think I'm gonna stay here. Where it's nice and safe."

"Isn't the good part of me supposed to be brave and valiant?"

"Maybe you're not as good as you think you are."

"What? What's that supposed to mean?"

"All those brave moments come from a place of personal gain. You thrust yourself into the line of fire not because it's righteous but because of your underlying vengeance for Loki. You became a detective not to save others but in hopes that you would find Skye, mostly because you lust for your mother's forgiveness. When was the last time you did something good without an anterior motive at play?"

"When was the last time you did something good," said Michael mockingly. "Shut up. You don't even know what you're talking about."

The barely detailed figure shrugged its shoulders. "Have fun. I hope you find what you are looking for."

"Yeah, with no help from you," said Michael dryly.

The further Michael roamed, the darker the cave became. The drubbing got louder. The ground beneath him tremored, as did the walls. The beating was so violent that part of him feared a landslide might occur.

He didn't know what would happen to him if he died down here, and unlike his previous self, not even five or so hours before, he wasn't exactly eager to find out anymore. He wondered if he would wake up at Dagrún Village or if death here meant a visit to Helheim or some other dastardly realm.

He chose not to dwell on that thought for too long. His ears were ringing too loud for him to focus. He reached an old water well that was larger than what he imagined one would look like. With each thunderous blow, the bricks surrounding it quivered, trembling like the house made of sticks from the *Three Little Pigs* fairy tale.

With all the courage he could muster, he unhooked the pail above and tied the rope securely around his waist. He thrust himself inside, gripping at the cord and dropping a few feet at a time. His forearms grew tighter with each drop, straining strenuously to keep hold, his hands burning at the jagged friction created by the rope.

He pushed past all the pain and descended deeper into the core of his subconscious. His muscles began to quiver, spasming up and down the entirety of his arm. He couldn't hold on any longer. His hands slipped from the rope, and he somersaulted like a yo-yo, spinning in circles until he belly-flopped along the surface of the water.

The water was uncomfortably hot, not enough to sear him but enough to discomfort him like that first full body dip into a hot tub. Otherwise, his mind was seemingly too preoccupied with the thought of what monstrous creatures might be lying beneath him to focus on the prickling, hot water.

His fear of the unknown quickly evaporated into a more centralized fear, the behemoth standing far and away above him. How Michael hadn't landed on top of the jotun-sized being was beyond him. Michael eyed the creature with fear, realizing that the being was a gigantic, aggressively pissed off version of himself. The monster was chiseled beyond belief and large enough that his sheer body mass gave Michael images of Surtr. His traps were large enough to fit a semi-truck upon, his back large enough to field a baseball diamond.

The creature flushed red at the sight of Michael. His face furled and scrunched; his eyes lit like a thousand suns. He thrashed at the water, sending tidal waves at Michael. Michael instinctively plunged as deep as he could go, his body rolling beneath with no control against the violent and monstrous waves above. He swam up for breath and noticed the water rising, surging rapidly, to the point that it now crested along with the rib cages of the behemoth.

Michael's initial thought was to ride out the storm. Hopefully, in doing so, the evil, vile version of himself would sink to the bottom, but just as quickly as that thought emerged, the behemoth grew tens of more feet, shattering that idea before it could elicit life. The water surged Michael upward like a surfer weaving through the waves. The behemoth stood waist level with the water once more, and that's when a sudden epiphany struck Michael leaving him to understand how to defeat the monster before him.

All of Michael's negativity, his self-confidence, his insecurities resonated inside this monster. Everything that Michael felt, on every plane of existence, this being felt as well, albeit on a much grander and cosmic scale.

The well, the water, it was all an analogy. The more Michael bottled things up, the longer he let his personal vendettas consume him, the longer he let this level of hatred fester inside of him, the larger this creature would become. If Michael stayed on the path he was currently on, eventually, this creature would consume him, becoming even larger and more barbaric than he was right now.

Once the water broke above the surface, Michael would no longer be in control. That was his figurative boiling point, a point Michael knew he couldn't afford to reach. If he didn't contain this being now, if he didn't confront himself, then he would be lost forever, and with that realization, the water stopped rising.

Michael could see through the crazed, destructive version of himself. He saw the good inside of him, the characteristics that the monster secretly enjoyed. No, it wasn't the good in him that Michael saw. That was nothing more than a silhouette that lived at the front of an imaginary cave. What Michael saw was himself. A pure form of himself, a form of himself that he had ignored for too long—a man who was in desperate need of healing.

It had always been him because that was all that it could ever be. Michael was in control, not the good him or the bad him or any of his emotions for that matter. He was the only one who could take reign of his destiny. He couldn't leave that up to some primitive monster he concocted and enslaved in the core of his subconscious.

Michael looked deep into the being's eyes, glimpsing and colliding with the behemoth's soul, which in turn was Michael's soul. He saw vengeance. He saw despair, guilt, regret, low self-confidence, and even less self-esteem. No, he didn't only see these things; he felt them and openly admitted to them for the first time.

He discovered the lack of faith and belief that he had bestowed upon himself for far too long. He was a prisoner of his own mind, unable to live with himself and his very own failures. They absorbed him, creating the obsessive, deranged being before him. The being that festered on hatred but ultimately yearned for approval and self-love.

And rather than learning from previous failures, he brooded in his losses. Those same failures amplified his increasing anxiety, which resulted in an even bigger fear than fear itself, his fear of failure. A fear of trying, so he lived by some stupid ass motto that he created many years ago, you couldn't fail if you didn't try. His fear of failure enriched his biggest fear of all, his fear that he would never be good enough. Good enough for Darrius. For Peter. For Konungr. For Steina.

But most of all, a fear that he would never be good enough for himself. His unreasonable expectations and his inability to forgive himself created this self-loathing monster, one that easily outweighed the good characteristics inside of him. His demons consumed him, tipping the scale and overbalancing any conceivable good that he could muster.

His fear of failure made him think of his best friend, Darrius. Michael heard him in resounding clarity, as if Darrius were speaking to him from beyond. *You can't save the world if you don't fix yourself first.*

It was unrealistic, irresponsible even to think that he could save his friends, save Alfheim, save the world if he couldn't even come face-to-face with the behemoth he stored within. He had to save himself from himself. This whole time he had been at war with Loki when in reality, Michael was his own worst enemy.

On some fundamental level, Michael had known this for some time, but he wasn't ready to acknowledge it then. It's why he was denied admission during his first visit here. At that point, a part of him still believed he could live with that much level of hatred. As long as they defeated Loki, it wouldn't matter how much affliction he harbored inside him, but one can only run from the truth for so long until those unorganized, strewn about skeletons topple over, opening that closet door for good. The only way for him to move forward was by forgiving himself, accepting who he was, and learning to let go.

The water spiraled, torpedoing to the bottom like a toilet being flushed. The water clanked at the sides of the well violently, both of them plunging with ferocity. Like a cockroach trying to escape a toilet bowl, they slithered along the edges attempting to grasp anything that would provide stability. Until, finally, they collided into one another, emerging into one.

As Michael became woven and entrenched with the behemoth, he felt everything subside from within. All his pain, his agony, his years of self-doubt had vanished. It was as if Michael consumed the suffering of the behemoth and the behemoth absorbed the misery of Michael, each of them washing away the pain of the other, becoming parasites of one another. A mutualistic relationship, benefitting both.

The water drained to the bottom, and as it did, it sucked Michael through. He plunged to the beginning of the cave, an engineering feat that made little sense, but Michael didn't complain about the architecture his inner self had constructed.

There waiting was the good Michael he had always aspired to be. No longer was he without detail. Now he was chiseled like a god, a man any would marvel at. The bustled, chiseled version of himself moved forward and congratulated him. "You've faced your inner demons. That's not an easy feat. Congrats," said the good him, extending his hand to help Michael up.

"Thank you," said Michael, grasping his hand and standing to his feet. "What does all of this mean? What's next for us?"

"It's time that we submerge. You've come to terms with the bad in you. Now it's time to accept the good."

"What of the bad in me? Will he ever reemerge?"

"Sure. He will always be there, deep within you. No one is whole-heartedly good. At least not all the time. We're emotional beings, and at times negative thoughts will arise. It's your job to control them. Future you may find yourself here again one day, but that's a you that you have yet to become, and his problems are probably far more significant than yours of today. One is always evolving, always growing. For now, we connect spiritually, and you embark on your next journey."

The newly improved, good version of Michael extended his hand out. Michael apprehensively stretched his right hand forth, and the two embraced upon a handshake. Just as Michael had intertwined with the bad, he merged with the good in him as well. The room spiraled, bringing the beings closer together until there was only one, only Michael.

Michael felt love. A love he hadn't felt ever before—a love for himself, a feeling of self-worth. For the first time he could ever recall, he accepted himself, all of himself. The good, the bad, and the ugly, but most importantly, Michael embraced his newfound mentality.

He was willing to fail. He no longer had that crippling fear of failure that had always tormented him. He now understood that failure was merely a word. A word that had no meaning unless he prescribed meaning to it. Failure could only exist in the eyes of the beholder, and he no longer believed in such a thing.

There was no such thing as failure, only lessons. With his newfound knowledge, he was ready to try again, this time with the willingness to put forth every ounce of him that he could offer. He knew exactly what he needed to do and where he needed to go. He just hoped that the council members he had left behind would forgive him.

CHAPTER EIGHTEEN

BROKKR AND EITRI

Michael awoke feeling physically and mentally rejuvenated, his stamina in tip-top shape and his wounds mostly healed as if yesterday's battle with Loki and Surtr had never happened. His heart still longed for Darrius and Konungr, but the only remedy for heartbreak was time, and that was the one thing Michael didn't have to spare.

He needed to get back to the shelter and make amends with the friends he left behind. Michael feared what sinister plans Loki might have left to unveil, but whatever it was, he knew one thing, he wouldn't be able to tackle Loki alone. He tried that and learned his lesson.

Steina was right; Alfheim did need him. This realm was dying, and it'd be an injustice to Darrius and Konungr to let it die without a fight. He owed them that much, and he was ready to prove that now. He exited the hut to a barely existing sunset. The false sun had seen better days, its power waning with every hour that passed.

With a refreshed body, he hustled back to the refuge, this time in a full sprint, reaching his destination in a little over an hour. He felt his hands flutter along the spine of the tent, fumbling to find its zipper. His hands were as nervous and unsteady as they were during his very first kiss. His mind and body grew angsty, scared of the rejection that may follow.

He took a deep breath and gathered himself. His legs were stubbornly rooted in place, both feet full of lead, but he found the strength to push them forward. He entered the tent to find a dejected and crestfallen Reynir near the entrance. Reynir's eyes were dazed, somewhere off in space, yet still full of unmistakable sadness.

Elation spread across Reynir's face as Michael entered. He burst to his feet and greeted him with a hug. "Michael! I was worried you weren't going to come back."

"Me too, but I'm glad I did," said Michael solemnly.

"I was on my way out to find you last night, but Steina stopped me. She thought it would be best for you to spend the night alone."

"She was right . . . I needed it. I was able to find the cave and enter this time."

"How was it?"

"It was humbling, to say the least. I have a lot of work to do on myself, but I thank you for sticking with me while I do it."

"Always, brother," he said, clasping Michael's hand.

"And listen, I'm sorry for leaving yesterday, Reynir. It won't happen again."

"You don't have to explain yourself. Everybody needs space. I'm sorry for not being there yesterday. I should have been fighting beside you all. Maybe then Darrius would still be alive. Konungr too."

"They wouldn't be, and neither would you. I'm only alive because Darrius sacrificed himself for me. Darrius is dead because of me. We should've left earlier, but I refused to . . . so it is I who is sorry. Because of me, we lost a brother."

"There was no way of knowing that you three would arrive at the precise time Loki and Surtr had. Had we known, we all would have shown up. Don't be so hard on yourself, Michael. I wear just as much guilt as you on the matter."

"I don't know about that, but I'm trying harder not to— about everything. Peter included. It's all a part of that transformation I'm on, I guess."

"Konungr would be proud of you."

"I can only hope so."

"Darrius too."

"Thank you," said Michael, nodding his head. "Where's Steina? I need to apologize to her."

"With Solfrid. She hasn't left her side. Follow me. Maybe I can convince her to swap shifts for a bit."

"And Ezra, is she okay?"

"She's in a lot of pain, but she will recover just fine."

Michael let out an internal sigh of relief. His heart punched inside his chest at the thought of seeing Steina. Their walk only building the anticipation that drummed inside him. Behind the closed tent of Solfrid's corridors, Michael and Steina locked eyes. His heart gallivanted even harder now, leaving him to feel like an animated character out of a cartoon.

Steina's eyes glimmered. The sparkle, the beauty, the hope that lied within them, still there. She rushed by Reynir and leaped into Michael's arms, hugging him tightly. His fingers gripped around her flesh, sinking into her soft touch. The smell of her hair intoxicated him, leaving him powerless.

He was weak for her. He was vulnerable in a way he had never felt before. She gave him hope that he could care again without the fear of being hurt because a life without her was far worse than a life devoid of feelings.

Michael felt love for the first time in his life. A sensual, romantic love. An "I can't live without you" type of love. He grasped magic at its core, and yet this felt more supernatural and magical than any spell he could contrive from his fingertips.

Their physical vessels interwove like puzzle pieces, locking together tightly in an embrace. Her flesh wrapped around his, yet he was numb to her carnal touch. All that Michael could feel was the warm, pacifying sensation that permeated between them as their auras gripped and clasped together tightly like a newborn unwilling to separate from the nipple.

With his hands nestled beneath her thighs, he lifted her higher, thrusting her legs around his waistline. Steina gripped the back of his head, pulling him gently. Michael fell into her gravitational pull, their foreheads crested on one another, lingering, as the anticipation of their first kiss mounted over them.

Michael peered into her eyes, no longer seeing hope but lust. A deep, lustful gaze consumed her. A longing desire for him, but before he could fulfill that passion, Steina pulled away.

"I—I can't, Michael," said Steina. "Not right now. There's too much at stake. Solfrid needs to see you."

"Solfrid needs to see me?" asked Michael. "Why would she want to see me of all people?"

"I don't know, but she said it was important. She has been asking about you all of last night."

"I suppose we should find out what it is then, huh?"

Steina nodded her head, leading him into the tent where Solfrid rested.

"How has she been feeling?" Michael whispered to Steina.

"Not too great," interrupted Reynir. "She's weaker than the past couple of days."

"Do you mind?" asked Michael, positioning himself by her bedside.

Reynir nodded his head in approval, allowing Michael to have his seat.

Michael placed his hands over her, siphoning his energy and funneling it into her. He was able to siphon enough orka to replenish Solfrid momentarily as she regained color and the strength in her arms. For the first time, she sat upright with a pillow placed behind her for support.

"Thank you," said Solfrid.

"Anytime," said Michael with a light smile, placing his hand on her shoulder gently.

"Time is now to launch sun. Upon Nidavellir, Brokkr, and Eitri's next of kin shall guide you. No longer can Alfheim wait."

"I agree. But how are we getting to Nidavellir without Darrius?"

"I think I can teleport us there," said Steina. "As sick as they are, the dark elves of that realm are still enriched with the blood of Alfheim. It should be enough for me to guide us there."

"Not to ruin your happy-go-lucky plan and all," said Reynir. "But I would have to imagine that launching an entrapped sun back into the universe must be a fairly excruciating task. And who's to say that Brokkr and Eitri even know how to do so? If it was such an easy task, any regular dwarf would have done it eons ago. Not to mention, is that not where Loki and Gullveig are stationed? We need a better plan than to show up, find some dwarves, and pray they can help us launch a sun."

"Brokkr and Eitri's next of kin," Steina coughed.

"Oh, whatever. Give me a break, will you?"

"Succeed, you will," said Solfrid. "Succeed, he will," she said, pointing at Michael.

"Me? Why me?" asked Michael.

"Because fate has written it long ago," Solfrid explained between hobbled breaths. "Weaved by the Norns. Come to fruition, destiny must."

"And let's say the Norns did weave it," Reynir interjected. "And the stars align perfectly, and Michael's fate is calling upon him. That doesn't change the fact that we are vastly under prepared for an expenditure of that magnitude. How have our other short-sighted plans worked out for us so far? By leaving, we will encounter repercussions of grave danger, none of which we are capable of handling right now."

"I agree," said Michael. "And your opinion is just and of sound mind, but we can't stay here any longer, Reynir. The longer we wait, the more we risk the others' health, yours included. I don't know what the right answer is, but I do know that our people will die here. The way I see it is, we die a valiant death on their realm trying to save Alfheim, or we die here and do nothing."

"He's right," said Steina. "You know it too, Reynir. These elves can't leave here. They are trapped with no means of escaping. Their hope lies in our hands. We must break the curse if they are to survive. That or launch the rune of Sól, but we only have one shot at that, so we better be certain when we do so."

"You're right," sighed Reynir. "You both are. We must lift the curse and save our people . . . But we can't just arrive there with some half-assed plan. How do we expect to find Brokkr and Eitri's next of kin?"

"I'm glad you asked," Steina grinned. "It's time we bring back our good old friend Fornviska. Last time I checked, you still owed us a sacrifice."

"That's Ezra and me, misses."

"No," said Solfrid. "Ezra made a sacrifice for my journey to Mimir. Only left, are you."

"Drats," said Reynir. "Fine. I will do it. But that means you or Ezra will have to stay behind to take care of everyone."

"Seeing as Ezra is in no condition to journey that leaves her here," said Steina. "I'm more than sure that she will not oblige."

"I agree," said Michael. "I don't see her arguing that. We can take the next few days to rest and plan some more, iron out any details along the way. That will give you more time to obtain the coordinates needed to deploy us there, Steina."

"Sounds good. Reynir and I could use those days to recharge. We will have to overcharge our orka, so we have some in reserve for when we arrive. It may be bad here, but Nidavellir has no sun whatsoever."

Reynir nodded his head. "I agree. Michael, what do you say to letting the ladies relax here while we go over some light planning? We can inform Ezra of the plan as well."

Michael glanced at Steina, sharing a moment's worth of eye contact with her. A glance just long enough for both to reciprocate their emotions, a mutual feeling of maybe next time or to be continued. Seeing no alternative in which he and Steina could be alone together, Michael followed behind Reynir. "Sounds good to me. After you."

They spent the next couple of days planning, with Steina and Reynir trying their best not to exert any of their orka, leaving Michael with the responsibility of replenishing and aiding Solfrid and the other ailing elves.

Solfrid spent most of her time resting, which left Michael with a lot of time to roam around his tireless, thought-invoking brain. He couldn't help but wonder, what was the point of trying if the Norns had already weaved and sealed his fate? If Ragnarök was, in fact, the inevitable doomsday that it was prophesized to become, then why even bother to try to stop it?

He thought of his destiny and how he was allegedly the one who would lift the curse of Nidavellir and save Alfheim. But that destiny never provided any specifics to the toll that it would inflict upon them. Would it cost him his fellow council members? Would it cost him the person he loved most in Steina?

He had already lost so much, and even though he'd found some inner peace within himself, he still questioned whether this game was worth playing. Whether his life was worth living if the ending had already been written in stone. If free will didn't exist, then who was he living for? Was he merely a pawn in some fascinating game that gods sat around and marveled at out of boredom?

Then he thought of his nefarious and wicked counterpart, Loki. Loki, a god, who had successfully altered his destiny and the events of Ragnarök. And even though Loki had changed them for the worse, it provided Michael with the smallest sliver of hope that maybe he could change his destiny too and alter Ragnarök or halt it entirely.

He had come too far to give up now. He couldn't give up on the family he had become a part of. They meant too much to him. If the only way to win the game was to play, then his chips were on the table, and he was all in. Ragnarök and glory would be his and if Loki stood in the way of that, then so be it. Michael had the Norns on his side, and that was all the assurance that he needed to come out victorious.

The day had finally arrived where Steina, Reynir, and Michael would venture to Nidavellir and attempt to lift its curse. Michael and Steina waited anxiously as Reynir scoured the woods for some last needed essentials, and no matter how much they asked what he was searching for, he only reiterated that he would be coming back with a surprise.

Their nervous energy was partly due to the treacherous journey they were about to embark upon, but mostly Michael and Steina's anxiety hemmed from their last moment alone. Ever since then, the tension between them had only built up more. To the point that it was now escalating and careening on a volcanic magnitude.

Michael felt like Mount Saint Helens around her, waiting to burst and ready to explode, physically and emotionally reeling in her presence. His magic erupted and overflowed in her company, hers doing much of the same. He could feel it just as she could feel his magic dance around her. Both pleading for one another's touch, but neither of them having had the time to make the move that would fulfill and satisfy their carnivorous and sexual appetites.

Michael didn't know what to talk about around her. He desperately wanted to continue their last conversation, but he thought it might be inappropriate considering the circumstances. Still, he had to say something. He couldn't stand idly by as their magic, unmistakably and obviously, frolicked around one another, playing a game of magical footsies.

"Nervous?" he asked.

"About?" replied Steina.

"Our trip."

"Duh. Aren't you?"

"Of course, but not for myself. I worry about what might happen to you or Reynir."

"Me too, but together we can do this."

"I know . . . I've just lost so much. I don't want to lose anyone else."

"And you won't. None of us will," she said, grasping his hand.

"Ahem," coughed Reynir straddled atop the magnificent dragon, Inon. "Don't forget about Inon."

"Inon!" Michael and Steina shouted in unison as the dragon filled both of their faces with wet and slobbery kisses.

"Oh, it's so nice to see you," said Steina, wiping away the globs of drool on her face.

Inon danced about emphatically, barreling at their sides, more than matching Steina and Michael's level of excitement. Like a Great Dane pretending to be a lapdog, he pranced atop of them, unaware of his sheer size and stature, before finally calming down and lowering himself to a level that Steina and Michael could reach.

They pulled themselves atop his scaly spine, holding onto the jagged spikes that ran along his backbone. They sat one after the other. Steina and Reynir sat with the ease and confidence of a jockey on his thousandth ride; meanwhile, Michael held on for dear life.

Steina rotated her right hand in circles, her left hand pointing towards the wisps of sparks that danced in the air. The portal grew larger with each rotation of her hand. "Nidavellir, here we come," she shouted.

At her command, Inon surged forward, thrusting through the portal and into the realm of the unknown. It was a realm entrenched and plagued by more darkness than Alfheim, a world shrouded in nightfall. Its only source of light was a mere and dimming waning moon off in the distance.

The wind rushed against their face, zipping at what felt like hyperspeed. With no landmarks around them or any way to see, it felt like they were going thousands of miles per hour. Butterflies gyrated in Michael's stomach as Inon danced in the wind, up and down, left and right, just like a rollercoaster.

Michael closed his eyes, bottling the butterflies even more as they shook and fizzed around, frantically searching for an exit. He tried his hardest to focus on anything that was man made, or dwarf made to be exact, searching for anything that nature did not make itself.

He may not have been able to see with his eyes, but he could view everything with precision as he remote-viewed the foreign terrain. It was as if he were observing the land through a set of night vision goggles. Mostly, he saw a desolate realm, a rocky landscape lacking trees or water. It reminded him of the pictures he had seen of Mars, a barren and clay-filled wasteland.

Michael concentrated harder, searching deep within the realm for the hidden city that supposedly lied beneath. He plunged himself into the earth, diving into it like a fox would the snow, carving his way into the realm's core until he had an up-close view of its anatomy. The sight left him speechless, like the beauty of an anthill, Nidavellir's core was simply mesmerizing. On the exterior, it was nothing, but below its surface was a city crafted in exquisite beauty, hidden to those above.

"The north mountain," said Michael. "That's our entrance. It's a few miles ahead. Take us to its opening, Inon."

Inon galloped in the air, bobbing and weaving excitedly, fluttering his wings faster and faster until the wind that surrounded them felt like that of a tropical storm approaching off the gulf. Inon plunged through the fissure of the mountaintop, descending deeper inside it, nosediving into a never-ending freefall.

The council traveled miles into Nidavellir's core until they could finally see light. Inon landed them safely upon some rocks below. They each eyeballed and gazed at the beauty of it all, buildings and sculptures to the likes they could never imagine thrived around them.

Architecture of new and old existed in unison, miles deep, in the heart of Nidavellir. An underground New York City, shining brightly like the stars above. Skyscrapers stood tall and mighty above them, some of them with no anchor to the ground. Buildings floated, as did the roads and highways. Trees, boulders, valleys, and mountains all synchronized together with technology unknown to any of them.

Restaurants, bars, banks, and different venues were carved into the stalactites that hung from the land's core. Stalagmites clumped together wildly from the ground, only to be chiseled into beguiling dwarven statues. Bridges made of rock and limestone connected the buildings up high as fluorescent neon lights enamored the city with every spectrum of the rainbow. A strip of casinos, lights flashing, danced about the town—their bright, open signs offering a friendly welcome.

Dwarves walked amongst the city just like any other, all of them burlier in size and nearly as wide as they were tall, maybe four feet in height altogether. A few of the dwarves would pass by and give menacing glares, but each of them would quickly glance the other way after noticing Inon.

They watched together in awe until finally, Michael broke the silence. "I guess you're up now, Reynir."

Reynir gave them a disgruntled look and palmed the dwarven-made artifact. "Fornviska,"Reynir stated. "In exchange for Brokkr and Eitri's next of kin, I choose to forfeit my position as next in line for head of council."

"No, you cannot do that," Steina pleaded. "I know how much that position means to you. I won't allow it."

"What is head councilor with no realm to look after?" Reynir asked. "Alfheim means more to me than a job description. Even if it is one that I have desired my entire life. Besides, you were made for the job. You are the youngest council member in history, remember," he said with a wink. "When the time comes, and Solfrid passes, hopefully, another thousand years from now, you will make her damn proud."

Steina nodded her head and proceeded forth with a small bow. "When that time comes, a thousand years from now, I won't let you down."

"I know you won't. That would be impossible."

The orb flickered to life, rolling in Reynir's hand, transforming into his very own handheld GPS. They followed the sphere as it guided them down the streets of Nidavellir. Each passing dwarf hawked them down, offering their services in one way or another, claiming to be able to craft anything that they desired. While tempting, the crew ignored their zealous solicitations and followed along the path blazed by Fornviska.

They walked many blocks, marveling at the beauty bestowed upon each corner until the orb settled at a location, *Brokkr & Eitri's Bar and Forgery.*

"I guess this is it," Michael said nervously as he grabbed the door handle. He pulled with minimal effort, expecting the door to welcome him, only for it not to budge. He gripped the handle once more, this time with both hands, and tugged at it, prying open the heavily weighted door.

The three tiptoed inside quietly, doing their best to bring the least amount of attention to themselves. In hindsight, Michael realized that it was rather impossible to camouflage oneself with a rather sizeable dragon trailing behind them. Inon's large hooves clanked along the metallic floor, bringing the tiny bar to a standstill.

All eyes were immediately positioned on them. The chattering stopped, and the bar went silent, minus some eerie dystopian metal music that played in the background.

"Were y'all raised in a barn or something?" asked the burly, bearded dwarf behind the bar. "Bringing a dragon into my bar. Fucking Midgardians, I tell ya what, waltzin' in like they own the place."

Reynir coughed. "Only one Midgardian," he said, nudging Michael slightly forward.

Michael turned his head, giving Reynir a bewildered expression. "What the hell, man."

"I'm only trying to get in his good graces, Midgardian."

"The dragon," the bartender barked sternly, banging his fist on the bar.

"Ahh, yes, our apologies," said Reynir. He patted Inon on the muzzle. "I think it would be wise if you were to wait outside, buddy. We will be out in a jiff. I promise."

Inon sauntered off, blazing small trails of fire from his nostrils, displaying his displeasure for the bar to see. He created even louder footsteps than before, rattling the glasses inside with each monstrous stomp. The dwarves eyed them with repulsion, their vision glaring and darting through them, peering at their insides.

"Well, be on with it," the bartender exclaimed, his voice sour and unwelcoming.

"We were hoping to find Brokkr and Eitri's next of kin," said Reynir. "We hoped that maybe one of you could guide us in the right direction."

The bar went quiet once more, all eyes darting to the back corner of the bar where two older, wizened dwarves spent their time nitpicking at one another's crafts. They stood over two blacksmith desks forging away, seemingly disinterested in the conversation that consumed the bar.

The dwarf with his back to them replied without turning around or even bothering to make eye contact. His sole attention on the crafts at hand. "Not interested. See them out, Admuck."

"With all due respect, sir," Michael asserted. "It's about the curse. We're here to lift it and resurrect your sun. I'm here to lift it. It's been written by the Norns themselves."

The two dwarves stopped their forging and turned their attention to Michael. The same dwarf that told them to go away responded once more. "Now I done said it nicely, we ain't interested. Is dat understood? Don't make me have to tell y'all again."

"Yes, sir," said Reynir. "Sorry for disturbing you."

The other dwarf, the one who had been quiet thus far, muttered words softly to his partner, yet loud enough that they still echoed off the walls for everyone to hear. "Let's just hear what they have to say, Brokkr."

Brokkr scoffed. "Be my guest."

The other dwarf, assumed to be Eitri, walked over to them and introduced himself. "Howdy, I'm Eitri, the third. That's my brother over there," he said, gesturing to the opposite end of the bar. "Brokkr, the third."

Brokkr grimaced at them and spit a gigantic wad of what could only be assumed as dip spit into a beer bottle while mumbling various profanities under his breath.

"Our grandfathers built this here bar from the ground up," said Eitri. "Built most of damn Nidavellir too. The finest craftsmen in our rich history."

"Pleasure to meet you," said Michael, extending his hand. Eitri accepted his greeting, wrapping his gigantic paw of a hand around Michael's. His hand was harder than steel, calloused with layers of thickened skin that felt as if his hand had grown biceps. "I'm Michael. This is Steina and Reynir," he said, motioning to each of them.

Eitri shook hands with the lot of them while his disgruntled brother continued to sit in the corner and glower at them. "The sun of Nidavellir. Now that's a damn good tale, I tell y'all what. And you claim to be able to resurrect it?"

"I suppose so. That's what Solfrid was told by Mimir at least."

"Solfrid? Ya hear that? They know Solfrid," said Eitri, yelling in the direction of his brother. "How's she doing?" he asked, turning his attention back to Michael.

"Not too great, unfortunately. That's why we need to break the curse and heal our land."

"A realm of darkness, I hear."

"Sadly, yes," said Steina. "Loki and Gullveig released Skoll and Hati. They devoured our suns whole. Our moons too. Solfrid ventured to Mimir afterward for his wisdom. His words were clear that we must resurrect your sun and rid both realms of the curse inflicted upon them. Then and only then can we live without a sun, and your community can bask in the glory of sunlight without turning to stone."

"I do reckon that would be mighty nice now."

"What do you say? Can you help us resurrect your sun?"

"Anyone over there in Alfheim mention why the curse ain't never been lifted yet?"

"No, not to my recollection."

"We ain't mind no stinking curse," Brokkr barked from the corner. "Our forefathers ain't mind no stinking curse neither. So, what, we ain't gets to see no sunlight. Who needs it anyway?"

"We do," said Reynir. "Direly, that is."

"That damn curse can only be broken by one with no dwarven blood," said Eitri ignoring his brother.

"In all of your years of trading, no one has ever offered to break the curse before?" asked Michael.

"'Fraid not. The one who breaks the curse can never return back to their home realm."

"That makes sense. That's why I must do it. I've already vowed to spend my life on Alfheim. If you can show me how . . . I'll do it. I'll lift the curse and resurrect your sun. I have no need to return to Midgard. My home lies on Alfheim."

"I got a trade for y'all," said Brokkr. "Y'all trade us your pretty lil' realm of Alfheim in exchange for this here piece of shit. How bout that? That way, we can finally rid ourselves of those pesky godforsaken dark elves."

"Yeah . . . that's not happening, pal, sorry," replied Michael.

"Hold on, Michael," said Steina. "This could benefit us. As the tale says, the sun of Nidavellir is brighter than the suns of Alfheim combined."

"Sure, but after we lift the curse, we will no longer need to rely on sunlight as we do now," said Reynir.

"Correct, but it's still essential to our livelihood. We don't know how big the rune of Sól will be," said Steina before shifting the conversation back to Brokkr. "If we exchange realms with you, will you agree to guide us and or give us the equipment needed to launch your sun?"

"Nah," said Brokkr. "That there's too much work. I was only yankin' your chains."

The bar erupted in laughter as the dwarves banged on the bar top and clanked their glasses amongst one another.

"I don't see why not," said Eitri. "We can finally have our own realm again. It'd be like the tales of our youth, told by our papas. We'd no longer have to hide down here below ground anymore. We can feel the warm sunlight shining pon' our faces for the first time."

"Blugh," Brokkr belched. "Fine, you can help launch that sun if you want some damn sunlight. Count me out. But we ain't trading no realm now, ya hear? Erthang is ardy built here. I'd like to keep her that way too."

"What is built can be rebuilt. Alfheim can be a fresh canvas. If we stay here, we'll have to rebuild above as it is. We can put our footprints on a new realm. We can be somewhere where we won't be overshadowed by our pops or grandpops no longer. Our destiny laid out by the Norns was that we'll rebuild a realm ravaged by darkness. What if it wasn't our realm they was referring to?"

"Too much work. I'm good."

"I understand. Your britches ain't big enough for that type of work. A blank canvas would only prove my superiority in crafting. Your reputation can't handle what I'd do to your sad, little shit you call work."

"Watch your fat, ugly mouth now before I shut it full of dragon shit. I'll make that dumbass trade and prove once and fer all I'm the superior brother and the superior blacksmith."

"We can't accept that," said Michael quietly to Steina and Reynir. "That's your home. You have a life there. Friends and family. Memories. There's too much history at stake."

"Alfheim can be rebuilt here," said Steina. "We will bring the other elves with us. Home is where the heart is, and as long as we have each other, Alfheim will always be home." She turned to Reynir for reassurance.

"That's up to you," said Reynir. "You are the assistant head of council now. I trust that you will make the right decision."

"Then we vote on it. If this is what it takes to save Alfheim, then count me in."

"Me too," said Michael.

"That makes three of us," said Reynir.

"If we trade with you, do we get to keep your architecture and creations already rooted here?" Steina asked the brothers. "It would be very beneficial, seeing as we have nothing remaining back home."

"Indeed, you would," said Eitri.

"And what of Michael? He vowed to Fornviska to return Alfheim to prosperity and never leave its side? Will he be trapped there?"

"Whodaya thank created Fornviska?"

"I suppose you did?"

"Well, it was our pops, but by resurrecting our sun, he will not only have restored one realm but two. As ya said, Alfheim is where the heart is. By healing and reconnecting the dark and light elves, he'll have done more for Alfheim than anyone in the history of that realm. It'll be the end of the Elven War. Fornviska will be more than grateful. I can assure ya of that. No punishment shall be rendered."

"Are there any repercussions that come with resurrecting your sun? Anything that will harm Michael in the process?"

"Only that he can't return to his home of Midgard."

"Who'd wanna return to that po dunk sack of shit?" Brokkr asked rhetorically.

Steina turned to Michael. "Are you sure that you are okay with this, Michael?"

"To be clear," said Michael to Eitri. "When you say never return home, that means never under any circumstances, right?"

"'Fraid so."

"Fine by me." Michael's heart longed to return home to Emma one day and tell her the truth, just as it longed to go back and put Konungr's and Darrius's souls to rest. Each of them deserved resolution, but that would be a problem for another day. People's lives were at stake, and he couldn't make a decision based on his own selfishness. Not anymore.

"Consider it a deal," said Steina, extending her hand forth.

Eitri shook her hand with delight. Everyone in the bar except for Brokkr erupted into cheers at the announcement of the trade.

"Shall we get to business?" asked Michael.

"I reckon we should, yes," said Eitri. "Let's gon and make our way to the vault. That's where we keep all the good stuff at. Follow me."

The three followed behind Brokkr and Eitri, but before they could leave the bar, they heard an ear-shrieking screech from Inon. Dark elves had swarmed the entrance as Inon did his best to fend them off. The elves stabbed at Inon with their spears as he hovered above for safety, firing molten hot flames in defense.

"Y'all go," Brokkr screamed. "I'll hold these here pistol willows off."

Reynir unsheathed his sword and rushed to Inon's aide. With a quick and powerful strike, he sliced the head off an attacking dark elf. He teleported a few of them elsewhere with his left hand, all while gouging his sword at the others with his right. "Eitri, guide them to vault. Brokkr and I can handle the featherweights here."

Michael, Steina, and Eitri watched cautiously, all of them charged with orka, ready to attack if needed.

"Get," hollered Brokkr. "I ain't need no help with these rat bastards. Gon' get that stupid sun now, ya hear?"

Eitri nodded his head, "Aye, captain."

Eitri guided them once again through the back door, which led them down a dark alley, through a welding shop, and into a factory that housed all sorts of iron and tools until they finally arrived at an elevator. The three of them got inside with urgency. Eitri stroked the numbers in sequential order, something that Michael made sure to focus on in case he needed to recall the memory at a later date.

"That's quite the code you have there," said Michael.

"Oh, that's nothin'," said Eitri. "It's just our grandpops birthday, our pops birthday, my birthday, and then Brokkr's birthday. Plus, my four kids and his three kids' birthdays. Do it once or twice an y'all a get the hang of it."

"Sounds easy enough," Michael chuckled.

The elevator doors opened to a large circular room with glass pods that encircled the perimeter. In the middle was another elevator, lacking any walls or support on its sides, only a circular platform instead. A sizeable cylindrical tube lied in the center of the platform, appearing to run through the entirety of the complex.

"I go no further," said Eitri.

"Why is that?" asked Steina.

"Ain't riskin' turnin' to stone. Not after what I seen happen to one of dem Ivaldi kids way back when. In the vault numbered nineteen, you'll find yourself a gauntlet. You'll need to equip that sucker before you seize the sun. Grab the goggles in vault ten as well. You'll need those there, so you don't burn your eyes out. After that, take the elevator all the way down to the bottom. That's where the sun is. You can't miss it. Grab her and put her in that pipe there and atta boy. It's a wrap."

"What can go wrong?" joked Michael. "We look forward to seeing you on the other side, Eitri," he said, shaking the gentleman's hand.

"Best of luck and Godspeed, young fella."

CHAPTER NINETEEN

THE SUN OF NIDAVELLIR

This was it; they were finally here. A few steps away from saving Alfheim and lifting the curse that had plagued the two realms for thousands of years. Michael and Steina walked to vault number ten as Eitri had instructed and grabbed the goggles enclosed inside.

Inside vault nineteen was a large and hefty, silver gauntlet, crafted long ago by Dvalin himself, resting there waiting for a soul brave enough to try her on. Dvalin's signature laid crested at the bottom in golden ink, shining like the sun, gleaming as freshly as if it had been scrawled the night before.

Michael reached inside and palmed the gauntlet. He held it in both hands, turning it over multiple times as he admired its intricate beauty. He slipped it on, and the gauntlet devoured his hand, consuming it whole, three sizes too big. The gauntlet tightened, growing smaller until it wrapped around his hand and forearm securely, gripping tighter than spandex. Above Dvalin's signature, an epithet started to appear in the same golden ink, engraving away with a mind of its own.

Michael Leitner, healer of Alfheim and savior of Nidavellir. Fated to die during the infamous battle of Ragnarök, and from the skies, he will be reborn.

The lines in Steina's face pressed and tightened upon reading. "We won't let that happen. We will make sure to put an end to Ragnarök long before then."

"I mean, hey, look on the bright side. At least I will be reborn. Whatever that means . . . but let's not mourn my future now. How about we finish playing god and reawaken this sun?" Michael put on his goggles, and just as the gauntlet did, they tightened around his head with the utmost precision.

Steina put on her goggles and followed behind Michael onto the platform in the center of the room. She pressed one of the many buttons, and the elevator descended, submerging them as deep as they could go into Nidavellir's core. The platform halted, and Michael and Steina exited, coming face-to-face with the imprisoned sun. The sun was etched into the wall, no larger than a basketball, leaving Michael to wonder how something so small and insignificant could entrap a realm's freedom for so long.

The sun's appearance was tiny and mundane, yet it still managed to captivate the entire room. It was the chamber's focal point, reminiscent of a night swim in the pool where one would open their eyes underwater only to be captivated by the tiny, circular pool light that orbited the deep end.

"You ready?" asked Michael, gesturing for Steina's hand as they stepped off the platform.

"As I'll ever be," she said, grabbing his hand and following behind him.

"Once I do this, there's no turning back. Svartalfheim or Nidavellir, whatever you want to call this place, will be ours, and Alfheim will be theirs. Are you sure that you're okay with that?"

"I am. I have never been more sure. As long as we have each other, that is all that matters. While Alfheim was glorious at its peak, it was destined to fall to Loki, and it did. Together we will make sure that this realm stands tall, and with our elven family here beside us, it will always be home."

A disturbing and ear-shrilling laugh filled the room, sending chills down Michael's spine, clutching his every last thought with terror. "Aww, how sweet, darling, but no one can stop us now," said the unmistakable and haunting voice of Gullveig.

Michael and Steina turned around to see Loki and Gullveig standing behind them, smiling devilishly, both sporting goggles similar to those they were wearing.

"How very sweet to find the two of you here," said Loki. "But I'm afraid I can't let you do that, Michael. You see, we need that sun right where it is. Surely you understand, don't you?"

"I'm afraid you left us with no other choice," said Michael.

"Steina, my dear," said Loki slyly, imploring his all too deceitful nature upon her. "Know that I meant every word that I have ever said to you. We can still have a future together, but you must trust me. Can you do that for me?"

"Why would I ever trust you again?" Steina asked sharply. "You're a piece of shit, Loki. I wouldn't trust you if my life depended on it."

"Ouch. So hostile. So malevolent. I've missed your feistiness and your passion. All the little things that make you, you. And while that hurts a little bit, I'm willing to look past it and forgive you for the greater good of Yggdrasil. There's more at play here than either of you understand, and you imbeciles keep getting in the way of all my hard work coming to fruition. I promise you when it's all over, and the dust has settled upon Asgard once again, we can be together, dear."

"I would never be with a scum like you."

"I'm afraid you already have," said Loki, licking his lips and unveiling his signature monstrosity of a smile. "I live inside of you. Inside your head. Inside your memories. Inside your every move.

You crave me, and deep down, you lust for the love of a god. A mere mortal, a mortal like him, can never give you the sensations that I have," he said, pointing disgustingly at Michael. "I am eternal, and I will always subside over you. I am now. I am always and forever, and in the end, we will be together once more."

"You are truly disgusting. You are nothing more than a despicable, lonely coward who will never know true happiness, and that will be your almighty downfall, and I can't wait to be there to enjoy every second of it."

Michael should've known better; he'd already let his emotions get the best of him twice now. Once, after Peter's death when he unsheathed Reynir's sword and attacked Loki with it. The second time he lost his cool, it cost Darrius his life. He knew better than to attack Loki, but his smug face and his stupid smile infuriated Michael. His hatred for Loki had no bounds. Loki had taken so much from him, and now it was Michael's turn to exact the revenge he had been plotting for two years.

Michael dug deep within, recalling the cave of self. He was reminded of the tumultuous monster he had faced there, a demon far scarier than either Loki or Gullveig. The monster that had lived within him all these years, and now he needed to become one with that beast again, last time to defeat him, this time to become him. If he was going to defeat Loki, he would need the most physically violent and repulsive version of himself to do so.

Michael made the mistake of charging at Loki already, neither time working in his favor. This time he was patient, listening to Loki's barrage of bullshit, and although the trickster was an amazing actor, Michael was having none of it, for he had seen firsthand the blood that had been shed by that monster.

Michael heard every lie unfurl from the lips of Loki, all the while he continuously charged his orka until that energy ruptured inside of him. His cup runneth full, overflowing with magic, maddeningly drunk off it. He felt like a tire overinflated with air and like that tire would need its valve stem for release, Michael needed the same, but his release came at the expulsion of a massive, fiery-red ball of destructive power that barreled Loki head-on.

The blast sent Loki pummeling across the room, battering him against the wall full force. Michael couldn't refrain the smile from emanating upon his lips. The taste of sweet vengeance was one he had long lusted after, but his victory was short-lived as Gullveig quickly greeted him and Steina with an onslaught of attacks.

Wisps of green, electrical energy crackled around Gullveig as she floated in the air. Two blades emerged from her hands, crafted by the orka she had generated. She thrashed relentlessly with grace and precision, leaving Michael and Steina on the defensive.

They each created an orka infused blade of their own, matching Gullveig's devastating weapons. Each of their strikes was met with a block from Gullveig. Even with both on the offensive, Gullveig was too quick and stealthy, her defense impenetrable.

Michael focused on Gullveig's right arm, visualizing it to be paralyzed in place until he was able to clench onto her shoulder and restrain her from attacking. Steina took advantage of Michael's telekinetic grasp and slashed at Gullveig's right shoulder, searing through her flesh to the bone. Gullveig's arm hung limply on its last thread like the loose tooth of a child too frightened to pull it.

Instinctively, Gullveig blasted Steina with her free arm, sending her in the air before she could attack again. Michael charged his orka, unleashing a powerful punch upon Gullveig's face with the hand that the gauntlet had been fitted to. The blow buckled her to her knees.

Michael released another jab, this one a devastating uppercut that sent Gullveig collapsing to the floor. Michael seized the momentum and mounted on top of her, landing one crippling haymaker after the other. The gauntlet connected with precision, drubbing her face with blistering contusions.

He pinned her injured arm beneath him with the weight of his knee and continued his assault. Michael maintained his leverage over Gullveig until she caught him off guard with a quick strike, thrusting her orka blade into his abdomen. The blow halted him just long enough for Gullveig to kick him off of her and free herself from his grip.

A searing, hot sensation singed through Michael's core as blood gorged from his abdomen in spurts. He winced in pain as he got to his feet and massaged his puncture wound with his left hand. He ushered his right hand forward, feeling his telekinetic grip grasp onto Gullveig once more, immobilizing her.

Steina shifted behind Gullveig, but the goddess broke free from Michael's stranglehold just as Steina got within striking distance. Gullveig teleported behind Michael and fired a staggering blast with her one and only abled arm. The orka attack sent Michael crashing fiercely into Steina, sending the two of them to tumble over one another across the floor.

Gullveig sprinted forward, one arm hanging loosely while the other held her orka blade. She thrashed her sword at them, but Steina was able to block it with an orka shield of her own. The force of their collision sent Steina and Gullveig spiraling back tens of feet. They each throttled towards one another, trading blows back and forth, one on offense, one on defense, both charging at the other tirelessly, waltzing together in what looked like a choreographed act of violence synchronized to perfection.

Michael hobbled himself off the ground, his core stinging from Gullveig's sweltering blade. He powered up once more, harnessing all the magic and energy he could withhold. The room quaked as remnants of metal and debris radiated around him. He fired his orb at Gullveig, this one larger and more calamitous than the one he had attacked Loki with.

Gullveig opened a portal before the blast, intercepting it, leaving Michael unsure of where she had sent it. His uncertainty didn't last long as the orb thrashed into his backside, whiplashing his entire body. He was gobsmacked by his own attack, clobbered like a quarterback hit from his blindside. He flew across the room and collided with the stiff and punishing wall.

Michael saw the night sky as he attempted to overlook the fight. His vision hazy as blinding black and white specks conglomerated together. It was as if he had rubbed his eyes fiercely upon waking. With widened eyes and panicked blinks, he was able to piece together the orka of Steina and Gullveig.

Their orka flared together rapidly like comets streaking across the night. Steina's orka resembled that of lightning, a dazzling yellowish-white that clashed against Gullveig's ominous green. They continued their flurry of attacks on one another, teleporting back and forth, both of them moving at fleeting speeds that were impossible to catch with the naked eye.

While the two traded blows, Michael limped towards the sun. He was unsure of what the hell he would do with it once he obtained it but equally sure that a sun was probably powerful enough to inflict an unhealable amount of damage upon his opponents.

Unfortunately for Michael, Loki had other ideas in mind. He tackled Michael to the floor before he could reach the sun of Nidavellir. The two wrestled, tussling above one another, trading grips and holds until another sharp stab to Michael's abdomen sent him gasping for breath. He blasted Loki off of him, bidding him a short allotment of time to aid his wounds.

Steina targeted Gullveig's injured shoulder, blasting it once more with orka leaving her arm to sway uncontrollably like a pendulum experiencing mechanical fits. Steina continued her merciless assault upon Gullveig, unveiling a melee of concussive blasts. Each menacing blow knocked Gullveig's head around until Steina held her in her clutches.

Steina lifted Gullveig into the air, planting her head against the wall firmly. Her grip was unwavering, etching itself tightly around Gullveig's throat, burrowing fiercely into her windpipe and collapsing it slowly. Steina had Gullveig on the precipice of death, albeit a short-lived death since the witch was incapable of truly dying.

With Gullveig's life in Steina's hands, Loki diverted his attention from Michael to Steina and swiftly grappled her to the ground. The two wrestled, vying for leverage until Loki laid atop of her, and the wrestling stopped. They shared a look of intimacy as they stared deep into each other's eyes, and for that one moment in time, Steina was powerless, trapped in the eyes of the man she had once fallen in love with on the mountaintops of Alfheim. Her vision emanated before her. Loki's captivating glance holding her prisoner.

Michael laid there despondently, too weak to intervene. The bad in him, the behemoth he called upon to start the battle, had exhausted him of all his energy. He channeled deep within, back to the cave of self. He had to release that being or risk being consumed by it for good.

Michael watched helplessly as Loki kissed Steina. He felt his heart tug inside his chest, pulling in each direction, swelling with indescribable pain and agony as he watched the two kiss each other with such passion and lust for one another. But it wasn't jealously that overcame him. It was pain, a longing pain, that he felt for Steina. Empathy even, she gave in to what she despised most, and it broke his heart to see that.

Steina pushed Loki off her gently, pulling herself away from their tender embrace. Her face crinkled with confusion as different emotions flooded her all at once. They stared into each other's eyes once more, both of them speechless.

"I missed you so much, Steina," said Loki, stroking the side of her face, running his fingers through her hair. "You must understand, I didn't mean for any of this to happen. I didn't slaughter that village, nor did I murder Peter either. I could never do those things. I am a victim. I am the victim of an elaborate ploy thousands of years in the making. I want nothing more than a life with you, and if you allow me to execute this plan, I can prove that to you. But I have to make things right first. Give me the opportunity to—"

Without warning, Gullveig fired a thunderous streak of lightning into Steina's skull. The blow knocked Steina unconscious upon impact. Gullveig's sinister cackle filled the air, throbbing inside Michael's eardrums as rage consumed him once more. No longer did he care about becoming that behemoth. He'd do anything to avenge Steina. He glared at Gullveig as a feeling of unquenchable malice slugged inside his chest. He charged his orka and prepared for his attack, but before he could do so, Loki had intervened.

"What have you done?" Loki screamed, trembling with a fervent passion. "This wasn't a part of the plan. She wasn't supposed to die."

"I improvised, honey," said Gullveig, shrilling with joy. "And your little lady friend here was trying to kill me. I'm unsure of whether or not you saw that. It was time I rid her from your life once and for all. She was . . . how should I say this? She was a succubus, darling."

Loki checked along Steina's neck for a pulse as relief spread across his face after discovering one. His face tightened, his teeth clenched, his eyebrows cocked with furor. His rage could be felt imminently as the floor quivered beneath them. The ceiling proceeded to unravel; scrap metal ripped off its hinges, circling Loki with ferocity. He charged at Gullveig, hitting her with a cataclysmic arsenal of blows. Gullveig fell to her knees, eating every one of Loki's vicious punches. Her high-pitched cackle becoming more deafening with every strike.

Loki wailed on her repeatedly with a combo of un-guardable orka blasts until finally, not even Gullveig could absorb them. She laid on the floor, limp and unconscious, no longer laughing maniacally. Loki slithered his way on top of her and placed his hand over her right cheekbone, injecting the switchblade from his wrist and thrusting it deep into her temple. A pool of blood spilled to the floor as Michael watched the light leave Gullveig's eyes.

A moment that should have delighted Michael infuriated him instead. He envisioned Loki slithering atop of Peter and impaling him in the same fashion he had just done to Gullveig. Adrenaline flooded Michael's arteries once more. The death of Peter replaying in his head filled him with the bloodthirst needed to continue.

His ears prickled with intense heat, his face flushing red. His orka levels spiked exponentially. The room surged in his wake, shriveling from the power he expelled. He now stood toe-to-toe with Loki, so close that he could feel the hot breaths from him trickle upon his face.

"You're gonna pay for what you did to Peter," said Michael. "To Konungr. To Darrius. To everyone. Now tell me where you're hiding my sister, you fucking pig."

Michael's body twitched with an uncontrollable rage. He was unable to stop it; it was as if he was hyperventilating on power. His body was housing an insurmountable level of orka, a level that was unsustainable to him. He was pushing his figurative RPMs past their limit. The pistons inside him rattled vehemently, feeling as if that imaginary engine would catapult from the hood of the car or, in his case, himself. He was entering dangerous territory, crossing a threshold that would cause his circuits to trip, but he couldn't let go. Not yet. Not with all this power surging through him.

"Your anger is misinformed," replied Loki. "As for your sister, I've never met her a day in my life. I have the slightest idea of her whereabouts, for that matter. You're not the only one who has lost things during this war. A war that began taking place long before you. A war that will long succeed you."

"A war that you created. Now, where is my sister?" Michael was no longer asking but demanding. He shoved his fists hard into Loki's sternum, pulsing orka into Loki's chest, defibrillating him with his touch. "I have visions that she is with you. Now tell me where you are hiding her."

"Visions?" asked Loki, visibly confused. "You've been having visions of her?"

"Visions where she refers to you as father, you lying, thieving, cold-blooded bastard. Don't play stupid with me," said Michael, shoving Loki once more. "I'll give you one more chance to tell me where she is before I pry the answers from your cold, dead body."

The angrier that Michael became, the closer he was to becoming the monster that consumed him within. The room constricted even more as power discharged around him, the walls slowly contracting and withering at the result of his wrath.

"I told you, Michael. I don't know your sister, nor do I know her whereabouts. Regardless of what you may have seen or seem to believe, this is only our second encounter together—the first being on Alfheim with Frey and Heimdall. I never killed Peter. Or Konungr. Or Darrius, as you have claimed. Only Heimdall, but that was an act of self-defense. And Heimdall himself will be reborn after Ragnarök. The gods have seemingly forgotten what life was like before this chapter dawned upon us.

"I've been framed, framed for as long as I can remember. But I do know who killed your friends, and with your visions, yes, your visions can lead us to him," said Loki, dropping to his knee, pleading his innocence like the slimy creature that he was. "This is our opportunity to take the advantage. Your visions . . . they can lead us to prosperity against the Allfather, Odin."

Michael's body, still convulsing and drunk with power, began to shut down, overwhelmed by more orka than he could absorb. He tried listening to Loki's words, but his ears were sweltering hot, buzzing too intensely for him to focus. His metaphorical well was on the verge of crumbling as it overflowed to its boiling point. He had to let go of all his power, or he would risk a permanent and irreversible transformation.

He crumpled to the floor; his body limp from all the strain placed upon it. His extremities felt like spaghetti, too weak to move a muscle, but his mind was still sharp. Sharp enough to use his last bit of remaining energy, and with it, he used his telekinetic power to wriggle the rune of Odin free from his pocket. He called it into the air and thrust it towards Loki. "If it's Odin you want . . . you got him," muttered Michael feebly.

The rune levitated in the air briefly before falling to the ground and clanking on the metallic surface. The two watched anxiously as the rune rattled and spun across the floor like dice tumbling across the craps table. Just as it seemed as if Michael had cast a dud, dust and smoke occupied the center of the room, converging about aggressively, spiraling like a dust storm from the Midwest and from the dust, appeared two ravens. Odin's ravens, Huginn and Muninn.

CHAPTER TWENTY

THE ALLFATHER

Huginn and Muninn scaled the room, circling the perimeter and cawing loudly. Their piercing caws transformed the atmosphere of the chamber into an eeriness that was typically attributed to death. Their wingspans covered five or so feet; their eyes beady and darting, locked in on Loki.

A burly, large chested gentleman walked through the smoke, emerging like a wrestler through pyrotechnics. He was chiseled, more so than anybody Michael had ever seen in his lifetime. Far more chiseled than Heimdall or Frey. He was as old as Konungr, if not older, yet he looked young and full of life at the same time.

The god was in immaculate shape; his broad shoulders and muscular build were enamored with too many scars to count. The wounds were memorable, leaving Michael with a feeling he'd seen those same scars somewhere before. Hints of déjà vu intertwined Michael's thoughts, but he was far too distracted to scour his mind on the abrasions of another.

Odin wore a horned helmet, which helped conceal his one and only eye. The other had been carved out and healed over, still leaving a rather deep indentation in its place. His chest plate and armor glimmered with gold. He stepped forward with a brash, unspoken level of confidence, a swagger that most would envy. Had Michael not been sure that he was there to help, he would have been absolutely terrified of him.

Loki tremored with fear. His lips quivered at the sight of Odin. "O-Odin. You, you called Odin. You fool," Loki said to Michael in panic. "He's the enemy. The man responsible for murdering Peter. The man who murdered Konungr and Darrius on Midgard. The man who's put an immeasurable price on my head and tarnished my reputation for eternity."

"Silence," said Odin, his voice strong and powerful as it bellowed throughout the room. The kind of voice that demanded respect from anyone who heard it. "My patience has worn thin with you, Loki. Your lips reek of betrayal and deceit. For that, I will sew them shut once more."

A thread and needle appeared on cue, striking fiercely into Loki's top lip. Loki wriggled and contorted his body, but Odin was too powerful. With Loki unable to move in Odin's grasp, the needle prickled up and down, sewing his lips together intricately. Tears rolled down Loki's cheeks as his face winced in pain with every strike. Each new stitch perforated his skin, lining his lips with blood. The blood dripped from his mouth, sloping down his chin and running across his neck like a river.

The sight filled Michael with bliss. It was all over; Loki could harm them no more. All the brave and bold sacrifices would no longer be in vain. They would finally have the meaning that they were worthy of. He could go to bed at night knowing that he made both Darrius and Konungr proud. He could forgive himself, now knowing he had given Peter the justice he deserved.

Tears welled in his eyes at the thought of it all. They had won at last. The sweet feeling of victory overcame him. The pain, the agony, the grief, it would all be over. Ragnarök would be delayed, the elves of Alfheim would be replenished, and most importantly, Loki would be bound once more, hopefully executed this time with no means of a return.

As Michael watched with triumphant joy, his eyes connected with those of Loki's. The exchange was awkward and unpleasant, but looking into Loki's eyes pained him with remorse, and he was unsure why. This was the man who had taken everything from him and his friends, yet somehow, he felt bad for him.

Loki's eyes had a sincerity to them. They were soft and reassuring, so much so that Michael began to second guess himself. Could Loki possibly be telling the truth? Steina seemed to believe he had some level of good in him, or else she wouldn't have kissed him. He was so damn believable too. Loki claimed to have not killed his friends, and yet for whatever reason, Michael believed him.

Hearing Loki's consistent begs and repeated lies that he had been framed brought Michael back to the cave with Konungr. Why couldn't Konungr have informed him of his suspicions? No, Michael thought, now wasn't the time for bargaining. He had witnessed Loki murder Darrius and Konungr. There was no mistake in the evidence that presented itself. Loki was a monster. Michael was resolute in that belief, and the sympathy that he felt for a brief moment in time was replaced with rage at the vision of his brother Darrius being skewered by Loki's spear, Gungnir.

Speaking of, where the hell was Gungnir? It appeared in every one of Michael's visions, and now all of a sudden, Loki doesn't have it anymore? It didn't make any sense. And where was Mjölnir or the sword of Frey? It seemed unlike Loki to harvest together such powerful weapons and not bring any of them to battle. Surely, he wasn't that cocky, was he? As Michael wondered quietly to himself, he noticed Loki's head tilt back and his eyes dart upward as if to get Michael's attention.

Michael followed Loki's eyes as they led him to Odin and his armor that glistened of gold. How Michael had missed it was beyond him. Maybe it was Odin's captivating entrance or his horrifying and ghastly ravens, but there it was, Gungnir, draped upon Odin's back. Its tip sharp and piercing, the width of it unsettling.

Michael shuddered as he saw the weapon that had slain Darrius and Konungr, a weapon that had inflicted so much pain amongst him. Why would Odin have it? That was Loki's spear, and it had been with Loki only a few days ago on Midgard. How could Odin have retrieved it in such a short timespan? And if he had succeeded in commandeering it, why would Loki still be alive to tell the tale?

The detective in Michael was rousing. The pieces to this elaborate puzzle didn't fit into place as he had expected they would. Something was missing, that much he was confident in. Unfortunately, he had the slightest idea of what the missing piece might be, but Loki was right about one thing; there was undoubtedly more to the story than he or his friends understood.

The needle stitched the end of Loki's lips together, and just as quickly as the needle and thread appeared, it had vanished. Loki's head fell to his chest. Whether from shame or fatigue, Michael would never know. Odin snatched Loki by his hair—in the same manner that Michael had seen Loki do to Skye in his vision—forcing Loki to administer eye contact with him.

"I would say that you would be welcome in Valhalla, but we both know that that would be a lie, now wouldn't we?" said Odin. "However, seeing as I am a god of sound mind and justice, I will make personal arrangements to guarantee your first-class ticket to Helheim," he said, shoving Loki forcefully to the ground and extending his spear high overhead.

It was a damn near-exact replica of Loki's statement before Darrius saved Michael's life on Midgard. That couldn't be a coincidence. The way that Odin unsheathed his spear, his mannerisms, the dialect in which he spoke, it was all Loki. Not the Loki before him now, but the Loki that had emanated in Michael's visions for far too long. The Loki that had killed Konungr and Darrius. The Loki that dragged him to Alfheim or wherever the hell when he was only five years old, and that's when Michael realized where he had seen those scars.

Odin, the broad-shouldered man, enamored with scars, was the same man who had thrust Skye into the dungeon the day she had been kidnapped. And there, chiseled upon Odin's cheek, was a freshly flayed scar, an exact match to the one Darrius had inflicted upon him with Hofud days prior.

Michael watched, conflicted, unsure of whom to believe, but instinct took over before his mind could convince him otherwise. He focused his energy on Odin, halting the Allfather's spear mid-strike, saving Loki from the fatal assault that Gungnir would have administered had Michael not intervened. Odin's hand quivered in Michael's grasp. He turned his body slowly towards Michael, his eyebrows tilted, his face perplexed. His confusion quickly shifting into that of a blood-boiling furor.

"The spear, where did you get it?" asked Michael, both his arms straining as they contained Odin's arm.

Odin quaked in Michael's presence, his power relenting and catastrophic, painting the room into a caricature of itself as their surroundings dwindled in the chaos. Michael's interaction allowed Loki just enough time to blast the spear from Odin's hands.

Gungnir rattled to the floor. Odin made a quick jab for it, but Loki blasted him backward before he could capture it. Loki swiftly snatched Gungnir in his presence. Odin cast a portal behind Loki and tackled him through it. The two of them tumbled through the portal to what appeared to be a volcanic wasteland. Michael could only assume the realm to be Muspelheim, Surtr's nightmarish paradise.

A place that Michael had no desire to visit, but he hurried to the portal in hopes that he could venture through, but it dissipated long before he could arrive there. He turned his attention to Steina, who still laid unconscious in the center of the chamber. Michael checked her vitals and found a heartbeat. He would have to wait to heal her. He couldn't jeopardize any more of his power. Not with Odin and Loki in the pursuit of battle, potentially returning to him at any moment.

He sat down and waited patiently, focusing in on the immense energy masses of Loki and Odin, hoping to locate them but ultimately came up without a trace. Not a glimpse of either being emerged within him. What had he done? he thought. Why would he stop Odin from killing Loki? Everything that he had worked so hard for was right before him, and he fumbled it all away, falling victim to Loki's smart mouth and deceitful ways.

Michael meditated quietly for minutes with no indications of either's whereabouts. A few minutes on Midgard could be hours on another realm or mere seconds. He had the slightest idea of how time operated here on Nidavellir. For all he knew, the battle could have already ended, and it scared him that he didn't know who he wanted to win. Maybe they would both die. That would end everything for good. No more gods and their power-hungry interests or their riddle twisted tongues.

Somewhere in the middle of Michael's angst, a sudden revelation washed over him. The entire reason he voyaged to Nidavellir was to launch the realm's sun. What the hell was he doing waiting for Loki and Odin to return and stop him? This was his opportunity to finish what the gods had started. Launch the sun, end the curse, and restore Alfheim and Nidavellir to their once renowned beauty.

The chamber walls had crumbled, shrinking the room's size in half. The place's infrastructure was buckling from the stress of battle, but somehow the cylindrical tube in the chamber's center stood mostly untouched.

Michael examined the sun, etched firmly into the wall. He excavated the debris that surrounded it and removed it out of the way delicately. He palmed the sun in his hand that wielded the gauntlet and felt an immediate surge of orka pulsate within him. A fiery, white-hot burst of energy flowed through his veins. He could feel the orka racing through him, throttling underneath his skin, replenishing his debilitated state.

Michael could sense Loki and Odin's return before they arrived back to the chamber. His senses were on fire, tingling from his latest resurgence. A portal reappeared, emerging both gods back into the room. Both their bodies were battered and bruised, pocked with gashes and scrapes, but it was Odin who held the advantage, pointing Gungnir directly into Loki's throat. Loki attempted to slither away on all fours, but Odin backed him into a corner, allowing him no escape, keeping Gungnir pressed upon him tightly.

"Do it," barked Odin, gesturing for Michael to launch the sun of Nidavellir. He kept a firm, unrelenting grip upon Gungnir, hoisting it deeper into Loki's throat. Both of Loki's hands flailed around the spear, struggling against Odin's sheer force. With Loki's lips still stitched together, he shook his head vehemently, all but begging Michael not to break the curse. "Now," continued Odin.

Michael studied the god's faces, examining their eyes, looking for any chink in their armor, any strains, any sudden blinks, anything that might display a sign of dishonesty. He didn't know who to side with. His mind begged him, telling him the clear and obvious choice was Odin. Odin was good; Loki was evil. End of story. Don't overthink it; his mind stressed.

However, his heart still tugged at him. Something about Loki's sincerity struck a chord within him, but most of all, Michael couldn't look past the fact that Odin had Gungnir. No matter what explanation he contrived, none of it made sense. Michael forced himself to put his internal dilemma behind him.

More important things were at stake. His decision to choose an alliance could wait for another day. He needed to resurrect the sun of Nidavellir. The elves of Alfheim were counting on him, and he couldn't let them down.

Still seizing the sun, Michael walked over to the cylindrical tube interwoven inside the platform and stepped aboard. Loki and Odin both eyed him intensely, still struggling in their game of tug-of-war for Loki's trachea. Michael ignored them both, too preoccupied with the mission at hand.

Excitement built inside him. He felt his heart throb and pound in his chest as he inched closer to the tube. It resembled a pneumatic tube like the ones seen at banks. Face-to-face with it, Michael gave one more look into Loki and Odin's direction. Loki's eyes were wide and full of terror, doing his best to fight Odin and express the grave concern of Michael's decision. Odin's face revealed the opposite, one of joy and zealous, his eyes sparkling at the sight of the reemerging sun coming to fruition.

There was no entrance or opening to the cylinder, just a transparent force field in the shape of a pipe that ran through the heart of the realm. Michael reached the gauntlet inside, sun in hand, and he felt the sun torque upwards with a powerful magnetic pull. Michael didn't fight it. He let the sun go, and away it went, shooting through the tube like a bullet exiting a gun. The sun expelled, too fast to see or comprehend, and just like that, it was gone.

Odin rejoiced; Michael wanted to join him but hadn't quite come to terms with what he had accomplished. He assumed it had worked, but until he could enter the surface and see for himself, he couldn't be sure, nor could he be sure of who to trust while he was down here. Only one thing was certain, one of the gods would die, and the victor would realistically eye Michael for seconds.

Before Michael could dwell on the matter any longer, smoke began to preoccupy the room. He was unsure if the smoke was hazardous, but he didn't want to stick around long enough to find out. Maybe it was a side effect to resurrecting the realm's sun, a trap set in place thousands of years before.

Michael rushed to Steina's side, desperately needing to teleport them to safety. His teleportation was spotty, and he had the slightest clue where they might wind up, but any place was better than here, he thought. He gripped Steina's arm, ready to bring her along before he heard Odin mutter profanities loudly.

"Where'd he go?" growled Odin. "Huginn. Muninn. Find him."

Through Odin's profanities, Michael realized the smoke was not hazardous but rather a clever smoke spell ushered by Loki, the opportunistic trickster who was clearly gunning for his escape. Once the smoke began to settle, Michael could see Huginn and Muninn etching their claws into a snake. The snake was about a foot long in length, resembling a garter snake, but it was clearly Loki in disguise.

The ravens double-teamed Loki, carrying him midair with their talons carved deep into his skin. They flailed and jerked violently, sending spasms throughout Loki's snake-like body. Loki shape-shifted back into the god he was, weighing the ravens down to the floor. He lunged at both ravens, trying to rid himself from their deadlocked grasp, but their talons were forged deep inside like a splinter. Loki transformed again, this time into that of a dragon. He stamped his head and rattled wildly, sending both ravens to retreat to safety.

Odin grew tired of Loki's antics and hurtled Gungnir at Loki's dragon-like form. Loki evaded the spear by transforming into a tiny, flamboyant hummingbird. The spear darted through the air, past Loki, colliding into one of Odin's ravens, tagging its wing and clipping it into the wall.

The raven stuck there, hanging by one wing and cawing in pain. It writhed erratically, dangling like an ornament in a tree. As a result of the raven's treacherous pain, Odin keeled over and moaned in agony. His hands wove around his head tightly enough to see the redness flush to his fingertips. He and his raven appeared to be interconnected in some form, and in the raven's pain, Odin had become afflicted too, his consciousness temporarily wounded.

Loki transformed back into himself. He gripped Gungnir and thrust it deeper into the wall, applying more pressure upon the injured raven. Odin's other raven, the one free from captivity, targeted Loki and hawked towards him. Loki unveiled his dagger from his wrist, shearing the wing of the other raven, sending it spiraling to the floor where it limped and fluttered in despair.

Loki sliced through his lips with the dagger in hand, removing the stitches that had been carved into them. His lips began to bleed profusely, more than they had before when Odin had sewed them shut. He focused his attention back on the raven that he had crucified into the wall and applied more pressure onto the raven's wing while his other hand pulsed blistering orka into the raven's chest.

Michael took advantage of Odin's anguish by targeting Odin's thoughts, looking to penetrate the mind of the Allfather. Odin grunted, tormented by Michael's assault, but Loki merely applied more pressure onto Odin's raven, allowing Michael to trespass into Odin's memories freely.

Memories scrolled past Michael in a chaotic whirl due to the tumultuous amount of pain Odin experienced. Michael had to be quick, thorough but quick. He didn't know how long Loki could fend off Odin.

He searched Odin's catalog of memories for himself, Michael Leitner, anxious to see what he might find. Sure enough, the memories appeared in chronological order, starting with the day Odin had abducted Skye, all while he had been impersonating Loki. Michael sifted through more memories with a sense of urgency, only to find Loki's words to bear the truth. It was Odin who murdered Peter. Odin who had murdered Darrius and Konungr.

Michael's brain faltered. He was numb with thought, and because of that, he lost his focus. Like a driver losing control of the steering wheel, he began to fishtail, hydroplaning away from the memories he coveted. Odin's memories became unorganized once more, gusting around him like a cyclone. Michael felt himself slipping from Odin's mind. The hurricane-force winds were too strong to fight, and he slipped, scuttling back into his body.

Loki seemed to have been pressing Odin while Michael had been extracting his memories, thus explaining how Michael could obtain those memories with such ease.

"Why?" asked Loki, pressing Gungnir deeper into the wall. "Why me, Odin? We were brothers. Why jeopardize that and assign me to a life of exile?"

Odin's teeth clattered, and his lips trembled as he tried to cover his mouth, refraining it from speaking, but Loki's power over him was too mighty. "Because you remembered the past," said Odin, still straining. "Remembered what was and the lifetimes before. After I hung myself upon Yggdrasil for nine days and nine nights, I was granted with wisdom and power unbeknownst before me, and with it, I cursed the gods and inflicted their memory. I couldn't afford for you to continue clamoring about our true nature of being reborn upon our deaths. Our true nature of the reincarnation that takes place after Ragnarök."

Michael watched in stunned silence. He couldn't believe his ears. Even after seeing the memories for himself, he still couldn't believe that Loki had been telling the truth the entire time. Michael spent the past two years with a consuming, misguiding hatred for Loki only to have learned that he was innocent. It was Odin who warranted Michael's vengeance, not Loki, and the entire time Konungr knew or at least had his suspicions.

Michael couldn't stand idly by any longer, not with the truth at his fingertips. "Where are you hiding my sister?" he asked Odin, filling with a renewed rage thanks to the temporary boost the sun of Nidavellir had provided him.

Odin grimaced, fighting to contain the answers that desperately begged to exude from his lips.

Loki applied more pressure onto Odin's raven. "Answer him. He deserves to know the truth."

"She is locked away on Asgard as my prisoner," Odin groaned.

"Why would you kidnap her?" asked Michael. "She was only a child. What good could she have done you?"

"After I drank from Mimir's well, I saw the future, and that future led to Skye Leitner. Skye Leitner would be my almighty downfall. A stupid little Midgardian girl. So, I kidnapped her and did what I had to do to protect myself. I trained her to become a fierce warrior, to fight at my side and never against."

"I don't understand. Why her? Of all the nine realms, my sister is at the epicenter. It doesn't make any sense."

"Oh, boo-hoo," interjected Loki. "Enough about Skye. What about me? Why masquerade around and pretend to be me, Odin?"

"I have a reputation," said Odin, struggling under Loki's grasp. "But you, Loki, you had nothing. You were a man that people we're lusting to hate. The men were jealous. The women scornful after your many twisted love affairs. The gods had already made up their minds about you. They already had preconceived thoughts. I just had to act upon them and bring those negative thoughts to fruition.

"It was too easy. Me kidnapping children, terrorizing realms, picking off gods one by one as I was disguised in your flesh. All those acts leading to the inevitable day where no god could overtake me. I have been inaugurating wars, rounding my plan into place. All under your very nose. It only took you a thousand years," said Odin, smiling with that same smile that he used to bear under the disguised skin of Loki.

Loki's hands slipped from Gungnir in a fit of rage. "And now you must atone for your sins." He let go of his grasp on the spear and throttled forward at Odin.

Odin's raven thrashed, severing its wing and freeing itself from Gungnir's grip splattering blood with each panicked flicker of its wings. The raven's release resulted in Odin being freed from the bonds that had controlled him.

Before Michael or Loki had the opportunity to stop him, Odin rounded up his ravens and teleported to safety, fleeing from Nidavellir in a flash. Michael stared, transfixed at the location where Odin resided moments prior, utterly bewildered at the events that had transpired.

"All along, you have been telling the truth?" asked Michael.

"I have," said Loki.

"Then why Gullveig? Why choose to conceal the sun of Nidavellir and torment the elves of those realms?"

"Not many are crazy enough to willingly battle Odin. Gullveig is one of them. Frankly, she was my only choice. She's as sinister as they come, but I needed her in our war against Odin. As for Nidavellir, I needed an army of dark elves to battle against Odin and whatever armies he has conjured beside him. Without that, our offensive has been weakened. You and I will need to work together to defeat him. I hope to have your hand in an alliance one day."

"One day . . . maybe. But damn sure not right now. You battled against us. You destroyed Alfheim. Blood is on your hands, Loki. All of that cannot be easily forgiven nor forgotten . . . but my hatred for you is no longer. That hatred belongs to Odin now and if defeating him means we must partner up in the future, then so be it, but you will have to earn my trust. Hers too," said Michael, motioning to Steina. "You can begin by helping me heal her."

"I understand. I look forward to proving my worth to you and exonerating my name."

Healing was less about healing and more about taking and absorbing the pain of another being, so while Michael still despised Loki, he needed him. Knowing that he was in no condition to heal Steina on his own, Michael did the unthinkable. He swallowed his pride and helped heal her with the assistance of Loki. Together they kneeled beside Steina, each of them gripping a shoulder and absorbing the pain inflicted by Gullveig.

Steina awoke in a weary state, that of lethargy. Michael began to feel overwhelmed as well. A groggy sensation flooded him after he healed Steina. It took a lot of orka to aid her to a functional state. His body ached from the pain he inherited from her. It ached from the pain of battle, depleted to its last bit from launching the sun of Nidavellir. With adrenaline no longer coursing through his veins, exhaustion overtook him.

He was now operating in between reality and a dream-like state, unsure if what was happening was real or a figment of his subconscious. It was Loki who was guiding them all the way to the platform where he and Steina both fell into the safe arms of Reynir, where Michael collapsed for good, his eyes too heavy to lift any longer.

CHAPTER TWENTY-ONE

FREY AND HIS BEAUTY

Michael and Steina both awoke a couple of days later, the battle exhausting them more than expected. Upon awakening, they gathered with their respective council members and briefed one another about the events that transpired in each other's absences.

During Michael and Steina's hibernation, Reynir and Ezra had gifted the rune of Sól to the dwarfs. They explained that Brokkr and Eitri happily accepted the gracious gift, yet they argued how it should be used. Eitri argued on behalf of using it on Alfheim while Brokkr grumbled about, stating that they should sell it.

With the assistance of Brokkr and Eitri, Reynir and Ezra were able to relocate the remaining elves of Alfheim, transporting them safely to their new home on Nidavellir. With the curse lifted, the elves were able to travel via portals with no harmful side effects. They also began assisting the elves who had been on Nidavellir as dark elves, helping to rehabilitate them into society after years of being hindered by a debilitating illness.

Greater news was that Solfrid was alive and as perky as ever. Michael was unsure of how many years she had left in her, but he was overjoyed to have her at their side. No longer was she bedridden, which was a huge relief, both physically and mentally.

Their new realm was beautiful. A vastly different kind of beautiful than Alfheim but exquisite, nonetheless. It was breathtaking to see the realm in the daylight, but thousands of years without a sun meant no trees or plants.

The terrain was rocky, a desert region consisting of mountains and peaks and valleys. A barren wasteland that was bereft of any man-made structures, at least atop the realm's core that was. The beautiful dwarven city still bustled below, but up above was dry and bare, an empty canvas for them to rebuild, and with that canvas, they chose to cast the rune of Frey.

"We wanted to wait until both of you awoke to cast the rune," said Ezra.

"After all, you are the one who lifted the curse," said Reynir, gesturing to Michael.

"Aww, nah," said Michael. "I couldn't have done it without each of you by my side. It was a team effort."

"I do hope that this is okay?" Steina asked Solfrid. "It was the only way we could get Brokkr and Eitri to agree to help us."

"Okay, it is," replied Solfrid. "I could not be more proud," she smiled, placing her arm around Steina.

"Together, we cast it," chimed Ezra with the rune cupped in both hands.

Everyone placed their hand in Ezra's, feeling the orka the rune of Frey generated within.

"To our fellow councilmen that we will see on the other side," said Reynir. "To Dafilrog, Ólafur, and Darrius. Cheers . . . One," he counted. "Two . . . Three," he shouted, and together the five of them cast the rune of Frey upon the barren land of Nidavellir.

And although Frey was dead, their god could still bless them once more and elicit a beauty that only he was capable of and elicit beauty, he did. The rocky and mountainous terrain that they harbored on stayed relatively the same, but from atop the peak of the realm, they watched as all five biomes emerged in unison and harmony, and what they couldn't see physically, they could feel.

Michael remote viewed the terrain in awe, marveling at Frey's astounding beauty. Even from beyond, the generous god delivered one last time. In the realms deep north and south, it snowed, and together they watched from afar as the snow crested upon the mountaintops. Polar ice caps emerged from nothing and sat gloriously amongst Nidavellir's oceans.

They saw forests emerge and encircle the realm. Temperate and tropical forests blossomed alike, spreading evenly across their new home. Black, white, and pink sanded beaches dispersed along the realm's coasts, some with palm trees surrounding, others with mountains, and some with rocks but all with grace and beauty. In the heart of the realm, large and magnificent grasslands sprouted the soils, completing the realm's transformation.

A new Alfheim, a virgin Alfheim, uninhabited by the waste of man. Even though Alfheim ran mostly on renewable resources and energy, it paled in comparison to a world untouched by man and man-made constructs.

Michael was overwhelmed with emotions as he watched the realm transform before him. That feeling of belonging that plagued him for so long was now absent as he sat on the mountaintops of Nidavellir with his family. This realm represented a new opportunity for all of them. It was the fresh start they all needed. A healing of their pasts and the pain that it hid.

He felt happiness, fascination, grief, joy, excitement, and uncertainty all in one. It had been a little over two years since he ventured on to Alfheim, and in those two years, he'd lived a lifetime. He experienced more heartache and grief than any man or woman should ever encounter. He felt the highest of highs and the lowest of lows. He saved two realms and felt the triumphant joy that came with it.

He let his hate for Loki fester into something that he wasn't proud of, but because of it, he was able to find love, an unconditional love for himself. Something that didn't exist back on Midgard two long years ago. With his newfound love, he was able to let go of his fear of being hurt or the resounding fear that he had of failure.

As a result of that release, he was ready to explore the relationship he and Steina had crafted. After a few days of social gatherings amongst the council, he finally got a moment alone with her. The moment he had been yearning for since their last private conversation got cut short.

They overlooked the realm's beauty together. Michael ached to break the silence between them, but lumps caught in his throat every time he attempted to do so. His brain racked every scenario imaginable, calculating any and every possible conversation that could possibly happen.

Finally, after what felt like an eternity of ear-stabbing, relationship-breaking silence, he spoke. "It's beautiful, isn't it?" He asked, mentally pounding himself at the vomit-inducing small talk he managed to regurgitate.

"It is," said Steina. "Thank you for being a part of it. We couldn't have done it without you, Michael. I'm glad you came back."

"Thank you for allowing me to be a part of it."

"Always," she said, staring at him longingly. "I want to apologize for everything that happened back there . . . in the chamber. I just," Steina paused, sighing deeply, trying her hardest to gather the words that eluded her. "We have something really special here, and I hope I didn't ruin that."

"You don't need to apologize, Steina. If it's at all possible, I think I admire you more now than ever before. But I do want to ask you something. I know we spoke about it briefly with the council, but Loki . . . do you think he's good? Like a good person?"

"I—I don't know. When we stared into each other's eyes, when we kissed, I could feel the good permeating within him. I could feel the kind-hearted passion that lives inside, but even if Odin spent a lifetime tarnishing his name, someone with that much dirt on their hands can never truly be clean. One cannot have that many allegations to their name without an ounce of any validity behind them.

"He is responsible for the fall of Alfheim. That is not something that can be taken lightly. Can we trust him in helping us defeat Odin? I believe so, but the question is, why? Why does he want Odin out of power so badly? I know Odin tarnished his name. I know about Ragnarök resetting the slate, but there are always hidden agendas with Loki. Always. I just wish I wouldn't have been so naïve not to have seen them when I was younger."

Michael nodded his head. "I agree. I don't know if he's the killer or the monster that history or Odin portrayed him out to be, but I damn sure don't trust him." Michael paused. "Do you . . . do you still have feelings for him?"

"No, I don't," said Steina sternly. "And I think I needed that kiss to assure that. And I'm so very sorry if I hurt you in doing so . . . for so long I didn't know what I wanted out of life, and then I met Lifthrasir or shall I say Loki, and he became everything that I wanted. I had never felt anything like it. He became my drug. He intoxicated me, and I consumed every ounce of him. I needed him. He took everything away. My insecurities, my pain, my doubt. He made me feel like I was worth something for the first time in my life, and because of that, I gave him everything.

"It was such a crazy passionate head over heels love. My heart still flutters at the thought of it, but it no longer leaps for him. There's a difference. One can still find joy in a chapter of their life without wishing to go back there, or go back to someone for that matter. Because one thing that Loki did provide me with is a feeling of self-worth, therefore, I can never regret him entirely. Even if he took that self-worth away, it meant that it existed, only this time it would be up to me to find it again.

"He was my first love, my only lover romantically speaking, and I put so much of myself into him that I never stopped to think about what I wanted from it all or what I wanted from myself. I only knew that I needed him. I thought that he was the one, and once upon a time, that was all that I wanted, so losing him hurt. It absolutely shattered me. Finding out who he really was, finding out that it was all a lie was devastating. A lot of time has passed since then, but it doesn't feel like it when you can recall every memory you have ever had with perfection.

"When we were together, in the chamber, no matter how wrong it felt, I needed that. I know it sounds crazy. It might not even make any sense, but I never got a proper goodbye. I never got goodbye sex or breakup sex, the longing not to let go during your last acts of intimacy or the cries and the laughs and the whole spectrum of emotions that encompasses it. I never got the closure that my heart desired.

"I thought that I missed him, so part of me needed that closure to see if I had really moved on. He was everything I thought that I needed at one point, but people change, and everything that I need is right here on Nidavellir. Those butterflies that I used to get with him, the same butterflies that I thought I would never experience again, I get those when I am with you, and I'm very sorry that I jeopardized that for some stupid closure. I caved in a moment of weakness. I'm overjoyed that everything turned out to be okay, but that doesn't excuse my behavior. I failed Alfheim. Most importantly, I failed you, and I am sorry for that, Michael. I hope you can forgive me."

"Are you kidding me?" questioned Michael. "You? Weak? You're the strongest person I know, Steina. You're so in tune with yourself, with your emotions, with every aspect of who you are. When I think about who I want to become, I aspire to be more like you. Finding the cave did wonders for me. I know what I need to do to become a better person, but you, you're already there. You always have been. From the moment I met you, and that's truer today than it was then.

"As for failing, you didn't fail. We're a team. Together we restored two realms and broke a thousand-year-old curse in the process. I mean, look at this place, it's beautiful. If not for you, it'd be the most beautiful thing I'd ever laid eyes on . . . if anything, I am the one that should be apologizing. I had Odin at my fingertips, and I let him go, but that's not a failure. It's merely a lesson, and whether it's Odin or Loki or Ragnarök itself, whatever it is that comes our way, I'm confident that we can handle it together," said Michael reaching for Steina's hand.

"Together," she said with a smile, placing her hand in his.

Her eyes glittered, dancing and sparkling as beautifully as the day Michael had met her, and no matter how lost he got as he gazed into them, he knew that he could never truly be alone with Steina at his side.

ACKNOWLEDGMENTS

To my amma, for your spirit and protection. From the moment I was born, you took care of me. Protected me and nurtured me in the way only a grandmother could. And although you are not here physically, I know that you are here in spirit. I never knew you as Steina, so to me, it's only a name. You were Amma. My Amma, and I hope that I was able to create a character and legacy that honors the strength and courage you exhibited.

To Anthony, for inspiring hope and imagination. No one will ever understand the in-depth world you created during your Wiffle ball games and bouncy ball extravaganzas. The multiple notebooks and countless statistics wouldn't begin to do it justice. When life forced me to become an adult far earlier than most, you provided me with the innocence and childhood I needed to continue. Your imagination inspired mine. You were once my biggest fan, and now I'm yours.

To Chloe, for your contagious joy and innocence. I'm not sure if life has hurt you yet, and if it has, you hide it well. But one day, life will throw its punches and when it does, never change. You're perfect, and I couldn't be more proud of the young lady you have grown up to become. Don't put up the same walls I've spent my entire life trying to take down. You are beautiful and amazing in every facet that life has to offer.

To my dad, for your strength and guidance. You were the strongest person I have ever met, and I hate that I never told you that. When everyone gave up on you, including me, you never gave up on yourself. You always told me how I made you proud, and while I always said the same, I can't help but feel as if I didn't say it enough. You were a true warrior, and I simply can't express how proud of you I am. Before your death, I had really begun to come in tune with my creative side of writing. I remember our phone calls where we brainstormed and pieced together the endings to my stories. So when you passed, I thought that was the end of that passion for me. I didn't believe that I was strong enough or good enough to carry on without you. Turns out I was wrong. While our time together was short, it was powerful, and I wouldn't change it for the world. Sometimes I still struggle going on this journey alone without you, but you left too much wisdom inside of me to ever truly die. Your Horcruxes remain, scattered throughout my heart, and through those memories, you will live eternally. We made a New Year's Resolution in 2012 to write a book. You were well on your way, but God had other plans. I just wanted to let you know that I held up my end, Pops. I love you.

To Jarrin, for your friendship and motivation. "First of all . . . Great job . . . I cannot stand Anthony . . ." I cackle every time I read this quote from you. I want to say the grandest of thank you's. You were the first to read Fielder's Choice after completion and, likewise, the first to finish Alfheim. You have been my biggest supporter and motivator during this daunting process. Thank you for believing in me, and thank you for your once-in-a-lifetime friendship.

To Leila, for unconditional love and selflessness. I was very selfish before I had you. I still am. Every day you help me to become a little less. You make me a better person. I know this is only a fantasy novel, but if life ever takes me away from you, I hope you can pick this up and find all the wisdom I have imparted in here for you. You inspire me every day. I love watching you grow into the incredible human that you are, and no matter what, I will always be proud of you.

To Matt, for sacrifice and commitment. I've been blessed to have two dads for as long as I can remember. It would've been easy to go your separate way after the divorce, but you never did. I don't know where I would be without you, but I know that I am who I am because of you. I've never met a harder working individual in my entire life, and thankfully that work ethic rubbed off on me. You instilled the hard work and dedication in me that was needed to complete this book.

To my mom, for a lifetime of compassion and support. It feels like sometimes you get the short stick when it comes to appreciation. I took you for granted a lot growing up, but that was only because I knew you would always be there for me. I now understand the fragility of life, and I want you to know how much I appreciate you and the sacrifices you have made for me. I will always cherish our long talks. Some of my favorite memories consist of me waiting for you to get off work so we can talk before I went to bed or the long vacation car rides where everyone fell asleep but us, and we would chat for hours on end. I love you, and I hope you're as proud of me as I am of you.

To Orlando, for helping me find myself. I know it may sound weird to thank a city, but I'm not sure I would ever know who I was without it. I moved to Orlando when I was broken and grieving. Ironically, I ran from my father's death, and it led me to the city he died in, but it was there that I was reborn. It was there that I discovered John Stoeter. And if I never see you again, I just wanted to thank you for everything you've done for me.

To my wife, for your everlasting love and belief. I'm pretty sure you believed in me before I believed in myself. You have sacrificed more for me than I deserve, and I truly am thankful. The very last paragraph of this novel reminds me of the time I got lost in your eyes at our wedding. Your beauty on that day and in that moment is something that I will never forget. From the shy girl who knocked on my door in her *Sublime* t-shirt to the amazing woman, mother, and wife that you have become. I have cherished every aspect of our journey, and I look forward to a lifetime of memories with you and our family. I love you.

9 781736 849903